PRAISE

The Silent Watcher

"*The Silent Watcher* is gritty and authentic and packs a punch. Victor Methos's own inimitable style is addictive."
—Robert Dugoni, *New York Times* bestselling author

The Secret Witness

"A red-hot suspenser aimed at readers for whom a single serial killer just isn't enough."
—*Kirkus Reviews*

An Unreliable Truth

"A straight-A legal thriller with a final scene as satisfying as it is disturbing."
—*Kirkus Reviews*

A Killer's Wife
An Amazon Best Book of the Month: Mystery, Thriller & Suspense

"*A Killer's Wife* is a high-stakes legal thriller loaded with intense courtroom drama, compelling characters, and surprising twists that will keep you turning the pages at breakneck speed."
—T.R. Ragan, *New York Times* bestselling author

"Exquisitely paced and skillfully crafted, *A Killer's Wife* delivers a wicked psychological suspense wrapped around a hypnotic legal thriller. One cleverly designed twist after another kept me saying 'I did not see that coming.'"

—Steven Konkoly, *Wall Street Journal* bestselling author

"A gripping thriller that doesn't let up for a single page. Surprising twists with a hero you care about. I read the whole book in one sitting!"

—Chad Zunker, bestselling author of *An Equal Justice*

THE
NIGHT
COLLECTOR

OTHER TITLES BY VICTOR METHOS

Shepard & Gray Series

The Secret Witness

The Grave Singer

The Deceiving Look

Desert Plains Series

A Killer's Wife

Crimson Lake Road

An Unreliable Truth

Neon Lawyer Series

The Neon Lawyer

Mercy

Vegas Shadows Series

The Silent Watcher

Other Titles

The Hallows
The Shotgun Lawyer
A Gambler's Jury
An Invisible Client

THE NIGHT COLLECTOR

VICTOR METHOS

This is a work of fiction. Names, characters, organizations, places, events, and incidents are either products of the author's imagination or are used fictitiously. Otherwise, any resemblance to actual persons, living or dead, is purely coincidental.

Text copyright © 2025 by Victor Methos
All rights reserved.

No part of this book may be reproduced, or stored in a retrieval system, or transmitted in any form or by any means, electronic, mechanical, photocopying, recording, or otherwise, without express written permission of the publisher.

Published by Thomas & Mercer, Seattle

www.apub.com

Amazon, the Amazon logo, and Thomas & Mercer are trademarks of Amazon.com, Inc., or its affiliates.

EU product safety contact:
Amazon Media EU S. à r.l.
38, avenue John F. Kennedy, L-1855 Luxembourg
amazonpublishing-gpsr@amazon.com

ISBN-13: 9781662528415 (hardcover)
ISBN-13: 9781662528439 (paperback)
ISBN-13: 9781662528422 (digital)

Cover design by Shasti O'Leary Soudant
Cover image: © Eddie Lluisma / Getty

Printed in the United States of America
First edition

He who fights with monsters should look to it that
he himself does not become a monster.
—Friedrich Nietzsche

1

The black Dodge Charger smashed through the chapel's doors, its engine roaring like an animal unleashed. Glass exploded inward, shimmering in the light before slicing through the air. Splinters of wood spun like jagged missiles and embedded into flesh. The impact hit the room like a bomb, shaking walls and rattling bones.

Guests hit the floor in panic, their screams swallowed by the deafening roar. The scent of flowers and perfume was overwhelmed by the acrid tang of rubber and hot metal. It felt like the end of the world.

Sixteen-year-old Brad Lowe instinctively turned toward his bride, Keri, his heart seizing at the sight. Her white dress was blooming with red, ribbons of blood trailing down her arms and face, where glass had sliced her delicate skin. Before he could process what was happening, the Charger lurched forward. The car clipped her hip, and she was flung into him like a doll. They crumpled to the floor in a tangle of limbs and lace, sliding into the terrified guests.

"Keri!" Brad gasped, clutching her tighter as her dazed eyes fluttered open. She was trembling, her breaths short and shallow. He touched her face, sticky with blood, and whispered, "It's okay. You're okay."

Screams filled the air. Brad's gaze darted wildly, locking onto his uncle writhing on the floor, blood pouring from a shard of glass embedded in his eye. The man's cries echoed in Brad's ears as he pressed his hand harder against Keri's back, trying to shield her.

The Charger's engine snarled again. Two figures stepped out of the car, their black clothes blending into the shadows and faces obscured by stark white skull masks. The driver, a hulking figure rippling with muscle, gripped a hunting knife in one hand and a gaudy, gold-plated handgun in the other. He walked with a predator's calm.

Brad froze. Keri was whimpering softly, her blood-soaked fingers clinging to his shirt.

"Stay down," he whispered.

"Please," the minister stammered, his voice trembling. He stood rooted in place, his glasses askew and his salt-and-pepper hair damp with sweat. "They're just teenagers. It's their wedding day. There's a safe in the back. I'll give you the combination."

The driver didn't pause. As he walked, he raised the knife and drew it smoothly across the minister's throat. The sound of the blade slicing through flesh was sickening, a wet, awful hiss. Black-red blood erupted, spraying in violent arcs and spattering the white skull mask.

The minister's eyes widened in shock as he dropped to his knees, clutching his throat. The gurgling sounds of his last breaths filled the chapel. A fresh wave of terror rippled through the guests.

Keri screamed, the sound raw and piercing. The masked man turned to her and yanked her up by the arm.

"No!" Brad shouted, his voice cracking as he lunged for her, only for the second figure to close in behind him. The butt of a shotgun slammed into the back of his skull, and his world exploded in pain. He hit the floor, vision swimming, popping colors blurring the edges of his sight.

"Brad!" Keri's voice was panicked, desperate.

Strong hands grabbed his hair and dragged him upright, his legs barely holding him as he was hauled toward the Charger. He fought, but it was useless. The grip on him was iron.

Keri's cries grew louder as she fought against the driver, her voice breaking. "Please, let us go! Please!"

The Night Collector

The trunk of the Charger opened. Brad was shoved inside with brutal force, his body slamming against the cold metal. Keri's small frame followed, landing hard beside him. She clawed at the masked figure and sobbed as the trunk slammed shut, plunging them into darkness.

Inside the suffocating space, Brad felt Keri shaking uncontrollably. Her breath came in ragged gasps, and her bloodied hands clung to him like he was the last solid thing in a world falling apart. "It's going to be okay," he said.

Outside, Keri's mother screamed, her voice echoing through the wreckage. "We don't have anything! Please, don't hurt them!"

The man with the gold-plated handgun turned to her, tilting his head as if considering her words. Then, with a sinister chuckle, he raised the weapon and shouted, "Bang!" Keri's mother flinched, her scream catching in her throat.

The Charger's engine growled to life again. Brad and Keri pounded against the trunk, their muffled cries swallowed by the roaring engine. The car peeled out, glass crunching under its tires as it tore through the remnants of the chapel. The wreckage faded behind it as the Charger disappeared into the neon glow of the Vegas night.

Inside the trunk, Keri buried her face against Brad's chest, her tears soaking his shirt. "Why?" she cried. "Why is this happening?"

Brad didn't have an answer.

2

Previous day

Lazarus Holloway sat in his black Chrysler, a torn jean vest on his back. A patch showed a Confederate soldier, half his face missing, teeth bloodied, eyes hollow.

Booker was next to him, smoking a primo—weed laced with coke. He had on a black shirt with red suspenders, and all Lazarus could think about was the Oompa-Loompas from *Willy Wonka*.

It was after nine, the sun long gone. Lazarus took a drag from his vape, tapped the rabbit-foot dangling from the rearview mirror, and stepped out of the car.

"Let's go," Lazarus said to Booker.

Booker extinguished the half-smoked primo, shoved it into his pocket, and climbed out of the car.

Down the street, a Metro SWAT van idled. Lazarus's partner, Kevin Riley, stood closer, leaning against a shack filled with tools and machinery. The watch commander had wanted him in the van with the rest of the team, but Riley hadn't listened. At six foot ten and over 350 pounds, the guy didn't have to.

Lazarus gave him a nod.

The handbag in his hand weighed heavy—one hundred grand in cash. He'd busted plenty of distributors when he worked Narcs in New Orleans, but he'd never handled this much money. It didn't excite him.

Didn't make him envious either. To Lazarus, money was just dirty paper stained with greed.

Dressed in black pants and a T-shirt, a man sat outside the warehouse door. The swastika on his neck looked like a fresh wound. He smoked, his eyes sweeping Lazarus up and down. As Lazarus and Booker approached, the man stood and flicked his cigarette onto the pavement.

"Spread your arms," the man said.

Booker grinned. "It's me, Jacob."

"Shut up and spread your arms."

Jacob patted him down, then turned to Lazarus. Lazarus lifted his arms without a word.

"Drop the bag."

"Brother, I got a hundred Gs in here. Ain't no way it's leavin' my hand until I give it to Deadeye."

Jacob's eyes narrowed, but after a moment he gave a nod and roughly searched Lazarus, hands sliding over his thighs, ribs, and arms. Satisfied, he jerked his head toward the door.

Lazarus had done his homework on the warehouse. It was a hollowed-out shell, part of a neighborhood that used to hum with life until cheaper labor sent the jobs overseas. For three years it had stood empty, buried under back taxes, not worth anyone's trouble—until six months ago, when it got scooped up by a sixty-eight-year-old retiree. She was the mother of the man he was here to see: Deadeye.

Inside, the place was just as empty. The entryway held a couple of filthy abandoned offices, papers littering the floor, shelves broken and scattered with old manila folders. Double doors led out to the main warehouse floor, and he could hear laughter coming from the office ahead.

A large man stood in the doorway, arms crossed, biceps bulging. He shot Lazarus a cold glare. Lazarus gave him a nod, then turned his eyes to the man behind the desk—a figure sitting like a South American dictator waiting to be addressed.

Phineas Walsh—Deadeye—didn't fit the image of the usual crew. He was in a white button-down, his tie loosened at the neck. His sleeves were rolled up, showing faded tattoos: Iron Crosses, knives, skulls, flames.

Deadeye was blind. He wasn't wearing his glasses, so the scars over his gray, useless eyes were on full display, the sockets a mess of old wounds. People said his father had tossed him through a sliding glass door and the shards had shredded his eyes, leaving them ruined.

But Deadeye wasn't some washed-up white supremacist stuck in the past. He was one of the founding members of the Steel Patriots, a prison gang born out of Texas, different from the others. They didn't just push guns and dope—they also invested. Treasury bonds, commercial real estate. They wore suits, waved American flags, and ditched the swastikas.

Still, Deadeye wasn't all in on their new-world act. Not fully. He cared more about cash than belief, running guns, girls, and drugs to anyone who could pay—Black Guerrillas, Latin Kings, MS-13. Over a wiretap Lazarus had heard him say once, "Green's the only color that matters to me."

A man like that could be flipped.

Sweat trickled down Lazarus's back. The summer heat had been relentless, pushing 122 degrees. Still, it beat the Louisiana bayou where Lazarus had started out as police—there, the air felt like a wall of boiling water.

Booker stood behind him, eyes darting nervously. The guy had only been an informant for a few months and hadn't worked a bust yet. Sweat poured off him, and Lazarus was thankful for the heat—otherwise, Booker's fear would've gotten their asses shot off by now.

"George, give us the room," Deadeye said, his voice smooth, calm, like sugary syrup dripping into someone's ears.

The muscle-bound man walked out, and Booker moved to follow.

"Not you, Book," Deadeye added, sensing his leaving somehow.

Booker froze. He glanced at Lazarus, trying to force a smile even though Deadeye couldn't see it.

"I gotta take a piss," Booker said.

"This won't take long," Deadeye replied.

Booker swallowed hard, looking again at Lazarus, who gave a barely noticeable nod. Booker sank into a chair against the wall, leaning forward, his face slick with sweat, like a wax mask melting in the heat.

"Where you been, Book?"

"Just tryin' to stay outta trouble."

Deadeye puffed on a cigar. "And you must be Hank," he asked, sensing the extra presence in the room.

"No, I'm Santa Claus," Lazarus said, tossing the bag of cash onto the desk.

Deadeye ran his fingers over the bag, found the zipper, and opened it. His fingers brushed the stacks of bills inside, light and deliberate.

"I love the smell of cash," Deadeye said, fingers still grazing the bills. "We've got Bitcoin, stocks, property—but for me, nothing beats cash. Every war in history's been fought for it. It's the great freer of races."

Lazarus said, "It's a slaver and we're its slaves. Some of us willingly."

Deadeye cracked a slight grin.

He reached into a drawer and pulled out a bottle of Wild Turkey and two shot glasses. "Have a drink with me."

"I'd rather just get the guns and get outta here."

"No time for even a drink?"

"I don't like carryin' this much cash, and I sure as hell don't like drivin' with a trunk full of guns. So if you don't mind . . ."

Deadeye sighed. "No one has any time for pleasantries these days."

The door swung open, and the man from outside stormed in and grabbed Booker hard by the collar. Booker's eyes went wide, panic setting in. "What the hell you doin'?"

George forced Booker to his knees. Lazarus felt a cold spike of adrenaline shoot through his gut.

Deadeye poured Wild Turkey into his glass, raised it to his lips, and took a slow sip.

"What is this?" Lazarus asked, his voice steady.

"Justice," Deadeye replied, a calm menace behind the word.

That familiar trickle of fear crept down Lazarus's spine.

"Book," Deadeye said, his voice low, almost casual, "I know you've been stealing from me."

Booker's panic hit hard, and George slapped him across the face.

Deadeye turned his head toward Lazarus, eyes blank but full of threat. "The question is whether I'm going to kill you, too. Life's all about decisions, isn't it?"

"We're rats in a maze with no cheese in sight," Lazarus said.

Deadeye chuckled. "I like you, Hank."

Booker tried to get to his feet, but George kicked him hard in the thigh, sending him crashing back down to his knees. Booker's voice cracked as he started to beg.

"I didn't do nothin'. I swear it. I'd never steal from you. You looked after my mama while I was inside. I'd never do that to you."

Deadeye leaned back in his chair. "One thing I hate more than a thief is a liar."

Lazarus stepped in, voice firm. "Easy there, hoss. I don't know what kind of beef you got here. I just want the guns I was promised, and me and Book are gonna leave."

"Can't let you leave."

"Sure you can."

Deadeye took another drink, his scarred eyes locked on Lazarus. For a second, Lazarus swore there was recognition in them, as if the man saw more than he let on. How much sight had he really lost?

"You know what makes people tick?" Deadeye said. "Fear. Sometimes you gotta get your hands dirty, make sure everyone around you feels it. Don't you think?"

Lazarus exhaled slowly. "You know what frustrates me about men with limited intellect? They always think they're original."

Deadeye grinned, slow and wide. "George, put a bullet in that thieving sack of shit's head."

Lazarus didn't hesitate. His hand slipped behind his back, fingers finding the grip of the Ruger LCP .380. The gun fit snug in its holster, designed for situations like this—when you needed to stay armed but look clean during a search. He drew it, smooth and fast, and leveled it at George, who had his own gun pressed against Booker's head.

"I can't let you kill 'im, friend," Lazarus said, his voice steady, eyes locked on George.

Deadeye leaned back, smirking. "What's he to you?"

"I got an interest in seein' him alive."

Realization flickered across Deadeye's face, his smile widening, mocking. "You're a cop. I thought he was just stealing, but he's a snitch, too, ain't he?"

Lazarus kept his aim steady on George, but his mind raced. Jacob was somewhere out there, by the door. If everyone rushed him at once, there was no guarantee Lazarus would get out of this alive.

"There's a SWAT team outside," Lazarus said calmly, trying to buy a few seconds.

Deadeye didn't flinch. "I don't really care," he said, taking another slow sip of Wild Turkey.

For a moment, the air felt thick, the room holding its breath.

A loud bang echoed through the hallway as Jacob slammed the front doors shut.

"Do it," Deadeye ordered.

Before Lazarus could react, George pulled the trigger. The shot rang out like thunder, and Booker's head snapped forward. Blood and brain matter sprayed the floor.

Time seemed to freeze, Lazarus's mind catching up with the chaos. The sharp smell of gunpowder hung in the air, mixing with the iron tang of blood.

Lazarus dove behind Deadeye's desk as bullets tore through the air. He rolled, bringing the Ruger up under the desk, and squeezed off two

The Night Collector

quick shots. One caught George in the Achilles, shredding it. George hit the ground, screaming, blood pooling around his leg.

Lazarus didn't hesitate. He lunged up, arm snaking around Deadeye's throat, and yanked him down behind the desk. Jacob was at the door now, Glock in hand, eyes wild.

"Easy, Jake," Lazarus shouted. "We can still work this out."

Before Jacob could fire, two massive hands appeared behind him. Riley, towering and silent, smashed Jacob's skull into the doorframe. The sound was brutal, like two bats cracking against each other. Jacob crumpled in a heap as if someone had flipped his off switch.

Riley had to duck to step into the room, his bulk barely fitting through the doorway. George was still howling on the floor, blood cascading from his torn ankle. Riley didn't bother with sympathy—he slapped cuffs on George and tossed him against the wall like a doll.

Lazarus hauled Deadeye to his feet and shoved him toward Riley. The big man grabbed Deadeye by the shoulders, locking him in place. Deadeye wisely didn't fight.

"Where my guns, Phineas?" Lazarus said, holstering his weapon.

"I don't know."

"Big man, break one of his arms."

Riley grabbed the man's wrist.

"No, no need for that. There aren't any."

"Aren't any *here*, you mean."

"No. We were just going to take the money."

"And kill us after?"

"Risk of doing business."

Lazarus gave a slight nod. "Fair enough. I won't take it personal then."

He slammed his fist into Deadeye's face, dropping him to the floor with a heavy thud.

"Consider us even," Lazarus said.

3

Lazarus had to give statements and hand over his weapon. Just procedure, nothing like the way things went down in New Orleans. Back there, you could be involved in a shooting—didn't matter if it was clean or dirty—and be back on the streets the same day, nerves frayed like a car-wreck survivor.

He sat on the hood of his car, vape pen in hand, waiting for Riley.

Booker had only been twenty-six. He'd taken care of his disabled mother, snitching to afford her prescriptions. Not a bad kid, really. But Lazarus knew better than most—the universe didn't care about that.

"You good?" Riley's deep voice rumbled as he approached.

"I'm good," Lazarus said, still watching the scene.

"You want help in the interview?"

"Nah. Phineas is a squealer. I can always spot a squealer."

Riley shrugged, taking a few steps back. "You sure you're good?"

"Fine," Lazarus said, eyes following the gurney as Booker's body was loaded into the ME's van. He exhaled a thin haze of vapor through his nose.

Deadeye sat in the interview room, staring blankly in one direction, dark glasses covering his ruined eyes. A black cane with gold trim and an eagle's head handle rested next to him, a necessity for balance from an old hip injury. He sipped from a Styrofoam cup, calm as ever, the faint hum of the air-conditioning the only sound.

It was late, the precinct settling into the eerie quiet of the overnight shift. Most desks were empty, the earlier chaos replaced by the occasional murmur of a phone call or the shuffle of papers. Outside the interview room, Lazarus stood near the one-way glass, arms crossed, watching. A single technician sat nearby, ensuring the audio feed was clear.

Lazarus walked in and took the seat across from Deadeye.

"You can't see it," Lazarus said, "but the ceiling's slanted in here. Apparently it disorients a lot of people. Something about exposure to odd angles. A lot of murder houses have slanted ceilings."

Deadeye grinned, but it didn't reach his eyes. "I like trivia, too, but can you tell me where the hell my lawyer is?"

"I haven't called him yet."

"Why not?"

"Because I think you and me can make a deal."

"I don't deal with your two-party, Jew-party government."

"Don't feed me that 'white is right' crap, Phineas. You don't believe it. You only care about yourself, and that's the road I'm offering."

Deadeye chuckled softly. "You want my boss?"

"Yes."

"And why would I help you? I'd be signing my own death certificate."

Lazarus leaned forward. "I don't think you realize it, but you're looking at death row."

"That right? For a few illegal guns?"

"No, not guns. This deal was the end of a six-month investigation. All I gotta do is call the US Attorney's office and tell them to push forward with the RICO case. Three hundred fifty-two charges. That's what they'll bring down on you. And with RICO, you get nailed for the crimes your dipshit underlings committed, too. Racketeering. The don goes down with the rest of the family. You'd get life for all that. But you're gonna get death because of Booker."

Deadeye's jaw tightened.

"Even if you don't get death," Lazarus continued, "your bosses up there in Idaho, playing soldier on their little compounds, are gonna see you as a liability. What do they do with liabilities, Phineas?"

"And what're you offering me instead?" Deadeye asked, the hint of a sneer still on his lips.

"Witness protection."

Deadeye laughed, a harsh, barking sound. "Witness protection? You think they can't find me? The government can't even protect the president. How're they gonna protect me?"

Lazarus calmly took a drag from his vape pen. "I heard your daddy did that to your eyes. That true?"

The laughter stopped. The room went quiet.

"Maybe you could protect yourself in there as a young man, but you're old now, Phineas. You can't protect yourself inside, not without your eyes," Lazarus said. "This is a onetime offer. Say no, and I leave. The marshals will pick you up and hand you over to the FBI. It's your call."

Deadeye leaned back in his chair, silent. After a few long moments, he finally spoke.

"What would I have to do?"

4

It was a Thursday night when Lazarus got home to his one-bedroom apartment, the clock ticking past midnight. Even at this hour the city sweltered, the heat clinging to him like a second skin.

He shut the door behind him, unbuttoning his sweat-soaked shirt. In the bathroom, he tossed it in the bin and caught a glimpse of himself in the mirror. His muscles were tight beneath skin that felt too thin and a heat rash spread on his ribs.

After stripping the rest of his clothes off, he turned on the shower. His hand brushed over his beard. Not long enough to trim yet. As he was about to step in, his phone buzzed on the sink. A text from Sandy, asking where he was. He'd forgotten about his promise to meet her at a bar tonight. He sighed and climbed into the shower.

The water was ice cold, numbing him until the heat of the day faded from his skin. He stood in silence, letting the chill seep in before grabbing the soap.

When he was done, he slipped on jeans and a T-shirt, his arms covered in the vibrant colors of tattoo sleeves. One glance in the mirror, then out the door.

He crossed the hall and left a twenty-dollar bill under the welcome mat of the single mother who lived there with her ten-year-old son, Isaac. She worked three jobs, barely scraping by. Isaac would find the money and stash it away for when they needed it.

Just off the Strip, the bar Sandy had picked was marked by a neon cowboy hat above the entrance and a patio where karaoke spilled into the night. Waitresses moved quickly, keeping the drinks flowing, ensuring everyone was good and drunk before the bills came with their blank tip lines.

Sandy was already surrounded by a group of guys buying drinks when she spotted Lazarus. She rushed over, throwing her arms around him, her breath heavy with booze.

"I'm so glad you're here!" she said, her voice loud and bright. "I missed you." She kissed him, her lips tasting like sugar and tequila.

She grabbed his hand, dragging him back to her friends. Lazarus had met them before, though they never seemed to like him much. That was fine. He stood behind them while they threw back shots, the men eyeing him with suspicion.

Sandy knocked back another shot of tequila and hollered like she was at a frat party. She held out a fresh shot for Lazarus.

"Don't feel like drinkin' right now," he said.

"Come on! Shoot it! Shoot it!"

Lazarus took the shot glass and poured the tequila onto the floor.

Sandy's face dropped as she stared at the liquid soaking into the filthy ground. "What's your problem?" she yelled over the crowd. "Why'd you even come here?"

"I don't know," Lazarus replied honestly. "Let's break up."

"What?" she said, laughing like she hadn't heard him right.

"Take care of yourself, Sandy," he said, his eyes going to the men hovering around her like vultures. "And you should stop drinkin'. These men are tryin' to get you drunk."

Without another word, Lazarus turned and left, driving through the city aimlessly before heading to the Last Chance Saloon—the only place in town where he'd ever drink.

The saloon was quieter than the bar he'd just left, but the people here carried heavier burdens. The owner, Bass—a massive man in a T-shirt, biker vest, and ripped jeans—sauntered over and slid into the booth across from him. He lit a joint, offering it to Lazarus, who politely declined while taking a hit from his vape pen.

"You want a drink?" Bass asked.

"No. Just needed to be somewhere else."

"I know the feelin'," Bass said, exhaling a cloud of smoke, his lips puckering like he was about to whistle.

"Where's your woman?" Lazarus said.

"She went home. Wasn't feelin' well. Speakin' of which, you look like shit."

"Feel like it, too."

"One'a them days, huh?"

"One'a them."

Bass leaned back, placing his joint on the ashtray. "You know what I do when I'm havin' one'a them days? I sit on the edge of this cliff near my house, look out at the city, and think about all the people who've lived and died and all the ones that'll come after. Makes me feel like a speck of dust."

"And that cheers you up?"

"Hell no. But it makes me forget whatever had me down for a while."

A shout for help came from behind the bar, and Bass stood and gave Lazarus a slap on the shoulder before he walked away.

Lazarus sat alone.

5

Detective Lou Hobbes stood in front of the Eternal Bliss Chapel, staring at the gaping hole where the wood and glass doors used to be. The one spot a car could crash through and still drive away. It was a mess of shattered glass and splintered wood, but it told a story.

There had been plenty of witnesses, mostly family, but Lou wasn't concerned about that. The place had a security system with video, thanks to the owner's wife, who'd insisted on it despite the fact they had nothing of value inside but Elvis costumes and Bibles.

Lou knew the minister. Will Dalton. They went way back, a decade at least. Will had belonged to the same church as Lou's ex-wife, and he'd been a stand-up guy, the kind of man who took in struggling families and gave them a roof for a while.

Now, Will was gone.

The medical examiner's team stood near the van, waiting to haul his body away. Lou clenched his jaw, forcing himself not to linger on the loss.

One of the forensic techs from CSI nodded in his direction and held up a clear evidence bag. "Found this near where the driver struggled with one of the vics. Doesn't belong to any of the guests."

Lou leaned closer.

The tech said, "Looks like a bracelet. But I can't make out the symbol. Maybe a crow holding a stick in its beak?"

"That's a sword," Lou said, squinting at the design.

The tech shrugged. "What's that mean?"

"How would I know?"

"Well, we'll be here for a while. I'll call you when we wrap up. By the way, Amanda Bines—mother of the bride—said she needs to talk with you."

Lou exhaled slowly as the tech walked off, turning his attention to Amanda, who was standing near the chapel's entrance. Her arms were crossed tightly and her face was a mix of panic and sadness, like she was barely holding herself together.

As he approached, he took note of her eyes—so dark they were nearly black, striking against the stress lining her face. She was a beautiful woman, which made Lou glance at her gangly, pale husband standing a few feet away and think, *Really? That guy?*

He nodded in greeting. "Amanda? I'm Detective Lou Hobbes. I'm sorry we're meeting under these circumstances."

"I need to tell you something," Amanda said, her voice trembling. Her eyes darted away, panic flickering behind them.

"What's that?"

She swallowed hard. "Who Keri's father is."

Lou sat in the parking lot of the apartment complex, staring at the familiar building. He knew this place—mostly full of newly divorced men trying to rebuild their lives. His father had moved in to a spot like this after Lou's mother left, and Lou had visited on weekends. It was a sad, quiet affair, full of strained conversation and empty space. Lou had felt the same after his own divorce.

Sighing, he got out of the car and headed up to the second-floor apartment. He knocked. It was nearly noon, but Lazarus looked like he had just rolled out of bed when he answered the door, shirtless, tattoos on full display. Lou's eyes flicked to the words inked across his chest: "NOBODY GETS OUT ALIVE."

"What do you want?" Lazarus grumbled.

"Can I come in?"

Lazarus left the door open and wandered toward the fridge. Lou stepped inside, glancing around. The apartment was nearly empty, as if it was a stop on the way to somewhere else. The only thing on the wall was a painting of a muscular, faceless figure pushing a boulder up a hill, muscles strained under the weight.

"Nice bachelor pad you got here," Lou said, watching as Lazarus guzzled milk from the carton.

"What do you want, Lou?"

"I need help with something."

"I'm busy."

Lou pulled out a small evidence bag and set it on the counter. "I think you'll want to hear this one."

Lazarus glanced at the bag before setting the milk carton down and picking the bag up.

"Found it at a scene over at the Eternal Bliss Chapel. Doesn't belong to any of the guests. Car crashes through the doors, two men kill the minister, kidnap the bride and groom, and drive off like it's just another Tuesday."

"Those places get hit sometimes like everywhere else," Lazarus said.

"Not like this. No robbery. Nothing taken from the guests, safe wasn't touched. Video shows them in and out in thirty seconds. They knew exactly what they were doing."

"You got the video?"

Lou nodded, pulling up the LVPD server on his phone. He found the video and handed the phone to Lazarus, who watched it twice.

"It's not two men," Lazarus said.

"How do you figure that?"

"The passenger's wearing baggy clothes to hide it, but that's a woman. Shorter gait, hip sway. Men and women walk differently, given the differences in external and internal sex organs."

Lou grimaced at the way Lazarus phrased it. Always something off with him.

"The bracelet," Lazarus said, nodding to the evidence bag. "That's a Mayan symbol."

Lou raised an eyebrow. "How do you know?"

"I've seen it before."

Lou stared at the bag. "What is it?"

"Buluc Chabtan. Mayan god of death. Priests used to wear that symbol." Lazarus put the milk back in the fridge. "Came across it when I lived in Mexico. Some remote villages still worship him alongside the Catholic God."

"What's that got to do with kidnapping?"

"Maybe human sacrifices."

Lou's jaw tightened. "You're saying they kidnapped those kids to sacrifice them?"

Lazarus leaned against the counter. "How the hell would I know? It's a guess, just like yours."

Lou studied him, not liking the nonchalant way Lazarus talked about it. "You seem to know a lot about this."

"I know the symbol. That's not the same as knowing *a lot* about this, Lou." Lazarus leaned forward. "So why are you here? You could've just googled all this."

Lou hesitated, then spoke. "There's something else. The bride—Keri Bines. Her mother is Amanda Bines."

Lazarus stayed silent.

"It should mean something to you. Since you were sleeping with her sixteen years ago. Exactly sixteen, right?"

Lazarus froze, tension creeping into his posture.

Lou said, "I know you're with the Intelligence section now, and I was hoping I could get some help. Considering . . . you know."

"Considering what?"

"Considering Amanda says Keri's your kid."

Lazarus was still, the silence stretching out between them.

Lou continued. "I talked to her myself. She says the kid is yours. She thinks this whole thing has something to do with you."

Lazarus shook his head. "No. It's got nothing to do with me. You want intel help, file a request like everyone else."

"I can't wait for that."

"Best things in life, Lou," Lazarus said with a shrug.

Lou's temper flared. "Quit farting around. Are you gonna help me or not?"

"Why should I?"

"How about because this might be your kid?"

"It's not."

"Fine," Lou snapped. "You can take a DNA test after we find her. But I need to find her first."

"I'm busy."

"You're a miserable bastard, you know that?"

He turned to leave, anger boiling in his chest. His hand was on the doorknob when Lazarus called out, "Hobbes."

"What?" Lou growled, turning back.

Lazarus tossed the evidence bag at him. "Don't forget your toy."

6

Piper Danes sat in the US Immigration and Customs Enforcement court, listening to the government attorney argue for the deportation of her client, Maria. Sixteen years old, sold into marriage by desperate parents who couldn't afford to keep her and had no other prospects in their village.

Maria had been lured to the States with the promise of marriage and a job in a garment factory. But Robert Gipp, the man who brought her over, had no intention of doing that. He was a pimp and a drug trafficker, and within weeks Maria had been forced into prostitution. Piper had taken the case as her guardian ad litem, representing the girl's interests since she was underage and had no one else.

The criminal case against Gipp wasn't looking good for the defense. Hundreds of text messages between Gipp, Maria, and her parents laid out the exchange in sickening detail. A young daughter for money.

But Maria hadn't testified yet. And because she was in the country illegally, Gipp's defense had alerted ICE, triggering deportation proceedings. Despite the criminal prosecutor's request for a special victim's visa to keep Maria in the US, ICE objected. The matter was now in the hands of an immigration judge.

The ICE attorney, stern and emotionless, reiterated his points. "Your Honor, while we acknowledge the tragic circumstances surrounding this minor, the law mandates deportation for individuals present in the US without legal authorization. Consistent application of immigration laws is crucial to maintaining the integrity of our system. There are established legal avenues for humanitarian relief, which require separate qualifications not met in this instance."

The judge, his slick hair glistening under the courtroom lights, nodded once and gestured for Piper to speak.

Piper stood and approached the lectern. Maria sat alone at the respondent's table, small and terrified. Piper had no obligation to be here, but she couldn't walk away from this girl.

"Your Honor," she began, "we stand at the intersection of justice and basic human decency. This young girl has endured horrors most people couldn't imagine. She's ready to testify against the criminals who exploited her. Deporting her now would not only silence a key witness but also undermine the principles we stand for.

"The law isn't just a rigid set of rules—it's a living system meant to protect the vulnerable and innocent. The U visa exists for cases like this, to protect victims who have the courage to stand against their abusers. Allowing her to stay and testify would show that we don't abandon those who seek our help."

She returned to her seat, heart pounding, but the judge didn't even pause. "I find the respondent does not meet the qualifications for the U visa and therefore grant the government's motion for deportation."

Piper sat frozen as they called the next case. A federal marshal approached Maria, who glanced back at Piper once before being led away. Piper could see the future unfolding—Maria deported back to her village and Gipp walking free without her testimony to nail him.

She took a deep breath, closing her eyes, then sighed it out before leaving the courtroom.

Outside, she sat in her Honda, gripping the steering wheel, fighting back the anger. She slammed her palm against the wheel once, but it felt childish. After a moment, she started the car and drove back to the office.

The GAL offices buzzed with Monday-morning chaos, attorneys scrambling to tackle a weekend backlog of cases.

"You all right?" Mike, her boss, asked as they went through the metal detectors together.

"Yeah, fine. Why?"

"You look distracted. What was this morning?"

They waited for the elevator.

"Deportation hearing. Didn't go well."

Mike shrugged. "Only so much we can do. How was your weekend?"

"I worked all weekend, Mike."

"Dang, really? I need to give you fewer cases."

"It's fine," she said, though the truth was the work kept her mind busy—off things she didn't want to think about.

The elevator doors opened and they rode up together, exchanging small talk. As soon as they reached their floor, Mike was swarmed by attorneys and staff asking for his time. Piper took the opportunity to slip away to her cubicle.

She sat at her desk, staring at her computer's blank screen. She couldn't dive into another case, not right now. She wasn't a robot.

She left her satchel on the desk and took the elevator back down to the café across the street. It was quiet for a Monday, and she ordered a croissant and a coffee, sitting by the window with a view of the street.

The croissant, buttery and flaky, brought back memories of Sunday breakfasts with her grandmother, Lake. They would sit out on the patio, chatting about nothing. Since Lake's murder last year by a man who had been stalking Piper, those mornings had turned into echoes. More than once, Piper had woken up thinking she heard her grandmother in the kitchen making breakfast.

When Lake died, Piper had inherited everything—her property, her possessions. Nothing had gone to her grandmother's three children, including Piper's own mother, who hadn't been seen in years. Piper's uncle and aunt had fought over retirement accounts, but she'd signed them over without a second thought, too disgusted by their greed to bother.

She had sold the house because she couldn't sleep there anymore, but the money from the sale had helped her buy a small condo. It felt distant, removed, but it was hers.

Her phone buzzed in sync with the crash of a dropped glass behind the counter, the barista's apology drowned out by the café's hum. The text was from a client's mother, asking if Piper could come to court early to review testimony again—for what felt like the sixth time.

Piper sighed, took one last bite of her croissant, and hurried out.

7

Lazarus Holloway stretched his back, feeling the stiffness set in after hours of paperwork. It was two in the morning and he'd had enough. He grabbed his jacket, along with his uneaten lunch—crawfish and potatoes—from the minifridge and left the office.

In the CIU, Lazarus no longer followed a dispatcher's orders. He picked his leads and hours, guided by quiet tips from informants or encrypted intel drops. His office—a clean, modern hideaway—felt like a private nerve center, not a chaotic bullpen.

Here, he sifted through financial records, intercepted calls, and found patterns others missed. By day's end, he didn't always have a suspect in custody, but he'd leave careful follow-up notes: a suspicious text to revisit, a whispered reference to a safehouse's location.

Working with colleagues required subtlety. A rumor about a gang's new supplier might earn a nod and a hint on which streets to watch at dawn. Follow-ups were precise—a quick call to a uniformed ally, a brief stop by the tech specialist's desk to confirm metadata from a burner phone. Sometimes he invited younger detectives into his sleek office, showing how the cartels coded phrases linked to offshore accounts. Bit by bit, Lazarus pieced together a world of hidden connections, all behind the scenes in the quiet efficiency of the CIU.

That's why Deadeye had gotten under his skin.

Six months of investigation meticulously piecing together a case, and now it was over. He felt jittery, empty, like an actor after a long-running show suddenly canceled.

The bust shouldn't have happened so soon. The lead detective from Narcs, Adams—a big Texan who always acted like he had something to prove—had asked the intelligence unit to help get Deadeye on a wire. Lazarus had fought hard against it. Six months of work, and he was close to getting a warrant for Deadeye's accounts, homes, even his yachts. A solid plan—get him arrested, then convince him that flipping on bigger players was his only way out.

"You convince him he'll walk away, he'll flip," Lazarus had said.

But Adams, cocky as ever, laughed it off. "I've been doing this thirty years, son. I know what I'm doing."

Knowing that Adams would go in guns blazing like it was the O.K. Corral, Lazarus had volunteered to handle it himself. He'd been allowed in but only with the stipulation that Booker, the informant, would wear a wire.

Lazarus had sent a single text to Adams after Booker's death: His dying's on you, dipshit.

As he drove home, the empty streets of Vegas stretched out before him, bathed in the city's glow. He got out of the car and stopped to look at the sky, though there was nothing to see. The ambient light was so strong it swallowed the stars whole, leaving nothing but black emptiness. It made him feel uneasy, like the earth was drifting in a void, a ship lost at sea.

As he walked toward his building, he heard shouting. Isaac's mother was at it again, arguing with the latest boyfriend. Lazarus tried to tune it out as he climbed the stairs, hoping Isaac was using the noise-canceling headphones he'd given him.

Inside his apartment, he tossed his keys on the counter and remembered the bracelet. Thinking of Lou Hobbes always left a bitter taste in his mouth—not that Lou was a bad guy, but Lazarus just felt better when he wasn't around.

The bracelet summoned Amanda Bines, raindrops streaming down his face as he crushed her heart that night. The thought of fathering her child had lodged in his gut like plutonium, poisoning him from inside. He'd never wanted kids and Amanda had known it. So why was she suddenly making these claims?

The bracelet had gleamed silver and obsidian, crimson-eyed crows staring from its surface. It had that unmistakable artisan quality; the kind found in mountain villages where craftsmen still worked silver by candlelight.

But this was different from typical thefts. Lazarus had seen desperate men take sledgehammers to display cases, even one would-be burglar who'd brought a construction crane to peel back a jewelry store's walls like a tin can.

But this? Nothing had been taken except the bride and groom. The motive wasn't money, and that bothered Lazarus. Money was the most common reason people hurt each other. When it wasn't about money, things got complicated.

He had always had a photographic memory, and he brought up the images of the bracelet in his mind as he took some paper and a pencil and quickly drew it. Then he walked to his bedroom and sat down at his desk. He searched "Buluc Chabtan" on his computer.

Chabtan wasn't just the god of violent death, but of destruction. He operated outside the influence of the other gods, embracing chaos as ultimate freedom—the freedom to kill, to destroy. It was myth, of course. But Lazarus knew myths were just religions people didn't follow anymore. Maybe someone out there was still practicing?

He scrolled down and saw an illustration of a priest in a headdress, cutting the heart out of a victim lying on a stone slab.

His mind drifted back to Amanda.

They'd been engaged, and he remembered loving her, whatever that meant. She would've told him if Keri was his daughter. Besides, she'd been on the pill. They'd even talked about not having kids.

Still, the words lingered in his mind: *A child.* The thought of it—even if it wasn't true—sent a wave of anxiety through him.

Lazarus tapped his fingers against the desk, then pulled out his phone. He texted Lou.

8

It was eight in the morning when Piper woke, but she didn't move right away. She lay there, eyes fixed on the ceiling, listening to the muffled hum of the city outside her condo's windows. The quiet whoosh of distant cars mixed with the softer sounds of a new day—somewhere, a pigeon—and the faint scent of brewing coffee from a neighbor's kitchen.

She felt that familiar chill again, the one that made her check closets and walls for hidden holes, a habit born from last year's case involving a stranger who lived secretly in his victims' homes. She told herself it was nothing, just old nerves, and finally pushed the sheets aside.

After a quick shower, she slipped into a plain gray suit, the fabric cool against her skin. Her fingers hovered over her ichthus necklace, remembering how it always brought a measure of calm to her otherwise-tense mornings.

The condo's clean, modern lines and the large balcony overlooking a patch of green and a small pond were small luxuries she allowed herself. As she stirred butter into a pan, the smell was comforting and homey. That's when her phone buzzed.

She glanced at the caller ID: METRO POLICE. Tensing slightly, she answered, "Hello?" Her spoon clicked softly against the pan as she turned the heat down. The quiet sizzle of eggs.

"How are ya, Dancs?" The voice had a West Virginia twang she hadn't heard in almost a year. Not since he had killed the man that murdered her grandmother. Everything from that time came back like a fist of emotion bashing into her. Instinctively, the condo's warmth seemed to drain away, replaced by a prickling unease. She gripped the handle of the skillet a little tighter.

"Lazarus?" She tried to sound casual but felt her voice catch. Outside, sunlight glanced off steel fixtures in the kitchen and the faint sound of laughter drifted through the balcony door. The contrast between the peace of her home and the tension in her chest was jarring.

"In the flesh, so to speak," he said, and for a moment she remembered the long hours they once spent on cases that left both of them hollowed out. "How you been?"

"Great," she managed, flipping her eggs as if nothing had changed. "You?"

"Good." There was a pause, the silence heavy enough that she could almost hear him leaning back, deciding how much to say. "I'm in the IU now."

"I heard. How's that?" She tried to imagine Lazarus in a cleaner, more controlled environment—no frantic calls, no exhausted uniforms. It didn't fit him.

"Well enough," he said. She heard a long pause and pictured him weighing his words. "Danes, I've got something I could use help on. You got time?"

Piper switched off the stove, the aroma of butter and eggs mingling with the jasmine from her diffuser. Outside, a small bird landed on the balcony railing, its head tilted as if eavesdropping. "Sure. What's going on?"

He explained the kidnapping at the Eternal Bliss Chapel—two teenagers dragged away on their wedding day. "The bride's only fifteen," he added. "Her family's panicking, and I need someone who can advocate for them. I'd like you to represent the bride when we find her."

Piper's heartbeat spiked, not just at the horror of it but at the thought of being pulled back into Lazarus's orbit. She tried to keep her voice steady. "You haven't found her yet then?"

"No," he said. "Does that matter?"

"I've represented wards in absentia," she replied, resting her elbows on the counter, "but never for a kidnapping. Usually they're runaways."

"This one's different," he said. "I want you to meet with the family. You're better with vics' families than anyone I've got."

His words were a small spark of warmth, a reminder that she was good at what she did. She looked around her condo—the neat shelves, the sunlight dancing on stainless steel—and felt the old tension bloom. "I haven't heard from you in almost a year, Lazarus. Now you call out of the blue?"

"The case is . . . complicated for me. I need someone I trust, and I trust you."

Outside, a breeze stirred the leaves near her balcony, and a faint rustle reached her ears. She closed her eyes, imagining the look on Lazarus's face: earnest, tired, a little desperate. He had to be to call her.

She breathed in slowly, letting the butter and eggs and sunlight anchor her.

"All right," she said. "Send me the reports."

9

Piper pulled up to the house and parked, taking a moment to gather herself. Before leaving her condo, she'd managed a brief back-and-forth with Lazarus and then her boss Mike—confirming that, as a guardian ad litem, Piper had authority to meet with the family and ask necessary background questions for a ward represented in absentia.

This wasn't really her job, talking to the mother of a missing girl, but she didn't mind. The police had likely given Amanda little information, leaving her to pace her house late at night, imagining every terrible thing that could be happening to her daughter. If Piper could bring a sliver of relief, she was willing to try.

She had also read the marriage license application and found out Keri was pregnant. It didn't list the father.

She walked up the driveway, noting the basketball hoop and the welcome mat that read "Blessed be the visitor." The house was modest but well kept, the kind of place where you'd expect family dinners and backyard barbecues.

The door opened and a woman appeared. Amanda. She looked younger than Piper had expected, her face free of makeup, smooth and unblemished, but her eyes told a different story—tired and hollow.

"Are you Amanda?" Piper asked.

"I am."

Piper pulled out one of her business cards. "I'm Piper Danes. I'm an attorney with the guardian ad litem's office. I was told you'd be expecting me?"

Amanda took the card, barely glancing at it. "Yes, come in."

The inside of the house was as neat as the exterior. The furniture was worn but well maintained, and religious trinkets adorned the walls. Piper sat on the couch as Amanda brushed aside a few toys and settled into a love seat opposite her.

"Sorry about the mess. My boys don't let anything stay clean for long."

"How many kids do you have?" Piper asked. People loved talking about their children, and she needed to put Amanda at ease.

"Three. Keri's the oldest, from a previous relationship, and me and my husband have two sons."

"How are your boys handling all this?"

Amanda's expression softened for a moment. "Kenneth doesn't say much, but Kendall's younger. He talks about it all the time. I don't know what to tell him to . . ." Her voice caught and tears welled up in her eyes. "Sorry. I was expecting her to be on her honeymoon by now."

"Keri's fifteen, right?"

Amanda nodded, wiping at her eyes with a tissue from the coffee table. "Yeah, the judge said they needed parental permission, and we gave it. I liked Brad. He was always so kind to her."

Behind Amanda, Piper noticed a collage of family photos on the wall. Keri's face smiled brightly in the center, a snapshot of innocence and hope.

"She's very beautiful," Piper said.

Amanda nodded, her hands twisting the tissue. "She's so much more than that. She doesn't care about the things other girls her age do—boys, looks, popularity. She's always been an old soul."

Amanda's voice trembled, and she dabbed at her eyes again, more to distract herself than to dry her tears.

"Detective Hobbes won't talk to me when I call," Amanda said. "I want to know what they're doing to find her. I've left him messages."

"In cases like this, things can be slow. If she was taken for ransom, it's just a matter of waiting for the kidnappers to contact you."

"And if it's not ransom?"

"Then it's most likely someone in her life, or Brad's. Someone who knows them and had something to gain from this."

Amanda shook her head, tears brimming again. "Who would gain from killing a minister?"

"I really wouldn't know," Piper replied, glancing at the family photos.

Amanda wiped her face again, her voice barely above a whisper. "The only thing I can think of . . . it might have something to do with her father. He always attracted the worst kinds of people. I told Detective Hobbes, and he said he was going to talk to him because they know each other. He's a police officer, too. Can you ask if Hobbes has talked to him?"

Piper's heart went out to Amanda. The grief and helplessness in her eyes shone through raw. A small part of Piper felt a pang of envy—envy for a mother who cared so deeply for her child. It was a feeling that was alien to her.

The last time Piper had seen her own mother, she'd been nine years old. Her mother had overdosed on opiates, and Piper called 911 before quietly returning to her spot on the couch, watching TV next to her mother's unconscious body, waiting for the ambulance. It had been so routine she hadn't even cried.

"Sure," Piper said, pulling out her phone and opening her note-taking app. "What's his name?"

"Detective Hobbes told me not to tell anybody. I don't know if it's okay or not."

"I think he would be okay with me knowing."

Before Amanda could answer, a young boy came racing around the corner and stopped in his tracks. He had wavy blond hair and wore a

T-shirt with a ripped collar, his cherubic cheeks flushed from running around outside.

"Mom, who's that?" the boy asked.

"Her name's Piper. She's a friend. We're talking about Keri."

Piper smiled at the boy. "Hello."

The boy stared at her, his face full of confusion. No sadness yet, just innocent bewilderment.

"When's Keri coming home, Mom?" the boy asked quietly.

Piper glanced at Amanda, who had gone distant, staring off into some faraway place, unable to answer.

10

Piper left Amanda's house and had driven halfway up the block before she realized she hadn't gotten Keri's father's name. The fact that Hobbes didn't want people to know who it was worried her.

If she was going to dig into the case, she'd need to talk to him. Most juvenile kidnappings involved parents who had lost custody and took their child rather than risk never seeing them again. But stranger abductions were a whole different beast—rare and terrifying in their randomness.

The last kidnapping case she'd worked had nearly broken her. Piper could still remember those sleepless nights, staring at the ceiling, guilt weighing so heavily on her that it made her physically ill. It was a burden she hadn't shaken, one that lingered in the quiet moments.

Her stomach growled, pulling her back to the present. She pulled into a diner she liked, ordered a burger and fries, and sat at an outdoor table. Some teenagers at the next table over were joking loudly about sex.

As she ate, she pulled up the rules on a guardian ad litem representing a minor in absentia. She had the same privileges as if Keri were present. It was a small relief, at least legally.

She skimmed articles on the kidnapping online. One in particular stuck with her—a brief interview with an older woman who had done the bookkeeping at the chapel. The woman described Dalton, the minister, as one of the finest men she'd ever known and said she would never be the same after witnessing the violence. The words tugged at Piper, a reminder of how brutal acts ripple outward.

The groom's stepfather had offered a reward for any information leading to the teens' whereabouts, but there hadn't been any updates. The fact was, with something this violent, if one thing went wrong, she guessed the kidnappers would kill the teens as coldly as they had the minister rather than risk getting caught with them.

Piper smirked when she saw a video of Detective Hobbes angrily swearing at a reporter who had ambushed him as he exited a bathroom, still zipping up his pants.

After finishing her meal, Piper tossed the plate into the waste bin and headed toward the police station.

The Metro PD building gleamed in the bright Vegas sun, the windows washed to a shine by workers on platforms. The station had a hum to it, with the sound of footsteps, phones ringing, and quiet conversations. It was oddly comforting to Piper—a place where the world still moved, despite everything.

At the front desk, she was directed to the fifth floor, where the Criminal Intelligence Unit was located. After being searched and going through security, she was stopped by another officer, who checked her ID.

"Who you here to see?" the officer asked.

Before she could answer, a voice from behind her said, "I'm guessin' it's me."

Piper turned to see Lazarus walking toward her. He wore black slacks and a white shirt with a loosened red tie. His beard was fuller than the last time she'd seen him, and she noticed a new tattoo on his arm—a dark, inked cockroach, its antennae curling to form hollow eye sockets, its abdomen distorted into a skull's grin.

He greeted her with a smile, and despite the year of silence between them, he wrapped one arm around her shoulders like an old friend. She hugged him back, catching the leathery scent of vape smoke clinging to his clothes.

"You look good," he said, pulling away.

"I've been working out every day. How are you?"

"Getting by." He sat casually on the security officer's desk, looking at ease.

Piper glanced at the officer and said, "Mind if we talk alone?"

Lazarus gave a playful smile. *"Mi casa es su casa."*

He led her through the office. The Criminal Intelligence Unit felt different from the other departments she'd seen—no cluttered cubicles, no worn-out desks. Everything here looked new, sharp, professional. As they walked past one office, Piper caught sight of a name on the door: "Det. Kevin Riley." The office was empty.

"I didn't know he followed you here," Piper said.

"More like I followed him."

They arrived at Lazarus's office, a corner space with two walls of windows that overlooked the city. It was an impressive view.

"Quite a step up," Piper remarked, taking in the spacious office.

"I never thought I'd care about things like a nice office, but I gotta admit, it beats the Dungeon." He settled behind his desk, leaning back in his chair. Piper sat across from him, sinking into a sleek gray chair that smelled faintly of coffee.

Lazarus's expression shifted. "How's everything going? Really."

Piper hesitated, then admitted, "Some days are better than others. Christmas without her was hard." She cleared her throat, uncomfortable with how much she was sharing. "Sorry I haven't called or stopped by."

"I get it," Lazarus said gently. "You see me and you remember."

The honesty of his words stung. "Sorry," she muttered, looking away. "You didn't deserve me just cutting you off without explanation."

"*Deserve* ain't got nothin' to do with it," he replied, taking out his vape pen and inhaling deeply. "What brought you by now?"

"I talked to Amanda Bines," Piper said, her voice steady again.

"What'd she say?"

"Not much, but it'll take a few meetings. I think I also figured out why Keri and Brad got married so young. Keri is pregnant."

Lazarus raised an eyebrow. "That probably explains the rushed nature of the wedding."

"Yeah. For a minor to get married, you need parental permission and a judge to sign off. Guess who the judge was? Judge Dawson."

"Really?" Lazarus asked, his tone thoughtful.

"Yeah, but there's only six juvenile court judges. It's probably just chance."

A small smirk crossed Lazarus's lips. "I don't think there's such a thing as chance when it comes to her." He took another drag from his vape and let the vapor linger in the air.

"Do you have anything so far?" Piper asked, changing the subject.

"Nothin'. We don't even know if they're alive or dead."

"They could've killed them there if that's all they wanted."

"True," Lazarus said, nodding.

"So, are you thinking ransom?"

"Usually with ransom they'd have contacted the parents by now, but there's been no word."

"So what are you thinking?"

Lazarus leaned back in his chair. "Not sure yet."

"What does Detective Hobbes think?"

"Hobbes doesn't think. Or when he does, he tries to get it over with as quickly as possible."

Piper chuckled, and Lazarus turned his monitor toward her. "You seen the video?"

"No. Just what was online."

He pulled up the security footage from the chapel, the video starting in color, showing the altar, the minister, and the couple standing before him. Brad looked like any regular teenage boy, but Keri—she was strikingly beautiful, looking far older than her fifteen years.

The black car crashed through the chapel doors. Even without sound the violence of the impact was palpable. Wood splintered, glass shattered, and chaos filled the room.

The two figures who got out of the car moved with eerie calm. The larger one—the driver—held a gun in one hand and a large knife in the other. Dalton, the minister, said something, but the figure didn't hesitate. In one swift motion the knife slashed across the minister's throat. Blood gushed from the wound and Dalton crumpled to the floor as the guests watched in horror, too scared to move.

The figure grabbed Keri and dragged her toward the car. Brad tried to intervene, but the second figure struck him with the butt of a shotgun, sending him to the floor.

In less than thirty seconds the teens were in the trunk and the car was gone.

"Notice anything?" Lazarus asked.

Piper shook her head, still processing the brutality. "One male, one female, I think. You're looking for a couple. And the driver didn't even hesitate before killing the minister. It was . . . casual, almost."

Lazarus nodded, exhaling vapor. "Like it was nothing. That only comes after a lot of killin'."

"Have you ever seen anything like this?"

He took another drag, eyes dark. "No."

11

The black Charger rolled to a stop at a gas station just outside the Nevada-Arizona border. Carlito Xibala stepped out and stretched his back, his caramel skin gleaming under the desert sun. His short, bright dyed-blond hair stood in contrast to the piercings on his face—three silver barbells in his cheek that caught the light.

It had been a long drive and his back ached. The grim reaper tattoo on his chest, partially exposed by the unbuttoned top of his shirt, shifted with his movements as he took in the dusty landscape. Denver was asleep in the passenger seat, her raven hair spilling over her chest.

Carlito filled the tank, then headed into the small gas station. The place was run down—a few sad rows of snacks, a large walk-in fridge for the alcohol, and a rack of well-worn magazines by the counter. He grabbed a six-pack of Tecate and approached the register.

A small bell sat on the counter, and Carlito tapped it once. Then again. And again.

Finally, a man emerged from the back—curly black hair, a faded tattoo on his forearm. "Easy, I'm here," the man grumbled.

Carlito didn't respond, just stared at the cashier as he scanned the beer.

"I like the work," the cashier said, glancing at Carlito's exposed chest.

"Excuse me?" Carlito replied.

"The work on your chest. The ink. You get it inside?"

Carlito cracked open one of the beers, eyes never leaving the cashier as he took a slow, deliberate drink. "Why would you ask me that?"

The cashier shifted awkwardly. "Didn't mean nothing by it. I've been inside, too. I know how the tats look different when you use sawdust in the ink."

"You ask every customer if they've been to prison, or just me?"

"Brah, I'm just making small talk. Didn't mean to piss you off."

"What *did* you mean then?"

The cashier stumbled over his next words, but Carlito had already turned his attention to the beer can in his hand. He finished the beer in a few heavy gulps, crushed it flat against the counter, the metal crumpling under his palm, and slid it across to the cashier.

"Throw this in the garbage over there," Carlito said.

The cashier—Rusty, by his name tag—hesitated, then picked up the crushed can. He moved toward the trash, but Carlito's voice stopped him.

"From here."

"What?"

"Throw it from here," Carlito repeated, flatly.

Rusty looked at the trash can, then back at Carlito. He tossed the can, and it missed, clattering to the floor.

"Pick it up," Carlito said.

Rusty bent down to retrieve the can, his movements slow, cautious.

"Bring it back here . . . good," Carlito said, watching closely. "Now, throw it again. And if you miss, I'm going to blow your brains over those porno magazines behind you."

Rusty's nervous chuckle died quickly as Carlito pulled out the gold-colored Glock tucked in his waistband and slammed it onto the counter. Rusty's eyes widened, fear seeping into him.

"Hey, seriously," Rusty stammered. "I don't want any trouble."

"Nobody wants trouble, Rusty, but that's life," Carlito said, his hand still resting on the gun. "Now, toss the can."

"I . . . I don't want to."

"Then you've made your choice?" Carlito raised an eyebrow, fingers tightening slightly on the Glock.

The Night Collector

Rusty's breath quickened, beads of sweat forming on his brow. "I don't know what to do."

"It's simple, Rusty. Take this can and throw it into that trash. From where you're standing."

"What if I miss?"

"I already told you what happens if you miss."

Rusty swallowed hard, glancing from Carlito to the trash bin. "Look, man, that doesn't even make sense. Why would I—"

Carlito lifted the Glock, aiming it squarely at Rusty's head. "I hate when people start sentences with *look*. Say it again, Rusty."

Rusty wiped his brow with a shaky hand, fear dripping from his pores. He held the crushed can as he looked at the trash bin six feet away. He closed his eyes, muttering a prayer under his breath. Then, with his eyes open and locked on the bin, he tossed the can.

It bounced once against the wall . . . and tumbled into the trash.

Carlito smiled, slapping the counter with his free hand before lowering the gun. "Good job, Rusty. I knew you could do it. Keep that can to remember me by."

He tossed a ten-dollar bill on the counter for the beer and started to walk out but stopped at the fridge, grabbing a Yoo-hoo before heading back outside.

Denver was awake now, her bare feet propped up on the dash as she painted her nails black. Her low-cut top showed more of her chest than Carlito liked, and he noticed a man stumbling as he walked by, eyes glued to her cleavage.

"Did you get me a Yoo-hoo?" she asked, not looking up from her nails.

"Of course, *mi amor*," Carlito said, handing her the bottle.

She took it and looked at him, raising an eyebrow. "What took you so long?"

"Just needed to motivate someone."

12

Piper washed her hands in the restroom, surprised by how clean it was compared to the run-down government building that housed her office. It was a relief to be in a place that didn't feel like it was falling apart. She glanced at herself in the mirror, took a breath, and walked back out into the lobby.

Lazarus was still pulling his car around, so Piper descended the stairs to where her and Lazarus's old offices used to be; a cramped basement they'd called the Dungeon. The elevator doors opened with a quiet hiss, revealing a space now serving as a storage room. Dim overhead lighting cast shadows on broken chairs and cracked monitors. Wires dangled from half-gutted water heaters and a haze of dust clung to everything.

At the far end of the room was a whiteboard, its surface coated with a layer of grayish film. Piper stepped closer.

The scent here was different from the upper floors: stale paper and mildew. She raised a hand to wipe the board but stopped inches from it. Through the dust, she could just make out faint outlines of old case notes—half-erased leads and the names of victims who still deserved remembrance, each one echoing silently in her mind.

In the corner, the word "Creeper" still faintly lingered in Lazarus's handwriting.

Her chest tightened. Memories flickered.

A victim's description scrawled in marker; Lazarus pointing at a scribbled time and date, his eyes bloodshot and raw from too much caffeine and no sleep.

She felt an odd nausea, as though the horrors mapped out here had seeped into the drywall. This place had once held a strange kind of energy. It felt hollow now.

Leaving the board untouched, she made her way upstairs and emerged into the harsh daylight, the heavy scent of city grime slapping her senses. Lazarus pulled up in his black Chrysler 300, the growl of its engine a welcome distraction. Piper slid into the passenger seat, grateful for the blast of cold air from the AC as they pulled away.

"Still got your rabbit's foot up on the rearview, I see," she said, gesturing to the little charm dangling.

"We all have our superstitions," he replied, pulling the car out of the lot and heading toward the freeway.

The silence inside the car felt heavy. Unspoken things hung between them, thickening the air.

"I guess we should talk about the elephant in the room," Piper said finally, glancing over at him.

"What elephant is that?" Lazarus kept his eyes on the road.

"Why we haven't talked for a year."

"I know why."

Piper sighed, leaning back in her seat. "It was nothing personal, Lazarus. I actually missed you. But I had a lot of healing to do, and you can't do it when you're constantly reminded of the thing you're trying to heal from."

"You said your piece, and I told you it's fine. Let's let this particular elephant out of the room, shall we?"

Her smile was small but genuine.

They drove on, heading deeper into West Las Vegas, where the neighborhoods were rougher and crime was on the rise.

Lazarus pulled into the parking lot of a dingy bar, the kind that reeked of stale beer even from the outside. "You wanna wait here?" he asked.

"No," Piper said.

"More work for you."

They went inside, and the smell hit her immediately—the stench of old booze, dried puke, and sweat from the heat. The bar was surprisingly busy for the afternoon, full of people drinking their days away.

Two men stood near a dartboard, tossing darts and sipping boilermakers. Lazarus approached them, with Piper a step behind. The bartender barely glanced in their direction.

The man tossing darts had shaggy black hair and wore a worn polo shirt and jeans. Lazarus stepped up behind him and said, "Brian."

"One sec." The man focused on the dartboard, brow furrowed in concentration. He threw a dart, narrowly missing the bull's-eye.

"What do you want, Lazarus?" Brian said, finally turning around.

"Need help on somethin'."

"So? You got the whole police force to help you. I ain't your CI anymore. So why're you in my bar?"

"Fine, let's call me a customer then," Lazarus said, pulling some cash out of his wallet.

"I need to know about a kidnapping at the Eternal Bliss Chapel. You hear anything?"

Brian shook his head but took the cash anyway. "Nah."

"A couple drove a car into the chapel, killed the minister, and took the bride and groom. Didn't steal anything, didn't ask for ransom. I need to know if anyone's heard anything."

"What you gonna do for me?" Brian asked, lazily tossing another dart.

"I just gave you a wad of cash."

Brian shrugged. "I can get cash anywhere."

Lazarus watched him throw another dart, then grabbed Brian's wrist before he could toss the last one. "I know you like gamblin'. How 'bout we make this interesting? We throw these darts right here. I win, you help me. You win, I owe you a favor."

Brian eyed him. "Any favor?"

"Within reason."

"You know I'm here all day, right? I do this a lot."

"Shouldn't be hard to beat me then," Lazarus said, stepping back.

Brian chuckled. "All right. Your dime."

"You first," Lazarus said, stepping aside.

Brian retrieved his darts and then approached the line. He threw the darts quickly, each one landing near the center but none hitting the bull's-eye.

Lazarus calmly pulled the darts from the board, then stepped up to the line. He took his time, exhaling slowly, eyes locked on the target. The first dart hit the bull's-eye dead-on. The second was off to the left, but the third hit its mark, knocking the first dart slightly aside.

Lazarus turned to Brian. "Find me something."

Brian scowled. "That was bullshit. You must've cheated."

Lazarus took a step closer, his voice low and cold. "I've been more than patient with you. You lost fair and square. A man that welches on a bet deserves whatever's coming to him."

Brian glanced away, clearly uncomfortable under Lazarus's intense stare. "All right, fine. No need for threats."

"Find me something," Lazarus repeated, his voice sharp as he turned to leave.

Outside, Lazarus snorted, like he was clearing the stink of the bar from his nose.

"I see you still have friends everywhere," Piper said, sliding into the passenger seat.

"This is where life is," Lazarus replied. "With the dirty bars selling coke out the back, the pimps and hookers on the corners, and the drunks puking in the gutter. And Brian knows all of 'em."

Piper buckled her seat belt as they pulled out of the lot. "Where'd you learn to play darts like that?"

Lazarus gave a half smile. "There was a time I wasn't doin' good. Mentally. The bar next to my apartment had a dartboard, and I spent my days there."

He turned onto the main road, his voice growing more distant. "First time I went in there, it was packed at three in the afternoon. Two guys got into a fistfight, beer flew past my face. They started laughing and drinking together afterward. The people were drunk, happy, horny. I thought, *this* is where real life is. The kind worth living."

"And?" Piper asked.

"And it never repeated. I played darts every day for hours, but never saw another fight, never saw the place crowded again. It was just that one day. A perfect storm of chaos, adding up to something beautiful. Made me realize the randomness of it, though. So I quit the NOPD and moved to Mexico for a while. Figured I needed a fresh start."

"And did it work? Running away?"

"No. Turns out, what you're running from is inside you. It comes right along."

13

Lazarus checked his watch. Judge Dawson would be in session, but he could wait. Working in the Criminal Intelligence Unit wasn't like being in Homicide, Major Crimes, or even Juvenile Crimes—those units thrived on grueling hours and immediate arrests. Intelligence was different. Success here meant knowing which leads to chase and which to toss.

Sometimes a "win" didn't come from cuffing a suspect, but from steering a team of detectives away from useless dead ends so they could focus on what really mattered.

As an intel officer, he provided a quiet backbone of information. The detectives outside those walls might be waiting right now for him to verify if a rumored safe house location south of the Strip was legit, or whether a certain nickname scribbled on a bar's bathroom wall meant anything. They needed his intel and on his timetable. That didn't mean he was slacking off; it meant he had the freedom to be deliberate, to pick his moments. If he chose to linger before seeing Dawson, so be it. They'd adapt. In Intelligence, he didn't check in with them—they checked in with him.

Lazarus walked to the courthouse entrance. He thought of Keri and Brad while he took the stone steps up.

Their violent abduction should have screamed *random*, but the chapel's wreckage, the captors' viciousness, and that symbol on the bracelet said something else. Nothing about this felt accidental, though everything pointed that way.

And the possibility that Keri might be his daughter squeezed his chest like a steel band whenever he let it.

He walked into the courthouse and nodded at the bailiffs as they let him pass through the metal detectors. He made his way up to Judge Dawson's courtroom. A juvenile, maybe ten years old, sat at the respondent's table. Two attorneys stood near the judge's bench, speaking in hushed tones. The boy's parents sat in the audience, hands clasped tightly. The mother's swollen eyes betrayed recent tears while the father's gaze was distant, lost.

Judge Dawson caught a quick glance at Lazarus—so quick, he doubted anyone else noticed. She had that ability, like a predator in the stillness of a forest, always aware of her surroundings.

The attorneys returned to their tables, and Judge Dawson announced, "We're continuing this matter to the twenty-second by stipulation of the parties." She addressed the parents and attorneys. "Thank you, everyone. Let's take a twenty-minute recess."

The bailiff instructed everyone to rise, and they did so with dutiful precision as the judge exited. Lazarus slipped out of the courtroom and headed to Judge Dawson's chambers. The door swung open, revealing her—no longer in her robe, but now in a sharp navy suit.

"I've only got a minute," she said, guiding him down a short corridor into her office. The space was modern and stark, its only decoration an aspen tree branch doubling as a coat rack.

She sat at her glass-and-steel desk and crossed her legs. Black leggings and shoes that matched her suit.

"You should add some decorations in here," Lazarus said, sitting across from her.

"Why's that?"

"So you can remember you're human."

"Do you have any in your office?" she asked.

"No." He smirked. "You look good. Trim."

"An hour of Pilates a day. It's the best exercise there is. You should try it."

"Work out, eat healthy, don't drink or smoke—die anyway. I'll take my pleasures while I can."

"You could live longer with delayed gratification."

"It's only delayed if you live that long. Since we don't know when our number's up, you're just putting off pleasure for something you might never get."

He took a hit from his vape, and she watched him, her expression unreadable.

"I read the article in the *Ledger* about your lawsuit. How are the twins? What are their names?"

She shifted slightly, only a flicker of discomfort. "Austin and Evan."

He nodded. "How's that going?"

"As expected. They've frozen all my assets. They're hoping to bleed me dry, force me into desperation."

"I don't think I'd want to see a desperate Hope Dawson."

She grinned. "No, you wouldn't."

Leaning back in her chair, she recrossed her legs. "Haven't seen you in a while."

"I'm sure you've kept tabs on me."

She gave him a faint smile. "And why would I do that?"

"You always keep tabs on people you think you can use."

Her lips pressed together. "I find it hard to use people who make a habit of staying a step ahead."

"Maybe. But you're always trying."

Her expression remained unreadable as her fingers tapped lightly on the armrests of her chair.

"Have you kept in touch with Ms. Danes?" Dawson asked.

"We talked yesterday for the first time in a year."

"Why so long?"

"She needed space."

"We all do." Judge Dawson exhaled softly. "But I assume this isn't a social call."

"I'm working a kidnapping at a chapel. I'm guessing you know about it, since you signed off on the wedding."

"I do. Yes. I liked Ms. Bines. What is it exactly you want to know, Lazarus?"

"The application said she was pregnant. Is that confirmed?"

"No test is required, but the parents confirmed it. Are you asking why I granted the license? If the parents agree, I see no reason to object."

Lazarus paused for a second, watching her closely. "No, I'm not asking about that. I just care that your name came up. I don't like when your name comes up in my cases."

"That's unfortunate, considering we work in the same field."

He ran a hand through his beard. "A guy walks into a chapel, slits a minister's throat like he's taking out the trash, kidnaps two teens whose parents don't have a dime. Then *your* name comes up."

Dawson's face remained impassive, but a flicker of something passed through her eyes. "And what does that tell you?"

Lazarus leaned forward slightly. "It tells me things aren't what they seem. And when you're involved, they never are."

"You give me too much credit," she said, her voice calm, measured. "There was something innocent about Keri. Like a puppy. As though she didn't understand what was happening. I felt pity for her. When I heard she was taken, I felt responsible since I granted the license."

She was giving him information, but Lazarus wasn't fooled. There was more—there was always more with her.

"If I can help," Dawson added, her voice soft and unreadable, "let me know."

He nodded, but his gaze remained on her. She was holding something back, but she wasn't flat-out lying either.

"What do you think so far?" she asked, her tone almost casual.

Lazarus inhaled deeply. "I've seen smash and grabs, but not like this. They were calm. He was calm when he slit the minister's throat. He's definitely the more dangerous one."

"I wouldn't be so sure. In couples like this, the female is often the more dangerous. Quieter, more patient."

"So you know it's a couple."

Her smile was thin, barely there. "Anyone who's seen the video would."

"Hobbes didn't."

"Hobbes has his uses, but careful analysis isn't one of them."

Lazarus couldn't help but grin. "Yeah, I noticed."

He stood to leave, but Dawson's voice stopped him. "Lazarus?"

He paused. "Yeah?"

Her eyes lingered on a piece of paper on her desk before meeting his. "Amanda told me who Keri's father is."

Lazarus didn't respond. He turned and left.

14

Night had fallen over Vegas, and Lazarus sat in his car, staring at the neon haze of the Strip. Tourists stumbled through the streets, liquored up and high, their laughter floating in the thick, sticky air. He could see the swarms jaywalking, the chaos that only Vegas encouraged. A weekday, but you wouldn't know it here.

Lazarus didn't care much about the legal weed—it had freed up resources to go after real problems. Drugs were a symptom. He wanted to go after the people that took their own pain and inflicted it on others.

He started the car and pulled away, cruising slowly past the casinos. A group of drunk women hollered at him from the crosswalk, but he didn't pay them any attention. His focus was on something else. Piper's address was up next, and tonight, he had work to do.

The condo complex wasn't much. White buildings with gray roofs. Simple, clean. A welcome mat outside her door read "Peace to all who enter here." He smirked.

He knocked, and after a moment Piper answered in a black skirt and blouse, sliding on an earring. She seemed composed, but there was always something guarded about her—something he didn't push.

"Hey," she said.

"Hey. So, do I get a tour?"

"Not much to see, but come in."

The condo was small and neat. Photos of her and her grandmother Lake dotted the walls, and Lazarus felt a sharp pang seeing the old woman's face. Lake had been good people.

He noticed a framed quote under one of the pictures: *The Lord is close to the brokenhearted.*

"Laz, you okay?"

"Yeah, just thinkin'. What did you say?"

"I asked if you want a Coke or something."

"No, I'm good."

"Well, I need one," she said, going to her fridge. "So what do you have so far? Anything new?"

"Looks more and more like a random smash and grab to me."

"I don't know. If I was going to do something like that, I'd target someone rich. Not teenagers that come from middle-class families."

"Never know. Desperate people do desperate things."

She grabbed her keys, and they headed out to his car.

"So, where are we meeting this guy?" she asked as they walked down the stairs.

"Pool hall."

"You're taking me to all the classy places," she said with a wry smile.

"Someone's gotta," he said, glancing at her as they got in the car. "You look fit. Been working out?"

"I run ten miles a day. Helps clear my head."

"You training for something?"

"No, just for me. Relieve stress. You got something like that for stress?"

"I drink."

She smiled but didn't press further.

They arrived at a run-down two-story building. The pool hall had large windows showing at least twenty tables, the glow of neon lights casting shadows over the players inside. Lazarus exchanged a few words with the bouncer, and they were let in.

"The guy at the counter just picked up the phone when he saw us," Lazarus muttered, eyes scanning the room.

"Who is he?"

"No idea. Go talk to someone. Act normal."

"Normal?" Piper snorted.

Lazarus moved off toward the back. Piper hesitated for a second, then walked over to two young guys in cowboy hats playing pool. Lazarus watched the man behind the counter fumble with a stack of pool cues. He glanced up, and the two exchanged a glance before he ran for a door.

Lazarus bolted after him.

The guy burst into the kitchen and yanked a pan of hot oil from the stove. He flung it at Lazarus, who raised his arm in time. The pan smashed into his elbow, and burning grease sprayed his neck, sending a sharp, searing pain through him.

Gritting his teeth, Lazarus went for his gun, but the man was already out the back door.

The alley outside reeked of garbage and piss, and the man didn't slow. Lazarus saw him scrambling up a fire escape and took off after him. His legs burned as he leapt two stairs at a time, the fire escape groaning under his weight. The guy was a few flights up, slowing, but still moving.

The rooftops loomed above him. As Lazarus reached the top, he spotted the man jumping to the next building, barely making the gap.

Lazarus didn't hesitate. He took the jump and landed hard, his knees buckling. The man was waiting with a piece of lumber and swung it wildly. Lazarus ducked under the first hit, but the second cracked against his shoulder, sending a jolt of pain down his arm.

The man was older with gray hair and a scraggly white beard.

"Easy, partner," Lazarus said, raising his fists. "I just wanna talk."

The guy kept coming, breathing heavily. Lazarus slipped a weak swing, then countered with two sharp blows to the ribs and solar plexus. The man crumpled, gasping for air.

"Now why'd you go and make me do that?"

The man wheezed on the ground, struggling to sit up. Lazarus lit a cigarette, watching him.

"I'm lookin' for Royd. I'm guessin' that's you. Why'd you run?"

"I want my lawyer."

Lazarus chuckled. "Who's your lawyer?"

"Colleen Redfern."

Lazarus whistled. "She's damn good. You must have been saving your pennies to hire her."

Royd sucked in air, his face a mask of pain.

"Here's what I don't get. How'd you know I was police so fast? You don't look like the smart type."

"I seen you before."

"Where?"

Silence.

Lazarus squatted next to him, blowing smoke into the night air. "I didn't bust you before. I remember every face I've ever busted. You? Not one of 'em."

Royd winced but didn't say anything.

Piper and a couple of bouncers came up onto the roof. Lazarus gave them a quick nod and told them it was under control, then turned back to Royd.

"You okay?" Piper asked.

"I'm fine. Gimme a minute."

Once the others were gone, Lazarus leaned in. "I got your name from a confidential informant. You know what that means?"

"Who?"

"If I told you, it wouldn't be confidential, would it?"

"I ain't done nothing."

"You've done plenty. You just don't know which thing I'm here for."

Lazarus lit another cigarette and offered it to Royd, who took it with shaking hands.

"My CI says you know about missing teenagers."

"Bullshit."

"Really? You got a rap sheet full of crimes against kids, going back fifty years. Ain't that something? But it all stops about eleven years ago, right around the time you got chemically castrated. You trying to tell me you're a changed man?"

Royd's breath was shallow, his lungs rattling with every exhale. Lazarus could smell the emphysema on him.

"What do you want?" Royd said.

Lazarus pulled up a photo of Keri and Bradley on his phone and showed it to him. "These two were snatched from a wedding chapel. The couple who took them killed the minister and left everything else behind. No ransom, no robbery. Just them. Now why would someone want two kids with no money?"

Royd barely glanced at the photo. "I've never seen them."

"I didn't expect you would."

Lazarus stood up, watching the old man struggle to breathe. "You're dying, Royd. I can almost smell it on you. Why not use what time you got left to fix a little of the mess you made?"

"What do I get?"

"What do you want?"

15

Carlito Xibala leaned back in the driver's seat, watching Denver step out of the car to make a call. She moved with a dangerous grace he loved—tight jeans, black blouse, heels that clicked against pavement. Her hair was pulled back into a severe bun, showing off her sharp features. Emerald eyes like a serpent's: cold but alive with something wild. The first time he saw her, those eyes had burned through him, daring him. She'd been sitting at a bar, smoking and watching the room like a predator.

He'd walked up to her.

"You're the only person here worth talking to."

"Yeah? And why's that?" Her voice was as hard as her look.

"Because I know you're the only one in here who'd have the balls to fight me if I robbed the place."

That had made her laugh, and that's when he knew he was in love with her, and he told her.

"You tell strange girls you love them before even knowing their name?" she had asked.

"Only the ones I'm in love with."

Carlito smiled at the memory as Denver hung up and slipped back into the passenger seat.

In the dim glow of the car's console, he caught the curve of her cheek and thought about how she had stroked his hair in bed until he fell asleep that first night he was out of prison. He remembered when she'd mended his jacket with careful stitches or the time she laughed at a dumb joke, her eyes crinkling in a way that made the world feel less jagged. There was love in him; love that smelled like engine oil and cheap soap, but love that insisted they could outrun the blood and regrets.

"Who was that?" he asked.

"My mom."

"It's good you still talk to her."

"You don't need to tell me things I already know."

He glanced at her. "You pissed about something?"

"Yes."

"What?"

"Who's Isabel?"

He paused, then chuckled. "Isabel's my aunt."

"She's been texting you. I saw your phone."

Carlito shook his head, amused. "You're the only one for me, *mi amor*. You've got a poet's tongue and a sinner's heart."

Her face softened. "I like the way you talk. I don't know anyone that talks like you."

Carlito opened the driver's door. "That's what happens when you're locked in a cell twenty-three hours a day. You either read or you go crazy. Or both."

As he stepped out, Denver started to follow, but he stopped her.

"No, this is me. Stay here."

"What are you doing?"

"Just finishing a promise I made. I'll be right back, *loca*."

He walked into the diner, the smell of grease and coffee thick in the air. The late-night crowd barely noticed him as he scanned the room. His eyes locked onto Nick, sitting alone by the window. Nick's bald head gleamed under the fluorescent lights and his saggy arms were covered in old, faded prison tats.

"Sup, brother," Nick said, standing to slap hands with Carlito.

"How's life treatin' you?" Carlito asked as they sat down.

"Like a baby treats a diaper," Nick replied, lighting a clove cigarette.

Carlito glanced at the half-eaten plate of pancakes in front of Nick. "You gonna finish that? Haven't eaten today."

Nick gestured to the plate. "Help yourself."

Carlito picked up the fork and dug in, savoring the sweet syrupy bite.

Nick blew out a cloud of smoke. "How long you been out?"

"Two months."

"First thing I did was grab my old lady. Took her to the parking lot and went to town. You?"

"I went to the library."

"The library?" Nick chuckled. "What the hell for?"

"If you have to ask, you wouldn't understand."

Carlito poured more syrup over the pancakes and took a large bite, his eyes not leaving Nick's face. The diner buzzed around them, oblivious. Nick took another drag from his clove cigarette, leaning back in the booth.

"So, what's this about?" Nick asked, growing uneasy under Carlito's steady gaze.

"You remember Little Puppet?"

"Yeah, I remember him."

"I got sick inside," Carlito began, his voice calm, almost conversational. "TB. Tight spaces, no ventilation—it spreads like rats. The doctor didn't care. I was going to die in there." He took another bite, then pushed the plate aside. "But Little Puppet—he had some favors owed him. Got me transferred to a real hospital. He saved my life."

Nick's face stiffened. He knew where this was going.

"Look, Carlito—" Nick began, but Carlito cut him off, leaning back in his seat, eyes hard.

"Nothing in life is free, Nick. Little Puppet wanted something in return for saving me."

Nick shifted, glancing around the diner, but there was nowhere to go. The exits were too far, and Carlito was too close.

"Carlito, man, that was between me and Little Puppet," Nick stammered, trying to keep his voice steady. "Ain't got nothing to do with you."

"You're wrong there."

Carlito pulled out his Glock and fired three shots into Nick's chest. The sound echoed through the diner, mixing with the sudden screams of the other patrons. The sharp scent of gunpowder filled the air, and Carlito's ears rang with that familiar, pleasant hum—the silence after chaos.

Nick slumped, blood pooling around his body. Carlito sat there, taking it in, before casually taking a sip of the lukewarm coffee from Nick's cup.

The diner erupted into anarchy. People ran for the doors, some stumbling over chairs in their rush to escape. Carlito watched them with mild interest, then wiped his mouth with a napkin, pocketed the pack of clove cigarettes, and stood. An elderly couple couldn't move quickly and ambled by his booth, and he smiled and nodded hello.

As he stepped outside, Denver was waiting, the window of the car rolled down, cigarette smoke curling from her lips.

"Who was that?" she asked.

"Just paying off a debt. It's done now."

He slid into the driver's seat and started the car. "I'm hungry. You feel like pancakes?"

16

Lazarus spoke with Royd for over an hour, the conversation circling through layers of filth and depravity. A world where flesh was sold like cattle, where lives were disposable. Royd was vile, but giving a good name was enough to keep him out of handcuffs, for now.

When Lazarus found Piper downstairs at the bar, she was sipping a soda, watching a game of pool.

"Sorry to keep you waiting," Lazarus said, sliding into the seat next to her. "Royd isn't the type to open up in front of women. He hates them."

Piper shrugged, though her eyes held unease. "It's fine. What did you get out of him?"

"He said he'd ask around. I'll lean on him for the next few days, make sure he does."

Piper nodded. "Could you use some help?"

"Maybe." Lazarus checked his watch. "I gotta meet somebody. Can you catch an Uber back?"

"Yeah," she replied, though confusion flickered across her face.

Lazarus left the bar and headed to his car, parked around back.

It was a forty-five-minute drive to the Sun Bella Apartments near Mesquite, Nevada. Lazarus had driven this stretch several times over the past few months. The desert stretched out like a barren wasteland dotted with neon oases—casinos and hotels rising like mirages in the sand. It was a strange kind of beauty, but one he had learned to like.

The apartment complex wasn't much to look at. The buildings were an ugly tan, trimmed in a hideous orange. In the center there was a sad little pool, a couple of tennis courts that looked like they hadn't seen a game in years, and a small workout center. Lazarus climbed the stairs to the second floor, the orange paint peeling under his fingers as he gripped the handrail.

He knocked on the door and waited, the dim blue light from a television flickering through the blinds.

"You in there, big daddy?" Lazarus called.

The door opened, revealing a hulking man who dwarfed the frame. Riley's shirtless torso bulged with unnatural muscle, skin stretched taut like it was inflated. Lazarus craned his neck but couldn't see past the guy's chest.

"What do you want?" Riley's voice was low, strained.

"Came to take you to dinner."

"It's late."

"Then call it breakfast."

Riley turned without a word, leaving the door open for Lazarus to follow him inside.

The studio apartment was a mess. Clothes were strewn everywhere, gym bags spilled open on the floor. The couch, which Riley collapsed onto, sagged in the middle from his weight. The big man stared blankly at the television, his bloodshot eyes rimmed with exhaustion, glazed over with something darker.

Lazarus sat down. "Thanks for helping me out with Deadeye. I'm sorry it went down like that. No one should've died."

Riley shrugged, his massive shoulders barely moving. He didn't say anything.

"What'd you take?" Lazarus asked, his voice calm.

"Xanax." The single word rumbled out of Riley's chest, thick and heavy.

"When was the last time you saw your kids, man?"

"I see 'em every other weekend," Riley replied, but there was no connection in his voice. Just a hollow fact.

For the first time, Lazarus felt a wave of pity. Not for the hulking frame in front of him, but for the broken man buried somewhere inside it.

Riley turned back to the TV, his eyes dead again.

"I've got something I may need your help on."

Riley grunted but didn't look at him.

Lazarus decided this wasn't the time to ask for his help with the kidnapping, and certainly wasn't the time to tell him Lazarus might have a kid. The mention of his kids had affected him in an odd way.

Lazarus stood and wandered into the kitchen. The fridge was nearly empty, just a few expired items and leftovers that looked like they'd been forgotten weeks ago. A few moldy vegetables in the drawer.

"Let's go, big man," Lazarus said. "I'll grab us some food."

"I'm not hungry."

"You gotta eat."

"I don't have to do anything!" Riley roared, springing to his feet. In a flash, his massive hand flipped the coffee table like it was nothing, sending it crashing against the wall.

The outburst was brief, but the shame that followed lingered. Riley's face twisted in regret, his hulking form deflating as quickly as it had swelled with anger.

"Sorry," he muttered, his voice barely audible.

"You up your T dosage?" Lazarus asked.

Riley nodded. "It helps with depression."

"It's bad for your heart."

"I don't care about my heart."

Lazarus watched as Riley bent down and effortlessly righted the coffee table.

"I, um, just wanted to check on you. I have something I could use your help on, but we can talk about it later."

Lazarus stood at the door, looking back one last time. He had known Riley for years—seen him in his prime, unstoppable, full of life. This man sitting on the couch was a ghost. And it wasn't just the drugs or the steroids. It was the slow decay of hope, of something vital being worn away.

He shut the door and left.

17

It was noon the next day when Lazarus walked into the Criminal Intelligence Unit offices. Given the sorry state of some of the other departments he'd worked in, CIU felt like a breath of air. They had everything: equipment, autonomy, and no one breathing down their necks. He could see himself staying here for a long time, though whether that was good or bad he wasn't sure.

He went to his office and stood by the large windows overlooking the streets below. From there he watched people swarm in and out of county administration buildings and greasy spoons. The nine-to-five grind. That routine life had never appealed to him. He'd rather ride the rails like a hobo or join some commune than waste his life behind a desk. At least he liked his job—or maybe *like* wasn't the word.

His office phone buzzed. "Detective, Piper Danes is here," his assistant, Anthony, said.

"Send her in. Thanks, Tony."

A minute later, Piper appeared in his doorway, taking in the sleek new surroundings.

She said, "I can't get over how much of a step up this is from the Dungeon."

"Not bad, right?"

"Did it come with a pay bump?" she asked, half smiling.

"Little one. What about you? Moved out of that lawyer's dump yet?"

"Nope, still a junior attorney. I don't mind, though. The more you climb the ladder, the more people you have to manage, and I hate managing people."

"Amen to that," he said, nodding.

"So, did Royd come through?"

"Old man actually did. He's got something. I'm meeting him at his place in about an hour to go over it."

"Mind if I tag along?"

Piper sat in the passenger seat of Lazarus's car as they drove, a soft bluegrass tune humming from the speakers. Lazarus had his window down, sleeves rolled up, letting the wind brush against the new ink on his arm.

"What do your tattoos mean?" she asked, curiosity winning out. "How do you choose them?"

"Each one marks a moment in my life I want to remember."

"What about that samurai?" She nodded toward the intricate design.

"Long story. But this flower here"—he pointed to a delicate white lily on his forearm—"that's for a woman I was in love with when I was eighteen. She was thirty-two. When she was done having fun, she told me she didn't want to see me anymore."

"Why do you want to be reminded of that?"

"Pain sticks with you longer than pleasure. You remember your pain, you can use it."

They fell silent as they approached the run-down neighborhood. The houses looked tired, with yards littered with rusting car parts and broken toys. A pit bull, chained in one of the yards, watched them with a wary gaze as Lazarus parked. He got out, knelt by the dog, and extended his hand, allowing the dog to sniff before giving him a scratch behind the ears. The dog wagged its tail in appreciation.

Piper followed Lazarus to the door. He knocked, and a moment later, Royd answered. The man's face was gaunt, his eyes shifting nervously. The smell of stale cigarettes hit Piper like a wall when the door cracked open.

"Can we come in?" Lazarus asked.

Royd shook his head. "Let's talk out here."

He stepped onto the porch, lit a cigarette, and took a drag, staring out at the street.

"You find what I asked for?" Lazarus said.

Royd nodded, exhaling smoke through his nostrils. "There's an auction Tuesday night."

"What kind of auction?"

Royd's eyes flickered toward Piper, then back to Lazarus. "Private. By invitation only. The kids you're lookin' for might be there if someone's lookin' to unload 'em fast."

Piper felt her stomach churn. "Excuse me, are we talking about selling people?"

Royd shrugged. "Call it what you want."

"Who's going to be there?" Lazarus said.

"Don't know. Usual types. People who buy for rich pricks who can get away with it in places that don't care."

"Where's it at?"

"In the basement of a bar. But you need invites to get in."

Lazarus stepped closer. "You're getting us those invites."

Royd looked panicked, backing away slightly. "I can't. I'll tell you where it's at, but that's as far as I go."

"That's not good enough, Royd. You're getting us those invites, and you're coming with us."

"No way," Royd stammered, stepping back farther. "These aren't people you mess with. You know what they'll do to me?"

Lazarus closed the distance, his face inches from Royd's. "Nothing half as bad as what I'll do to you if you don't."

"What are you even gonna do? Walk in and say you're a cop? They'd shut everything down in a second."

"That's not what I do anymore. I'll be there to gather intel, talk to people. See if I can get some information on where those kids are. And if you don't help me, Royd, I'm gonna be gunnin' for you. You don't want that."

Piper shifted uncomfortably. She had seen Lazarus cold and calculating, but this was different. Personal.

"Lazarus," Piper said softly, "we'd have a better chance of getting in with Royd's help."

"There's no women allowed," Royd cut in, eyes darting toward Piper.

"Even if I don't take you, I want two invites," Lazarus said. "But Royd, if anything happens, I'll make sure you wish it hadn't."

18

Piper spent the day at the office, but her thoughts were miles away. The image of teenagers, right here in the US, trapped in a world of sex slavery haunted her. It wasn't just the horror of it but also the helplessness—the fact that these kids had no escape, no one to protect them. The weight of it sat like a heavy stone in her chest.

For Piper it went beyond the job or the official guardianship. If these kids vanished—just numbers on a roster or names on a report—then what good was her training and her hours at the courthouse negotiating for children? She could feel something bigger at play; a chance to prove that people like her and Lazarus could still make a difference; that the system wasn't just an empty promise.

She needed clarity, perspective, and there was only one person she trusted for that—Bonnie Epps. Bonnie had been a prosecutor with the attorney general's office, specializing in human trafficking cases before retiring to open a restaurant with her husband. If anyone understood the scope of this nightmare, it was her.

It was late, well past dinner, but Piper knew the restaurant would still be open. She grabbed her things and made her way out of the office.

As she stepped out of the elevator on the first floor, she ran into Mike, her boss.

"Hey, where you headed?" he asked, smiling in that easy, familiar way he always did.

"Just tracking someone down," Piper replied, her mind still preoccupied. "What about you?"

"Grabbing my stuff, was about to head out. You eaten yet? Let's grab something."

"I can't tonight," she said, shaking her head.

"Oh, okay, no worries," Mike said, his voice a little softer than before.

As she walked past him, Piper replayed the conversation in her head. He had seemed more disappointed than she expected, and that threw her. She had always seen him as a colleague, a friend, nothing more. Had he been thinking differently?

She got into her car and headed to Casa de Asada, the Salvadoran restaurant Bonnie owned. It was a cozy, unpretentious place, one level, with Salvadoran decor. Piper had only been there once, at the grand opening, but she remembered the food being good.

When she arrived, the restaurant was still humming with activity. A young hostess with jet-black hair greeted her.

"Just one today?" the hostess asked.

"No, actually, I'm looking for Bonnie," Piper replied.

The hostess smiled, nodding. "I'll grab her for you."

Piper stood in the small waiting area, her eyes landing on a painting—a faceless man on a mule, both slumped in exhaustion under an unforgiving sun. Beaten down by life and the heat.

"Piper!" Bonnie's voice cut through her thoughts.

Piper turned and smiled as Bonnie, all warmth and familiarity, wrapped her in a quick hug.

"It's been too long," Bonnie said.

"It has," Piper replied. "How's life treating you?"

"Busy, but we've been blessed," she said, waving her hand dismissively. "You look great, by the way."

"So do you," Piper said.

"Eh," Bonnie grumbled. "Just an old lady trying to keep it together. Work keeps me going. My dad always said never retire—your body knows it when you do."

"I'm hoping that's not true, because I plan on retiring and doing absolutely nothing," Piper joked.

Bonnie chuckled. "Come on in, let's get you fed. You look like you could use it."

They found a quiet table near the back, away from the noise. After disappearing into the kitchen, Bonnie returned with two vibrant-green drinks.

"Tastes better than it looks," she said, setting one down in front of Piper.

Piper took a sip and raised her eyebrows in surprise. "This is amazing."

Bonnie grinned. "My mom used to make these every Sunday. Brings back memories."

Piper smiled politely, but didn't have much to say. Her relationship with her parents didn't stir fond memories.

As they settled in, Bonnie's warmth helped ease the tension that had been building in Piper's mind all day.

"How's the legal world treating you?" Bonnie asked.

"Still at the GAL," Piper replied.

"That's been, what, four years now?"

"Yeah, I like working with kids. It feels . . . important."

Bonnie nodded, understanding. "Those cases stick with you. Even the good ones. But the bad ones haunt you."

Piper took a deep breath. "That's why I'm here, actually. I need your advice."

Bonnie's expression shifted, more serious now. "What's going on?"

"I'm representing a ward in absentia—a favor for someone. She was kidnapped from her own wedding. She's only fifteen."

"I saw something about that on the news. You think it's trafficking?"

"The detective on the case thinks so. Just a random kidnapping for quick money. I trust him, but it's just . . . Why would they target two teenagers? Why go to those lengths?"

Bonnie leaned back, considering. "That's not how trafficking usually works. It's not the movie version, where people get snatched off the street. It's slower, more manipulative. They groom these kids, build trust over social media, get them to think they're running off to something better."

"But Keri was just grabbed," Piper said. "She wasn't groomed."

"Then they must've been desperate. Or, they knew she'd be worth a lot. Underage, blond, and white, from a middle-class family? She's a prime target for high-paying clients."

Piper felt disgust. She wondered how they would exploit someone carrying a child.

"If it is trafficking, how fast could they move them?"

"Very fast. They could have them out of the country within days, maybe less. Mexico's the easiest route, then she's gone. Thailand, Saudi Arabia, anywhere. They'll sell her to the highest bidder. You have maybe a few days before no one will ever see them again."

Piper stared down at her drink, her stomach sick. "I can't believe this is still happening. Slavery."

Bonnie's expression softened. "It's happening everywhere, Piper. More now than ever. And you need to be careful."

"Why?"

"You're dealing with people who see human beings as things. When someone thinks like that, they're willing to do anything without feeling bad about it."

19

Lazarus stood across the street from the half-finished casino, watching workers heft beams and weld supports. Occasionally, developers offered behind-the-scenes tours before opening day, and he never missed them. He loved seeing a place in its untouched, pristine state, then returning later to witness how time—the great equalizer—left its inevitable mark.

The workers looked like ants swarming a hill, and tourists crowded the sidewalk, snapping photos. The hotel and casino were going to be two towering buildings connected by a walkway—one of the largest, glitziest additions to the Strip.

When Lazarus first moved to Vegas, he hadn't understood why the city council and state officials kept green-lighting more casinos. To him, it seemed like more competition meant less profit for everyone. But now he knew there was a backroom culture calling the shots, determining the course of the city. Those were the people he wanted to meet someday.

He got into his car and drove across town.

The house was a pleasant two-story in a neighborhood filled with young families. Riley and his wife, Shelby, had moved in when they first got married and liked it so much they never left.

Lazarus knocked and checked his watch. He had waited until Shelby got off work. A petite blonde in jeans and a button-up shirt answered the door, her smile quickly fading when she saw Lazarus.

"How are ya, Shelby?"

Her face hardened. "Fine."

"How are the kids?"

"They're fine, too."

"You're not gonna make it easy on me, are ya?"

She didn't respond, folding her arms instead.

"Can I come in?"

"Why?"

"Why are you angry at me? Did I do something?"

She stared at him for a moment, then exhaled deeply. "No, no, I'm sorry. I just assumed you were here to . . . I don't know. Something."

"I saw him yesterday."

"How is he?"

"Not good. He's taken vacation time, but it'll run out."

"So, what? You're here to ask me to take him back?"

"At least go see him. I think it'd help him get straight."

"I can't."

"Why not? You two shared time together."

"I never got his time. Never. I was alone raising the kids, alone through breast cancer, alone, alone, alone. It was easier without him home because I had a routine. Then it was better without him here at all."

"A man's gotta provide for his family and spend time with them. It's not an easy balance, and there's no instruction manual."

"He could've found another job or transferred. He didn't. He let things get worse and worse."

Lazarus looked behind her at the home. Photos of Riley weren't up anymore.

"He's a good man, Shelby. Good men in this world are rare. You hang on to 'em when you find 'em."

"I know he's a good man, and I wish him the best. But I feel like he ruined his family for his job."

"That's not how it was."

"You don't know how it was. You weren't here."

Lazarus could see the rimmed eyes of someone who'd been crying recently, makeup attempting to cover the evidence.

"Aren't you lonely?" he asked.

"We're all lonely."

Lazarus breathed out, resignation settling in. "If you need anything, let me know."

He turned and walked to his car. Once inside, he glanced back and saw Shelby peeking out through the window, watching him. He started the engine and pulled away.

———

Lazarus called and texted Riley several times over the next day but got no response. Finally, he decided to drive down to his apartment.

Last night, he'd dreamed again. Usually his dreams were brimming with screams and blood, but this one had slipped into silence. In the blackness, Keri Bines stood still, no whisper of movement or sound. Her face, half lost in shadow, mirrored his own. When he woke, an ache had lodged itself in his chest, a sadness he couldn't shake.

He wanted to bury himself in the Deadeye case—focus on that twisted figure warping young minds into foot soldiers for chaos. People like Deadeye had a sickness that infected everything it touched, and Lazarus longed to cut it out before it spread more. But Keri's image had kept surfacing, uninvited, hovering in front of every thought.

He was facing unknown odds, and if he had to walk blind, he wanted people he trusted with him. Until recently, Riley had been that man—no layers to peel back, no hidden motives—just honest eyes and a steady hand. Now, Lazarus wasn't so sure.

The summer sun glared overhead and the heat shimmered in waves, bending the air like glass. The complex was alive with the sounds of kids playing outside—it was Friday, a short school day.

He parked and went to Riley's door, then knocked hard. No one answered. He tried again, but nothing. Peering through the window, he could see Riley sprawled out on the couch, snoring like a bear.

"Big man, you okay?" Lazarus knocked on the window, but there was no response.

The door was unlocked.

The apartment reeked of booze, and not the good kind—the rotgut you chug just to get drunk. Riley was snoring loudly, his breath stinking of cheap liquor.

Lazarus checked his watch. It wasn't even afternoon yet.

The place was a disaster: litter scattered across the floor, trash overflowing from the bins. Lazarus rolled up his sleeves and started cleaning.

The garbage on the floors filled two full bags, and he needed another two to clear what was already overflowing under the sink. The bins were out back, so he hauled the bags outside and dumped them into one of the large trash containers around the building.

When he got back inside, Riley was sitting up on the couch, groaning.

"Kinda early to be tying one on, big daddy," Lazarus said.

"You're one to talk."

Riley dragged himself to the fridge, yanked out a gallon of milk, uncapped it, and started chugging it like water. He downed a quarter of it before letting out a long burp, then wiped his lips with the back of his arm.

"You my mother now?" Riley said.

"Just a friend."

"I don't need either."

Lazarus sat back on the couch, watching as Riley pulled some frozen chicken breasts from the freezer and tossed them onto the counter to thaw.

"I got somethin' a few days from now I need help with."

"What is it?" Riley asked, not looking up.

"Auction."

"For what?"

"People."

Riley stopped. "You serious?"

"Yeah."

"Why isn't Vice taking it?"

"They will once we know what it is for sure. Hobbes is the lead; I'm just support. I'm thinking this was a random smash and grab. They saw two vulnerable kids and thought it was a quick payday. This auction might be for them. I need someone watching my back."

Lazarus hesitated, debating how to phrase the next question.

"You good for it?"

"What's that mean?"

"You're drunk all day, man. I've never seen you like this."

"You don't got the right to tell another man how to drink."

Lazarus leaned forward, elbows on his knees, interlacing his fingers. "If you want her back, you should quit the force. Find something else to do."

"Can't do that."

"Sure you can."

"My dad was a cop. So was his dad."

"So? We don't have some destiny written in a book. We make our own lives."

"I'm not good at anything else."

"You've never tried."

Riley slammed the fridge door shut with enough force to make the contents rattle. "What the hell is this?"

"I'm worried about you."

"I don't need you to worry about me. I'm a man, and men go through shit. It happens."

Lazarus nodded. "Point taken. You going back to work when your vacation's over?"

"Yeah."

He rose. "It's on Tuesday night. I'll be by to pick you up." He turned to leave, then added, "Better come packing, just in case."

20

It was around two in the afternoon on a Monday when Lazarus met Piper at a diner near the courthouse. The place had a classic, retro vibe—black-and-white photos on the walls and checkered tablecloths. She had chosen a booth against the wall, next to a photo of one of the first casinos built on the land that would later become Las Vegas.

As Piper spoke, Lazarus listened. She described the past year without her grandmother, and Lazarus stayed silent, offering no advice.

"Are you happy?" he finally asked when she stopped speaking.

"You're the only person who ever asks me that."

"People usually ask where you live, what you drive. They don't ask if you're happy."

"I think I'm getting there. What about you?"

"I'm breathing. That's enough."

"Plants breathe, too. That's not enough."

The waitress came by and Lazarus ordered a black coffee. Piper stirred her soda, watching the bubbles rise and pop in the red plastic cup, her thoughts distant.

"So, you're really doing it?" she asked. "Going to bust an auction?"

"I'm not busting anything. I'm there to get intel. See if I can find out where they're holding Brad and Keri. Just in case, I'm bringing Riley along."

A small smile crossed her face. "How is he?"

"Been better. You know he got divorced, right?"

"I didn't. What happened?"

"Same thing that always happens. People start growin' apart and don't talk about it."

"Are you sure it's smart to take him with you? Someone like him draws a lot of attention."

"Maybe they'll focus on him and not notice what I'm doin'."

She let go of the straw and placed her hands in her lap. "Do you really think they'll be there? Keri and Bradley?"

"I doubt it, but it's possible. Most of these deals go down through photos. They keep the vics somewhere else in case things go south. That way they can use 'em as a bargaining chip. 'Cut a deal and I'll tell you where they are; don't and they starve to death.'"

Piper shook her head. "I still can't believe this is happening in one of the most advanced cities in the world."

"It's always been happening. We just see it a little better now."

"How does someone even find out about auctions like these?"

"Word of mouth. They pay off cops to make sure they're left alone and no one gets too curious."

"How do you not sound upset when you say that?"

"Because I accept things as they are. Corruption's everywhere. You're never gonna get rid of it all. You can only hope to keep it at an optimal level."

The waitress refilled Lazarus's coffee. He took a deep breath, letting it out slowly.

Piper said, "What are you going to do if they're not there?"

"Just talk to everyone I can, see if I can pick up tidbits, maybe dates of other auctions or things people have heard. It's a long shot, but what else we got right now?"

21

Ryan Montgomery sat two tables behind Judge Hope Dawson at the country club and watched her sign the check.

He guessed she was at least twenty years older than him, maybe more. He'd always liked older women. His last girlfriend had been older than the judge.

Ryan worked as an assistant at a security firm. He didn't love being out in the field, especially on a tail job. Most rookies liked chasing suspects and flexing muscle, but he wanted other things in life. An office on the top floor where he could be seen by the firm's executives every day and get noticed.

Judge Dawson rose from her seat, her Gucci bag draped over one shoulder, and headed for the door. Ryan left a ten on the table—enough to cover his soda—and followed her outside.

She climbed into a brand-new black Bentley. It gleamed in the sun, more like a jewel than a car. Ryan got into his Camaro and followed at a safe distance.

Everything about her—her clothes, the way she sipped her wine—was refined, almost hypnotic. He could see himself falling for a woman like that. But she wouldn't give him a second glance. Not yet. Someday, when he was pulling seven figures like the top execs at his firm, maybe then.

They drove about twenty minutes into an even more exclusive neighborhood than the one with the country club. Judge Dawson handed her car keys to a valet in front of a place called the Clementine—a private bar with tinted windows and a discreet sign. Ryan managed to park around back, then tried to enter through the front. A brawny security guard put a hand on his chest.

"Members only," the guard said.

Ryan's gaze slid over to Dawson. She was already seated, her back turned to him.

"Fine," Ryan said, "I'll buy a membership."

"Costs ten thousand a month."

Ryan blinked. "What are you serving in there that costs ten grand a month?"

"Whatever it is, you ain't getting it without ten grand."

The guard didn't crack a smile. Ryan gave a nod and backed off.

He returned to his Camaro to keep an eye on the front. After forty-five minutes, Judge Dawson finally came out. She took her Bentley from the valet and drove off. Ryan started his car, then nearly jumped out of his skin when someone knocked on his window.

A police officer stood there, eyes locked on Ryan, motioning for him to roll down the window.

"Step out of the car," the officer said.

Ryan felt his stomach twist. "Did I do something wrong?"

"Out. Now."

A second police cruiser arrived. Ryan sighed and popped open the door.

They searched him, questioned him about following a judge, then checked his private investigator's license history. When it was over, three hours had passed. Judge Dawson was long gone. Jobs paid a bonus when you didn't lose a tail the entire shift.

Damn. I needed that bonus.

He trudged to his car, cursing under his breath. Overhead, the moon was faintly visible. A woman's voice startled him.

He whirled around and found Judge Dawson standing there, wearing a fitted jacket.

"You did well," she said. "You lasted longer than most of them."

Ryan tried to play it cool. "I don't know what you mean, ma'am. And, honestly, I don't—"

She stepped closer, and her tone went cold. "Let's not insult each other. How much do my brothers pay your firm?"

"What?"

"They hired you to follow me. They even broke into my house. You might not know that part, but you know they're your clients. So how much are they paying?"

Ryan swallowed. "I think it's three thousand an hour."

"And you get what, fifteen percent?"

"Twenty."

Dawson raised her eyebrows. "Twenty. That's high." She paused. "What's your name?"

"Ryan Montgomery," he said quietly.

"Well, Ryan Montgomery, I'll pay you a hundred times that amount for one task."

He let out a half laugh. "For what?"

"I want to know what my brothers have on me—everything. I want my files *and* their files, everything your firm dug up on them when they signed the contract."

"We don't keep files on clients," Ryan said. "They're the ones footing the bill."

She gave him a pitying look. "Ryan. Grow up. If your firm charges three thousand an hour, they investigate the clients without telling them before taking a job. I want those files."

Ryan shook his head. "I wouldn't even know where to start."

She smiled, slow and confident. "I'll tell you exactly where to start."

22

Keri Bines slumped against the cold wall, ropes gnawing her wrists. Eleven days since the kidnapping—nine in some dank basement, the last two here, wherever "here" was. No voices, just the faint skitter of something small nearby. Their captor had left food and a bucket but hadn't spoken—just a hulking silence.

She glanced at Brad, slumped beside her. He leaned against the wall, too, his head tipped back, eyes closed like he was somewhere far away. Peaceful. She was jealous of that, even if it wasn't real. Her own head was a storm—memories of her mom, her messy room, the little fish tank she used to ignore. Now all she wanted was to see those things again, just once.

She sniffled, tears slipping out before she could stop them.

Brad stirred, his eyes fluttering open. "What's wrong?"

"Nothing. Go back to sleep."

He sat up a little, scanning the room like he might find a crack in the wall they'd missed. But there wasn't anything. They'd spent hours pulling at the knots, only to have them cinch tighter. Whoever had tied them had known what they were doing. The thought sent a chill through her; you'd have to have done this a lot to know how to tie knots like that.

Brad moved closer, his arm brushing hers. "We're gonna be okay," he said. "Cops are probably looking for us right now."

Her laugh was bitter. "We don't even know where we are. How do you think they're going to find us?"

"I just know."

"You're so stupid sometimes," she said, shaking her head.

Brad smiled faintly. "That's why you love me, isn't it? Can't have a guy who's smarter than you."

She almost smiled, almost let herself fall into the comfort of his teasing. But the damp, musty smell of the room reminded her where they were. Dust covered everything, thick enough to choke on, and the moonlight sneaking through the gap under the metal door only made the shadows move and look alive.

"Are you scared?" Brad asked softly. "Sorry, stupid question. I'm just talking."

"I'm scared of him," Keri said, keeping her eyes down. "Not the dark."

"Really?"

"Yeah." She hesitated, then said, "When I was twelve, I got drunk with my best friend and stumbled home. Charlie convinced my mom to send me to one of those scared-straight wilderness camps."

"You never told me that."

"I don't talk about it."

"Why not?"

"It was hell," she said bluntly. "The counselors had fun torturing us. But there was one guy, probably in his thirties, who wasn't like that. He was funny and taught us survival stuff—like how to find water or stay cool in a desert. He acted like he cared."

Brad waited, his silence patient. That was his way. He didn't push.

"One night," she said, her voice trembling, "he came into my cabin."

Brad stiffened beside her, but he didn't interrupt.

"He didn't . . . you know," she said, her relief still raw. "But I woke up with him touching me."

"What'd you do?"

She smiled, despite herself. "Grabbed his balls and twisted as hard as I could."

"No way," Brad said, grinning.

"Way. He screamed loud enough to wake everyone up." She leaned her head back, staring at the ceiling as if the memory were playing on it. "When I got home, I told my mom, and you know what Charlie said? 'Boys will be boys.' Then he went golfing."

Brad's jaw tightened. "That's messed up."

"Doesn't matter now," she said, her voice dull.

"Why do you do that?" he asked. "Talk like nothing good ever happens?"

"Because it doesn't. Look where we are."

Brad had no answer. He looked away, his fingers twisting nervously at the ropes on his wrists.

The sound of an engine roared outside, cutting through the silence. Tires crunched on gravel; then a car door slammed.

Keri froze, her breath catching in her throat.

Brad's hand brushed hers. "We're gonna be okay," he whispered again, but this time he didn't sound convinced.

23

Carlito Xibala woke up around one in the afternoon and rolled over to kiss Denver. Since the night they met, they hadn't slept apart.

She wasn't in bed, but he heard the toilet flush. She emerged from the bathroom in nothing but panties and a crop top, her smooth legs revealed in the dim light.

"What?" she asked.

"You're beautiful. Like a snake."

"You think a snake's beautiful?" she asked, crawling onto the bed on all fours, her emerald eyes gleaming like a predator's.

"People are afraid of snakes because they think we're separate from nature. We're not. That's why it's all beautiful."

He gently brushed her hair aside, looking into her eyes.

"And now you've bitten me," he said. "Your venom is in me. I'm helpless."

She straddled him. "Don't say things you don't mean."

"I never do."

They kissed, their bodies moving together as if magnetized. It didn't take long before they made love.

Afterward, Carlito pulled on a black sleeveless shirt and a pair of worn jeans. "You sure about this?" he asked.

"Which part?" Denver said.

"We're going to piss off a lot of people."

Denver snorted. "So what? We're the ones risking our asses. We deserve more cash. They don't get their hands on anything till we get some cash."

Carlito nodded, leaning in to press a quick kiss on her cheek. "I'll be back."

Denver slept a bit longer before getting out of bed. The apartment belonged to one of Carlito's old cellmates. He owed Carlito a favor, though she didn't know what kind. It was clean enough, but the neighborhood was terrible. Graffiti and trash and the wail of sirens.

After getting dressed, she looked out the window. She could see into the building next door. A man sat by his window, smoking. She'd seen him watching them before, his eyes following her.

He grinned at her from his window and waved.

The phone rang, snapping her attention away. Denver answered her mother's FaceTime call. Her mother's face appeared on screen—aged, lined with the scars of a hard life.

"How are you?" her mother asked.

"I'm okay. Just working."

Her mother scoffed. "What work are you doing with him?"

The way she said *him* dripped with venom.

"We take care of each other."

"You still think he's going to marry you?"

"Yes."

Her mother let out a bitter laugh. "He's not the kind of man that marries. He uses women and throws them away when he's done."

"I don't need advice on men from you."

The words hit like a slap, and her mother went quiet.

"Sorry, *mami*," Denver muttered.

"It's okay. I shouldn't say anything. You're in love and won't listen anyway."

The Night Collector

Denver sighed. "What did you want?"

"I want you to come home. I haven't seen you in a long time."

A knock at the apartment door interrupted them. Her mother's voice was curious. "What's that?"

"Someone's here. I'll call you back." Denver hung up and went to the door.

When she opened it, a tall man with wide shoulders and prison tattoos on his forearms stood there, a grin plastered on his face.

"Hi," he said.

"Yeah?" she said, folding her arms.

"Guess you know why I'm here," he said with a smile.

"No, I don't. And I got shit to do. Bye."

She went to shut the door, but he blocked it with his foot.

"Now that's rude. I'm a nice guy." He forced his way inside, pushing her back.

He was big, over six feet tall, and reeked of booze. He shut the door behind him.

"Get out," she said.

He took a step forward, his grin widening. "You were supposed to deliver something to us. I was there. I was there a long time, like an idiot just sitting there checking my watch, but nobody showed up. Now that wasn't nice to do, was it?" He glanced down the hallway, clearly checking if anyone else was there. She figured he had been waiting outside until Carlito left.

"You don't get them until we get more cash."

He shook his head. "I wasn't the one you made the deal with. It's not nice to change a deal after you've made it. Where are they?" He took a step forward. Denver didn't back away.

"Get out."

"You should be nicer to strangers. Maybe you need to learn some manners?"

"Get. Out."

His hand flashed out and slapped her hard across the face. The pain exploded across her cheek, nose, and lips. Denver was knocked off her feet, landing hard on her back as blood began streaming from her nose.

Before she could react, he kicked her in the ribs, flipping her over. She gasped for air, the breath knocked clean out of her lungs.

"What's wrong? Can't breathe?" he mocked.

He threw her onto her back and straddled her, his hands closing around her throat. Denver clawed at his fingers, but his grip was like iron.

Denver's vision blurred, and for a moment she was no longer in the apartment. She was eight years old again, hiding behind the couch as her father's drunken fist flew into her face. The sound of her cheekbone cracking and her father's slurred threats.

Desperation flooded her. She yanked one hand from her throat and sank her teeth into his thumb, crunching bone. Blood flooded her mouth as she clamped down harder. The man howled, then slammed a fist into her face, nearly knocking her out.

"You bitch!" he screamed, cradling his mangled hand. Denver spit out the chunk of thumb she'd bitten off and laughed—a blood-soaked, maniacal laugh.

He stared at her, eyes wild with rage. "You wanna play?"

Grabbing a handful of her hair, he yanked her up, then threw her across the room into the kitchen. She slammed into the cupboards and crumpled to the floor.

He strolled toward her, calm now, amused. "You got fight in you. I like that."

Denver was on her knees, gasping for air. He bent down, getting in her face.

"Go ahead," he taunted, pointing to his chin. "Take your best shot."

Her fingers curled around a shard of glass from a broken plate. She drove the glass deep into his inner thigh and ripped downward. Blood sprayed from the wound as he screamed, stumbling back.

Denver spit out blood and a tooth, laughing even harder.

The man roared and rushed her, flinging her into the wall. She vomited before he grabbed her hair again and threw her into the bathroom. Glass shattered as she hit the mirror, the medicine cabinet crashing to the floor.

Denver grabbed a toothbrush, the only thing within reach, and stabbed it into his eye. He howled in agony, blood pouring from the socket as he reeled back.

Still dizzy, Denver forced herself to stand. She grabbed a jagged shard of mirror and stabbed it into the soft flesh under his chin, over and over until her arm burned and the glass was slick with blood.

The man's hands were shredded and his neck a pulpy mess. He swung wildly and connected with the side of her head. Denver hit the floor, gasping, her vision swimming.

The man collapsed against the wall, blood pouring from his neck and pooling on the floor. His eyes, filled with terror, locked onto hers.

"What the hell is wrong with you?" he croaked.

Denver just laughed. She couldn't stop.

24

Judge Hope Dawson's dining room shimmered in the candlelight, the polished mahogany table reflecting warmth.

Each of her eight guests—figures who held influence—found themselves seated with precision, their names spelled out in calligraphy on pristine cards.

Dawson sat at the head of the table in a silk blouse, watching her guests with a genteel smile. They had come expecting polite society and conversation. They had not expected intimacy: each dish before them was an unsettling secret.

The banker's braised duck simmered in a sauce he'd praised at a charity gala. The surgeon's childhood comfort meal—a fish stew fragrant with herbs she'd never admitted to loving—steamed gently. The journalist's truffle pasta made by his mother's recipe.

The utensils chimed against porcelain, and the conversation began on safe ground—compliments on textures and flavors, but she knew they felt uneasy. These were people accustomed to commanding rooms, but Dawson's quiet demonstration of their private tastes rattled at least some of them. Power always shifted subtly.

The banker said, "So, what's been happening with your brothers' lawsuit?" He then slid a piece of glistening duck between his lips.

"They're winning," Dawson said, barely holding back her revulsion while she watched him chew. "They're trying to take everything I have."

The banker's wife leaned in with fake sympathy. "Oh, Hope, that's just terrible."

Dawson let her eyes rest on the woman's face just a second too long. "You would know, wouldn't you, Pamela? You have brunches with Austin's wife every Sunday."

The woman cleared her throat awkwardly and seemed almost to shrink into her chair.

Dawson said, "Before this lawsuit, I told them I'd have to air their dirty laundry as they will mine. And theirs is much worse."

The banker, feigning ignorance, raised his brows. "Worse how?"

"They've been involved in seedy affairs. More than once, they visited a certain island notorious for its . . . shall we say, 'loose morals.' I wonder, Fredrick, if you've ever visited that island with them?"

The man opened his mouth but changed his mind on speaking.

Dawson's eyes roamed over each face. Every person here might testify against her soon.

She smiled. "Anyway, enough dark thoughts. Tonight's dessert is a croquembouche."

Her tone brightened as she unveiled the elegant tower of caramel-glazed pastries.

Dawson switched on soft chamber music.

She laughed at their anecdotes, pretended sympathy, matched them sigh for sigh. But inside she felt a single emotion: disgust.

A tax attorney known for his smoothness finally set down his fork and said, "Hope, this meal—these meals—are remarkable. How did you know everybody's favorites?"

Dawson's eyes caught the candlelight, carving lines of shadow along her cheekbones. "People reveal more than they realize. If you watch them carefully, they'll reveal everything you want to know about them." She raised her glass to her lips. "Or perhaps I just asked your secretaries."

The guests chuckled, but the sounds came out uneasy.

"But really," the attorney said, pretending a casual tone, "how did you know?"

She tilted her head, voice almost tender. "I like to know my enemies personally," she said. "To speak to them and see how they respond. How they lie to my face with a smile. I like to watch them lie to me and see the shame in their eyes, but something else, too. Something that makes them do it despite the shame. Some sort of pleasure."

Silence fell.

A few people watched Hope, and a few looked away. Seconds ticked by before anyone moved or said anything.

The lawyer finally cleared his throat and placed his napkin on his plate as he rose. "I think maybe we've worn out our welcome."

When the doors closed behind her guests, Dawson cleared the table. She moved through the rooms like a ghost.

In the gold-hued bathroom, she disrobed and stepped into a hot shower, water hissing against marble.

She lathered and contemplated the equations of her evening: Every guest was aligned against her, but they were weak. Pliable to pressure. Soft like dough.

She turned the shower off and got out, slipped on a robe, and dried her hair in front of her mirror. She caught a glimpse of her steel-colored eyes. She had never seen herself as beautiful and disliked mirrors.

She carried a glass of wine onto her balcony. The city spread in front of her like an animal, its lights flickering.

Her phone buzzed. She answered and said, "It's late. Are you drunk?"

Lazarus's voice crackled over the line. "I am not."

"Then a social call?" She sipped her wine, letting her eyes drift over the skyline.

"Something like that."

She let a quiet breath escape through her nose. "What do you want, Lazarus?"

"I want to know about these kids."

"Because she's your daughter?"

"Because they don't deserve this."

"What is it about having a child that frightens you so much you can't even speak about it?"

Silence flickered on the line.

"I don't think I feel like talkin' about that right now."

"You want to talk about who took them." She swirled her wine. "You may find out or you may not. They might vanish—gone as if the earth swallowed them. People disappear; you know that." She paused, enjoying the quiet tension. "You talk about randomness, but you never see it when it's in front of you."

"You think it was random?"

"They were children. What could they have possibly done to earn that?"

He let out a breath. "Random would be bad. Random would mean I got no real leads right now."

She took a sip of her wine. "Were you in love with her mother, or was it some sloppy one-night stand?"

"You have yourself a good night, Hope."

When he hung up, Dawson went back inside. She couldn't stop grinning.

25

Carlito liked old cars. One of the few good memories he had of his father was sitting in the garage on Saturdays, watching as the old man fixed Mustangs and Camaros. It was probably the only time during the week his father wasn't drunk.

He pulled up to a run-down trailer park in Glendale, one of the worst parts of the city. Around here, the police were practically invisible. Drug dealers hung up flyers announcing their next rounds of business like clockwork, and nobody gave a damn. Carlito never blamed them for it—they were just surviving like everyone else.

He stepped out of his car with a bag of groceries. A couple of kids playing next door eyed him, and he shot them a wink before walking up to the door of a dilapidated trailer. He didn't knock.

Inside, his mother and aunt sat in worn-out chairs, the small color TV humming in the background. His aunt was on disability because of her weight, and his mother was paralyzed from the waist down after a drunk driving accident. His father had been at the wheel the night he died.

"You bring some food?" his mother asked, her eyes dull but sharp enough to notice the bag in his hand.

He set it down on the table, glancing around the small, dirty space. "This place is a mess. I'm hiring you a housekeeping service."

"You can't afford that."

"I will soon. I'll get you out of here, into a real house." His tone was even, but something in his voice said he meant it.

"You always say such things," his aunt muttered in Spanish, still glued to the TV.

He ignored her and sat with them for a few minutes, pretending to watch the talk show they were glued to.

When they started eating, Carlito told them he'd bring more food later and left.

Carlito got back to the apartment complex and took the stairs two at a time. The door was open a crack. He froze, his senses going into overdrive. His hand moved to his waistband and pulled out his pistol before he pushed the door open with his foot.

The scene inside was chaos. The coffee table shattered across the floor, the TV on its side, and blood splattered across the walls like a painting.

He crept forward. He peered around the corner into the hallway that led to the bedroom.

That's when he saw her—Denver, slumped against the wall. Her face was a mess of cuts and bruises, her hair matted with blood. One of her eyes was swollen shut, and her lips were split. He swallowed hard, the bile rising in his throat, and took a step toward her.

But then his gaze fell on the man.

He was lying against the opposite wall, still breathing—barely. His face was as mangled as Denver's, his neck torn to shreds, blood seeping out of a gaping wound in his thigh. Carlito didn't recognize him.

"She's crazy," the man gasped, his words thick with blood. "I was just walking by . . . She attacked me for no reason, man."

With a swift motion, Carlito drew a blade. The sound of steel slicing through flesh. The man's throat opened like a macabre smile. Blood gushed, staining the floor crimson as the man collapsed, gasping futilely for air.

Carlito turned back to Denver, his hands trembling as he knelt beside her. "What did he do to you, *loca*? What did he do?"

The Night Collector

She flinched, fighting him off weakly at first, but when her good eye recognized him, she managed a bloody smile. Relief flooded him.

"You're gonna be okay," Carlito whispered, crouching beside her. He glanced at the man's lifeless body one last time, then snatched a few essentials—keys, phone, gun—and shoved them into a bag. With a quick breath, he scooped Denver into his arms, her body limp against him, and bolted out of the apartment.

He drove like a madman to the hospital, weaving through traffic and running red lights. He didn't care if the cops chased him. He wasn't stopping for anything.

After he skidded to a stop outside the ER, he bolted inside. "I need help!" His voice was raw, frantic.

A nurse rushed over, and soon a gurney was brought out. Carlito laid Denver on it, his hands shaking uncontrollably. The sight of her, broken and bloody, gutted him.

The doors to the trauma ward swung open, and Carlito tried to follow, but a nurse stopped him. "Sir, you can't go back there."

"I'm going with her," he growled, his eyes wild with fear and rage.

"Sir, please. You've done all you can. Let us take it from here."

Carlito's eyes filled with tears he refused to let fall.

"Without her in it, this world is nothing but ashes to me."

The nurse's face softened. "We'll take good care of her. I promise."

He stood there, helpless, as the doors closed behind her, sealing him on the other side.

26

Lazarus lay in bed, frozen. The faint glow of moonlight slipped through the blinds, slicing the ceiling into uneven bands of light and shadow. He couldn't move—sleep paralysis held him in its fist. Only his eyes could dart, locking on the mirror across from the bed.

In the reflection, he saw himself lying still, but then his double moved, though he hadn't. Slowly, the figure turned its head and grinned. The skin peeled away from its face in wet, sloughing strips, revealing a bare skull.

A blaring alarm shattered the silence, yanking him out of the nightmare. He bolted upright, gasping for air, his hands pressing against his temples as if to keep his skull from splitting. His heart hammered like a war drum.

Sleep paralysis was no stranger to him—it was his oldest enemy. The neurologists had written it off as stress-induced hallucinations, but they didn't see what he saw: bleeding skies, crumbling cities, the dead walking on a broken earth. Visions of humanity's end, no different from the billions of species that had gone extinct before it. And if he didn't act tonight, Brad and Keri would be the first to fall.

He threw the blanket off and stumbled to the shower, and the icy water bit at his skin. It was the only thing that could shock him out of the darkness clawing at the edges of his mind after sleep.

Freezing needles stabbed his chest as his mind raced—every hour without a lead shrank the kids' odds. No breakthrough tonight at the auction and death would win.

He dressed quickly: dark suit, no tie. He strapped a gun with a filed-off serial number to the small of his back. His department-issued piece stayed in the drawer. It was for men who still had faith in the system. Lazarus didn't. Not anymore.

Standing before the mirror, he ran a hand through his damp hair, staring at the man who stared back. Bloodshot eyes, beard darkening his jawline, and a look that told the story of too many lost nights.

Somewhere out there, Brad and Keri were fighting for their lives, and the clock was ticking.

He grabbed his keys and left to pick up Riley.

Fifteen minutes passed before Riley finally lumbered out of his apartment. When he got into the car, it tilted under his massive weight, reminding Lazarus of the *Flintstones*, with the mammoth-size ribs that flipped the car over.

Riley was crammed into Dockers and a suit coat, his biceps straining against the fabric like they were ready to explode.

"How much you benching these days?" Lazarus asked as they pulled onto the street.

Riley grunted. "Seven eighty."

"Seven hundred and eighty pounds? You can bench half a ton?"

"Yeah, but I pay for it. My joints feel like they're gonna snap every morning when I wake up."

"So why do it?"

Riley stared out the window for a long moment. "Why do people drink? Why do they snort chemicals or whip themselves? Something else is hurting us and we don't know what it is."

"Don't know or don't wanna know?"

Riley didn't respond. The conversation drifted into silence as they drove across town to the auction. It was being held at an exclusive club that didn't advertise—one of those places you only found if you already knew where it was.

They arrived at an old building that had been gutted and turned into something modern on the inside. Steel stairs led them down to a speakeasy-style restaurant. The lights were dim, and shadows clung to the corners. Cigarette smoke curled from the mouths of rich patrons as soft, ambient music played from hidden speakers.

At the entrance, two men were checking IDs. Lazarus recognized one of them from Metro—Kenny Perks, a DUI patrol officer working side gigs to make ends meet.

"That's Perks," Riley muttered. "You know him?"

"I've seen him around. Vouch for him?"

"I don't vouch for anyone."

Royd appeared from around the corner, looking jumpy. "I've only got two invites," he muttered.

"That's why there's two of us," Lazarus replied, not bothering to reassure Royd, who seemed like he was about to pass out from anxiety. "Give me the invites and get outta here."

The tickets were white with gold trim, advertising a charity auction for Tibet. The real auction would come later.

They passed through security and entered the restaurant. The waitresses, in elegant evening gowns, floated between tables and offered drinks. Everything gleamed and glittered, but it all felt off—like a stage set for something else.

Riley ordered a beer while Lazarus kept his eyes on a man with a ponytail, walking from table to table and showing photos of prizes to the patrons. A BMW was drawing a lot of attention. After a few minutes, Ponytail noticed them and made his way over.

"Evening, gentlemen," he said, scanning their tickets with an app. "Are you here for the auction or just looking to gamble?"

"Auction," Lazarus said.

"Then I'll see you in the back for the special prizes." Ponytail gave them a wink and moved on.

The auction began with all the exclusivity money could buy. The room was hidden behind an unmarked door. Dim lighting glinted off polished tables and a brass-railed bar stocked with bottles worth someone's rent. The air carried cigar smoke and expensive cologne, softened by a low hum of jazz.

About thirty people sat in leather armchairs arranged in loose rows, their murmurs sharp and deliberate. Most were men in tailored suits and gleaming shoes, with a few poised women mingling among them. Power was clear.

Lazarus stood near the bar, one hand grazing the small of his back, where his gun rested. He scanned the room, noting how some bidders leaned forward, their attention cutting through the casual atmosphere.

After the public auction, Ponytail led them to a private room in the back. This was where the real business happened. The lighting was dim, the blinds drawn. Other men began to file in, all of them stone faced and silent. It wasn't until Ponytail handed Lazarus a set of photos—photos of expensive cars parked on random street corners—that Lazarus realized something was wrong.

"What is this?" Lazarus asked.

"Special inventory," Ponytail said with a smile.

"This isn't what I came for."

"I'm sorry, but that's all we have tonight," Ponytail said, his tone dismissive as he walked away.

"We got made," he muttered to Riley.

"How?"

"I don't know."

Outside, Lazarus quickly dialed Tony from CIU and ordered surveillance on the building. But he knew Bradley and Keri weren't here. They would keep the real merchandise far from this place, leaving no evidence behind.

As they waited for their car, Ponytail approached again, holding out a key.

"I believe you forgot this," he said, handing Lazarus the small key, with a placard that read "lounge." Before Lazarus could ask anything, Ponytail was gone.

"What now?" Riley asked.

"Let's find out."

They found the lounge hidden away in the basement. The steps down were lined with tiny ambient lights casting shadows on the walls. Two men stood by the door, and when Lazarus showed them the key, one unlocked the door and let them in.

Inside, the atmosphere shifted. The room felt like a private club for the wealthy—a place to gamble, drink, and keep secrets. Dark wood paneled the walls, gleaming under the amber glow of sconces shaped like lanterns. Pendant lights cast soft pools over green-felt tables, leaving the corners in shadow. A faint trace of cigar smoke lingered, mingling with the scent of whiskey.

Men sat around the tables, their faces blank. No one smiled or laughed. Lazarus's gaze landed on a man near the back, lounging with a drink. He recognized him—a casino owner from the Philippines.

Years ago, the man had been tied to a murder: a young girl strangled after being last seen with him. The charges never stuck. Lazarus still remembered his smug face leaving the courthouse, free. Now he sat here, sipping scotch.

Something felt off. Too smooth.

"That was too easy," Lazarus whispered.

Ponytail appeared again, but this time his tone was different, almost apologetic. "Gentlemen, I regret to inform you there will be no auction tonight. Unforeseen circumstances. Thank you for your understanding."

No one protested. No one even looked surprised. The crowd silently filed out one by one without a word.

Lazarus and Riley followed.

"What the hell just happened?" Riley asked.

"I don't know," Lazarus said, watching Ponytail disappear around a corner. "But I know who does."

Lazarus and Riley sat in the car, waiting. It was nearly two in the morning, and the streets were quiet as the club down the block emptied out. The patrons left in clumps, laughing and stumbling. It didn't take long before the staff started leaving as well. Ponytail was among the last. He stepped out wearing a black London Fog jacket with the collar turned up and strolled around the block.

Lazarus pulled the car forward, keeping the engine low. Ponytail's walk was casual, no hurry. He stopped in front of a sleek Cadillac, paused for a second, and glanced back at them—just a brief uninterested look.

"Want me to grab him?" Riley asked.

"Not here." Lazarus eased the car forward, then made a U-turn farther down the block, watching as the Cadillac merged onto the main street.

"Run the plates," Lazarus said, keeping his eyes on the car ahead.

Riley tapped into his phone and made the call. "Omer Kassim Abdulla, forty-two. Listed as a host at Clive's Bar and Grill."

"I don't know many restaurant hosts that drive hundred-thousand-dollar Cadillacs."

They followed the car at a comfortable distance. Neither of them spoke. Riley, fidgety, eventually reached for the radio and turned it on. Some bluegrass came through the speakers, and he asked, "Is this satellite?"

"Seriously? That's what you're thinking about right now?"

Riley shrugged. "I want some music."

Lazarus switched to a '70s rock station. They passed the glowing neon of the Rio, its pink lights flickering against the backdrop of the dark casino building. The city slowly slipped behind them as the Cadillac pushed farther out, moving away from the lights and into the quiet edges of Las Vegas.

Lazarus had trained in surveillance back in his rookie days, but following someone in a single car was always tricky. In the academy, they'd drilled into them the importance of having multiple vehicles on a tail. Ideally, three cars—each keeping distance, switching positions, using traffic as cover. But with just one car it was harder to stay discreet. They'd need to rely on luck, using side streets, trying not to be too obvious.

Lazarus clenched the wheel, the Cadillac's taillights flaring like embers ahead. Time bled away—push too hard, spook Ponytail, and the lead could vanish. Or worse, a shoot-out could put another body in the morgue. He had to stay fast but steady.

After thirty minutes of following the Cadillac out of the city, they reached a secluded, upscale neighborhood. The homes sat perched on a cliff, overlooking the glittering lights of the city far below. Omer turned onto a quiet cul-de-sac and pulled into the garage of a sprawling white mansion, its bay windows reflecting the lights from the city.

Riley said, "How fair is it that a piece of shit like that gets to live in a house like this?"

"Karma, big daddy. Getting money's one thing, keeping it's another. Most people don't hold on to it for long." Lazarus opened his door. "You stay here."

"Why?" Riley's brow furrowed.

"In case anyone shows up," Lazarus said, already stepping out into the dark.

Riley grumbled but didn't argue. Lazarus didn't want to admit it, but Riley's head wasn't in the game tonight. Lazarus needed to focus, and having to babysit the big guy wasn't going to make this any easier.

The street was mostly empty. Dirt lots and half-finished construction projects surrounded the area. The nearest streetlight was at the entrance to the cul-de-sac, leaving Omer's house bathed in shadows. Lazarus moved silently across one of the lots, slipping through the dark.

At the front door, he knocked, rang the bell once, and waited. The faint sound of footsteps approached from inside, and the door swung open. Omer stood there, a puzzled expression crossing his face as he took in the sight of Lazarus standing on his doorstep at two in the morning.

Lazarus grinned.

Before Omer could react, Lazarus popped him in the nose—a quick, sharp jab. Nothing devastating, just enough to let him know how this was going to play out. Omer staggered back, stunned, as Lazarus shoved him inside, closing the door behind them with a quiet click.

27

Piper drove through the desolate streets, her stomach knotted tight. Sleep had eluded her, and the hum of the engine was the only thing that quieted her thoughts.

This part of the city, far away from the crowds on the Strip, felt hollow. Its silence broken only by the occasional buzz of a flickering streetlight. On a few corners, women lingered, their eyes vacant.

The thought that in this city, traffickers could be holding people, stacked like inventory waiting to be shipped, was something she couldn't shake. She hadn't even known that was a reality until recently. Watching an FBI seminar on human trafficking had opened her eyes. The video of those young women—college students—being kidnapped by men in police uniforms still haunted her. The women hadn't fought, hadn't screamed. They were convinced the officers were real and had walked calmly to their fate. That fact dug at Piper. That someone could trust so completely only to be betrayed like that.

She parked in front of her apartment building and walked inside, still replaying the seminar in her mind. She was distracted, her thoughts circling back to Keri and Bradley, wondering if they were suffering somewhere just like those women in the video.

When she got home, she quickly changed into sweats and headed to the kitchen table. A manila folder was waiting for her, sitting next to an old plate with the remnants of dinner she'd forgotten to clean up. The folder contained a list of known traffickers that Bonnie Epps had managed to pull together for her. Piper grabbed the dirty dish and put it into the sink, then got some warm milk before sitting down to sift through the documents.

As she flipped through the names, she felt a sickening weight in her chest. There were so many of them. Known traffickers—men who sold human beings—and so many were still out there, living free. Men of all races and backgrounds; some as young as teenagers and others in their seventies.

She got to work cross-referencing each name, checking criminal histories and eliminating those who were locked up on the night of Keri and Bradley's kidnapping. Then a name jumped out at her: Randy Keller.

Her fingers froze on the page. Randy Keller. She knew that name—he was the stepfather of one of her former wards, Mathew Dyer. Mathew had tried to get emancipated from his parents, claiming abuse. Piper had been his attorney. When the court denied Mathew's petition and forced him back into the home, he'd run away. She hadn't heard from him since.

She dug out her old files, her mind racing. Cross-checking the details, she confirmed it was the same Randy Keller. Back when she was representing Mathew, the investigators had uncovered quite a bit about Randy. He had been a low-life pimp and small-time drug dealer since his teenage years. Piper remembered he was so broke during the trial that he couldn't afford a private lawyer. Randy was the kind of guy who made money only to watch it vanish into a black hole of his own making.

Her decision was made. She had to talk to him.

28

"Who the—"

Lazarus popped Omer in the nose again, cutting off his words. Omer wasn't a man built for pain, and the punch left him wide eyed, fear written over his face. Blood trickled from his nostrils, and he cupped his hand over the wound like he was dying from it.

"Why'd you cancel the auction?" Lazarus asked.

Omer shook his head, pulling his hand away to stare at the blood streaked across his fingers. "I don't know."

Lazarus took a step forward, and Omer stepped back.

"Bradley and Keri," Lazarus said. "Where are they?"

"I don't know."

Lazarus delivered another sharp jab, the thud of knuckles against flesh louder this time. Omer let out a yelp, his hand darting back to his now bloodier nose.

"Shit! Stop that!"

"Then start talking."

"I'll call the police," Omer threatened weakly.

"I am the police. Now sit down."

He motioned to the dining room table with a tilt of his head. Omer hesitated but complied, moving slowly, like a man walking to his execution.

They sat, and Lazarus pulled out a pack of gum, offering a piece to Omer. It was a deliberate pause, a way to stretch the tension. Omer accepted the gum with trembling hands. They chewed in silence, Lazarus's eyes roaming the room.

"Nice place. You from UAE?" Lazarus asked.

"Yes." Omer's gaze flicked to the blood drying on his fingers.

"Had a buddy from the Emirates once. Went back home for a visit and I never saw him again. Never did find out what happened."

Omer stared at him. "Why are you doing this? I swear, I don't know anything."

"You know enough," Lazarus said. "Enough to help me find those kids you were planning to sell tonight."

Omer shook his head again. "I just set appointments. I don't know anything."

"Now that right there is a lie," Lazarus said, leaning back. "You know why the auction was canceled. The real reason."

Omer shifted uncomfortably, his eyes darting toward the kitchen. "I need a paper towel."

Lazarus's hand drifted toward the gun tucked at the small of his back. "Go ahead."

Omer stood slowly, retrieved a roll of paper towels, and held some to his nose, wincing as he dabbed at the blood. "I don't know why it was canceled. That's the truth."

"Why do auctions usually get canceled?"

"I don't know. This is the first one I've handled."

"Bullshit," Lazarus said.

"I swear it! I'm just an accountant. I have a degree in accounting."

Lazarus chewed his gum, watching Omer. "You're gonna tell me why that auction got shut down. And you're gonna tell me now. Who can you call to find out?"

"Nobody," Omer stammered, panic flooding his voice. "I can't just call these people. If they suspect something, they'll kill me."

Lazarus leaned forward, his voice dropping to a dangerous whisper. "You're scum, Omer. You sell children. If anyone deserves to die, it's you. So I don't care who you're afraid of. You're going to call them."

He pulled the gun and set it on the table, the metal gleaming under the light. "I don't think anyone would miss you if something happened tonight."

Omer's face went pale. He removed the soaked paper towel from his nose and stared down at it for a long moment.

Omer swallowed hard and pulled out his phone—a dated BlackBerry, the kind politicians and high-level criminals used to avoid hacks. His thumb hovered over the keypad, his eyes darting nervously between Lazarus and the phone.

He dialed a number, and Lazarus stepped in close enough to listen. A man answered on the other end, his voice carrying a slight Arabic accent. Omer spoke in Arabic, the conversation short, tense. Lazarus couldn't understand the words, but he watched Omer's body language, searching for any sign of betrayal. He would have no idea if Omer had just told the man on the other end of that phone to send a hundred killers with rifles over.

The call ended after twenty or thirty seconds, and Omer slid the phone back into his pocket with a defeated slump in his shoulders.

"The supplier never showed up," Omer muttered.

"The supplier?" Lazarus repeated, leaning closer.

"Someone was supposed to deliver the merchandise. They never showed up to drop it off."

"Why not?"

Omer shrugged, blood still trickling from his nose.

Lazarus stepped closer, his face inches from Omer's now. "You're going to take me to the man on the other end of that phone."

29

When Piper arrived at the Keller home, it looked exactly as run down as she remembered—unkempt lawn, bent chain-link fence, and a house that seemed to sag. She hesitated at the front gate, recalling her last visit here. The Kellers hadn't exactly been thrilled when she was trying to help their son get emancipated from them.

She knocked on the door and Daphne Keller answered. She looked older, worn out. Her once-bright blue eyes were dulled with fatigue and her face gaunt. She wore torn jeans and a faded Ozzy Osbourne T-shirt and her hands were speckled with age spots.

"What do you want?" Daphne's voice was cold, like she'd been expecting bad news.

Piper smiled awkwardly, trying to ease the tension. "Guess you remember me."

"What do you want?" Daphne repeated, no warmth in her voice.

"Is Randy home?"

"No."

"Can I talk to you for a minute, then?"

Daphne looked ready to shut the door in Piper's face, but Piper quickly added, "I came here alone—no police. I don't want to cause you any trouble."

For a second, Daphne just stared at her. Then, understanding the unspoken message, she stepped aside and let Piper in.

The house smelled of old smoke and stale air, just like Piper remembered. Inside, it was cluttered and dimly lit. Daphne walked to a worn armchair and collapsed into it like she had no energy left. Piper stood near the doorway, taking in the scene. No photos of Mathew on the walls. It was like he'd never existed.

"How is he?" Daphne asked.

Piper shook her head. "I haven't spoken with Matt since you got him back."

"He was here for about a month, then took off."

"Do you know where?"

"No. I woke up one morning and all his clothes were gone. Just like that. Never saw him again."

"Did you file a missing persons report?"

"What would be the point? He ain't missing, he just don't wanna be here."

Piper nodded. "I'm sorry for how it all turned out."

"You can save your sorries. Doesn't matter now."

Piper bit back the urge to argue. She'd fought harder for Matt than Daphne ever had. It was clear that Randy had been a monster, and Daphne had done nothing to stop him.

"Where's Randy now?" Piper asked.

"Still in lockup. Got a few more months."

"You gonna let him move back in when he gets out?"

"Why wouldn't I?"

"Maybe Matt would come back if Randy wasn't around."

Daphne looked down at the ashtray on the coffee table, her expression softening into something Piper could almost call regret. "Why are you really here?" she asked, her voice quieter now.

"Randy might have information about two missing kids."

Daphne took a long sip of her energy drink, then leaned back, her eyes distant. "Like I said, he's in lockup. You wanna talk to him, go talk to him."

It took only one phone call to the warden and Piper had her visit lined up. Being with the guardian ad litem's office had its perks, and prison administrations were usually cooperative. Still, as she drove to Desert Plains, unease clung to her like a second skin.

Desert Plains Correctional looked more like a research facility on a barren moon than a prison. Its white, flat buildings spread out in the shadow of a single towering guard post. Piper had always felt unsettled here. The energy was off—stuck, like her grandmother used to say.

After the usual routine of scanning and searching, she was led to the professional visitation room. It was the bare metal tables and benches under fluorescent lights that gave everything a washed-out, sickly glow.

Randy Keller shuffled in, dressed in his orange prison jumpsuit, with his hands cuffed in front. Two guards loitered near the door, chatting. Randy sat down across from her with a look that had aged more than she'd expected. His mustache drooped into his scruffy goatee, and a bald patch marred the right side of his mullet.

"How's life, Randy?" Piper asked, though she already knew the answer.

"I'm locked in a cage. How the hell you think?"

"I suppose that's fair," Piper said, suppressing the distaste that welled up at the sight of him.

Randy glanced back at the guards. "What'd he do now?"

"No. I haven't heard from Matt since he left. Do you know where he is?"

"Shee-it, I forgot what he even looks like. His mama wanted him back, but I didn't care if he stayed gone. One less mouth to feed, you know?"

Piper bit her tongue. She needed something from him, and it wasn't the time to remind him how despicable he sounded.

"So, if this ain't about Matt," Randy said, leaning forward, "what's it about?"

"I want to talk about something off the record."

He looked amused. "Off the record, huh? Must be damned important then."

Piper held his gaze, trying to keep her tone neutral. "I need information. I know you've worked with gangs before, moving girls across state lines. I'm not asking you to admit anything. I'm just saying I know you were involved."

Randy leaned back, a smirk on his lips. "I ain't lifting a finger for you. I remember how you made me look like an idiot in court."

"You made yourself look like an idiot."

Her mouth said it before her brain could tell it to stop.

"I'm not here about that, Randy. I'm here because two teenagers were kidnapped. The families have no money, so it's probably trafficking. I need some help."

Randy laughed. "Last time I saw you, I was wondering what it would feel like to wrap my hands around your throat."

A cold shiver ran down Piper's spine, but she forced herself not to look at the guards. She wouldn't give him the satisfaction of seeing her rattled.

"You're wasting your time," Randy said, his grin widening. "You can't get me to help."

"I'll trade for it. Gotta be something you want."

"Take off your shirt."

"What?"

"Your shirt. And your bra."

Piper felt a wave of disgust. "How about money for commissary?"

"I don't need you for that. I can get money."

"Only if you're selling drugs."

He shrugged, unapologetic. "Drugs are cheap in here and the guards bring 'em in. It's all a system. You gonna preach to me about the system?"

"I don't care about that. I just want a name. Someone I can talk to about this."

He grinned again, nastier this time. "Then pull up your shirt."

"No."

He began to rise. "Then we're done here."

Piper panicked. "Wait. There's something else, right? Something you want. There has to be. Everyone wants something."

Randy scratched his stubble. "When they busted me, they found five grand in cash. The cops took it."

"They confiscated it under civil forfeiture."

"Yeah, well, that's bullshit. It was my money. I want it back."

"If they think it's tied to a crime, they can take it."

"They got no evidence. You get me my five grand back and I'll give you a name. Otherwise, don't bother."

30

It was past midnight and Lazarus sat in his car, eyes fixed on the house Omer had pointed him to. An address and a name in exchange for Lazarus forgetting he'd ever seen him.

Iqbal Hussein. A man with dual citizenship in the US and Saudi Arabia and a graduate of Yale Business School. Lazarus had tried to find a criminal record, but nothing showed up—not that Saudi police would be rushing to send over anything even if there was one.

His phone buzzed. It was Piper.

"Yo," he said, still eyeing the house.

"Sorry if you were sleeping."

"I don't sleep. What's up?"

"Where are you?" she asked.

"Just waiting for someone."

"I need your help. There's a guy in jail—Randy Keller. He says he has a name connected to the auction from last night. But he says the cops took five grand from him when he was arrested, and he wants it back. The case file doesn't mention any cash, though. Could be civil forfeiture, but I'm not sure."

Lazarus glanced again at the quiet house. "You think the cops pocketed it?"

"I don't want to jump to conclusions, but it's possible, right? And I'm not the best person to go accusing police officers. Can you check it out?"

"Yeah, I'm on it," Lazarus said.

He pulled up Randy Keller's case file on his phone. There was no mention of the five grand. Lazarus knew the two uniformed officers who'd been on the domestic violence call that night. One of them, Richard Stanley, had worked with Lazarus a few times. A decent cop but the kind of guy who seemed like he thought everything was beneath him. Randy could be lying, sure—but it wasn't outside the realm of possibility that Stanley and his partner had swiped the cash.

He called his assistant and asked him to send someone down to watch Iqbal's home until he could get back. Then he asked for Stanley's home address.

Stanley lived about thirty minutes outside of Vegas in a cookie-cutter desert suburb. Tan houses with flat roofs stretched out in every direction, the occasional cactus breaking up the monotony. Beyond the neighborhood, sand hills rolled on endlessly.

Lazarus knocked on the door. Stanley answered in jeans and a dirty T-shirt, his hair slicked to the side and his mustache looking like a droopy caterpillar. His eyes were bloodshot and he had the vibe of someone coming off a long night of drinking.

"Something wrong?" Stanley asked, his voice heavy with irritation.

"Nah, nothing wrong. Just need to talk."

"Now?"

"Yes, now."

Stanley glanced back over his shoulder. "Can it wait? I've got company."

Lazarus leaned a little to the side and caught sight of a young woman lounging on the couch. She was dressed in cutoff shorts and a tight tank top.

"She's pretty," Lazarus said.

Stanley shifted uncomfortably. "Yeah, well, I'll see you tomorrow."

He tried to close the door, but Lazarus slapped his palm against it, holding it open. "It can't wait."

Stanley sighed, stepping out onto the porch. Lazarus turned his back to the house, looking up at the empty sky, where stars blinked into existence.

"I'm gonna need that five K you took from Randy Keller," Lazarus said.

A long pause. Stanley said nothing, and that silence told Lazarus everything he needed to know.

"Why?" Stanley asked finally.

"The guy wants it back."

Stanley snorted. "You know how many times I've been to that house? Guy beats his wife so badly she spends days in the ER. Don't you think he's owed a little karma?"

"That ain't why you took his money," Lazarus said, turning to face him. "You took it because you could and because you're greedy. But I'm not here to judge you. I just need it back."

Stanley crossed his arms. "No."

Lazarus leaned against the porch railing, his posture relaxed, eyes fixed on Stanley. "I have to insist."

Stanley's face tightened. "All these criminals with big bankrolls, and I can't even afford a decent vacation or car. You think that's fair?"

"No. But that's a rationalization. And one you came up with after you already took the money."

Stanley glanced at the woman inside, then back at Lazarus. "I already spent it."

"On what?"

"A vacation."

Lazarus shook his head. "You're lying. If that was true, you'd have told me from the start."

"I'm not lying."

"You are. And I still need that money."

Stanley took a step closer. "Or what?"

"Don't be like that, Stan. Own up and be a man. I'm not asking you to tell anyone. Just give it back and we're cool."

"So that's it? You're playing errand boy for a scumbag like Keller?"

Lazarus pushed off the porch railing, closing the distance between them. He pulled up the photos of Brad and Keri on his phone and held them up to Stanley's face.

"These two were kidnapped. If they're not already halfway to the Middle East, they will be soon. That money is going to a man who can give me a name, someone who might know where they are."

Stanley stared at the photos, his face hard. "Sorry. No."

Lazarus pocketed his phone, his gaze narrowing. "If you're telling me no after hearing that, it means you don't respect reason. And I don't respect people who don't respect reason."

"Get off my por—"

Lazarus didn't let him finish. His fist connected with Stanley's mouth, sending him stumbling back. For a moment, it looked like Stanley was out, but then he swung back with a wild right hook. His knuckles crashed into Lazarus's cheek, and Lazarus staggered back, feeling the dull throb of pain flare up.

Stanley's hand shot up, palm out. "Wait!"

He spat out blood onto the porch. Lazarus noticed the girl inside was watching them but didn't seem particularly surprised. She sipped her drink.

"Why do you care so much?" Stanley asked, wiping his mouth with the back of his hand. "Why them?"

"That girl might be important to me."

"Why?"

"None of your business. Now go get the cash or come at me again, brother."

Stanley glanced back at the woman, then sighed. "Wait here."

Lazarus watched as he disappeared inside. The woman on the couch didn't flinch.

A moment later, Stanley returned, tossing a brown paper sack into Lazarus's hands. Lazarus peeked inside.

"All here?" he asked.

"I spent a little."

Lazarus nodded. "Thank you."

Stanley's jaw clenched as he stepped back. "I won't forget this." The door slammed shut behind him.

31

Piper waited for Lazarus outside Daphne's house, scrolling through an article on sex trafficking. Much of it centered on the Middle East and parts of Asia. Saudi Arabia was mentioned several times—a dictatorship run by a single family. The article explained that Saudi Arabia wasn't even called that until the royal family took control and renamed the nation to solidify its power.

It painted a world where powerful princes, shielded by near-absolute impunity, maintained sprawling harems reminiscent of the Middle Ages—lavish, guarded enclaves filled with women held under their control, echoes of ancient feudal rights. One prince, interviewed anonymously, bragged of keeping over a thousand women on his sprawling property.

A knock on the window startled her.

"You okay?" Lazarus asked, grinning as she rolled down the window.

"You're like a cat. I didn't even hear you."

"I brought you a present," he said, handing her a brown paper sack filled with cash.

Piper took it, feeling the weight of it in her hands. "Feels a little gross giving this back to him."

"Let the small fish have what they want so you can use them to catch the big ones."

Piper handed the money to Daphne and waited as she called Randy to tell him. She had hoped Randy would spill what he knew over the phone, but he refused—smart on his part considering all prison calls were recorded. A few years back they'd landed in trouble for illegally recording attorney-client conversations, hunting for evidence to build more charges against inmates. They claimed the practice had stopped, but few people believed it.

After both drove to the station, Lazarus parked his vehicle and said, "You drive. I've never been in your car."

Piper's beat-up car wasn't flashy, but it was functional. She couldn't justify buying a new one when the old one got her where she needed to go without any trouble. Lazarus stayed quiet most of the drive and Piper found herself grateful for the low hum of the radio.

"I haven't seen Riley in a while," she blurted, more out of discomfort than concern.

"You hate silence, don't you?" Lazarus asked, watching her closely.

"Yeah."

"It makes us stronger."

"I don't need to be stronger. I need to talk."

"So, are you really asking about Riley or just talking to talk?"

"I'm really asking."

Lazarus sighed. "The divorce hit him harder than he expected."

"I've handled hundreds of divorce cases in custody battles. Eventually people find a way to make it work. If they don't, their lives are just one miserable moment after another."

"Some people don't mind misery. It can be comfortable, too."

"Judge Dawson told me that about you once," Piper said, glancing over at him.

Lazarus gave her a sidelong look. "You still talk to her?"

"Occasionally. Sounds like things aren't going her way right now."

"I think her brothers made a bad bet. She's too smart to lose a lawsuit when they're trying to take everything she has. They made her desperate, and that won't end well for them."

"What do you think she'll do?"

"Anything she has to."

Piper let it drop as they arrived at the prison. Lazarus lingered in the lobby, chatting with the guards, while Piper went back to the attorney-client room. Randy was brought in after almost twenty minutes, slumping into the chair across from her.

"Seems like you're startin' to enjoy visiting me," Randy said with a grin.

"I did what you asked."

"Yeah, that was impressive. Shows how much bullshit is in the system when a lady like you can get that much money back from the government in one night."

"I had help. Now give me the name."

Randy leaned back, his smirk widening. "I feel like I should ask for more."

A flash of anger swept through Piper and she struggled to hide it. Randy chuckled, clearly enjoying the reaction.

"I have nothing else to offer, Randy. I did what you asked. If you're the kind of man who has no honor, there's nothing more I can do."

Randy spat on the ground. "Arab guy. Iqbal. Don't know his last name."

"That's it?"

"What more do you want?"

"Details. Anything. Car he drives, tattoos, something useful. I can't track someone down from a first name alone."

Randy scratched at his chin, thinking it over. "He owns a building downtown. Stardust Offices. Named it after one of his old girlfriends, Stardust. You ask me, you name your daughter something like that, you're just asking her to end up on a corner somewhere."

Piper jotted down the information in her notes and made several mistakes she had to delete and rewrite. She was moving too fast, her thoughts spinning ahead as the clock ticked down. What if she was already too late? If the teens were on a boat, drifting somewhere in the ocean, her chance to find them could already be gone. The thought tightened her chest.

"Anything else that could help?"

Randy flashed her a lecherous grin. "Not with your clothes on."

Back in the car, Piper handed her phone to Lazarus. He glanced over the notes and nodded.

"I know this guy," Lazarus said. "Saudi businessman."

"How do you know him?"

"Long story." He checked his watch. "I've got his address. Feel like taking a little drive tomorrow morning?"

32

The sun was already at its peak when Lazarus picked Piper up from her apartment complex. He handed her a coffee, and she thanked him.

"Where is this place?"

"Far. Maybe wanna do some work on your phone if you can."

The drive took over an hour, leading them to a quiet rural town. The place seemed to exist solely for workers at the nearby solar plant. As they passed through, Piper noticed only a handful of buildings: one grocery store, a gas station, a post office, and a couple of restaurants.

"It's peaceful here," Lazarus said, letting his arm hang out the window. "Almost like you can hear the earth breathe."

"You like it better than the city?"

He shook his head. "This isn't where life happens. It's a facade—cardboard and tape holding it together. But it's peaceful."

"I can't think in the city sometimes. We need quiet."

"Quiet doesn't last long."

They pulled onto a long dirt road that led to a sprawling estate—a mansion complete with stables and horses. A muscular young man tended to one of the horses, his gelled hair and tight shirt making him look out of place on the ranch.

Lazarus stepped out and the man turned to them, eyeing them curiously.

"I'm looking for Iqbal," Lazarus said, flashing his badge.

"He's inside," the man replied in a heavy accent.

The man led them through the mansion's front doors, which were framed by marble pillars and gleaming doorknobs that looked like real gold. Inside, they were directed to wait in the atrium. Lazarus admired the high ceilings, but Piper's attention was caught by a photograph—a shark tearing apart a smaller shark, the violence captured beneath a blue sunlit sea. It was brutal and eerily beautiful.

"Can I help you?" a smooth voice asked from the staircase.

A young Middle Eastern man descended, rolling up his sleeves to reveal a gold watch.

"Iqbal?" Lazarus asked.

"Yes."

"I'm Detective Holloway with Metro PD."

"Do I need my lawyer?"

"No."

Iqbal studied them for a moment, then gestured for them to follow. He led them outside to a lavish backyard, complete with fake grass, a pool, and an infinity hot tub. A woman in a bikini lay tanning nearby, her skin glistening with oil.

They sat at a shaded patio table. Iqbal gave them a warm, friendly smile. "What can I help you with?"

"You're about to tell me a bunch of lies," Lazarus began, "and I'm going to sift through them to find what I need. But I'd rather we skip that. Wouldn't you?"

"Yes."

"Then let's be honest. You buy flesh and send it back home. I'm not worried about that right now. I'm focused on two kids. Tell me where they are, or at least point me in the right direction, and I'll leave you be."

Iqbal leaned back, his expression unreadable. "You speak like a gentleman. So let me be clear—I don't kidnap anyone. We pay consorts."

Piper's face tightened. "Consorts? That's what you call them?"

"Yes. And we pay them well. You'd be surprised how desperate they are. Young people willing to sell their bodies for a shot at insta-fame and a seat on a private jet. Why break the law when they'll hand themselves over willingly?"

"So you're not a slaver?" Piper asked, her voice sharper now. The way he dismissed the lives he manipulated made her stomach churn.

"Maybe my ancestors were. But with enough money, you don't need to be."

Lazarus cut in. "Two kids were going to be sold at an auction, but it was canceled."

"I had nothing to do with that. I don't deal in underage consorts. They can't consent."

"Let's say, hypothetically, you did know these people," Lazarus said. "Why would an auction like that get canceled at the last minute?"

Iqbal's eyes drifted to the woman by the pool. "Hypothetically? Maybe the supplier couldn't deliver."

Lazarus leaned forward, a hint of excitement breaking through. "Tell me about the supplier."

Iqbal shrugged, clearly enjoying the power shift.

Lazarus pressed. "We agreed to be honest, remember? If I wanted to find this supplier, where would I start?"

Iqbal gave a tight smile. "If I had to guess, you'd find someone like that in prison."

Piper saw through the deflection—Iqbal was trying to pin this on Randy. But before she could say anything, Iqbal added, "But he wouldn't be in prison now, would he?"

Lazarus rose, signaling the end of the conversation. "Thanks for your time."

Once they were back in the car, Piper frowned. "Why'd we leave? He didn't give us anything."

"You gotta read between the lines with guys like him. The smart ones don't get caught. They deflect."

"So, we're looking for someone in prison?"

Lazarus shook his head. "No. Our boy's a recent parolee."

33

Carlito woke up around nine in the morning, groggy and disoriented. His body felt like it had aged decades, stiff and aching—a testament to the life he had lived, the kind that etched years into his bones. He ran his hand through his hair and looked up to see a doctor standing before him, wearing a smile.

"She's stable," the doctor said, sitting down beside him. "She's got internal injuries but no active bleeding. Knock on wood," he added, tapping the chair. "There's a fracture in her orbital socket, which will take time to heal. She'll need to take it easy for a while. We also detected a slipped disc in her back. She'll need physical therapy, and we can explore other options if that doesn't help."

"Can I see her?" Carlito asked.

"Yes, she's awake."

Carlito stood, every joint in his body protesting the movement. He felt ancient—but for the life he had lived, the things he had seen, the pain was a fair trade.

He entered Denver's hospital room to find her sitting up in bed, staring blankly at the ceiling. A black patch covered one eye, and her arms were wrapped in bandages. Carlito forced a smile and pulled a stool next to her. He took her hand and squeezed it gently. She tried to squeeze back, but her strength wasn't there.

"I like the eye patch," he said softly. "You look like a sexy pirate."

She smiled, then winced in pain. "Don't make me laugh. It hurts."

"What happened?"

She shook her head, trying to hold back the tears building in her good eye. "Doesn't matter now."

Carlito's face darkened. "I never should've left you alone in that place."

"You didn't know," she said, trying to push herself up in bed, despite the pain.

Carlito gently pushed her back down. "Stop. You need to rest."

"No. We got things to do. We can still make the first drop. I'll make up some excuse why we weren't there."

"Doesn't matter anymore."

"What do you mean?"

"I canceled it," Carlito said.

"What? Why?" She pushed herself up again, groaning through the pain. "That money was how we were gonna get out, Carlito!"

"Money's just dirty paper."

"You're so stupid sometimes!" she snapped. "I can't take this city anymore. The stink of this place, the noise . . . I need to get out. I'm going crazy."

Carlito stared at her, sadness creeping into his voice. "Love will do that to you. It's a type of insanity. Life would almost be easy without love, wouldn't it?"

Denver let out a long, shaky breath. "I need to leave this place, Carlito. I don't know how much more I can take."

"And you will," he promised, gripping her hand tightly. "I'll take care of it."

"How?" she demanded. "How are you going to fix this?"

"The gods don't want us to ask how. They just want us to ask what, and they'll take care of the rest."

Denver let out a sigh, her anger still simmering. "Just . . . give me my phone."

Carlito drove up to TJ Storage, a facility on the outskirts of the city, nestled in the desert, where jurisdiction got fuzzy. It was the kind of place you used when you didn't want something found. He scanned his key card, and the gate creaked open. The facility was a maze of gray brick buildings, each lined with steel doors, red stripes running along the sides. Carlito made his way to the back, where he kept his unit.

He punched in the code, unlocked the door, and rolled it up. The front of the unit was cluttered with old car parts, motorcycles, and scattered tools. But farther inside, past the junk, was something else. Plastic bags of food, a roll of toilet paper next to a bucket, and two kids—Brad and Keri—tied to the pipes.

It had only been a couple of days since he'd last been here, but they looked worse than he expected. Their faces were pale, their skin greasy, and their clothes filthy.

"You two need a shower," Carlito said, crouching down to their level. "We'll get you one on the way to Paz Vieja, and a change of clothes. You'll love the city. It's the most beautiful part of Mexico. I was born there."

Brad's throat worked to swallow. "Is that where you're going to kill us?"

"You know, the Mayans used to worship their sacrifices. They were revered because they were about to meet the gods."

He sat cross-legged on the cement floor. "If you could see what it's like in the next world, you'd be amazed. We're radiant spirits trapped in rotting meat."

He paused, studying their faces. Keri's panic was building; her breathing was shallow, her lips trembling. She was beautiful in the traditional sense—perfectly shaped, flawless—but Carlito found her beauty dull, almost offensive. There were millions like her, all assembly-line perfection. He preferred the beauty of the ugly and the damned. People like Denver, who carried their pain on their skin.

"But don't worry," Carlito continued, his tone almost soothing. "You wouldn't be worth much to me dead. I guess maybe I could sell you to a butcher's shop and say you're pork." He laughed at his own joke, but Brad's eyes widened in horror.

"I'm kidding," Carlito said with a grin. "I wouldn't do that. It's disrespectful."

"What are you going to do with us?" Keri said.

"You're going to be sold. That's the fate the gods have chosen for you. It's nothing personal."

"I'd rather die."

Carlito's smile faded into something sad. "Me too."

"I just want to go home," Keri pleaded.

"You don't have a home anymore," Carlito said. "Sometimes, there are things in life we can't control, and we have to accept it."

"I don't want to accept it!" Keri screamed, her panic finally breaking through. She thrashed against the ropes, sobbing uncontrollably. Her hysterics filled the unit, echoing off the cold walls, and Carlito watched her with sympathy; to see someone fight against fate was pitiful, even embarrassing.

"It's useless to fight," Carlito whispered, almost to himself.

Brad, calmer, more controlled, asked, "What happens if we don't sell?"

Carlito's smile returned. "That's why I like you, Bradley. You think things through."

He sighed and stretched his legs. "If you don't sell, they'll slit your throat to save the cost of a bullet and dump you in a ditch. But don't worry. You'll sell. If nothing else, they need workers in places no one else wants to go. You'll probably die quickly there, which might be a blessing."

Brad's body began to tremble uncontrollably.

Carlito rose to his feet, brushing the dust off his pants. "Let's go. We've got a long drive ahead of us."

34

Lazarus didn't have many contacts left in the prison system. The few he knew wouldn't take his calls. Piper, however, had better luck. The warden liked her, which got her a meeting with Steven Malloy, a social worker at the Department of Corrections, to go over a list of recent parolees.

They didn't meet at the prison itself but in an administrative building downtown, where some of the DOC satellite offices were housed—likely for the staff who preferred to keep some distance from the prison.

Piper and Lazarus walked into the building. No metal detectors, no real security—just a hollow, heavy atmosphere, like the prison. A large woman sat behind a plain desk and Piper asked for Steven Malloy. The woman led them through the maze of bland hallways to Steven's office: simple and functional with a couple of motivational posters on the walls.

Steven, a young man in a collared shirt and jeans, sat behind the desk, eating a cucumber sandwich. A mountain bike leaned against the wall and an IRONMAN race poster hung over his desk.

"Hey, you," Steven said, wiping his hands, flashing Piper a smile.

"Hey," Piper replied, sitting down across from him. "Thanks for making time."

"For you? Anytime. You're one of my favorites," he said with a grin before glancing at Lazarus. "And you are?"

"Lazarus Holloway," Piper introduced.

Steven nodded a quick hello. "All right, who are we hunting down today?"

Lazarus, leaning casually against the doorframe, cut straight to it. "We're looking for a recent parolee with a violent streak—a guy who's slippery, smart, and probably started his record young. He'd be connected, well enough to pull resources and stay one step ahead. Someone who knows the right people and isn't new to crossing lines, or borders. Most importantly, they need ties to a criminal group—something organized. They'll need resources to move people quickly."

Steven let out a low whistle. "Sounds heavy. This about that wedding couple?"

Piper nodded. "Yeah, can you help us?"

Steven sighed, scratching his head as he pushed his chair back. "Give me a couple hours. I'll dig through the parole database and see what I can find. I'll call you when I have something."

Before Piper could respond, Lazarus said, "We'll wait."

After fifteen minutes of small talk in Steven's office, it became uncomfortable, so Lazarus and Piper stepped into the hallway and sat in the worn-out plastic chairs. Lazarus stretched his long legs out in front of him, fingers steepled over his stomach, his eyes half closed. Piper fidgeted.

"I think I need you to talk to Hobbes," Piper said.

"Why's that?"

"He told Amanda not to reveal who Keri's father is."

"You haven't looked on the marriage certificate?"

"It lists John Doe because she's underage." She paused, staring at his face. "Why would he tell her to do that? I mean, even if it is a police officer?"

He glanced at her and then away. "I think you already have an idea why that is."

The two looked at each other.

"No," she almost gasped.

"Remember when I told you I was engaged? Amanda was who I was engaged to."

"Did you know?"

"Of course not."

She stared at him. "Is she sure?"

"She says she is, but no paternity test yet. She never lied to me before."

"Do you," she said, her voice careful, "wanna talk about it?"

Lazarus's face remained unreadable, but his fingers tensed slightly over his stomach. "About what?"

Piper frowned, frustrated by his cool response. "About what? Are you kidding me? Lazarus, she might be your daughter."

He sighed deeply, staring up at the ceiling as though the question had been hanging there all along. His jaw tightened, a muscle twitching at the edge of his temple, but when he spoke, his voice was flat and calm. "I shouldn't be anyone's father. If she is mine, we're both better off not knowing."

"And you really think you can just ignore it? That having a child out there won't eat at you?"

There was a flicker in his eyes—something barely noticeable but there. Piper didn't push, but the silence between them felt loaded.

"Guess we'll see," he finally said, his tone resigned, though his body betrayed a hint of tension as he shifted in his seat.

Steven called from his office. "Got some names for you."

They went back inside. Steven was printing out a stack of papers. He handed the sheets to Lazarus. "I found eighteen parolees from the last three months that fit your criteria. A few are back in custody for parole violations, but there's still some out there."

Lazarus thumbed through the pages, scanning the names and the booking photos. "They all got ties?"

Steven nodded. "Yeah, a mix of cartel, street gangs, white supremacists, and some of the nastier biker gangs. I filtered for guys with histories of kidnappings and violence going back to their juvenile records."

Lazarus flipped through a few more photos, his expression unreadable. "Thanks," he said flatly before heading for the door.

Piper gave Steven an apologetic smile as she followed Lazarus. "He's a man of few words, but we appreciate it."

"Anytime," Steven replied, then hesitated before adding, "Hey, by the way, there's this U2 concert coming up. I've got two tickets if you're interested."

Piper blinked, caught off guard by the sudden shift. "I appreciate the offer, but things are really hectic right now."

Steven, eager to downplay his request, pressed on with a smile. "It's just a concert. Two hours max—we can leave whenever."

Piper shot him an awkward smile. "I really am swamped, but maybe another time."

Steven nodded, but the moment lingered just a little too long, the invitation hanging awkwardly before she turned away.

As they were leaving, Steven's tone shifted, more serious now. "Be careful. Some of these guys get another arrest and it's life. People get desperate when they've got nothing left to lose."

35

Carlito pulled into the hospital parking lot and cut the engine. Brad watched as Carlito stepped out of the car. He had changed into a white sleeveless shirt, revealing intricate tattoos that wove down his muscular arms—ancient warriors with knives, blood, and skulls, all done in deep, precise lines.

Carlito lit a clove cigarette, leaning against the hood. "Now listen, kids," he said, exhaling smoke, "if either of you scream for help, I'll shoot you both." He paused, turning his gaze toward them through the windshield. "And then I'll have to shoot anyone who sees me. You'll be responsible for a lot of death. Better to sit quietly, no?"

Brad felt Keri tense beside him.

A nurse wheeled a woman out of the hospital entrance. She wore an eye patch over one eye, her other eye gleaming with intensity. She stood slowly, her movements stiff, like she was holding back a wince with every step. Carlito wrapped his arm around her waist and kissed her gently.

He walked her to the car, and despite her obvious pain, the woman held her posture rigidly, as though she wouldn't allow herself to show weakness in front of anyone.

"Brad," Keri whispered, her voice trembling. "What are we gonna do?"

"I don't know," Brad whispered back. "This guy is crazy."

Carlito opened the passenger door and eased the woman in. She settled into the seat, her gaze locking onto Brad and Keri in the back. Her beauty was cold, almost serpentine. Brad felt a pang of guilt—despite the terror, he couldn't stop looking at her.

"You have to help us," Keri pleaded, her voice cracking. "He's going to kill us."

Brad pulled her close, his voice low but soothing, "It'll be okay."

The woman gave a small smile. "Listen to your man," she said. "Everything's going to be just fine."

Carlito started the engine. "One big happy family," he quipped with a laugh. "Can you imagine us with kids?"

"Yeah, I can," the woman said dryly.

Carlito grinned. "A little baby, huh? I can't see you changing diapers."

"I'd do what I had to for my kids," she replied. "Are you going to drive with these two tied up in the back?"

"I thought about it," Carlito said, glancing at Brad in the rearview mirror. "We could get pulled over, though."

"Then we kill the cop," she said matter-of-factly.

Carlito laughed again, but when the woman didn't laugh along, he grew serious. "Nah, we'll be fine. Me and Bradley have an understanding." His eyes rested on Brad in the mirror again. "Right, Bradley? If you try anything, I'll sell you as pork. How's that sound?"

His laughter rang out, but Brad felt a tightening grip in his stomach. Keri was trembling, her sobs quiet now.

Carlito turned on the radio, searching for a station. "You like country music, Little Bird?" he asked, looking over his shoulder at Keri, though she barely lifted her head.

"She likes country music," Brad answered for her.

Carlito's face lit up. "Ah, good taste! I love country music. Johnny Cash, Willie Nelson, Merle Haggard—they knew what pain was."

A slow country song filled the car. Carlito tapped his finger on the steering wheel as though it were a cheerful tune, entirely out of sync with the heaviness.

The freeway stretched out in front of them, growing more desolate as they left the city behind. The stale air from the car's AC didn't cool them.

"I need to use the bathroom," Brad said, his voice breaking the silence.

The woman—whom Carlito had called Denver—exhaled a long stream of clove smoke, her lips curling. "Hold it."

"It's number two," Brad said, cringing as the words left his mouth.

Carlito laughed, but Denver's one good eye narrowed, venomous.

"Fine," Carlito said, turning off to a road that led to a run-down gas station. He stopped in front. "I'll take him in."

"Get me a Yoo-hoo," Denver called after him, flicking her clove cigarette out the window.

Brad was out of the car. Carlito followed closely behind, hand resting casually on his gun. The station was a mess—filthy floors, shelves lined haphazardly with junk. The bathroom was tucked around a corner. Carlito leaned against the sinks as Brad went into the first stall.

Minutes passed and nothing happened.

"I can't go," Brad finally said.

"Why not?"

"Because you're standing right there."

"So?"

"It's making me nervous," Brad said.

"So? Don't be nervous."

"You've joked about selling me as pork twice today. I can't not be nervous around you."

"Fair enough," he said, pushing off the sink. "I'll wait outside."

Brad waited for Carlito's footsteps to fade before moving. His eyes darted to the small window at the back of the bathroom. He could probably fit through it but thought Carlito would be expecting that.

His heart hammered against his ribs, every nerve in his body screaming at him to act—but his mind was clouded. He cracked the bathroom door open. The hallway was empty, the music from the station's speakers loud enough to mask any small sounds he made. He stepped out, scanning for Carlito, but saw no one. If he could make it to the car and get Keri, they could run across the freeway and stop someone.

Brad bolted toward the store's front. But as he reached the main aisle, he felt an iron grip on his arm. It felt like being grabbed by a machine.

Carlito's voice said, "That was fast."

Brad's throat went dry. "Yeah . . ."

"Grab some candy bars for Little Bird," Carlito said, his voice suddenly cheerful.

Brad's hands shook as he fumbled through the shelves, picking random candy bars. His mind was spinning, everything surreal. He joined Carlito at the register, every instinct screaming to make a move, to shout, to run, to do something.

Outside, a semi pulled up to the gas station. Brad could feel the adrenaline coursing through him, drowning out everything else.

He had one chance.

He ran, bursting through the door, his legs carrying him toward the truck and his voice hoarse as he screamed for help.

But before he reached the truck, his vision exploded in pain. He hit the ground hard, his head spinning. When the dizziness faded, he saw Denver standing over him, her gun pointed at his forehead.

"That's twice I've had to knock your little ass out," she said.

"Leave him alone!" Keri shouted from the car.

Carlito strolled up, munching on a donut. "I'm disappointed, Bradley. Now I'll have to restrain you. It's a shame."

"Let me shoot him," Denver said, her finger on the trigger.

"No, *loca*. We need them alive," Carlito said with a sigh. "Even if they are a pain in the ass."

Brad felt the muzzle of the gun press against his forehead, his breath coming in shallow gasps.

"Please don't kill me," Brad whispered.

Denver pulled the gun away, grabbed him by the collar, and dragged him back toward the car.

36

Lazarus had spent the day on the phone, glued to his computer or out in person chasing down parole officers, arresting officers, and social workers and caseworkers from the Department of Corrections and Family Services. His eyes throbbed with strain from crossing names off lists and digging into backgrounds. He'd managed to whittle down the list of potential parolees, but he was still missing something.

As evening fell, he stretched his neck, feeling the weight of the day settle into his bones. His body was tired in ways he'd never noticed before. Once, he could crash on any couch, sleep on floors, or survive on scraps of rest and feel fine the next day. Now even the most comfortable chairs hurt. He knew time chipped away at everyone, but it had a cruel way of letting you feel invincible until you weren't.

He chuckled grimly to himself, imagining what Piper would say about his morbid thoughts. She'd probably try to shake him out of it, find some silver lining.

Checking his watch, he debated whether to pick her up for the next part of his search. After a moment he decided against it. He'd bring Riley instead.

When he got to Riley's apartment, the door was unlocked. A bad sign.

"Riley?" Lazarus called as he stepped inside. No answer. The apartment was empty but the faint smell of something bitter lingered. Lazarus headed to the bathroom and opened the medicine cabinet. It was worse than he'd expected. Percocet—enough to dull an elephant, along with insulin, growth hormone, and at least four types of testosterone. It was a minipharmacy. No wonder Riley had been so distant, his thoughts fogged.

Closing the cabinet, Lazarus sighed. He locked the door on his way out and drove down to the Last Chance Saloon. The cracked and dusty parking lot felt as worn as the people who stumbled in. He kicked the dust off his boots before walking inside, the heat of the pavement still clinging to the soles.

Bass was behind the bar.

Lazarus took a booth and ordered two Midnight Porters, a half-beer, half-coffee concoction that most people gagged at the thought of. He popped one open and leaned back, sipping slowly. His eyes studied the bottle's design as he idly peeled at the label.

Bass ambled over. "Mind if I sit?"

"Your bar."

Bass slid into the booth, took a pill from his pocket, and swallowed it dry. "How you holding up?"

"Okay," Lazarus said. "You?"

Bass shrugged, not really answering.

"Haven't been sleeping much," Lazarus said.

"Wife got me some sleeping pills when I was struggling. Knocks me right out," Bass said.

"Doesn't work for me."

"Why's that?"

"You ever hear of sleep paralysis?"

"Like nightmares?"

Lazarus took a long drink before answering. "Not just nightmares. It's when you're awake and asleep at the same time, seeing and feeling things that aren't real. It's like your body's frozen but your mind's stuck in a world of demons."

Bass let out a low whistle. "That's heavy, man. What do the docs say?"

"Usual stuff—could be this, could be that. The mind's a mystery." Lazarus stared into his drink. "I'm working a kidnapping. Two teenagers, probably about to be sold overseas. You ever hear of the club messing with human trafficking?"

Bass leaned back. "Hell no. The old-timers in the club would never sell Americans. They were rough bastards, but they had lines they wouldn't cross."

"You know anyone who did?"

"Not personally. But I kept my distance from that. Flesh is a shady game. We stuck to guns, drugs, and booze."

"Booze?"

Bass grinned. "Moonshine. People love it, brother. It's a special kinda drunk, the kind where you forget everything. Good money, too, until the ATF started wasting taxpayer money chasing us down."

Lazarus chuckled. "The biker gangs ain't like they used to be."

"No, they ain't. The new generation's in it for the money. All the old ideals—freedom, brotherhood—they're gone. Just dollar signs now."

Lazarus tapped at his bottle, half lost in thought. "You know that people with depression score higher on tests of realism and IQ? High intelligence is indicative of mental illness and depression. When our minds understand reality too much, they try to destroy themselves."

Bass grimaced. "That's about the worst thing I've heard today."

Lazarus smiled faintly, but his mind was already moving. After a few more minutes of small talk, he finished his drinks and left.

The drive took him to the other side of the city and Lazarus let his mind drift as the traffic crawled. Bass had been through hell, just like him. He thought back to the day he met Bass—back when Bass's son was found murdered, his skull bashed open in the street. No arrests were made, but Lazarus knew someone had seen something. People just refused to talk. It still gnawed at him.

Finally, he arrived at the address he was heading to, an apartment on the first floor of a complex. The man who opened the door was older, bent with age, walking with a cane. "Can I help you?" he asked.

"Just needed to cross you off my list," he said vaguely, not bothering to explain.

Lazarus's next stop was a known cat burglar. He'd always admired their kind—thieves who turned crime into an art. Years back, in New Orleans, he'd met Slippery Sal, a pickpocket so slick he'd lifted Lazarus's watch without him noticing. When Sal realized Lazarus was a cop, he returned it with a grin. A real pro. Too bad his luck ran out—beaten to death over a wallet in some dive bar.

Lazarus got to a run-down brick building around ten. He had tried the man's phone several times—"Carlito" was all the voicemail said. No answer.

The neighborhood was one Lazarus knew well. It was a breeding ground for informants, fueled by poverty and desperation. He entered the building and headed to the fourth floor. The scent of mildew and rot clung to the walls.

As he passed the first apartment, he could hear the unmistakable sounds of people having sex. Lazarus kept walking, indifferent. Passion was a mystery to him. It wasn't part of his world.

He knocked on Carlito's door. No answer.

After a moment's hesitation, he tried the knob and found it unlocked. Quietly, he pushed the door open, his hand moving to his weapon.

The apartment looked like a war zone. Blood smeared the floor and was splattered across the walls. A shattered glass coffee table and an overturned television, the screen cracked. Lazarus drew his weapon.

A large man was slumped against the wall, his throat slashed open and blood pooling around him. Lazarus examined the deep gash, noting the grisly precision of the cut. It was done up close—personal.

He listened, holding his breath, but the apartment was silent. Moving carefully, he checked the kitchen and bedroom. Nothing.

Holstering his weapon, Lazarus pulled out his phone to call it in.

He stared down at the body.

Looks like your last move was a bad one, partner.

37

After Lazarus's call, Piper sent a couple text messages and then dialed the GAL's general investigator, Gwen—a no-nonsense operator who got results.

"I just sent you a name. Carlito Xibala. I need everything—associates, arrests, whatever you can dig up."

"Give me five minutes," Gwen said.

Four and a half minutes later, Piper's phone buzzed. An email from Gwen had landed in her inbox: Carlito's life, neatly packaged in a PDF.

His criminal record read like a nightmare: assault, assault with a deadly weapon, mayhem involving bodily mutilation, burglary, larceny, arson . . . the list stretched from when he was twelve years old. Year after year, Carlito added more crimes to his rap, except for a break in his early twenties when he served two tours in Iraq before being dishonorably discharged. There were no records detailing why he had been discharged.

Piper had a few other cases waiting, but this one consumed her attention. It wasn't just about the law anymore—this world of trafficking, where human beings were commodified and discarded like waste, gnawed at her. This was a darker dimension of society she had never explored. She was used to exposing hidden truths, but this felt different.

As a guardian ad litem, Piper had spent years uncovering people's secrets. She knew everyone left traces, and with enough persistence you could always find fragments of their true selves.

With reclusive subjects, she questioned delivery drivers, who were invisible witnesses to the patterns of people's lives. Bartenders held stories that you could piece together about regulars. Friends of teenage girls would spill secrets buried in texts. But ex-cons like Carlito needed something else. Prison, with its isolation and the constant presence of others, revealed more than most people realized.

She dialed Steven Malloy, the social worker from the Department of Corrections, hoping he could provide more information on Carlito's past cellmates. Just before the call connected, her mind went back to his recent concert invite. Her "maybe" hung awkwardly between them.

Steven was attractive, and they shared a professional rapport that sometimes felt like it could be more. Still, the idea of mixing work and her personal life made her uncomfortable.

When he picked up, Piper quickly refocused on the case. "Hey, Steven. Got a minute?"

"Hey, you. Yeah, I've got the info you asked for. His old cellmate let him take over the apartment when he was paroled."

"Do you know where the cellmate is now?"

"He's out, working as a diesel mechanic. I sent his address over, too."

"Thanks, Steven. I really appreciate it."

"No problem."

Relieved he hadn't brought up the concert again, Piper grabbed her car keys and left.

The garage where Jaxon Briggs worked was small, just outside downtown, and shared space with a convenience store. The mechanics hanging around watched her curiously as she walked in. One of them, a slim man with short hair, stood behind the counter, staring at a computer screen. His hands were stained with grease and his shirt was dirty from the day's work.

"Help you?" he asked without looking up.

The Night Collector

"I'm looking for Jaxon Briggs," Piper said.

He glanced up at her, wiping his hands on a rag. "He's on break. Probably out back."

She thanked him and walked around the building. Out back, Jaxon sat on a crate, smoking and sipping an energy drink. He was built like a tank—short and squat with a belly that pushed against his mechanic's jumpsuit. He looked like a puffed-up creature who felt threatened.

"You Jax?" Piper asked, standing a few feet away.

"Yeah."

"I'm Piper Danes. I'm a guardian ad litem. I represent children in legal matters."

He chuckled, his deep laugh making his chest heave. "I ain't no kid, lady, so you ain't got no reason to be talking to me."

"I'm here about your former cellmate, Carlito Xibala."

Jaxon's demeanor shifted slightly, a subtle tension in his body. "He finally do it?"

"Do what?"

He shook his head. "Never mind. Why do you wanna know about him?"

"I think he's involved in kidnapping two kids, and there was a dead body found in your apartment that the police need to talk to both of you about."

Jaxon's laugh this time was bitter, amused. "Whatever."

"Can you at least tell me what he was like? What types of things was he into?"

"I dunno. Same shit as everybody else, I guess. He's into the Mayans, though—lining up stars and gods and blood. Crazy shit."

"He's religious?"

Jax shrugged. "I guess. He thought he was related to them or something. He was prolly right."

"Did he ever talk about what he planned to do once he got out?"

"If he did, I ain't telling you. Carlito never did me wrong, and I won't do him wrong neither."

Piper nodded, not surprised by his loyalty. "I understand. Can you at least tell me how I can get in touch with him? Maybe a phone number?"

"I don't have it. Don't talk to him much these days."

"Did he have anyone waiting for him when he got out? A girlfriend, maybe?"

"Yeah, there was a girl. Had a weird name I can't remember. Dumped his wife for her."

"His wife?" Piper asked.

"Yeah. Weren't married long, though. Her name was Savannah."

Jaxon crushed his cigarette underfoot and stood, signaling that their conversation was over. "I gotta get back to work."

"Thank you for your time," Piper said. She stood her ground as Jaxon walked past, muscles rippling with tension. She wasn't about to let him see her nervous, but the reality was clear—he could break her in half without trying.

Once Jaxon disappeared into the garage, Piper immediately pulled out her phone and texted Lazarus.

38

Lazarus didn't speak much on the drive to the home of Savannah Taylor—formerly Savannah Xibala. The neighborhood was calm, a typical lower-middle-class haven with well-kept lawns; the kind of place where young families start their lives. A clean red Toyota sat in the driveway, and bright flowers were planted next to the porch. Lazarus parked at the curb and quietly glanced at his phone, pulling up Carlito's criminal history as they walked to the front door.

"This level of violence," he muttered, shaking his head. "How the hell this guy even pass the psych eval to get into the military?"

Piper pressed the doorbell. The chime echoed softly inside. After a moment the door opened and revealed a woman in a yellow top and a skirt. Her blond hair fell neatly to her shoulders, framing a pretty but tired face.

"Savannah?" Piper asked.

"Yes?" The woman's voice was cautious.

"I'm Piper Danes, an attorney with the guardian ad litem's office, and this is Detective Holloway. We wanted to talk to you about your ex-husband."

Savannah's face immediately hardened, a silent understanding passing across her features. "What did he do?"

Piper glanced at Lazarus, then back to Savannah. "May we come inside?"

There was a brief hesitation, but Savannah stepped aside, allowing them in. The house was clean and orderly. Framed photos of Savannah with a handsome man and two young boys lined the mantle. Piper sat on the love seat while Lazarus leaned against the wall.

"You have a lovely home," Piper said.

"Thank you." Savannah sat on the couch, folding her hands in her lap. Despite her calm posture, Piper noticed the subtle tremor in her fingers and the rapid tapping of her foot.

Piper leaned forward slightly. "I'm sorry to bring up Carlito."

Her eyes remained fixed downward. "Just ask what you need to ask."

"Do a lot of people come by asking about him?" Lazarus cut in.

"Every now and then," she replied. "Usually the police. But it hasn't happened for a while, not since he was in prison. I guess he's out now?"

"He hasn't contacted you, then?" Piper asked.

"No, and he has no reason to."

Piper shifted her focus to the pictures on the mantel. "Are either of those children Carlito's?"

"No, thank heaven."

Lazarus crossed his arms. "Why thank heaven?"

"If you're looking for him, then you know why."

Lazarus's eyes narrowed. "People like that don't change much. I'm guessing you're not surprised to hear he's involved in something violent again."

Savannah let out a dry, humorless laugh. "People getting hurt because of him was the story of my life—until I scraped together enough money to leave."

Piper said, "You left him? He didn't leave you?"

Savannah nodded, her gaze drifting to the window. "I left. But he wasn't always like this. When I met Carlito, he was"—she hesitated, choosing her words—"magnetic. He made you feel like you were the center of the universe. Do you know how attractive that is to an eighteen-year-old girl who's been ignored her entire life?"

"When did he get violent?"

"Back then, he had a temper, but nothing like it turned into later."

"What changed?" Lazarus asked.

Her lips pressed into a thin line. "Whatever the army made him do in that desert, he brought it back with him. That darkness snuck into our home. I had to get out of there."

"And he let you go?" Piper asked.

"Yeah. I told him I was leaving, and he just looked at me. He nodded like I'd asked him to pass the salt or something. He signed the papers and didn't fight me on anything. That was Carlito. When he decided something was done, it was done."

Lazarus said, "Cold."

"*Cold*'s a good word for it," Savannah said, folding her arms across her chest. "Like I said, people getting hurt because of him was my life. I wasn't going to stick around and be next."

"Do you know where we can find him?" Lazarus asked, leaning slightly forward. His tone was calm, but there was a quiet pressure behind it.

"No idea."

"Has he ever mentioned any places he might go if he were in trouble?" Piper asked.

Savannah's foot tapped faster, her fingers fidgeting with the hem of her skirt. "I don't know where he is. But I know him well enough to know he doesn't care about things like money. If you're chasing him for that, you're wrong."

"Then what is it?" Lazarus asked.

Savannah hesitated. "Fear. He told me once that, as a kid, he used to start fires in trash cans just to watch people panic. He liked the fear in their eyes."

Piper leaned forward, her expression softening. "Savannah, I'm trying to find two teenagers who were taken. Carlito is probably involved. I promised one of the mothers I'd do everything I could to bring her daughter home." She pulled out her phone and showed

Savannah a picture of Keri. "I know this is hard, but if there's anything you can tell us . . ."

Savannah glanced briefly at the photo and then turned away. "I don't know where he is. I really don't. But"—she paused, her voice softening—"he has a storage unit. It was his father's. He worked on old cars there. If he's not hiding out, he might stop by to check on it."

Piper nodded. "Do you know the name?"

Savannah bit her lip, thinking for a moment. "It's at TJ Storage, on the outskirts of the city. I haven't been there, but that's the only place I can think of."

39

Piper stared out the passenger window as they drove toward the storage unit. The facility wasn't even on her radar—tucked behind a small mountain, hidden from the freeway, with no signs or markers. Just desolation. Whoever used it had chosen it for a reason.

"I heard Steven ask you out," Lazarus said, breaking the silence.

Piper shot him a look. "Why do you say it like that?"

"Like what?"

"Like you found a note in middle school you weren't supposed to read."

Lazarus chuckled, his hands loose on the wheel.

"Are you jealous?" Piper asked, half smiling.

He took out his vape pen. "I don't get jealous of relationships. No matter how it plays out, they always end in tragedy. One of you will always die first."

"You don't talk like this when you go on dates, do you?"

Lazarus just took another drag on his vape.

———

The freeway exit bled into a dirt road that snaked around the base of the mountain. The landscape turned alien, barren. Dust devils whipped across the plain, throwing up red clouds that blurred the horizon behind them. The freeway vanished into nothing.

Her stomach tightened as the tires crunched over gravel.

This was it.

She turned the scenarios over in her mind, each worse than the last. What if they were too late? What if Keri Bines was already dead or being smuggled somewhere they'd never find her? What if their arrival spooked whoever was holding her and she ended up caught in the crossfire?

She glanced at Lazarus. He stared straight ahead, his jaw set with hands steady on the wheel, but she wasn't fooled.

This wasn't like any other case. If Keri was his daughter—and Piper was starting to believe that she was—this was personal. If the girl died, Lazarus would lose his only chance to know her. He'd never admit it, but Piper knew it would eat at him, leaving a wound that would never close.

"I don't think a place like this is meant to be found," she said.

"Then we'll make sure they know we found it."

Piper had spoken to the facility's owner earlier. He was just an absentee landlord who didn't even know Carlito's father had passed. The unit had been rented for decades, practically forgotten by the company.

The storage facility appeared like a mirage—long rows of units painted in rust-red to blend with the rocks. A low office building sat out front, looking as lonely as the landscape. A tall chain-link fence surrounded the compound, with a sign bolted to it: "DANGER—ELECTRIFIED FENCE."

"Someone doesn't want us peekin'," Lazarus muttered as they parked a ways out. "Wait here," he said before Piper could respond.

He stepped out into the dust storm that was beginning to pick up. But he had seen worse storms than this before, ones that swallowed the horizon and turned the sky black, as if the world had ended. But this chaos felt fitting—Carlito's kind of place. Violent and unpredictable with short patches of calm.

He opened his trunk and grabbed a small tool bag.

At the entrance to the facility, a thick yellow-and-black wire ran from the electrified fence to a power box just inside. No easy way to cut power from this side. His eyes landed on a dirty rubber mat at the entrance. He lifted it, grimacing as years of grit and dust filled the air. Tossing the mat over the fence, rubber side down, he climbed over quickly, the rubber insulating him from the electric charge.

On the far side of the compound he found Carlito's unit. The lock was heavy, but a small bolt cutter from his tool bag made quick work of it. He crouched, listening for any sound from inside before rolling up the storage-unit door.

Lazarus froze.

Car parts were strewn across the floor—engines, tires, rusted metal, all haphazardly tossed in piles. Posters of vintage cars lined the walls, and a grease-stained workbench held a row of empty beer cans.

But it was what lay beyond the car parts that stopped him.

A bucket with a roll of toilet paper sat against the wall. Nearby, strands of rope littered the ground, stained with dried blood.

Lazarus felt his chest tighten. He had seen enough crime scenes to know this wasn't just a storage unit—it had been a prison.

Shit.

40

Judge Dawson walked into the country club with the calm air of someone who belonged there. The landscaping was immaculate, flowers imported from all corners of the world. The chef had once worked in five-star restaurants across Europe. It was the kind of place her husband, Charles, had introduced her to. Even now, she found it unsettling to think of him when she came here.

He had been charming at first. Handsome, pedigreed, the kind of man whose credentials made even CEOs envious—Harvard, then Harvard Business School, a CMO role at a Fortune 500 company. On the surface, he was everything her father had probably hoped for. But when the doors closed and no one else was around, Charles was something else entirely: insecure, irrational, violent, and psychotic. A reflection of the man her father would have handpicked.

She pushed the memory aside as Derek arrived. He strode into the room, cutting an imposing figure in black slacks, a black shirt, and a black leather jacket—despite the sweltering heat outside. An American-flag pin gleamed on his lapel and at the base of his neck was a tattoo of an eagle, a globe, and an anchor—the symbol of the US Marines.

Dawson studied him as he sat across from her. "I've never seen you without that jacket," she said.

He leaned forward, his elbows on the table. "First wife gave it to me. Before she died."

"I'm sorry, Derek. What happened?"

"Overdose," he said matter-of-factly. "Got hooked on pills. Went downhill from there. But what the hell can you do, right?"

A server came to take their drink order. Dawson ordered the lightest beer they had—Derek's preference. Once the server left, Dawson's eyes went to the files Derek had pulled from his satchel.

"You don't usually meet in person unless you've found something," she remarked.

Derek was the best private investigator in the state. A former marine, then a police officer and detective with Metro, and later a DEA special agent, he'd seen it all. He'd retired after operations in South America left him disillusioned.

"You were right," Derek said, sliding the files across the table. "Carlito's no joke."

Dawson opened the folder. The photo staring back at her was unsettling. Carlito Xibala was handsome in a feral way, and his eyes—empty black holes—held no warmth. They stared out from the photo like a void. His face was marred by three silver barbells piercing his left cheek and a scar above his right eyebrow.

"This seems like a man she would fall for," Dawson mused.

Behind the photo were images of a dilapidated room, tiles of moldy green and dull white walls. Bodies, dark skinned, lay in pools of blood on the floor. One of the bodies wore an Iraqi military uniform.

"Did he do this?" Dawson asked, a hint of excitement in her voice.

Derek nodded just as the server returned with their beers. He took a long drink, foam clinging to his upper lip. "Yeah. But it started earlier than that. Traffic stop over there went south. Some poor bastard pissed him off. He cut him up, real brutal. The guy wasn't even an insurgent—just an electrician. Instead of kicking Carlito out of the military, the CIA scooped him up."

"Why?"

"They had intel they needed and Carlito was their leverage. They told him they wouldn't charge him with murder if he did some work for them. He butchered six more at Abu Ghraib—like they were cattle. Might've been more. After that, they gave him a discharge and a free pass."

Dawson traced the edge of the folder with a finger. "I assume this is all classified. Should I ask how you came by it?"

Derek grinned. "What, you wanna steal my source?"

"No, just impressed," she said, though her mind was already turning over the potential uses for a man like Carlito. "What else do we know about him?"

Derek leaned back, still holding her gaze. "He's a violent son of a bitch. Grew up rough. Parents moved him here from Mexico when he was a kid. Same year, he put a pencil through a school cop's eye. Spent the rest of his childhood in and out of juvie."

Dawson reviewed the criminal history laid out in front of her, reading over the details of each charge with measured interest.

Derek took another swig of his beer. "You said something about trafficking. Honestly, it's a crap game. You make more moving dope."

"There are certain advantages," she countered. "Drugs are easy to trace. People . . . not so much. You can grab four or five in one night and have them across the border before morning."

He shrugged. "I don't know. Sounds like paranoia to me."

Dawson smiled faintly. "The Dark Ages lasted a thousand years—filled with murder, genocide, and pestilence. What makes you think our technology has changed human nature?"

Derek drained his beer, clearly not interested in a philosophical debate. "I ain't here to fix the world. Just trying to make my slice of it a little nicer." He grinned. "Speaking of which, I saw that fee hit my bank this morning. Thanks for the tip."

"I pay well for work performed well." She closed the folder, but Derek wasn't finished.

He pulled out another, smaller file and set it on the table. "Got some photos of a recent crime scene in here for you. Know you like that stuff."

"Thank you." She slid the folder into her bag without so much as a glance inside. "I've got another request. There's a young man from Citadel Investigations who's about to pull files on me and my brothers. I'm sending extra funds to your account for him. Get those files and return them directly to me. I'll pass along his details."

He shrugged. "So, I drop off some money and pick up some papers? We can just call it a favor, you don't have to pay me."

"I don't like getting favors. Even from people I like."

He raised a brow. "Well, thanks, I guess." Derek paused, eyes narrowing. "Mind if I ask something?"

"Depends on what it is."

"I know this is need-to-know, but why the sudden focus on Carlito? You've already got plenty going on with your brothers suing you."

"They overplayed their hand," she said. "I'm just showing them mine."

He finished off his beer with a sharp tilt of the bottle, then set it down. "I'm guessing they won't like how that turns out."

41

Lazarus leaned against the hood of his car, waiting for CSI to finish processing the storage unit. The criminalists here were among the best in the country. After the TV show took off, forensic schools saw an influx of students with big dreams. But most of them quickly realized the daily grind of the job—sifting through monotonous, gruesome scenes—wasn't glamorous. When you're being paid to do it, the excitement fades and it just becomes work.

He'd already seen the footage from the facility's cameras. Carlito Xibala and a woman had driven into the facility. A few days later, Carlito had driven the kids out in the same car, alone. The woman had been identified as Denver Hartley, a known associate of Carlito, with a criminal record as long as his.

Piper joined him on the hood, silently watching the techs comb through the site. After a moment, she spoke.

"He's moving them somewhere to sell fast, don't you think?"

"Unless they're already dead."

"They're worth more to him alive."

"It'd be more rational to kill them now and lay low."

"How can you talk like that? One of those kids might be your daughter, Lazarus."

He didn't respond right away, his jaw clenching. He stared ahead.

"You get his face out there?" she asked, changing the subject.

He nodded, taking a drag off his vape pen. "Airports, bus stations, ICE—all notified. Roadblocks at the border. If I were him, I'd make for Mexico. Dump them there, then vanish."

Piper shook her head. "Their families aren't gonna forget about this. Neither are you, Lazarus."

He finally turned to face her. "You want to catch people like this? You have to see the victims the way they do. I can't afford to see her as anything else."

"That's heartless."

"That's survival. Now can we stop talkin' about it?"

A heavy silence settled between them as they continued to watch the techs.

"What about Denver?" Piper finally asked. "What's her story?"

Lazarus exhaled vapor from his nose. "Her father was a pimp and her ex-husband was a pimp. She's been used her whole life."

"And now Carlito's using her, too." Piper shook her head. "She never had a chance."

"Man's the cruelest animal."

Before Piper could respond, one of the techs, a young guy named Davies, approached them, holding a clear evidence bag.

"Found this," Davies said, holding up a crumpled receipt inside the bag.

Lazarus examined it. "He was feeding them," he said. "At least we know he wants them alive."

A news van rolled up around the bend, then parked in front of the facility. The Channel 13 logo stood out in bright blue and yellow on the side of the van. An attractive blond woman in a business suit hopped out, followed by a cameraman in basketball shorts and a T-shirt.

"Who the hell called them?" Davies said.

"One of you, probably," Lazarus said, handing the evidence bag back. Davies didn't reply, instead hurrying off, looking awkward.

"You want me to get a uniform to send them off?" Piper asked.

Lazarus stood and stretched. "Nah, I'll handle it. We need 'em this time."

He approached the reporter, Kendra—something. He'd dealt with her before. She greeted him with a sly smile, her ruby-red lips curling in amusement.

"Been a while, Detective," she said. "How come you don't call me anymore? You and I had a pretty good professional relationship, if I recall."

"I remember askin' you to keep something quiet and it was on TV that night. Didn't even make it a full day."

"That was news. What do you expect me to do with it?"

"I expect you to keep your word. Without that, we're just parasites floatin' in the sun."

Her cameraman, a scruffy guy named Terry, was unloading his gear as she tilted her head, curious. "So what are you after?"

"I need you to air a segment. In return, I'll give you an exclusive interview with everything you want to know about what's going on here. But only if you let me say what I need to say."

Kendra grinned. "Terry, let's set up around the back of the van," she said, leading Lazarus around the side of the vehicle for some privacy.

42

Carlito pulled the car in at a diner about an hour from the border. The building sat alone surrounded by dusty parking spots and a flickering neon sign that advertised "Best Steak in Town." Food was one of Carlito's few indulgences, but even that was occasional. He preferred fasting for long periods, finding that when all his desires funneled into a single craving—hunger—it was easier to control them. A man with one need could manage. It was when desires ganged up on you that you became a slave to them.

He brought Brad in with him, leaving Denver and Keri alone in the car. Carlito figured it was better this way—they would be easier to control one at a time. A hostess, a young woman who looked of Japanese descent, smiled at them as they waited for their table.

"You have Japanese ancestry?" Carlito asked her, his dark eyes watching her with an intensity that made her slightly uncomfortable.

"I do," she said, still smiling but with a hint of hesitation now.

"It adds an exotic beauty to you. You shouldn't hide it under blond hair and pink nails. Uniqueness is beauty."

"Uh, thanks," she replied. "John's your server. He'll be with you in a minute."

Carlito watched her go, then turned to see Brad staring out the window toward the car. The young man was nervous, a ball of tension barely holding itself together.

"She'll be okay," Carlito said. "No need to be so scared."

Brad swallowed hard. "Are you going to kill me?"

"I haven't decided yet."

"That's better than yes."

Carlito laughed softly. "I like you, Bradley."

"Then why are you doing this?"

Carlito glanced out the window at Denver, sitting in the car, watching the light play off her hair. There were moments, even now, when he marveled at her—how a man like him could have someone like her. Sometimes, it felt like he had stolen something precious he never deserved.

"I have an ancestor," Carlito began, turning his focus back to Brad. "He wanted to marry a chief's daughter. But he was just the son of a poor priest, so the daughter was promised to the richest man in the tribe. On their wedding night, my ancestor snuck in while he was taking her virginity and killed them both. Sawed them into pieces."

Brad's eyes widened, the horror evident in his face. "What happened to him?"

"The tribe tore him apart with their bare hands. And the head priest cursed my family's bloodline. But it wasn't a curse; it was a gift. That suffering made us stronger. You've never suffered in your life, Bradley. Now that you are, you're asking questions like 'Why?' There is no *why*. We suffer. That's it."

Before Brad could reply, the server approached and Carlito ordered steaks and beer. As the server left to get the beer, Brad sat in silence, nervously tearing at the edge of the straw wrapper.

"What's going on in that head, Bradley?" Carlito asked, leaning back, relaxed, as the server brought back a bottle of beer and a cold mug before leaving again.

Brad hesitated. "I'm just wondering how many people you've killed."

"Depends what you mean by *killed*."

"There's more than one kind?"

"There's murder, which is illegal. And then there's killing, which isn't." He took a long gulp of beer. "In Iraq, Bradley, I killed plenty there. But it wasn't murder. The government wanted those people dead."

Brad studied him. "But you've killed other people, haven't you?"

"Some people need killing."

Brad's voice cracked slightly. "I don't want to die."

Carlito sighed, the first sign of weariness showing in his usually controlled expression. "I'm saving you from something far worse. Nations are rotting from the inside. Soon, the whole world will fall into chaos. I'm sparing you from watching everything you know die."

The server returned with their food a bit later. Carlito dug into his steak with enthusiasm while Brad poked at his plate, pushing the food around without eating. Carlito watched him, chewing slowly.

"Do you know the gods are jealous of us?" Carlito said, his voice almost reverent. "Because we die. Our lives are short, so everything is temporary. The gods are eternal. They don't know true loss, like whispering goodbye to someone you love, knowing you won't ever see them again. Immortality is their curse. Death makes us beautiful, so they're jealous of us."

Brad, unable to respond, let his gaze drift to the people in the diner, hoping one of them might see his desperation. His eyes fell on the TV behind the counter, where a news segment was running with closed captions.

On the screen, the words scrolled by quickly: *Public is asked to call 911 if they see them*—The mug shots of Carlito and Denver were staring back at him from the screen.

Carlito noticed the change in Brad's expression. "What are you smiling about?"

Brad quickly looked away from the screen. "Nothing. Just thinking about something."

43

Denver absentmindedly filed one of her nails, though it hardly mattered. She glanced at her hands. Another nail missing, thanks to that psycho they'd sent when they hadn't dropped the teens off. She'd have enjoyed being the one to kill him, but Carlito had claimed that for himself.

Her body was one big ache—eye, ribs, hands, back, every space between joints screaming with pain. The pills they'd given her stayed untouched. She needed to think, and those meds fogged her mind.

From the back seat, Keri's voice cut through the silence. "He loves you," she said.

Denver didn't bother turning around. The sight of Keri—blond, beautiful, innocent—made her stomach twist with disgust. Something about that kind of beauty made Denver itch to destroy it. She could put a bullet in her right now. They could find another blond idiot to replace her.

"I think Brad loves me," Keri continued, nervously picking at the seat belt. "He's told me, but some people just say it, you know? I think he means it, though."

"Why are you talking?"

"I'm nervous. I talk when I get nervous. I'm sorry," Keri stammered, her words tumbling out faster now. "But I think you love him, too. I can tell."

"Shut your mouth."

"I can't. I'm just scared, okay? I'm sorry. I can't stop." Tears welled in her eyes as she rambled, panic creeping in. "You love him a lot, don't you?"

Denver glanced at her in the rearview mirror. Keri's wide, terrified eyes reflected back at her. "What's the matter, Daddy didn't teach you manners?"

"That piece of shit isn't my dad," Keri shot back, staring out the window. "My dad took off when he found out my mom was pregnant."

Denver paused. "You're better off. I wish I didn't know mine."

Keri let out a nervous laugh. "Yeah, right. Look at where I am. I'm gonna be sold or killed for no reason."

"Not for no reason."

"You don't believe the same stuff he does," Keri said. "About the gods and all that. I can tell because you roll your eyes when he talks about it."

"You don't know shit about me."

"I know you don't believe it."

Tears streamed down Keri's face now, and her voice trembled. "Brad and I aren't allowed to live together until we're married. It's one of the things my mom's husband said. So we sneak out. Sometimes I wonder if he's really the one. I mean, how do you know, right? What if the person you're meant to be with is in Paris or something and you never meet them?"

Her sobs grew loud and messy, but she wasn't wiping the tears away anymore. Denver thought about slapping her, but something held her back.

She lit a clove cigarette and leaned back against the seat, exhaling as smoke filled the car. She wished Carlito would hurry the hell up.

When Carlito returned, he opened the door for Brad to climb into the back seat. The to-go boxes were handed out and Carlito slid into the driver's seat. He started the car, tuned the radio to a country station, and began the drive back to the freeway.

Brad gripped Keri's hand, squeezing harder than he meant to, trying to offer comfort he didn't feel. He wanted to tell her what he knew—that the cops knew about Carlito and Denver—but fear kept him quiet. If Carlito found out, he'd kill them and leave their bodies in the street and probably laugh while he did it.

"Where are we going?" Keri asked, her voice rising with panic.

Carlito met her gaze in the rearview mirror, his expression unreadable, then turned back to the road without a word.

Keri snapped, her composure crumbling. Tears streamed down her face as she screamed, "Just kill us! I don't want to be sold—just kill us already!"

"I can't, Little Bird."

"Stop calling me that!" Keri screamed, her voice piercing the car.

Carlito didn't flinch. It was as though Keri's screams were nothing more than background noise, the creak of an old floorboard or the hiss of static.

Brad whispered into her ear, "Don't say anything. The police are looking for us."

Carlito, catching the movement in the rearview, turned the music down slowly. His eyes fixed on Brad.

"What are you whispering about?"

"Nothing."

Carlito's gaze held steady. "Don't be stupid, Bradley."

Brad swallowed hard, his mouth dry. "I won't."

44

Lazarus finished the interview and shook hands with the reporter. He'd seen other male detectives treat her differently from her male colleagues, but he always made a point of treating reporters the same way: as though he didn't like any of them.

Afterward, he headed back to the car, where Piper sat on the hood talking with Davies, who was clearly flirting with her. Lazarus ignored the interaction and slid into the driver's seat, where he waited for Piper.

"You okay?" she asked, climbing in beside him.

"Media leaves a bad taste in my mouth," he said, starting the car.

The streets were unusually quiet, an empty lull on a Friday night. It was the time when gamblers disappeared into bars or hotels to fuel up on booze, drugs, or food before heading back to the tables. Lazarus could still feel the pulse of the city, though. Like a living thing.

He rolled down the window, the dry air cooling his face as he took a drag from his vape pen. "You got other cases?"

"I did. I asked for them to be covered for a while."

"You didn't have to."

"What are friends for?"

There was silence in the car a few minutes until they stopped at an intersection.

"I had a case like this once." Piper's voice was soft.

"What was it?"

"It wasn't exactly like this, but similar. A twelve-year-old girl claimed her neighbor kidnapped her. The police didn't believe her because she had a so-called promiscuous history. Whatever that means for a twelve-year-old."

She recalled with bitterness the first time she had heard that term applied to a child. She had to push it out of her mind because it was too infuriating.

"I was her guardian and I didn't push hard enough. I was new. I thought if the police thought it was nothing, then it must be nothing."

Lazarus glanced at her. "What happened?"

"The neighbor raped her while her parents were out of town. A few weeks later she took an entire bottle of codeine with strawberry schnapps. She died on the way to the hospital."

Piper stared out the window as the light at the intersection turned and they began to drive.

"The strawberry schnapps stuck with me," she said. "Her house had plenty of other alcohol—things that would've done the job quicker. But she chose . . ."

"Something a child would choose," Lazarus murmured.

She didn't say anything.

"You didn't believe her?" he finally asked.

"I think I did. But I got caught up in it. The system makes you do what you can and move on quickly because there'll always be another case. But I swore I'd never do that again. If I took a case, I'd see it through, no matter what." She turned to him. "Have you talked to Amanda yet?"

Lazarus exhaled, the vapor curling out of his nostrils. He pulled into the parking lot where her car was and parked. Without looking at her, he said, "I'll call you if we find anything."

Piper hesitated, as if she wanted to say more, but then she got out and he drove off without another word.

The Night Collector

Lazarus walked into the dimly lit Last Chance Saloon. Something inside him felt coiled tight, like a spring.

The place was busy. A rowdy group of bikers crowded the back, drunk but not causing trouble. Nobody dared at Bass's place.

Lazarus downed beer quickly. Despite the caffeine in the porter, it calmed his nerves. As he finished a second bottle, he logged on to the Metro PD's network, then pulled up Amanda Bines's current address.

Same house. A small rambler in a quiet suburb. White picket fences, porch swings, and mailboxes on the corner. The kind of place people moved to when they were ready to settle down, to try to pretend the world wasn't what it was.

When he parked outside the house, he spotted an old man on the neighboring porch, his cigarette glowing in the night like a firefly. The old man took a drag and the ember flared bright before fading again. Lazarus counted the glow three times before stepping out of the car.

The air was warm, the night thick with the scent of cut grass. Lazarus walked up the short path to the porch. The sound of a television hummed from inside the house. He knocked and a middle-aged man answered the door. The guy had perfect anchorman hair, the kind that made Lazarus wonder if he worked for the same news station he'd just given an interview to.

"Charlie Bines?"

"Yeah."

"I'm Detective Holloway, Metro PD. I was hoping to speak with your wife."

"Oh, um . . . sure, but Detective Hobbes didn't mention anyone else coming by tonight."

"I'm here on my own, just helping him out."

Charlie hesitated. "Okay, let me get her. Would you like to come in?"

"Nah, I'm good out here."

As Charlie went inside, Lazarus glanced at the old man again. He was still watching, his cigarette now just a glowing nub.

"You havin' a good night, old-timer?" Lazarus called out.

"Above ground and got a fresh beer. What else does a man need?"

Amanda Bines appeared at the door, freezing when she saw him. Her eyes went to the neighbor then back to Lazarus. "Let's take a walk."

They walked in silence, her shoes clicking softly on the pavement. It wasn't until they were a block away from the house that either of them spoke.

"You look good," he said quietly.

"You too." She gave a small smile. "I like the new car."

"It's not new. Had it ten years. But I take care of my things."

"You always hated the idea of buying new stuff."

"Things that last tend to keep lasting."

They crossed a street, and Amanda stepped over a cracked section of sidewalk where an anthill rose up like a tiny mountain. Lazarus sidestepped it, watching the ants scurry about.

"You didn't tell Charlie about me?" Lazarus asked.

"No."

"Who did you tell him Keri's father was?"

"Does it matter?"

"No, guess not."

There was a beat of silence.

"Did you ever get your doctorate?" he asked.

"No. I decided to stay home with the kids."

"You decided, or Charlie?"

She shot him a look. "I don't think you get to ask me questions like that."

"You're right," he said. "I apologize."

He took out his vape pen, the familiar action grounding him as he took a long drag. "Is she really mine?"

Amanda didn't answer right away. They turned down another street, this one leading to an empty lot. Covered in graffiti, a "FOR SALE" sign stood at the edge, like a wound on the pristine suburb.

When they were on the other side, she finally spoke. "Yes. She's yours."

"You sure?"

"If you're asking if I was with anyone else, I wasn't."

"Why didn't you tell me?"

She stopped walking and turned to face him, anger and hurt etched into her. "You called off our engagement like it was nothing. You showed up at my house, drunk off your ass, and said you never wanted to see me again. You think I'd raise a child with someone like that? I knew I could do better on my own."

Lazarus stood there, taking it. "Fair enough. But you still should've told me."

Amanda looked down, biting her lip. "You're right. I'm sorry."

"You want me to . . . spend time with her now?"

"I know men like you, Lazarus. Men who are going to self-destruct. My father was like that, right before he put a gun in his mouth. I don't want my daughter to go through that."

"I can at least help with the bills," he offered, his voice softer.

"I don't need your money. I make my own."

Tears welled in her eyes as she spoke again, her voice breaking. "Do you know what happened to her, Lazarus?"

"I'm gonna find out."

Her gaze bored into him. "Is it because of you? Did she get taken because of you?"

"I don't think so. We got a name, an ex-con, who we think has her. I haven't seen any connection between him and me, or you and Keri. We looked into Charlie, too. Nothing. Makes me think it was a random smash and grab. Quick payday. They probably found out about it in the *Ledger*. It has wedding announcements from the local chapels."

"If it was money, they would've asked by now."

He knew she was right. Amanda had a sharp mind, sharper than his. She'd been getting her doctorate in criminology when they'd been together, and they used to spend hours talking about deviant behavior and criminal analysis.

She looked up at him, tears streaming down her face. "Lazarus, what are they going to do to my daughter?"

"I think they're taking her to Mexico," he said softly, "to traffic her."

Amanda gasped, her hands flying to her mouth as she sobbed. Lazarus watched her, feeling powerless. She fell into him, sobbing uncontrollably. He put his arms around her, feeling her warmth, her familiar scent—vanilla and cinnamon. It was the same bodywash she'd always used, the one he liked.

"Why did you leave me?" she said quietly.

He swallowed. "If life only gives you bruises, you don't know what to do with a gentle touch."

They stood like that, wrapped in each other's arms, as the world moved on around them.

45

Carlito pulled into the parking lot of a dingy motel near the Mexicali border, sweat rolling down the back of his neck from the heat.

The run-down sign flickered weakly, casting uneven light over the asphalt. Barred doors lined the units and their paint peeled in the dry desert air. Cooling units jutted from open windows, humming like dying animals.

"Make sure the kids behave," he said, stepping out of the car.

The front office smelled like sweat and stale cigarettes. He tapped a bell on the desk. Behind it, a poster of a woman in a bikini, faded at the edges, hung crookedly. A tubby man with a beard and a dirty cap shuffled out from the back.

"How are ya?"

"Good. Need a room."

The man scratched his gut, waddled behind the desk, and pulled up something on the computer. He burped silently, then asked, "How many nights?"

"Just one."

"That's sixty-two ninety-five and a fifty-dollar deposit."

Carlito pulled a few bills from his wallet and laid them on the counter. The man stared, his eyes growing wide. Carlito followed his gaze. A TV mounted on the wall flickered with an Amber Alert:

Armed and dangerous . . . please call law enforcement . . . kidnapping victims . . .

Carlito's picture appeared in the corner of the screen. Denver's face followed.

"I hate that picture of me," Carlito muttered, half to himself.

The man swallowed hard. "I don't want trouble."

Carlito turned slowly to face him. "So what should we do?"

"How about you pretend you didn't come in and I pretend I didn't come out?"

Carlito chuckled. "I like poor neighborhoods. People know how to mind their business. Okay, amigo, I'll take my money back then."

The man's hands shook as he handed the cash back but Carlito was already reaching for his pistol. One shot through the man's forehead. Blood sprayed across the bikini poster and the man's body jerked, knocking the computer and phone system to the floor in a crash as loud as the gunshot.

Carlito tucked the gun back into his waistband and jogged out to the car. Denver sat in the passenger seat, chewing gum, watching him. The kids in the back were pale, the girl sobbing quietly. Brad wasn't crying.

Carlito slid into the driver's seat. "We need to cross Mexicali tonight. It can't wait."

The engine rumbled to life, but before Carlito could lock the doors, he heard them open. Brad bolted from the back seat, dragging the girl with him. They sprinted across the parking lot fast enough that Carlito didn't have time to react.

"Shit!"

He kicked the door open and leapt out.

46

Piper sat at home, staring at the clock. It was a Friday night and she had no plans. Her life had become a series of mundane routines, but the repetition helped. It kept her grounded, kept the memories away. She tried to focus on the good times with her grandmother, but no matter what, the image of Lake Danes torn apart in a bathtub haunted her. Before she'd looked, Lazarus had told her not to.
You don't want this in your head.
She should've listened.
She started the shower and was barely in when the doorbell rang. She turned the shower off, straining to hear. It rang again. No one was supposed to be coming over.
She wrapped a towel around herself, slicked her wet hair back, and hurried to the door. Looking through the peephole, she saw Lazarus standing there, dressed in a black button-up, holding a six-pack of beer and a pizza.
"Can you open up? This pizza's burnin' my hand."
"One sec."
She rushed to throw on some sweats, then opened the door.
"You hungry?" Lazarus asked.
"Starving."
She let him in, and he set the pizza down on her glass dining table—the one she'd picked up from IKEA on discount. As he sat, she

suddenly felt self-conscious. The condo was small, the furniture cheap. Normally she didn't care what people thought of her things.

From the kitchen, she grabbed plates and glanced back at him. He was staring at his reflection in the glass tabletop, lost in thought.

"So what's the latest?" she asked.

"Everyone's notified, and their pictures are out. Border Patrol's on alert. Mexican police, too. Unless Carlito's planning on swimming, he's not crossing that border."

"You figure out why?"

"No connection to anyone. I think he saw some easy money and took his shot."

She brought the plates over, placing one in front of him. He took two bites of pizza, then pushed the plate away and reached for his beer. What started as a sip turned into a long drink.

"I saw Amanda," he said finally.

"And?"

"She says Keri's my kid."

"You believe her?"

"She wasn't ever a liar before."

"You could get a DNA test before you do anything."

Lazarus nodded. "Yeah."

Piper took a bite of her slice and chewed slowly. "How long were you engaged to her?"

"All of six months. Then I called it off. Woke her up in the middle of the night and told her she was the type of person I hate: banal and obvious. Told her I never wanted to see her again."

"Wow. What did she do?"

"Nothing. Didn't fight me on it. Like she'd been expecting it."

He let out a long breath, his fingers tapping the table absently. "She asked me once how I felt about kids. Looking back, I think she was pregnant then, testing the waters."

"What did you say?"

"That I would never, in a million years, bring a kid into this world. Not with her, not with anybody."

"Ouch."

"Yeah," he muttered, draining the rest of his beer.

His phone buzzed on the table. He glanced at the screen and answered. "This is Holloway . . . You were right . . . What is it? . . . Uh-huh . . . Which motel? . . . Anything taken? . . . There video? . . . No, I know where it is."

He hung up, already standing.

"What is it?" Piper asked, pushing her plate aside.

"Motel clerk shot near the border. Nothing taken. Nobody shoots a clerk with cameras behind the desk unless they're desperate. They're getting the footage now, but I'm betting that's him."

"I'm coming," Piper said, standing up.

"No way."

"Those kids could be there. They might need someone."

"I'll call you when they're safe."

"You're not my boss, Lazarus."

"And you're not a damn cop, so stop acting like one."

The silence that followed was thick, the kind of silence where words weren't going to fix anything. He rubbed his neck, regret creeping into his expression.

"Sorry," he said.

Piper folded her arms. "As soon as those kids are safe, I want you to call me."

Lazarus headed to the door. "I will."

47

Brad ran so hard it felt like his legs were going to snap. Not the kind of burn you get from running laps in gym class—this was different. This pain told him that if he didn't keep going, he was dead. He knew it. This was the second time he had tried to escape. There wouldn't be a third.

He and Keri bolted from the motel, sprinting down a side street and into a quiet business park. A few scattered cars were there, engines cold. They tried the doors to one of the buildings—locked. They kept running, lungs burning, muscles screaming.

Keri's voice cracked as they reached a run-down office building. "I have to stop."

"Just a little longer," Brad panted.

"I *can't*, Brad."

He saw a row of dumpsters behind the building and yanked her over, pulling her down behind them. They collapsed onto the concrete, their breath coming in ragged gasps, hearts pounding like jackhammers.

"Did he follow us?" Keri asked, her voice barely a whisper.

"I don't know. I didn't look back."

They sat in silence, straining to hear anything—footsteps, voices, an engine. But all they heard was the wind through the empty lot.

"What's wrong with them?" Keri said.

"I don't know," Brad muttered. He didn't have answers.

He leaned his head back against the rough wall of the building, staring up at the sky. "My mom's probably freaking out. Her anxiety's so bad she can't get out of bed. This is probably making her crazy."

"Mine's probably sitting by the phone waiting. She's like that. Waits for things to happen instead of doing anything about it."

"I like your mom. I don't even mind Chuck."

"He's awful. He's so . . . obvious."

"There's worse stepdads." Brad wiped spit from his lips, his breath finally calming.

A car. Slowly creeping through the parking lot.

Headlights swept over the dumpsters and lit up the area behind them. Brad held his breath, his heart hammering. Keri squeezed his hand and her nails dug into his skin.

The car rolled around the lot, idling for a second, then drove off in the opposite direction.

Brad didn't waste time. "Let's go."

They dashed out of their hiding spot, moving in the opposite direction of the car. The street ahead stretched out, lit by flickering streetlights. On one side, a row of dark retail shops. On the other, empty fields. Then, in the distance, a gas station. Its lights glowing. A person was leaning against their car, pumping gas.

Keri started to cry, her shoulders shaking with sobs. Brad swallowed the lump in his throat. They were close.

Tires screeched as the engine revved behind them.

"Run!" Brad shouted.

They sprinted toward the gas station, but the car was closing in too fast. They wouldn't make it. Not to the gas station. Not with the car barreling down. His eyes darted to the left. Across the street—a parking garage. Multilevel and next to an office building.

He grabbed Keri's hand and yanked her toward the garage. They dashed across the street and made it past the security booth. The booth was empty. No phone. Just a ramp spiraling up into the dark.

They ran up the ramp, shouting for help, their voices bouncing off the concrete walls, but they only heard echoes in reply.

They reached the second level. A few cars were scattered around, but not enough. The sound of the engine below them rumbled through the structure, reverberating up the ramp. Carlito's car. The one he loved so much because it was loud. Alive.

Keri was gasping for air, her body giving out. "I can't run anymore," she choked, sitting on the stairs as they neared the third floor.

"We're almost there," Brad urged, pulling her up.

"Almost *where*?" she cried. "They're not going to stop."

"The cops are looking for us. We just need to hide until they find us."

He squeezed her hand, trying to keep her grounded. "Just a little more. I promise."

They jogged up the next set of steps. When they reached the third floor, Brad spotted a row of cars lined up against the wall. He pulled Keri behind one, and they pressed themselves against the cold concrete. They crouched low, the city lights in the distance beyond the open side of the garage.

Then they heard it. The unmistakable rumble of Carlito's engine, louder now, closer.

"If they come up here," Brad whispered, "I want you to run. Run down the ramp and don't stop."

"I'm not leaving you."

"They won't chase both of us. If you get away, you can call the police."

Keri shook her head, tears streaming down her face. But Brad wasn't backing down. He wasn't brave. He didn't know what it meant to be brave. But if Carlito and Denver were going to catch one of them, it would be him.

The car rumbled louder, echoing up the ramp. Brad could hear Denver's voice shouting, telling Carlito to go up another level. The sound of her voice sent a chill up his back.

The headlights pierced the darkness and the car crept up the ramp, the engine purring.

Brad's pulse pounded in his ears. Denver's voice rang out again, impatient.

"They're up here. There's nowhere else they can go."

48

Lazarus grabbed Riley from his apartment, neither of them saying much. Riley was sober, which was rare, but he still wasn't talking. Lazarus didn't mind. The drive was long and he didn't need the distraction.

Lazarus sped down I-8, nearing Mexicali, the needle climbing higher with every mile. Six hours from Vegas, but if he pushed hard enough, maybe four.

Riley broke the silence. "You got a death wish?"

He let out a humorless laugh. "What are you talking about?"

"You're doing a hundred and twenty."

Lazarus glanced at the speedometer, the car trembling beneath him. He hadn't even noticed. He slowed.

"I've seen men who wanted to die," Riley said, his voice flat. "When I was in the marines. They always smiled the biggest and told the dumbest jokes. Made sure everybody thought they were fine. Then they'd run straight into a firefight or race Humvees down roads with mines. Is that what you're doing?"

"I don't want to die, but I'm not scared of it either. Are you?"

Riley shrugged. "No. When you don't have much to live for, it doesn't sound so bad."

Lazarus glanced at him. "Why're you talkin' like that? You don't know it's over. Couples break up all the time, get back together, then break up again. It's like gluing a lamp back together. Every time, it's uglier, but you still keep using it. You'll get another shot, even though you probably shouldn't."

"You can't say that. You've never loved anybody."

Lazarus didn't respond. His phone buzzed on the console, and he pressed the button for speaker. Tony's voice came through.

"We just had a uniform interview someone from housekeeping, boss. She said there were three people in the car—two younger and a woman in the passenger seat. Bad news, though—no video. Camera's just for show."

"Doesn't matter. It's him," Lazarus said. "Good work."

He pressed the gas, pushing the car back to a hundred. The road blurred, but he wasn't slowing down. He flicked the radio on. A sad song filled the car, some guy singing about a woman who stole his breath and never gave it back.

Riley shifted in his seat. "Why'd you bring me? You think I'm gonna off myself, so you don't wanna leave me alone?"

Lazarus stayed quiet. He knew better than to lie again. Cops like Riley saw through everything.

"Thought crossed my mind," Riley said.

Lazarus gave a slight nod. "Everyone thinks about it sometimes. It's about control. Knowing you get to decide when it ends, not fate."

He glanced at Riley, then back at the road. "What stopped you?"

"My kids. I can at least not do that to them."

"You're a good father, Kevin."

The silence settled between them again, the song still crooning in the background. Lazarus passed a semi, the speedometer inching higher.

49

The car rolled to a stop near them. Brad bit down hard on his lower lip. His body trembled and he could feel the warmth of panic building in his chest. For a split second he thought he might piss himself, but somehow the thought of Keri being even more terrified than him stopped it. If he freaked out, she'd fall apart.

The engine cut off. The doors clicked open and Brad's heart skipped. Muffled voices and footsteps followed.

"Stay here," he whispered, moving to get a better view.

Keri grabbed his arm. "Don't go."

"I'm just gonna see if it's them."

"Of course it's them. Don't be stupid, Brad."

He hesitated, then sat back down. They both crouched behind the cars, their breaths shallow. They didn't move, didn't even breathe too loudly. Just listened. Footsteps, voices—but nothing close.

"You think they're gone?" Brad whispered.

"I don't know. We just need to stay quiet."

More footfalls. Closer this time.

"We can't stay here," he whispered. "We have to move."

"No. We need to hide," she whispered back.

"They're going to find us. We have to get out."

Brad squeezed her hand. When he felt her calm, she nodded. They crept to the bumper of the car, peering around. The level wasn't crowded—maybe a dozen cars. There was a ramp leading down to the lower level on one side and another ramp going up to the fourth floor on the other.

Brad motioned for Keri to follow as they crouched low and dashed across the lot. They moved between cars. Lungs on fire.

The moonlight caught her tears and Brad suddenly noticed how beautiful Keri was and he hated himself for never telling her.

The sound of footsteps echoed. Brad stopped, holding his breath. The ramp down wasn't far—maybe thirty, forty feet. But the dark corners of the parking garage looked like shadows waiting to swallow them.

"I think they went upstairs," Brad whispered. "Is that what it sounded like to you?"

"I don't know," Keri said, shaking her head.

"We need to—"

Denver's hand shot over the hood of a car, grabbing Keri by the hair. Keri screamed as she clawed at Denver's arm. Brad froze, terror paralyzing him. His mouth hung open and his body went cold.

Denver yanked Keri to her feet. Instinct kicked in and Brad grabbed Denver's arm with both hands, using his body weight to pull her down. Denver hit the ground and let go of Keri's hair.

"Run!" Brad shouted, shoving Keri to get her moving.

Keri stood frozen, staring, but then her legs kicked into gear, and she ran. Brad bolted in the opposite direction, pounding on car hoods, setting off alarms. One blared across the level, echoing off the concrete walls. He kept shouting, kept pounding. Anything to distract Denver. But when he glanced back, Keri and Denver had already disappeared down the ramp.

Carlito emerged up the ramp, gun in hand. Brad's stomach dropped. He sprinted up the ramp to the next floor, rounding the bend, legs burning, lungs screaming for air. He slapped another car as he passed, setting off another alarm.

He dove under a minivan, flattening himself on his back. His chest heaved and he had to force himself to slow his breathing.

Carlito's footsteps echoed up the ramp, slow. He wasn't running. He didn't have to.

"Bradley, I'm disappointed," Carlito called out, his voice calm. "I thought we had an understanding."

The footsteps stopped maybe ten feet away. Brad could see Carlito's boots as they turned, scanning the area. Carlito wasn't moving. He was listening.

"Come out, come out, wherever you are."

Brad squeezed his eyes shut, trying to block out the fear. He thought of his parents—his mom, whose anxiety would tear her apart when she heard what happened. He thought of Keri. He thought of marrying her. His parents had only approved of it because he lied and told them she was pregnant.

If I get out of this, I'll tell them I love her and I don't care what they think.

Then, a miracle—a car engine. It rumbled through the parking garage, the sound bouncing off the walls. Carlito's boots moved, fading away. Brad's breath came in shallow bursts, his body shaking. He waited until the sound of Carlito's footsteps disappeared, then crawled out from under the van.

He ran for the ramp, shouting, "Help! Help me!" His voice echoed, loud and desperate, and there was no sound of boots behind him.

He had made it almost to the ramp when a gun barrel pressed against his temple. He stopped dead, his breath catching in his throat. Carlito stood beside him, calm.

"You almost did it," Carlito said, his voice admiring.

Brad shook his head, panting. "Just . . . do it. I can't run anymore."

Carlito hesitated. Just for a second.

Then headlights cut through the shadows, and a red SUV came around the ramp. Brad saw the woman driving, blond, her face frozen in shock. Carlito glanced at her. A second of distraction.

Brad ran.

He bolted across the lot, his feet pounding the concrete. He darted toward an elevator.

"Bradley!" Carlito's voice boomed behind him, but Brad didn't look back. He ran to the end of the row of cars and to the elevator. He slammed the button repeatedly.

"Come on, come on, come on."

Carlito was coming, walking fast, his eyes full of something Brad hadn't seen before—anger. Real anger. It made him realize how terrifying Carlito really was.

He glanced over the edge of the garage. Four stories hadn't seemed like much until now. The ground below was a black pit. If he jumped, he'd break every bone in his body.

The elevator dinged. The doors slid open.

"Bradley! Don't!"

Brad jumped inside and slammed the button for the top floor. The doors closed, sealing him inside. He collapsed, leaning over, hands on his knees, trying to breathe.

The doors opened. Brad stumbled out. His legs were jelly, and he could barely stand. There were fewer cars here, less cover. He sprinted to the other side, but his body was failing him. His side burned, and hot sweat stung his eyes. He couldn't hear anything but his own blood pounding in his ears.

The elevator dinged again.

"Bradley," Carlito's voice called. Calm. Steady. "There's no reason for this."

Brad turned, breathing hard. "It's you. It's not fate, it's not gods. It's just you doing this."

Carlito paused, almost like the words stung. "You don't know what you're saying, Bradley. I know the gods are real because I've seen them. But it's okay. I forgive you."

Brad backed against the stairwell doors. Locked. Nowhere to go. He climbed up onto the railing, balancing on the narrow strip of concrete. He kept his eyes on Carlito.

"Bradley, you're not going to jump. You want to live. I know you do."

"If you know that, why would you sell me to people who might kill me?"

Carlito extended his hand. "Stop this. Let's go."

"I'm not going with you."

Carlito lowered his hand. "Okay, then jump. I'll wait."

Brad swallowed hard and glanced behind him. The fall looked endless, like a black hole waiting to swallow him.

"You see, don't you?" Carlito's voice was smooth, coaxing. "The futility of it. There's no escaping fate."

Brad took a breath. "How can you sell people?"

Carlito's eyes hardened. "I don't need to explain myself to you. Now get down or jump." He took a step forward.

"Stop," Brad warned, inching back.

"What are you going to do? Die for certain now or live longer and see what happens?"

A scream shredded the night air. Brad's pulse spiked—Denver was out there, hurting Keri, and that cry was hers.

Carlito lunged. Brad stepped back, his foot slipping. He lost his balance. His arms flailed as he tried to grab onto something, anything.

"Bradley!" Carlito shouted, diving forward, his hand snagging Brad's shirt. For a moment, it held. Then, the fabric tore and Brad's body tipped backward.

The world spun and he fell into darkness.

50

Carlito watched the boy fall. No screams—just a silent descent through the black. When Brad's head hit the barrier ten feet from the ground, his neck snapped back violently, and his body crumpled to the pavement like a discarded doll. The sound of bone on concrete echoed up to Carlito, but he didn't flinch. He'd seen worse.

Carlito ran down the stairs. The boy might still be alive. He'd seen crazier things—a man in Iraq blown off a rooftop by a mortar, only to walk away. If the kid survived, maybe he could still sell him. Damaged goods, but someone would pay.

Maybe.

When he reached the ground, he found Bradley lying face down. The boy's arm was twisted behind him at a grotesque angle, his legs spread awkwardly, one knee turned almost fully backward. His body was a broken mess.

Denver stood nearby, staring at the body, her hands clenched into tight fists.

Without warning, she whirled on Carlito, punching him hard in the chest. Her wiry strength caught him off guard, nearly knocking him back.

"What the hell, Carlito! What are we gonna do now, huh?" she spat, fury radiating off her in waves. "You're so stupid sometimes!"

"I didn't want him to die," Carlito said, his voice low.

"Who gives a shit what you wanted!" she shouted, her fist slamming into his chest again. "He was half our money!"

"Not half," Carlito said, taking a breath to steady himself. "You said the girl's the one he really wants. Maybe we can still get enough for her to make this work."

He stepped closer, his tone softening as he reached out and brushed Denver's cheek with the back of his fingers. Her anger wavered a little.

"Your anger makes you strong. It's power, *mi amor*. But don't waste it on me."

Carlito glanced toward the exit of the lot, where the red SUV had screeched away seconds ago. The driver was probably calling the cops by now.

"We can't stay here," he said calmly, heading to the driver's side of their car.

Keri's terrified screams echoed from the trunk, the pounding growing frantic. It made him grin.

Denver slid into the passenger seat, still seething. Carlito paused, catching a glimpse of Brad's lifeless body.

The grin he'd had a moment ago faded. "I hope the gods welcome you, Bradley."

―――

Carlito pulled into a small apartment complex a few miles from the border. He knew every hotel and motel around would be watching for him after he'd killed that clerk. The situation was delicate—close to the endgame. And that was when people made mistakes.

"We need to spend the night here. Maybe a few nights," Carlito said.

"We're too close. We need to get out of here."

Carlito turned the car off. "If a wise man is given ten seconds to complete a task, he will spend nine of them thinking and the last second acting. I need space to think."

"Space? You're crazy. We need to go."

"I'll be right back," he said, ignoring her frustration. He stepped out of the car before she could argue more.

The complex was old, with faded stucco walls and narrow windows. Eight buildings, three stories each, spaced just far enough apart to feel isolated.

Carlito's eyes scanned the last building, farthest from the road. A small pool sat between it and the one before, with a few scattered patio chairs and rusty benches. He walked over and sat on one of the benches as he pulled out a crumpled pack of cloves from his pocket. He lit one with his father's lighter, the only thing he'd kept from the man.

The building was quiet. Dark. Only a handful of apartments had their lights on. Carlito could see into them from where he sat. The first floor held a young man in a tank top, beer in hand, moving around in his kitchen. Carlito tilted his head, watching him. The man's lips moved, but was he talking to someone? Carlito couldn't tell.

He finished the clove, stood up, and walked closer to the building. The man looked young but worn, his face already lined with the marks of life. Not the kind of life that left proud scars. This man carried the weight of bad choices. He wasn't one of those who'd lived through hell and emerged stronger. His kind of suffering was the kind that just wore you down until you crumbled.

Carlito walked to the door and knocked.

51

Lazarus had to stop for gas and the delay gnawed at him. He cursed himself for not filling up earlier—Mexicali was only an hour away, but every second wasted felt like another nail in the coffin. If Keri wasn't already dead, she was running out of time.

Riley sat quietly in the passenger seat, his arms crossed, offering nothing but one-word replies.

Once the tank was full, Lazarus got them back on the freeway, flooring the gas pedal to make up for lost time.

"You won't help anyone if we die," Riley muttered, breaking the silence.

Lazarus eased off the gas. "He speaks."

"I talk when there's something worth saying," Riley said. "Why do you care so much about this one?"

Lazarus shifted in his seat. "Why do I care about two kids being sold into slavery?"

"Happens every day. What makes this one different?"

Lazarus hesitated. "She might be . . . relations."

Riley turned to him. "*Relations* how?"

"I told you I was engaged once. She says she was pregnant and never told me."

Riley snorted, shaking his head. "You serious?"

"Yeah."

Riley chuckled. "I can't picture you as a father."

"Thanks," Lazarus replied dryly.

"You wouldn't be good at it. That's just the truth."

"I'd be fine. I'd just do the opposite of everything my stepfather did."

"That's not how it works," Riley said. "Once you've got kids, they push against you, and whatever's inside you comes out. And what you've got inside isn't good for a kid."

Lazarus glanced at him. "I liked it better when you weren't talking."

A small grin tugged at the corner of Riley's mouth, and for the first time in hours, Lazarus felt a little more at ease.

"So what's the plan when we get there?" Riley asked.

"He won't cross the border now, but he's not heading back either. He'll lay low, think things through. Unless he's insane, and then he might try to shoot his way into Mexico, but my money's on him hiding."

"How you gonna find him?"

"I don't know yet."

As they neared Mexicali, Lazarus felt that familiar cold pinch in his stomach—the electric connection he sometimes got with the men he was after. A small, invisible thread tying them.

His phone rang—it was Tony. Lazarus hit the speaker button.

"Yeah," Lazarus said.

"They found Brad Lowe."

"Alive?" Lazarus asked.

A pause, a beat of silence that stretched too long. "No. And the girl's still missing."

Lazarus's jaw tightened. "How did he die?"

"Not sure yet."

"Send me the address. I'm close."

When they arrived at the parking structure, police cruisers and an ambulance were already there. The paramedics were standing around the doors of the ambulance, chatting casually—not a good sign. Lazarus parked near the entrance, stepping out as a young officer moved to block his path. Before the cop could speak, Lazarus flashed his badge.

"Detective Holloway. Someone should've called."

"I got it, Billy," said a heavyset man with a thick mustache. He wore a gray suit jacket over Dockers and extended his hand. "Frank Dillard."

"Lazarus Holloway. This is Detective Riley."

Frank nodded toward the ME's people, who were lifting a black body bag onto a stretcher. "Sorry about the kid," Frank said.

Lazarus glanced at the bag.

"Is it him for sure?" Lazarus asked.

"Yeah, it's him. Kid didn't stand a chance."

Lazarus gave a slight nod and looked at the location where the body had been and then glanced up to the structure.

Frank said, "ME still needs to sign off on it, but it looks like the fall killed him. Might've been thrown off."

Lazarus shook his head. "If he was thrown, he'd be farther from the building. He fell straight down."

Frank frowned. "Maybe it was the better alternative."

Floodlights illuminated the scene as the ME's crew continued documenting the area. The cops were packing up, the investigation winding down.

"My guess?" Frank said. "Xibala—Carlito—he'll make a run for the border. Probably hopes Border Patrol hasn't caught wind of him yet."

"Maybe," Lazarus said.

"We've got men on the freeway and at the border and the National Guard's been notified. He's got nowhere to go."

As Frank spoke with one of the officers, Lazarus stepped back into the shadows, slipping away from the main group.

Carlito would need a quiet place to hide. The border towns were full of decaying, forgotten corners, where generations of families had slowly thinned out, leaving the elderly to live in isolation. Carlito would find an old couple, take them hostage or kill them, and live off the grid for weeks, maybe months.

He pulled out his phone and dialed Kendra, the reporter he'd spoken to earlier.

"Twice in one night?" Kendra answered. "You must be desperate."

"I need a favor," Lazarus said.

"Already?"

"Yes. It's the only way we're going to catch this guy. I need to get on live TV down here. Now."

"I can't do that again."

"You did it once. Get the local stations to do it. Journalists help each other out the same way cops do."

"It's not that easy."

"I've never known you to back down from a fight."

A long sigh. "Fine. I'll see what I can do. But this better be good."

52

Carlito dragged the body into the bedroom closet and pushed the door closed. He quickly scanned the apartment. No women's clothes, no kids' toys—nothing to suggest the man had anyone else in his life. He lived alone. That was good.

He texted Denver, telling her it was safe to come in.

Minutes later, she strode in and sprawled across the couch like she owned the place.

"What are we gonna do, Carlito?" she asked, exhaustion clear in her voice.

"We're going to wait here until people forget about it."

"People aren't that stupid."

"A person is smart, but people are stupid. Give it a few weeks and they'll be distracted by something else. We'll get across then."

"*Weeks?* And what, we just live here?"

Carlito glanced around the apartment. "It's not so bad. Better than our place."

He held out his hand and she took it, wincing slightly as he pulled her to her feet. She pressed a hand to her side, where the bruises were deepest, but she didn't complain. He admired that about her—how she bore pain without letting it show.

As he pulled her close, her breath brushed his cheek, sweet and warm like cinnamon. His gaze flicked to the cuts on her face, now thin lines of red against her skin.

He pressed her hand to his chest, letting her feel the steady beat of his heart. They swayed in a slow dance, no music playing, just the quiet rhythm of their breathing.

"It's only you, *loca*," he said. "Nothing else matters. Where I live, what I eat, who I am . . . none of it. Only you."

He kissed her, tasting the salt on her lips. "I should get Little Bird before she makes too much noise," he said, turning to leave.

But Denver didn't let go of his hand.

"What is it?" he asked, pausing.

"We're going to die tonight, aren't we?"

He laughed softly. "We're not."

"How do you know?"

"Because the gods tell me these things," he said, his voice sure. He kissed her again. "You will not die tonight. I promise you."

He stepped outside, the warm air brushing against his face, dust kicking up from the wind. Carlito always liked these small border towns—their old mission churches and crumbling history, remnants of a time before the United States existed. They felt disconnected from everything, like time had slowed down here.

As he walked to the trunk, he thought of Mexico. His memories of it were faint, hazy, like smoke slipping through his fingers. He should've remembered more, since he wasn't that young when they left, but all he could remember clearly was a local bureaucrat, Señor Marcos, who had tormented his father.

Señor Marcos had a thing for Carlito's mother, and every chance he had, he'd humiliate Carlito's father—a violent, cowardly drunk, who'd take out his shame on Carlito with whatever was handy. Belts, tools, cigarettes. One time, a table leg, which fractured his skull.

Carlito hated his father, but he hated Señor Marcos more. He had hoped his father would finally snap and kill Marcos. At least then his father would have done one right thing. But instead, Marcos died of a stroke and his father died in a car accident. Too quick, too easy for men like them. But it taught Carlito something: The gods had their own reasons for things, reasons men would never understand.

When he reached the trunk, he could hear Keri pounding from inside, her screams muffled. He popped it open, and she tried to jump out. Her fingernails raked across his face, one catching his eye. He slapped her hard, sending her back into the trunk, where she sobbed.

Grabbing her by the arm, he yanked her out roughly. She struggled, but when he raised his hand to strike her again, she turned her face away and covered herself. He didn't hit her.

"Don't do that again," he said coldly, dragging her back to the apartment.

Once inside, Carlito threw her to the floor. She looked up at him, wide eyed, trembling.

"Where's Brad?"

Denver smirked. "He's dead."

Keri's face crumpled. "You're lying."

"You think so?" Denver taunted, leaning in closer.

Keri's head dropped, her body shaking as she wept. "No . . ."

Carlito felt a heaviness settle into his bones. Everything hurt—his skin, his muscles, his mind. He sank into a chair at the glass dining table.

"He died painfully," Denver added, her voice cutting through the sobs.

"Denver," Carlito said, shaking his head.

Her smugness faltered, replaced by a look of frustration, but she fell silent. Carlito stood up, stretching his aching limbs. "I'm going to lie down."

He made his way to the bedroom and collapsed on the bed, flipping on the TV. He wasn't in the mood to watch, but he needed to see if the police were talking about him. Going through the channels, he stopped at a local news broadcast. The headline at the bottom read *POLICE NEED YOUR HELP.*

The reporter was discussing the case with a man Carlito had seen before—a cop, the same one from the TV earlier. A good-looking guy, calm, collected. His beard was neat, hair slicked back. Carlito's eyes caught something—a tattoo on the cop's arm, visible when he scratched his face. A cockroach in the shape of a human skull.

Beautiful.

Carlito mumbled the name aloud as it flashed on the screen. "Lazarus Holloway. Who are you, Lazarus Holloway?"

The detective didn't talk like most cops, with generalities. He wasn't talking to an audience—he was talking to Carlito.

"Yes," Lazarus said in response to the reporter's question, "I believe Carlito's near the Mexicali border, likely hiding out. What I'm hoping is that he contacts me so we can talk, man to man."

Carlito grinned. He watched the way Lazarus's eyes never wavered, how his voice carried no fear. This cop knew who he was up against, and he was inviting Carlito to reach out.

"I'm asking him to contact the number on the screen," Lazarus continued. "It'll connect to my assistant at Metro PD, who will get ahold of me."

Carlito grabbed his cell phone and punched in the number.

53

Lazarus paced outside the diner, the glow from the neon sign casting long shadows on the cracked pavement. His stomach was doing somersaults, and the jittery feeling running through his veins made him restless. Inside, Riley sat at a booth, eating fried steak and eggs. Each bite was slow and deliberate. Lazarus could tell by the far-off look in his eyes that Riley wasn't even tasting the food.

Lazarus checked his phone and texted Tony again.

Anything?

Tony responded quickly.

About a dozen nutjobs. Maybe next time tell me before you post my number on TV.

Lazarus smirked, but the tension in his body wouldn't ease. He paced, pulling on his vape and glancing down the street. He needed this to work. Carlito had to be watching the news, monitoring the situation like Lazarus would in his position. It was the only shot they had.

The door to the diner creaked open, and a young woman stepped out, fiddling with a cigarette that refused to light. Lazarus saw her struggle and pulled his lighter from his pocket, then flicked it on without a word. She gave him a quick "Thanks" as she lit her cigarette and exhaled smoke.

"No worries," Lazarus said, slipping the lighter back into his pocket.

She took a long drag, blowing the smoke out through her nose like she'd been holding something in for too long. "So, you're a cop, huh?"

Lazarus blinked, about to ask how she knew, but then he glanced down and saw the badge clipped to his belt.

"Yeah," he said.

"My father was a cop," she said after a pause. "He hated it."

"Opinions vary," Lazarus replied.

"He was a cop in Guadalajara. A good man. He wouldn't take any money from the cartels. That's when they don't trust you."

Lazarus's interest was piqued. "What happened to him?"

"They shot him in the back while he was dropping me off at school," she said, her voice flat, emotionless. "I was still in the car."

"I'm sorry to hear that," Lazarus said.

She smoked in silence a while. Then she tossed her cigarette to the ground and crushed it under her boot before walking to a beat-up Dodge parked nearby.

"Have a good night," she said, pulling the car door open.

"You too," Lazarus said. He watched the taillights fade into the distance.

He was about to head back inside when his phone buzzed in his pocket. It was Tony.

"Yeah," Lazarus said, pressing the phone to his ear.

"I think I got someone for you to speak with," Tony said. "He said to tell you the gods want you two to meet and that he'd like his bracelet back."

Lazarus froze. "Those were his exact words?"

"Yeah, he's on the line right now. It's his cell phone."

"Transfer him."

A click, then silence, followed by slow, steady breathing on the other end.

"This is Detective Holloway. Who am I talking with?"

A beat, then a voice, smooth. "I think you know, Detective Holloway."

Lazarus kept his tone calm. "I have to be sure. Lotta people wanting attention."

"Yes, there are," Carlito said. "But you wouldn't have taken the call if you didn't think it was me."

"True."

"You said you wanted to talk. So talk," Carlito said.

"I wanna meet."

"I'm not new at this, you know."

"No tricks. Just me and you."

"Why?" he asked, suspicious.

"I like looking a man in the eyes when I speak to him. Especially if we're tryin' to work out a deal."

"A deal, huh?" Carlito paused, letting the silence stretch out. "There's a church five blocks into Valadez. San Pablo. In the town's center. I'll be there. If anyone shows up but you, I'll kill the girl. Understood?"

The line went dead before Lazarus could respond.

54

Lazarus dropped Riley off at the sheriff's station and drove to Valadez alone. The town was dead quiet, the old church looming in the center. Its dark wood doors were splintered and the quarter moon cast a sickly glow over the decaying building.

Frank had offered to wire him up, but Lazarus had refused. This wasn't a sting operation—this was personal, a reckoning.

The air was thick with dust and it clung to Lazarus's skin as he approached the massive front doors. A "condemned" sign was slapped across them, warning that the building would soon be demolished, like all remnants of the past.

He pushed the heavy doors open, the wood groaning under the strain. Inside, beams of fractured moonlight spilled through shattered stained glass and painted the air with swirling dust.

"Do you believe in fate, amigo?"

The voice came from somewhere in the darkness, smooth and unhurried.

Lazarus paused, his hand instinctively drifting toward his firearm. His eyes hadn't adjusted, and the space was just a cavern of shadows. "Depends on your definition."

"That your life was written in the stars before you were born."

"No."

"Why not?"

"Because that would mean we're helpless to avoid it."

"Or it could mean we're free from regret. No choices, no mistakes—only the path you were always meant to walk. Peace."

Lazarus stepped forward cautiously, the floor creaking beneath his boots. Every muscle in his body tensed. He imagined Carlito hidden in the shadows, a rifle trained on his chest. One squeeze and it would be over.

"Kinda hard to take advice from a voice in the dark," Lazarus said.

"I like the dark. It's where the gods speak to us—voices carried through time."

Lazarus's eyes adjusted slowly, revealing outlines of decaying pews, a crumbling altar, and the hulking shape of a decrepit organ, its pipes rusting and broken.

"The gods made you take those kids?"

"No," the voice said, a flicker of humor in it. "But if I took them, the gods wanted it. Just like they wanted us to meet."

Lazarus shifted his gaze toward the organ. For a moment, all was still. Then, a subtle movement caught his eye—a glimmer off to the side. He tightened his grip on his weapon.

"And what do you think they want from us now?" Lazarus asked.

"That depends," Carlito said, his tone darkening, "on what kind of man you are."

Carlito was kneeling in front of the altar, shirtless, surrounded by a ring of unlit candles, which he began to light one at a time. A massive tattoo covered his back—priests sacrificing bodies on a pyramid, skeletons piled at the base of the stone steps. In front of him was a bowl. Lazarus watched, keeping his footfalls loud so Carlito could hear him. But Carlito was entranced, sliding a large knife across his wrist. Blood dripped into the bowl, and when it was full enough, Carlito lifted it to his lips and drank.

Lazarus took a few more steps forward, but Carlito didn't react until he smeared blood across his forehead in the shape of a cross. He inhaled deeply, as though the ritual had given him strength, and finally turned to face Lazarus.

Carlito was shorter than Lazarus and his chest was inked with a grim reaper, black against his skin. His close-cropped hair was bright under the dim light, and his face, though rough, was undeniably handsome.

"I'm surprised there's no graffiti here," Lazarus said, his voice casual.

"The kids know better. There's some things even they respect."

Lazarus scanned the room, looking for Denver. "You almost made it."

"Not over yet, amigo," Carlito said, his smile slow, deliberate.

"That's true, but your face is everywhere. Stealing kids on a slow news day wasn't your best move, I'm guessing."

Carlito shrugged. "No, it all slipped through my fingers. But that's life, isn't it? The most ironic outcome is always the most likely."

Lazarus took out his vape, inhaling slowly before exhaling a cloud. "You don't talk like a prison hound."

"Thank you. I read a lot—every book in that prison library. When they got ebooks, whew, it was over for me. I read day and night. Kept to myself. That's how you get by. Don't sleep with whores, you won't wake up with whores."

"Not the worst advice I've heard."

Carlito ran a finger over the fresh wound on his wrist. "Do you know why I agreed to meet with you?"

Lazarus shook his head. "No."

"Because I can see it in your eyes. You have it, too."

"And what do you think I have?"

Carlito sat down, resting his arms on his knees, his gaze never leaving Lazarus. "My father asked me once, 'Is it better to die young in a blaze of glory or live a long, quiet life? Pissing yourself, forgetting who you are and what you love, but alive.'"

"What'd you say?"

"Nothing. My father liked to talk without waiting for answers. But I've thought about that question a lot. Do you?"

"From time to time," Lazarus said. "When the mood strikes me to think about the meaning of things."

"And what do you think the meaning of things is?"

"The meaning is whatever keeps you from killing yourself."

Carlito let out a soft laugh. Lazarus offered him his vape. Carlito took it and inhaled deeply. "That's good. You should try the tobacco in my hometown. Best in the world. Tastes like the lips of a woman. I'm going to miss it. I'm going to miss a lot of things. I should've spent more time enjoying them."

"Wisdom comes at a hell of a time, don't it? Youth's gone, fire's dimmed, and all the pretty girls went home."

Just then, the front doors creaked open. Lazarus turned to see Denver enter. She wore jeans and a black shirt, her hoop earrings catching the faint light. Even in the dark, her beauty shone like fire.

"I told you not to come here," Carlito said.

"What are you doing?" Denver asked, confused, her eyes darting between Carlito and Lazarus.

Carlito had a gun tucked into his waistband. "This was all me, amigo. She wasn't involved."

Lazarus kept his expression neutral but nodded. "Sure."

Denver looked at Lazarus, then back to Carlito. "Who is this?"

Carlito sighed, running a hand over his face. "You chased me across the state," Carlito said, his eyes narrowing at Lazarus. "Most cops would've let the locals handle it or called Border Patrol. Why did you come yourself?"

"The girl's important to me," Lazarus said.

"Who is she to you?"

Lazarus said nothing but regretted it instantly. The silence told Carlito everything he needed to know.

He laughed. "I can see the resemblance now. See? Ironic?" Carlito said, his voice laced with amusement. "My first real kidnapping, and it's the daughter of a policeman."

"Maybe kidnapping's not your game," Lazarus replied coolly.

"No, it isn't. I let myself get talked into it, and I shouldn't have. Well, the girl's tougher than she looks. She'll be stronger for this. She's in the apartments down the street. First floor. I forget the number."

Lazarus nodded. "Thank you."

Carlito gave a small, almost courteous bow. Lazarus put his vape away, the weight of his gun pressing against his ribs.

"I know what you think you need to do," Lazarus said. "Don't. Take the charges and fight 'em in court."

Denver glanced between the two men again. "What's he talking about, Carlito?"

"He's talking about fate, but he doesn't understand it," Carlito said, a strange smile playing on his lips.

"What the hell does that mean?" she demanded.

"It means I love you, *loca*. More than the stars love the night. You made my life shine for a while."

"Carlito—"

Before she could say another word, Carlito reached for the gun in his waistband. He tugged it free, but his movements were sluggish, lacking conviction. Lazarus drew faster, firing two rounds into Carlito's chest before the other man could get his gun up.

The sound was deafening as the gunshots echoed through the empty church. Carlito flew back, the bullets hitting with wet, heavy thuds.

And then screaming.

The worst screams Lazarus had ever heard.

Denver collapsed, her face twisted in horror, her screams primal and raw, echoing off the church walls. She scrambled to Carlito's side, shaking him.

"Don't you die! Not you, Carlito! Don't you leave me here alone."

Carlito's eyes were glassy, blood trickling from the corner of his mouth. He looked at her, a weak smile tugging at his lips before his body went still. His final breath was a rattling whisper.

"No, no, no!" Denver sobbed, clutching his body. "Don't leave me! Not you! Please, Carlito, please!"

Lazarus lowered his gun.

Denver's sobs turned into deep, guttural cries. Like a wounded animal's. She turned to Lazarus, her face twisted in rage, teeth bared. "I'm gonna kill you," she spit.

Lazarus holstered his gun, pulling out his cuffs. "Maybe one day. But not today."

55

Lazarus paced outside the Vista View Apartments, anxiety gnawing at him as the California Highway Patrol cruiser idled nearby. He had called Piper three times now and she hadn't answered. On the third ring, it went to voicemail again. He hung up and immediately dialed her back. This time, she picked up.

"Hey."

"I need a warrant," Lazarus said.

"Hello to you, too."

"Hello. I need a warrant."

"For what?"

"They've got her stashed in an apartment. If no one answers, I want in. I'm not waiting."

"In California?"

"Yeah."

"I'm not licensed there, Lazarus."

"So, there's nothing you can do? I thought you were more creative than that, Danes."

She sighed. "Give me the county. I'll see what I can do."

"Make it fast," Lazarus said. "Please. Someone asked Denver if she'd tell us where Keri is and she kicked the officer in the crotch."

"I'll do what I can."

When he hung up, Lazarus scanned the parking lot. The momentum had stalled. Troopers were leaning against cars or sitting on the curb, their energy fading with nothing to do but wait.

He stepped forward and raised his voice. "Ladies and gentlemen, we may as well get to it. Mark any first-floor apartments where no one answers. If someone opens the door, ask for permission to search and make sure your body cams catch their consent. A warrant's coming, and as soon as it gets here, we'll go into the apartments where no one's home."

The troopers were slow to react until Frank spoke up. "All right, you heard the man. Let's get moving. Sooner we get this done, sooner we're out of here. Except you, Dawkins. You're staying behind to write an apology letter for kicking down the wrong door last time."

A few troopers chuckled as they spread out into the complex. Lazarus followed.

He knocked on the first apartment door, waiting as the sound echoed through the quiet complex. The building was old, government-subsidized housing stuck in the middle of the desert. No schools, no churches, no community. Isolation.

An old man in pajamas eventually answered.

"Police. We have reason to believe a kidnapping victim might be in one of these apartments. Mind if I look?"

"Oh, wow. Sure, come in," the man said, stepping aside.

The apartment was tiny, just a single bedroom and a cramped living space. Lazarus scanned every corner, looked under the bed, behind the doors. Nothing.

He left, moved next door, and repeated the process.

The warrant finally came through after what felt like hours. Lazarus had canvassed most of the complex by then. They had four apartments marked—no one had answered the doors.

Frank handed him the document with a smirk. "Someone's got some pull."

"Why's that?"

"A state supreme court justice woke up a superior court judge for this. They didn't want to sign off at this hour, but apparently you know someone important."

Lazarus nodded, not surprised. "Let's get to it."

The sergeant standing behind them spoke up. "We're ready, Detective."

Lazarus was the first to reach the apartment they had marked. The locks weren't standard locks; they looked thick and were made of a dark brushed metal. The keyholes had odd shapes. Lockpicks wouldn't work.

No manager or custodian was on-site, and at this time of night, that meant kicking doors down.

Riley stood back, his face tense. Lazarus could see the hunger in him, the need for action. It was the same hunger Lazarus recognized in himself sometimes. Riley didn't want to sit on the sidelines—he wanted to charge in, feel the rush. That was dangerous. Needing a high could make a man willing to do anything to feel alive.

"Police, search warrant!" an officer shouted, as another swung the battering ram against the door. The lock shattered and the door flew open, slamming into the wall. A team of six officers flooded inside, guns drawn.

Lazarus stood outside, listening for any sounds of resistance, but all he heard were shouts of "Clear!" echoing through the apartment.

A large SWAT officer emerged after a few minutes, shaking his head. "Nothing."

Lazarus clenched his jaw, the tightness in his chest growing.

"Let's hit the others," Frank said, already moving to the next apartment.

Each door they hit was the same. It was well past midnight, and the hallway lights flickered in the stale, cramped corridors. One after another, they broke down doors, cleared rooms, found nothing. Lazarus's frustration boiled beneath his skin, but he kept it in check, methodically following the officers from apartment to apartment.

By the time they reached the final apartment, a knot of dread had settled in his stomach. He watched as the troopers took their positions, ready to repeat the process.

This has to be it, Lazarus thought. *It has to be.*

56

Piper stood on Judge Dawson's balcony, gazing out at the endless lights of Las Vegas. Sometimes she would forget how the city appeared to outsiders and would try to see it with fresh eyes. An oasis of glitz and glamour in the middle of a barren desert, hiding graves of those killed and buried by organized crime.

Judge Dawson stepped out in a silk robe, carrying two wineglasses. She set them on the patio table and pushed one toward Piper. Despite the late hour, the judge lifted her glass for a toast. "To catching the bad guy."

Piper took the smallest sip she could and placed the glass down. The wine was sweet, almost like cake. "I'm sorry to come over like this," Piper said. "I didn't know anyone else who could get me a warrant that fast."

Judge Dawson waved it off. "It's not a problem."

"I know, but it's been so long since we've talked, and here I am at—"

"Piper," the judge interrupted, her tone gentle but firm, "it's fine. It's good to see you. You look exhausted, though."

"I am."

"Do you regret getting involved?"

"No," Piper said.

The judge leaned back. "Because you get to help Lazarus meet his daughter?"

Piper stiffened slightly but didn't deny it. "I'm surprised you didn't tell him."

"It's not my place," the judge said, taking a small sip of her wine. "What does he think about it?"

"He doesn't."

A grin tugged at the corners of the judge's lips. "It would be . . . unusual to see Lazarus as a father. From what I know, a parent is someone who sacrifices themselves for their children. I'm not sure he's particularly good at that."

"Were your parents like that?" Piper asked, her curiosity piqued.

Judge Dawson gave a small laugh, almost bitter. "No. My mother died in childbirth with me, and my father was a cruel man. Exceptionally so. Enough that I knew I never wanted children of my own."

She downed another swallow of wine. "What about you? Do you see kids in your future?"

Piper shook her head slowly. "Probably not."

"Why?"

"I'm not . . . in the right place for that. And I don't know if I ever will be."

The judge nodded. "You mean you're not healed yet. It takes a lot of time and energy. It's difficult."

Piper shrugged, her gaze falling to the city again. "I don't even know if it's healing I want. I just want to feel content. I don't need to be happy—just . . . content."

"Contentment can be dangerous," she said, her voice sharp. "Charles—my ex—when he committed suicide, we had spent the day together. I've gone over that day a hundred times in my mind. Every word, every action. What he ate, what he read. I wanted to understand what he was thinking when he decided to end his life. And you know what I realized?"

Piper looked at her, waiting.

"I think he was content," the judge said, her voice cold, almost detached. "That's the danger of contentment. It numbs you. It numbed him. Don't settle for it, Piper. Contentment can be taken from you in an instant."

Piper's phone buzzed in her pocket. She glanced at the screen and saw the message from Lazarus: Got the warrant.

"I can't believe you got the chief justice to wake up a superior court judge," Piper said, trying to lighten the mood.

Judge Dawson smiled slightly, though her eyes stayed distant. "Not that impressive. His wife's a friend."

Piper put her phone away but lingered on the last message. A knot of anxiety twisted in her stomach.

"You're worried about him," the judge said, her voice gentle.

"I guess I am."

The judge swirled the wine in her glass, her eyes distant again. "He's not who you think."

"What do you mean?"

"He has layers," the judge said, "and you can't tell which one is truly him."

"I've known a lot of terrible people," Piper said. "Lazarus isn't one of them."

Judge Dawson's smirk returned. "No, he's not terrible. But he's dangerous. He's dangerous because he doesn't know himself."

"I'm pretty sure you could say that about anybody."

"Yes, I suppose you could."

A distant ambulance wailed somewhere in the city.

"I'm sorry about the lawsuit," Piper said, shifting the conversation. She'd seen a gossip site earlier, detailing personal dirt on Judge Dawson, primarily concerning her husband's suicide and some real estate deals with shady partners, hinting at a small but vocal movement trying to unseat her from the bench. Piper chose not to bring that up.

The judge waved a dismissive hand. "Thank you, but it all could've been avoided if my brothers had listened to reason. Instead, they figured airing our family's dirty laundry was the best way to shame me."

"Do they have a real claim?"

"Unfortunately, yes."

"I'm guessing you didn't have a good relationship with your father?"

The judge let out a small, humorless laugh. "That's an understatement." She stared into her wine again, watching the way the moonlight reflected off the liquid. "My mother died giving birth to me," she said, "and my father never forgave me for it."

Piper blinked. "I'm sorry."

The judge's eyes flicked to Piper, catching the dim light. "I had a nanny growing up. Celeste. She protected me as best she could and I loved her like a mother—more than a mother. When she died, I didn't shed a tear. But when my father died, I wept."

"Why?" Piper asked.

Judge Dawson turned her gaze to her glass, lips tight. "Because I fed on hatred for so long, I didn't know how to live without it."

57

The last apartment had all the lights off. As Lazarus stood outside, the crowd of curious neighbors grew, drawn by the noise and the flashing lights. More shouts of "Clear!" echoed from inside, but then Lazarus heard something that made his stomach drop: "Got someone!"

His instincts kicked in and he rushed through the apartment door, shoving past two SWAT officers. Their CO was too busy to tell him to stand down, so he barreled forward toward the bedroom, his heart pounding.

Inside, the sight that greeted him stopped him.

A young man lay on the floor of the closet, clearly dead. Blood had trailed down his face and soaked his shirt. It was gruesome, but almost serene, like some Renaissance painting. The man had likely been shot when he opened the door and his body dragged into the closet afterward. But what caught Lazarus more was the girl—Keri—bound on the floor next to the body.

She wasn't moving. Her eyes were glassy, distant, as though she couldn't even see the officers pointing rifles at her, screaming for her to show her hands.

"Her hands are tied, idiot," Lazarus snapped, slapping the barrel of one officer's rifle away as he pushed forward. He knelt down beside her, pulling out the knife from his ankle holster and cutting the ties from her wrists. She didn't flinch. Didn't move.

"Keri?" Lazarus asked softly. "Can you hear me?"

Nothing. She stared through him, lost in shock.

He reached out gently, taking her hand in his. "Can you walk?"

There was no response, but he slowly helped her to her feet, careful not to startle her. She was completely dissociated from the world around her.

He regretted not bringing Piper; she'd know what to do.

They made their way outside, and as soon as they exited the building, paramedics rushed toward them. Lazarus watched them load her into the ambulance, her face still blank, her body limp. He felt a knot in his throat as he saw a flash of something—something that looked like his own reflection in her hollow eyes.

The Imperial County Sheriff's Station was unremarkable—just an office building with a sign slapped on the front. Lazarus stood outside, texting Frank.

Riley stood next to him, staring at nothing.

"You okay?" Lazarus asked.

"Fine," Riley replied, but his voice was flat. Distant.

"Don't seem like it."

"I am."

Lazarus greeted an officer walking by with a nod.

"You need some more time off," he said to Riley. "You need to get your head straight."

"And do what?"

"Go do something where you can find your core, man. Wander. Go to Thailand, Spain—anywhere. People are born wanderers."

"I don't want to wander," Riley said, his voice hardening.

A pair of uniformed deputies passed by, glancing at the two men. Their looks lingered on Riley's hulking frame, but neither said a word.

After they were out of earshot, Riley turned back to Lazarus. "I know you saw her," he said quietly.

Lazarus took out his vape. "I thought she wasn't talking to you?"

"I went to the house. I had to see the kids."

Lazarus inhaled, the vapor swirling in the air as he exhaled slowly. "What happened, man? You didn't cheat, didn't beat her. You were a good daddy. Why'd she leave you?"

Riley looked down at the pavement, his voice dropping. "Doesn't matter. Love's just time. I wasn't there to give her time."

"She didn't try to work on it?"

Riley hesitated. Lazarus could see the internal struggle, the way Riley was building up the courage to say something deeper.

"I think there's someone else," he finally said.

"Why you think that?"

"Because I'm a cop. She's been going to the salon more. Being secretive with her phone, her Instagram. I heard her talking to someone at night and she said it was a friend that needed advice. That's never happened before. All the little things add up."

"You gonna find out for sure?"

Riley shook his head. "No."

"You don't wanna know?"

"I know," Riley said, the sadness in his voice cutting.

A sedan pulled up and Frank stepped out, jogging up the steps like a man excited for the spotlight. Lazarus could tell he was ready for the interviews, the media attention. Some cops loved the limelight, eager for the brass to notice them, to give them promotions and cushy desk jobs. Lazarus would never be that, and he was fine with it.

"I wanna talk to her alone," Lazarus said as he followed Frank inside.

"Not a chance," Frank replied. "You can be in the room, ask a few questions. That's it."

Lazarus didn't argue. Being allowed in the room at all, out of state and without proper jurisdiction, was already a favor.

They walked through the lobby, passing bulletin boards covered with flyers: internship announcements, job postings, notices about an upcoming softball game between the cops and firefighters.

They reached the interview room—basic, no frills. No one-way glass, no recording equipment. Just a table and a few chairs.

"Bring the big man with you," Frank said, nodding at Riley. "We're gonna intimidate the hell outta her. She's weak. I can tell. She'll talk in ten minutes, tops."

As they entered the room, Lazarus saw Denver sitting at the table, handcuffed. She wasn't cowering. She wasn't intimidated. Frank had misread her. There was a strength there, an intensity that radiated from her like heat from a fire. Lazarus could feel it immediately and knew right away she wasn't giving them anything.

"You want something to eat or drink?" Frank asked as he sat down across from her.

Denver barely looked up, her eyes flicking over him with disdain. Lazarus leaned against the wall, watching. Riley sat next to him, quiet as usual.

When Denver finally glanced up at Frank, it wasn't curiosity or fear in her eyes. It was boredom.

Frank waited a beat, then shrugged. "No food or drink? All right, let's get to it. We've got you on kidnapping, child endangerment, human trafficking. Maybe even murder, if we can tie you to that boy's death or the motel clerk. You're looking at the death penalty."

Denver said nothing.

"Don't you feel bad?" Frank pressed. "A sixteen-year-old boy is dead because of you."

Her eyes grew colder, retreating inward, shutting him out.

Frank's frustration began to show. "I'm trying to help you here. I don't wanna see you strapped down and injected like a rabid dog. Help me, and I'll help you."

Denver smiled with a dangerous, seductive glint in her eyes. "Take off these cuffs and I'll help you."

Lazarus hoped Frank wasn't dumb enough to actually take them off.

"You think you're smart," Frank said, leaning in. "But you're not. If you were, you wouldn't be here. We've got enough evidence to bury you."

Denver laughed softly, muttering something in a language Lazarus didn't recognize.

Frank clenched his jaw, tapping the table with his knuckles. "Whose idea was it to kidnap the kids?"

"Your mother's," Denver said.

Frank's face turned white, his jaw tightening. Whatever nerve Denver had hit, it was deep.

Lazarus saw the pain flash across Frank's face and knew Denver saw it, too. He quickly sent Riley a text. A moment later, Riley stood and slipped out of the room.

Frank leaned in closer. "You killed that boy. You know what felony murder is? Someone dies while you're committing a felony, it's murder. Death penalty, even if you didn't pull the trigger."

Denver leaned forward, her eyes locking onto Frank's. "Your mother's in hell getting raped by the devil."

Frank's face drained of color. Lazarus could see the barely contained rage in his eyes, but before Frank could react, his phone rang.

"What?" Frank barked into the phone. "Now? Fine."

He hung up and stood, giving Lazarus a sharp look. "Emergency call. I'll be back."

When Frank left, Denver's eyes didn't leave Lazarus.

"That was harsh," Lazarus said. "His mama probably died recently."

"If he can't run with the big dogs, he should've stayed on the porch."

Lazarus pulled the chair over and sat beside her, not on the other side of the table. A slow burn of anger twisted in his stomach—this was the woman who had taken Keri.

Keri, his daughter.

That word still tasted strange, as if it belonged to someone else's life. He had expected it to hit him like a shock wave, but all it brought was a numb, hollow sort of grief.

He took out his vape, took a long drag, and held it out to Denver. She leaned forward, wrapping her lips around the vape, her eyes locked on his, sucking softly before pulling away. She exhaled the vapor slowly, blowing it into his face and bathing him in it like a curse.

"I figure Frank would just about have died from a hard-on, you doin' that, but it don't work on me and it's degrading to us both. Knock it off."

For the first time, she looked hurt, retreating into herself.

"Did Carlito ever teach you to speak Tzeltal? I figure he spoke it since it was the language of his gods."

She said nothing.

"Did he take the time to teach you about the gods?" Lazarus asked, but there was no reaction.

He changed tactics. "I want to hear your side. Just you and me. No bullshit."

Denver spit on him.

"The best day of my life will be when I kill you," she hissed.

The door opened and Frank came back in. "What are you doing?" he asked.

Lazarus didn't answer. He stood up, leaving the room without another word, Denver's eyes burning into him the whole way.

Outside, Riley was waiting in the hallway. Lazarus groaned as he sat down next to him, pulling out his vape again.

"What'd you say the emergency was?" Lazarus said.

"Family. When they put him on the line, I told him I was calling about his car warranty."

Lazarus chuckled before taking another drag from the vape. The memory of Denver blowing vapor in his face lingered.

"She's something, isn't she?" Lazarus muttered, turning the vape pen over in his hands. "A woman like that could give a man meaning."

"Only thing she'll do is get a man killed."

Lazarus exhaled slowly, nodding. "Yeah. But it might be worth it."

Lazarus dropped Riley off at a hotel and made his way to Holy Cross Hospital, a run-down facility near the border, often overrun with patients who couldn't afford medical care. It was one of those places where, despite the grim surroundings, doctors were obligated to treat everyone. The emergency rooms overflowed on weekends, and now wasn't any different.

He checked at the nurse's station. No officer was assigned to the room where Keri was staying—not a move he would've made, but the immediate threat was gone.

Lazarus walked down the hall and found the door. He paused for a second, collecting his thoughts, then stepped inside.

Keri lay in bed, a hospital gown draped over her frail body, her bright-blond hair still matted from the chaos of the past day. She was reading *The Bell Jar* by Sylvia Plath. Lazarus had read it, too, when he was around her age.

Across the room, her mother, Amanda, was asleep in a chair, her head tilted awkwardly.

Keri noticed him and lowered the book. Lazarus grabbed a stool and quietly slid it next to her bed. Her blue eyes, so much like his own, met his. A bracelet on her wrist caught his attention—delicate and pastel-colored with the name "Suzy" written on it.

"Who's Suzy?" he asked softly.

"My best friend," Keri replied, her voice thin and tired. She flicked the bracelet gently. "She moved to Wyoming. We talked for a while, but then we stopped."

Her eyes didn't leave the bracelet, her voice cracking slightly. "Brad's gone, too, isn't he? She wasn't lying. I know because she looked happy when she saw how much it hurt me."

"Sorry, Keri." His gaze went to her mother, making sure she was still asleep. "The doctors told me you're not pregnant. What were you trying to do?"

Tears welled up in her eyes, but her voice remained steady. "Brad's parents hated me. His mom called me a slut. They never would've let us get married, so we told them I was pregnant. They thought they were forcing us, but we wanted to. We were gonna run away. You can get an apartment if you're married, even if you're not eighteen."

"Did your mom know?"

"She liked Brad," Keri said with a nod. "She didn't mind me marrying him. Her friend's a judge, and she said it was totally normal and that she'd do it for us."

Lazarus felt his heart skip. "What judge?"

"Her name's Hope," Keri said. "She did our marriage license. Why?"

"How does your mom know Hope?" he asked, keeping his tone calm.

"I don't know."

Lazarus glanced over at Amanda. He pushed the thought aside for now.

Keri's voice trembled as she took a deep breath. The tears that had been threatening finally broke through. She put her face in her hands and sobbed, the sound raw. It wasn't the cry of a young girl anymore. Youth had ended.

"They said Carlito's dead," Keri said after a long moment. Her voice was quieter now, barely above a whisper. "Is he?"

"Yes."

"You're sure?"

He nodded. "Yes."

"What about her?"

"She'll be put on trial for murder," he said. "She's going to spend the rest of her life in prison."

Keri's tears slowed, though the sadness in her eyes didn't fade. A slight sniffle. A brief moment of relief. But Lazarus knew better. The monsters never really left—they just hid.

Keri glanced at her mother, and Lazarus saw Amanda was now awake, watching them quietly.

"Sorry," Lazarus said. "Didn't mean to wake you."

Amanda rose from her chair, stretching slightly. "I should get up anyway. I want to take her home as soon as they let us. Walk with me down to the cafeteria?"

Lazarus nodded and stood. He turned back to Keri. "Get some rest. You'll be going home soon."

As he went to leave, Keri reached out. "Will you come back and wait here? Until I can leave, I mean?"

Lazarus glanced at Amanda, then back at Keri. "Sure."

The hallway echoed with the sound of their footsteps as Lazarus and Amanda walked side by side toward the cafeteria. The sterile hum of the hospital followed them, though the emergency room chaos buzzed past the double doors.

The cafeteria was small and dimly lit, with tables that had seen better days. They grabbed coffee, and as they sat in a booth, Lazarus watched Amanda absentmindedly stir Splenda into her cup. She was on autopilot, her movements mechanical.

"Thank you," she said softly. "Thank you for saving my daughter."

"You're welcome."

She took a small sip of her coffee, then put it back down. "Why didn't you tell her who you were?"

"Didn't seem like my place."

"Or are you waiting for a paternity test?"

"You never lied to me before. No reason to think you'd start now."

Amanda gazed across the room at a couple eating in silence. "I thought you'd scream at me when you found out. I'm glad you didn't."

Lazarus took a sip of his coffee, wincing at the bitterness.

She said, "I thought you would hate me."

"Why would you think that?"

"For keeping this from you."

Lazarus shook his head. "It was my fault. I don't blame you."

Amanda looked down into her cup, her face lined with quiet sadness. "Do you wish I'd told you?"

He weighed the question. "I don't know that it would've made a difference." After a moment, he added, "She looks like my mother did at her age."

Amanda's eyes widened slightly. "Really? You never showed me any pictures."

"I don't have any."

Amanda leaned forward. "You never talk about your parents."

"There's not much to say," Lazarus replied. "My mother left my father in the middle of the night and married a man with two wives already. We moved to the desert for him, and he treated us like slaves. My mother thought she'd done it all for love."

"She didn't love him?"

Lazarus shrugged. "She didn't know what love was. When you don't know what love is, you mistake horrible things for it."

Amanda exhaled slowly, her hands wrapped around her cup. After a long pause, she asked, "What's going to happen to that woman?"

"They'll charge her with everything they can," Lazarus said. "But they don't like giving women the death penalty. Seeing a woman strapped down and injected doesn't sit well with juries. She'll get life, or something like it. She'll be an old woman when—if—they ever let her out."

Amanda's face softened slightly. "I've never liked Brad's parents, but I can't imagine what they're going through. I should call them."

"Maybe give them a bit."

Amanda rubbed her face with her hands, taking in a deep breath. Lazarus took another sip of his coffee, the silence between them stretching longer. There wasn't much left to say.

58

It didn't take long for Piper to get notice about the charges brought against Denver Rose Hartley. She sat in a café, waiting for her coffee, reading the information from the district attorney's office:

Human trafficking, first-degree kidnapping, conspiracy to commit kidnapping, child endangerment, contributing to the delinquency of a minor, and a slew of lesser crimes. No murder charges.

Piper frowned at her phone. She sent a quick text to her friend Penny, now at the DA's office, and got the scoop: They were charging Denver for what they could get here, and after that, she'd be extradited to California to stand trial for the felony murder of Bradley Lowe and the motel clerk. It made sense, but something felt off. Denver was just as liable for the minister's murder as Carlito. Why weren't they charging her with that?

Penny said it got political when a case got too much attention, but there was something else here. They were targeted on their wedding day in front of fifty people. Why? Why not wait for them when they were alone? It was like Carlito and Denver wanted to make a show of it. The DA's office's theory was that they saw the wedding announcement in the *Ledger* and knew with the teens' age and good looks they could get a lot of money for them. It was the most likely motivation, but the most likely hardly meant it was the truth.

Then again, Lazarus always told her the world was one random event after another. It was entirely possible they saw this as a quick payday and it had nothing to do with Keri and Brad; it was just their misfortune to be in the paper that day.

She skimmed the list of witnesses and victims. Her own name was next to Keri's, labeled as her attorney. She got her coffee to go and left.

It was a scorching Tuesday afternoon, the temperature near 110. Piper didn't mind the heat. Growing up, she'd come to associate the sunbaked pavement, the thick smell of exhaust, and the city's simmering garbage with something safer. She'd walk to friends' houses whenever she could, spending as little time at home as possible.

Amanda Bines lived on the edge of town. It was a longer drive than Piper wanted, but she didn't hesitate. As she drove, she listened to *In Cold Blood*, an audiobook she'd always meant to get around to. She loved the writing but hated how much it had drawn her in. She knew people like the Clutter family and was saddened because she knew what was going to happen to them.

When Piper arrived, she parked and put up the windshield heat blocker. Amanda answered the door in a tight black yoga outfit, her face drawn with exhaustion.

"Hello again," Piper said, offering a warm smile.

"Hi. Come in."

The house was tidy, as if Amanda had spent all her nervous energy cleaning. The coffee and cake on the kitchen table felt staged, like a photo in a magazine. The tablecloth was spotless.

"How's Keri doing?" Piper asked as Amanda poured herself some coffee.

"She went back to school, but she's not the same," Amanda said, shaking her head. "She doesn't see her friends anymore. She just stays in her room and listens to music."

"Has she talked about what happened?"

"No. And if I try to bring it up, she shuts down. The only time she'll say anything is when she's half asleep, when her guard is down. She told me Carlito said he was going to sell her." Amanda's voice trembled. "What fifteen-year-old can handle that?"

"Not many," Piper said softly. "Keri's strong."

Amanda wiped her eyes quickly. "What's going to happen to her?"

"Psychologically? It'll take time. Is she in therapy?"

Amanda shook her head. "No, not yet. I don't even know where to start."

Piper nodded, already mentally noting a therapist she could recommend. "I know someone. She's great with traumatized kids."

"I'd appreciate that. Thank you. I just—sometimes I feel so lost. I don't know what to do."

Piper offered a small, understanding smile. "That's natural. You've both been through a lot."

Amanda's lips trembled. "I thought I'd lost her. When she was gone, it was like part of me had died. I couldn't breathe. I . . . I didn't know how to go on. They always say no parent should have to bury their child, but until you feel that kind of terror, you don't know what it means."

Piper let the silence hang. Amanda was unraveling and she needed the space to do so.

"What's going to happen with court?" Amanda asked, her voice shaky but trying to stay composed.

"Keri will have to testify. It's going to be painful, but I'll be there with her. As her attorney, her well-being is my only priority. No one will push her into anything she's not ready for."

"Does that mean she has to see that woman again?"

"Yes," Piper said. "But it'll be in court. She won't be alone. There'll be plenty of security. She won't get hurt."

"Hurt again, you mean."

"Yes," Piper said. "Hurt again."

They chatted a bit longer about the case and what Keri could expect in court. After a while, the front door opened. Keri came in, her backpack slung over one shoulder. She gave them a quick glance.

"Keri, this is Piper," Amanda said. "She's your lawyer. She wanted to meet you."

"Hi, Keri," Piper said gently, smiling. "I'm sorry to catch you after school. I know you probably need to decompress."

Keri shrugged, not meeting her eyes. "I'm gonna lie down."

The two women watched her retreat down the hall and shut the door behind her.

Amanda sighed. "See? That's all she does. Comes home, hides in her room. She doesn't talk to me anymore."

"She's still in survival mode. It might seem like she's pulling away, but when she starts processing all this, she'll need you. You're her anchor, Amanda."

Amanda ran her thumb along her wedding ring, spinning it absently. "Lazarus met her," she said after a pause.

"He didn't mention that."

"He came to the hospital. He talked to her, but he didn't tell her who he was."

Piper tilted her head thoughtfully. "Did you?"

"No."

"It's not my place, but would it be so bad for her to know she has a father out there who's a good man?"

Amanda's face hardened. "Good man? Does a good man come to your door in the middle of the night and tell you he never loved you? I cried for months. I couldn't even go to work. He destroyed me. I was picturing a life with him—a family. Growing old together."

She looked away and Piper could see the wounds were still raw.

"Do you know how I was going to tell him about Keri?" Amanda's voice cracked. "I bought a stuffed bunny. It said 'It's a girl' on its little feet. I was going to surprise him with it. Three days before, he shows up drunk and tells me he never wants to see me again."

Piper's heart tightened. "Lazarus has demons," she said gently. "But I think, deep down, he's trying to do the right thing. Maybe getting to know him could help Keri—help her see how a real man should treat her."

Amanda narrowed her eyes. "Because right now, every man is Carlito Xibala."

Piper nodded, but added quietly, "And Brad, too. She lost him after what was supposed to be the happiest day of her life, and now all she's left with is tragedy. It's a lot of pain to carry. Maybe having Lazarus in her corner could give her another way to see the world—and to see men. She needs someone to show her that not everyone is going to leave her broken."

59

Piper finished speaking with Amanda Bines, gathering every piece of information she could about Keri—her habits, her favorite foods, books, television, even the clothes she favored. Children often had no clear sense of who they were, but their unconscious minds knew. Piper believed that those deep-seated motivations, the ones people rarely understood, ran their lives. And most just called it fate.

Piper's goal was to help Keri bring her trauma to the surface. What Carlito and Denver had done to her couldn't stay buried. It would eat away at her if she didn't process it. Piper's job was to guide her through that darkness, to help her reframe the memories and give her back some control.

As they stood at the door, Piper asked, "Mind if I give Keri my card?"

"I can give it to her," Amanda said.

"I'd like to do it myself, if it's okay."

Amanda hesitated but then nodded. "Sure. You know where her room is."

Piper made her way down the hall and gently knocked on Keri's door. A soft voice answered, "Come in."

The room surprised her. It wasn't a typical teenager's space. Books were stacked on every available surface, and the posters weren't of pop stars or teen idols but of classic film covers like *Gone with the Wind* and *Casablanca*.

"Are you a fan of old films?" Piper asked, standing back to give Keri space.

"Yeah," Keri mumbled, not looking up from her phone.

"How'd you get into that?"

Keri shrugged, still staring at her screen.

"I love *Casablanca*," Piper continued. "I must've seen it three times when they played it at the dollar theater near my house."

Keri finally glanced up. "Everyone's so elegant in that movie."

"They are," Piper agreed. "Did you know Humphrey Bogart had to stand on milk crates to look taller next to Ingrid Bergman? He was really short. It's funny how the screen can make people seem larger than life."

"You expect them to be like the picture in your head, but they never are," Keri said, her eyes drifting back down, but she wasn't entirely closed off now.

Piper took a step closer and sat down on the edge of the bed. "Do you want to study film when you're older?"

Keri's tone shifted, a little sharper. "I know what you're doing."

"What's that?"

"You're trying to build a connection so we can get this over with."

"That's not what I'm doing," Piper said. "I'm here to get to know you. My only job is to help, that's all. If there's anything you need or questions you have, I'm the person to ask."

Keri met Piper's gaze fully. "Is Denver going to get out and kill me?"

Piper smiled gently, though her heart ached at the fear in Keri's voice. "No. I wouldn't be surprised if she never gets out. And if she does, it'll be when she's old and frail. You won't have anything to worry about."

"So, you're my lawyer?" Keri asked, her curiosity slipping through the defensive wall she'd built.

"Yes."

"And you'll do anything I ask?"

"Yes, within reason."

"I want to see his grave. Carlito's," she said. "They wouldn't let me see his body. I want to see his grave. You're my lawyer, right? I want to see it."

Piper hesitated. "I don't think that's a good idea."

Keri's gaze dropped back to her phone, her voice cold again. "So, you won't do anything I ask. *Within reason.*"

Piper felt the prickle of being watched. She turned and saw Amanda standing in the doorway, her eyes full of heartbreak. Amanda gave a small nod, barely noticeable.

Piper took a deep breath. "Okay," she said. "Let's go."

Piper parked the car at Hillside Cemetery, the quiet settling around them as they stepped out. Keri was already moving ahead, her pace fast and determined, while Piper followed slowly. The cemetery was unsettling, perched on a hill that overlooked Las Vegas. The graves seemed dug into the slope at odd angles, as if the earth couldn't hold on to the dead and was ready to release them to tumble down into the city below.

They descended stone steps that led them through the uneven rows of tombstones. Piper spotted the grave first. It was simple—no frills, no grand epitaph. Just "CARLITO SAUL XIBALA" engraved into the weathered stone. A few flowers lay scattered at the base, likely left by the only people who might have cared—his mother, maybe an aunt.

Keri stood in front of the grave, motionless, her eyes locked on the stone as if waiting for something to happen. Piper stayed silent, folding her hands together, giving the girl space to process whatever was swirling inside her.

After what felt like minutes, Keri's voice cut through the stillness. "I thought he was going to rape me," she said, her voice flat, emotionless. "But he never touched me. Not like that."

Piper stayed quiet.

"Is Brad buried here?" Keri asked, her eyes still locked on Carlito's name.

Piper remembered the chaos surrounding Brad's funeral. How Keri had been inconsolable to the point of needing sedation. Her mother had made the tough call to keep her away, fearing it would break her even more.

"No, he's buried in town," Piper said softly.

Keri nodded, though her expression didn't change. Her gaze fixed on the tombstone.

"You really loved him?" Piper said, treading carefully.

Keri shrugged, her shoulders barely moving. "I don't know. What does it even feel like?"

Piper hesitated. "I'm not sure. I thought I was in love once, but now I don't think so. But the fact that you miss him, that you're here—maybe that means something."

Keri didn't respond right away. The wind picked up, carrying dead leaves past them, swirling briefly before dropping again.

"Why did you want to marry him?" Piper asked, trying to keep her voice light, casual. "You two were so young."

Keri's blank expression faltered, just a flicker of something beneath. "Brad wanted to get emancipated. Divorce his parents. He hated them. He said if we got married, we could get our own apartment—be free."

Piper nodded, understanding. "That's true. You would have been legally emancipated."

"He told me the only way they'd let us was if I said I was pregnant. His parents wouldn't want an abortion, and they wouldn't want the baby born outside of marriage." Keri's voice wavered, then settled into the same empty tone.

The air between them grew heavy again as Keri stared at the gravestone, her face unreadable. The breeze moved around them and dead leaves skittered across the ground.

"This didn't do anything," Keri finally said, her voice hollow. "I thought maybe it'd feel good. To see where he's buried. But it doesn't. It doesn't change anything."

Piper didn't respond.

"Brad never hurt anybody," Keri added, her eyes welling up. "He was a good person."

Piper stepped closer, her voice gentle. "The world hurts good people, too, Keri. Sometimes it hurts them the most."

60

After dropping Keri off, Piper headed to the office to tie up loose ends on other cases. One in particular weighed on her—a case involving an elderly widow who needed to be placed in eldercare. The woman refused to go, clinging fiercely to the little independence she had left. No family was willing to take her in, leaving Piper to make the decision she dreaded: signing off on the commitment papers to have her placed in a care facility against her will.

It was the worst part of her job, taking away someone's freedom, even when she knew it was the right thing to do. After filing the papers, a wave of sickness hit her, the kind that made her question why she had to be the one to make these decisions. But there was no one else.

With that handled, Piper grabbed her satchel and left the office. She needed to clear her head and decided to stop by the district attorney's office to check on Denver Hartley's prosecution—it bothered her that she hadn't been getting the updates she expected. As she stepped into the hallway, her phone buzzed with a text from Lazarus. He was worried about Keri, wondering how she might be coping. Piper could feel his hesitation in every word, as if he wasn't sure he had the right to ask. She typed a quick reassurance that Keri was holding up—at least outwardly.

The DA's office was a sterile, modern building, almost too polished. Piper had always found it unwelcoming, a reminder of her law school days and the distasteful experience of applying for clerkships. The glances from partners, more interested in her legs or her chest than her credentials, had been enough to make her realize she was never going to survive in corporate law.

After she passed through security and showed her bar card, the receptionist called up to the prosecutor handling the case. "He's ready for you," she said. Piper thanked her and headed down the narrow hallway toward James Porter's office.

His workspace was as bland as she remembered—tidy but soulless. Brown binders stacked neatly, case law books lining the shelves, not a single personal touch. James hadn't changed much either. Middle aged, with the start of a belly and a head of curly hair that he was already fighting to keep from going fully gray.

"Long time no see," he said, leaning back in his chair with a heavy sigh.

"Yeah, it's been a while," Piper replied, keeping it casual. "How's everything?"

"Same grind, different day. How about you?"

"Pretty much the same."

They exchanged pleasantries, but Piper could tell he was eager to get down to business.

"I heard you're the GAL for Keri Bines," James said.

"I am. I wanted to get an update on where things stand."

James gestured to the stack of papers in front of him. "We've got everything we need—witnesses, video evidence, Keri's testimony. It's a slam dunk."

"So you think Denver will take a plea?"

He shook his head. "Not with Gideon Malloy as her lawyer. She's not going to plead to anything."

Piper knew Gideon Malloy—an ethically questionable but highly skilled defense attorney who'd gotten more than one guilty client off the hook.

"How did she afford him? I thought she didn't have any money."

James shrugged. "I have no idea who's footing the bill, but it doesn't matter. Gideon can't do anything with the evidence we've got. He's good, but not that good."

"If the evidence is that strong, why wouldn't he recommend a plea deal?"

"Because he's Gideon Malloy. He'll go to trial just to make a show of it."

"What are you offering?"

"Life without parole," he said flatly.

"Not with parole?" she asked, pushing back slightly.

"For this? No way," James replied, a flicker of annoyance crossing his face.

"If that's the deal, I don't see why they wouldn't go to trial. Gideon isn't going to accept that, and you know trials can be unpredictable."

"I know what I'm doing. This case is airtight. You're Keri's GAL, and that's fine, but leave the prosecution to me."

It took everything in her not to snap at him. His arrogance grated on her, but she forced herself to stay calm, remembering her grandmother's advice: When you're angry, smile.

She smiled, soft and polite, and said, "We're getting off on the wrong foot. My only goal is to protect that girl. Any information you can give me helps me do that."

James sighed, leaning back in his chair. "Tell Keri she has nothing to worry about. Denver Hartley is never going to hurt anyone again."

61

Lazarus had barely slept when the sun finally began to rise. He dragged himself out of bed after a sleepless night helping Narcs with a drug trafficking case.

He showered and dressed in black slacks and a white shirt with a red tie, skipping the suit jacket. The heat was unbearable—120 degrees by the morning—and the air seemed thick with it. His phone felt hot in his hand as he saw a message from Tony:

Did you know Riley was quitting?

Lazarus frowned, texting back immediately.

He quit?

Just a few hours ago. Turned in his badge and left. The watch commander was shocked, said Riley was blue through and through.

He is.

Lazarus pocketed his phone and left the apartment, driving aimlessly around the city. The noise of Las Vegas—the tourists, the drunk ramblings, the city's buzz—slowly became background static.

Sometimes, when things got too loud inside his head, he found driving through the noise brought clarity.

He didn't understand why Riley had quit. Riley came from generations of cops, dating back to the old Irishmen who crossed Ellis Island. This wasn't something he would do lightly.

Lazarus's thoughts kept spiraling and he finally decided to get some answers. He drove to Riley's apartment and parked outside, watching from a distance.

Even with the AC on full blast, Lazarus was sweating through his shirt. He sipped from a warm water bottle, his eyes glued to Riley's building. After what felt like an eternity, Riley emerged in shorts, his massive calves on full display, and got into his truck without even glancing around.

Lazarus trailed him, keeping just far enough behind not to be noticed.

Riley's truck went up Sahara Avenue and down I-15, eventually pulling into a parking lot outside an office building downtown. Lazarus knew the place—it was where Riley's wife worked, the accounting firm. He parked at a distance and watched as Riley backed his truck into a spot, facing the entrance. He was drinking, though Lazarus couldn't tell what from this distance. Alcohol likely. Riley had always had an incredible tolerance for booze, once drinking fifty beers in a single sitting.

Then a black Tesla pulled into the lot, parking near the entrance. A man got out, sharply dressed in a dark-gray suit, his hair slicked back in a neat part. Riley kicked open his truck door. He moved too fast.

"Oh, shit," Lazarus muttered under his breath.

The man by the Tesla looked up, eyes widening as he dropped his satchel and bolted in the opposite direction. Riley ran after him, and Lazarus, already sprinting, followed right behind.

The man was fast, but fear drove him faster than his body should have allowed. Riley, despite his bulk, was faster. They raced through the alley, Riley's rage a palpable thing, a force that Lazarus could feel radiating off him like desert heat.

Riley cut to the right, disappearing from Lazarus's sight. When Lazarus rounded the corner, he saw the man sprinting straight ahead—and Riley, like a truck on two legs, barreled into him. The man went flying, crashing hard onto the pavement. Riley loomed over him, face red, sweat dripping, fury etched into every feature.

"Kevin, stop!" Lazarus shouted.

Riley barely acknowledged him, his breathing heavy, eyes filled with a mix of rage and despair.

"Don't do this, man," Lazarus said, stepping in between Riley and the man on the ground. "She's not your wife anymore. She can do what she wants. That's the truth."

Riley's jaw clenched and Lazarus saw the hurt in his friend's eyes. Words like that cut deep, especially when you knew they were true.

"I know why you quit," Lazarus continued. "You respect the badge. You knew a badge shouldn't be part of this, so you turned it in. That means you know this is wrong."

"I'm going to kill him," Riley growled.

"I won't let you."

"You standing in my way?"

Lazarus became suddenly aware of how high he had to look to keep eye contact with Riley.

"You're drunk and pissed off. Let's get some coffee and talk this through."

"Get out of my way," Riley barked.

"If you hit this guy, even once, you'll cave his skull in. You'll end up in a cell with your kids visiting you behind bars. Is that what you want?"

Mentioning his kids landed. Riley's eyes shifted, the rage still there, but now something else had crept in—shame.

The man on the ground stirred, his voice trembling as he stammered, "You've got the wrong person. Please—"

"Shut up," Lazarus snapped.

Riley's breathing slowed, his face still red, but the fight was draining out of him. Lazarus took a step closer.

"Let's go, big daddy. You're blue, through and through. You don't want to be remembered for this."

Riley hesitated, but then he turned, lumbering back toward his truck.

The man on the ground exhaled in relief, pushing himself to his knees. "That guy's crazy! I'm going to call my lawyer and—"

Before he could finish, Lazarus clocked him in the face, sending him sprawling back down.

"That's for sleeping with another man's wife," he said, turning to follow Riley.

62

Piper dressed in a beige suit paired with black shoes and glanced at her reflection in the mirror. She'd never been particularly concerned with her looks, brushing off any notion of beauty as a fleeting asset, but she liked dressing up for court. As a child navigating the system herself, she'd been impressed by the men and women in fancy clothes, tossing around words she didn't understand. They had seemed like they lived in a different world, far from the messiness of her own life.

Her phone chimed. A text from Amanda.

Piper had done her best to keep Amanda in the loop, providing updates on motions and hearings—though Amanda's replies tended to be short, more about Keri's well-being than legal strategy. They weren't exactly friends, but Amanda was opening up to her more about life at home and the struggle they'd been having raising a smart, rebellious teenage girl.

As she buttoned her blazer, she thought about the woman's last message: Should I come to the hearing today?

Piper typed a quick reply, reassuring Amanda that she'd let her know if the DA needed her to attend. There would be time for testimony down the line.

The case was solid—a slam dunk, as James had said. Carlito and Denver hadn't exactly been subtle about their crimes. But Gideon's unwillingness to plea nagged at her. James was meticulous, always ready to pounce on any error, but Gideon wasn't bound by ethics. The man played dirty and didn't care who got hurt in the process.

Piper arrived at the courthouse early. After passing through security, she watched the families huddling together, some on the verge of tears, waiting for the doors to open. It was a criminal calendar today, the usual chaotic blend of anxious families and silent individuals who had no one with them.

She took her seat behind the prosecution's table, the room quiet except for the low murmurs of public defenders whispering to their clients. The bailiff called the courtroom to attention as Judge Franklin Hayes entered, a small, sharp man with a penchant for overexplaining his decisions. Piper had appeared in front of him before, and while his thoroughness could be tedious, she preferred it to the alternative.

"Please be seated," Hayes said in his soft voice, barely above a whisper, but with enough weight to carry through the room. "We're waiting on the district attorney's office. We'll begin shortly."

Piper checked her watch. The judge had been punctual as ever, entering the room exactly at eight thirty, not a second early or late. James Porter arrived moments later, along with Tami, a young Korean prosecutor Piper had met before. They exchanged quiet nods before taking their places.

The doors behind her opened again and Gideon Malloy entered like a man completely at ease. His bright-blue suit stood out, loud and immaculate, and the gold ring on his pinkie seemed excessive even by Las Vegas standards. He walked with the confidence of someone who knew he was the smartest person in the room, his motions precise and smooth as he approached the defense table.

"Good morning, Mr. Malloy," Judge Hayes said, glancing up from his computer. "Would you like to call your matter?"

Gideon stood, his posture perfect. "Yes, Your Honor. Number twelve on the docket—Denver Hartley."

The bailiffs were already bringing her in from the holding cells. When Denver appeared, shackled and dressed in an orange jumpsuit,

Piper studied her. There was no emotion in Denver's face—not fear, not anger, not even defiance. Just blankness. She looked around the courtroom with the same detachment, as though the proceedings were happening to someone else.

Men around the courtroom stole glances at her, their attention drawn like a magnet, but Denver didn't acknowledge any of it.

"Ms. Hartley," the judge began after confirming her identity, "we're here today for an arraignment. What are we doing, Counselor?"

Gideon handed out copies of a motion—one to the prosecutor, one to the judge. "We're entering not-guilty pleas, waiving the preliminary hearing, waiving jury trial, and requesting the next available bench-trial date."

Piper felt a knot tighten in her stomach. Waiving everything to rush to a bench trial? This wasn't a strategy she expected, and from the look on Judge Hayes's face, he hadn't seen it coming either.

"Mr. Malloy, she's facing a life sentence," the judge said, eyes scanning the motion.

"I am aware, Your Honor," Gideon replied.

The judge turned his attention to Denver. "Ms. Hartley, do you understand what your attorney is asking?"

"I do," Denver said.

The judge explained her rights carefully, making sure she understood the gravity of waiving both the preliminary hearing and a jury trial. Denver confirmed each point, and the judge leaned back, considering.

"Well, Mr. Malloy is an excellent attorney," Judge Hayes finally said, "so if this is what you want, I see no reason not to proceed. We'll set this matter for the next available bench trial."

James stood, clearly unsettled but his tone measured. "Your Honor, I have witnesses that need to get work off, detectives that need other cases covered, I need—"

Gideon said, "I . . . I . . . I . . . All I'm hearing from the State is their needs and their wants. This is Ms. Hartley's case, not Mr. Porter's. Let us have our day in court or release her, Your Honor."

The judge thought a moment longer. "I think she's too much of a flight risk with these types of charges, but I will grant the defense's motion for an expedited bench trial. Please have any motions in limine filed by Monday of next week. If there's anything else that comes up, feel free to email me and cc all counsel. My clerk will schedule the dates with you. Good to see you both, gentlemen."

Piper could almost hear James grinding his teeth. He tried again, emphasizing the magnitude of the charges, the need for proper preparation, but Gideon cut him off at every turn, twisting the narrative to make it seem as though the prosecution was dragging its feet.

Finally, the judge ruled. "As I said, gentlemen, I'll grant the defense's motion for an expedited bench trial. I won't release Ms. Hartley, given the nature of the charges, but we'll move forward quickly."

With that, court was adjourned. Gideon leaned in to whisper something to Denver before she was led back in cuffs, while James threw him a dark look.

Piper wasn't surprised when Gideon approached her outside the courtroom.

"Ms. Danes," he said with that smooth smile. "Mind if we chat for a moment?"

"Not at all," she replied, though she was already on the defense.

They sat on a bench, his posture as immaculate as his suit. Piper set her satchel down.

"I'd like to interview Ms. Bines before trial."

"She's already given several interviews to the police," Piper said.

"Yes, but the police aren't asking the right questions."

Piper hesitated, then shook her head. "I don't think that would be in her best interest."

Gideon gave her a sharp, calculating look. "It'll be more upsetting when I question her on the stand and she's blindsided."

"I'll think about it," Piper said.

Gideon smiled, rising to his feet. "That's all I can ask. Have a pleasant day, Ms. Danes."

As he walked away, Piper saw Lazarus leaning against the wall, watching Gideon with a look of quiet disapproval. When Gideon disappeared around the corner, Lazarus approached.

"I haven't eaten," he said, his voice gruff. "Let's grab something."

―――

They sat in the small café on the courthouse's first floor, a no-frills diner serving up comfort food like burgers and fried chicken. It was a known spot run by a retired cop, and Lazarus always said cops knew the best places to eat. The room was filled with the steady hum of police officers and court employees grabbing a bite between cases.

"What do you think about all that?" Lazarus asked as they sat down by the windows after placing their orders.

Piper sighed, still trying to process the morning. "I don't know. I've never seen anyone push for a bench trial on a case like this without even a preliminary hearing. James said it's a slam dunk with a jury, so I can't imagine how it'll go with just the judge."

"Gideon's no fool," Lazarus said, leaning back in his chair. "He wouldn't do this unless he's got something up his sleeve. I need to figure out what."

"How are you going to do that?"

"Thought I'd drop by his office and ask him myself. It's the last thing he'd expect."

She chuckled. "Bold move. Couldn't hurt, I guess. Did you see Denver in court?"

He nodded, his expression darkening. "Yeah. Did you see the way the men looked at her? Even the judge was hypnotized. She walks in, and it's like everyone forgets where they are. Voodoo."

Piper shook her head, still not fully understanding. "She's beautiful, sure, but I don't get it. There're plenty of beautiful women in Las Vegas. I don't understand why she has that effect."

"You're not a man," Lazarus said simply.

Their number was called and Lazarus went to grab the tray of food: two sandwiches and a pile of chips. He sat back down, rolling up his sleeves and tossing his tie over his shoulder to keep it out of the way.

Piper took a bite of her sandwich, the flavors doing little to settle the unease she felt. "Have you spoken to Keri at all?"

"No."

She set her sandwich down. "Are you going to take a paternity test?"

Lazarus didn't look up. "Amanda's no liar. Doesn't matter anyway."

Piper's frustration bubbled up. "How can you say that? Lazarus, you might have a child. *Your* child."

"There's nothing I could offer," he said.

"I don't believe that. I think you have a lot to teach."

"All I could teach her about is dread. She might learn it anyway, but not from me—not this young."

"She's already learned it, Lazarus."

Lazarus was quiet for a moment, staring at the table as if trying to see something beyond it. "Yeah," he said finally. "I guess she has."

63

The law offices of Gideon Malloy were nestled in the swankiest part of town, on the ninth floor of Two Summerlin. A gleaming monument to the kind of wealth most people could only dream of. Lazarus knew it was all for show. Gideon worked alone, with just a paralegal to back him up, but his reputation preceded him. The rich and guilty flocked to him, desperate for someone who would go to any length to win.

Lazarus walked past a sleek conference room and into the back offices. Gideon's paralegal was hunched over paperwork, while Gideon sat behind his desk, still in his suit coat despite being indoors. Lazarus figured the suit was for him, part of the performance.

"Detective Holloway, good to see you," Gideon greeted, his smile tight, controlled.

"You too," Lazarus said as he sat down. He took in the office—clean, minimalist, nothing personal on the walls, just a desk, a computer, and a few law books on a shelf.

"You could expand, you know," Lazarus said. "Bring in a few young lawyers. You'd have a whole team to do the heavy lifting, and you could spend your days on the golf course like the big firm partners."

"Not my style. If you're not in court every day, you're not a real trial lawyer. Courtroom skills need to be maintained."

"You've got the skill, no doubt. If I ever found myself in trouble, you're probably the guy I'd hire."

That seemed to relax Gideon a little, the compliment softening his edges. "I appreciate that, Detective. So, what can I do for you?" Gideon asked, getting straight to business.

Lazarus leaned back, keeping his tone casual. "Saw what happened in court. I'm curious—why'd you waive everything and push for a bench trial so fast?"

Gideon let out a laugh, though it sounded forced, like a man unused to the sound of his own laughter. "You think I'm going to tell you that? I'd be disbarred in an instant, and rightfully so."

"Figured it was worth a shot. Worst you could do is say no."

Gideon smiled faintly, nodding. "I can appreciate that. Life's about risk, after all. How dull would it be without it?"

Lazarus decided to press. "Why not take a deal, though? You've got to know the odds are against you."

"Because I can win."

"I don't see how."

Gideon leaned forward slightly, his tone turning reflective. "You've been a police officer a long time. When you've done something long enough, it narrows your view. You see the world through only one set of eyes."

Lazarus grunted. "Fair enough."

Gideon's gaze sharpened. "You've never come to my office before, not even during our homicide cases. Why now? Why does this kidnapping have you so interested? Is it because you feel guilty about shooting her lover?"

Lazarus felt a flicker of something—regret, maybe. Carlito Xibala wasn't someone he'd wanted to kill. He'd had no choice, but the guilt still lingered, heavy and stubborn. And underneath that guilt was something hotter: anger.

Carlito had taken his daughter—stolen her, used her as leverage. Any pity Lazarus felt was tangled with anger that Carlito's death hadn't fully extinguished. Carlito had deserved worse.

He met Gideon's gaze and said nothing, locking it all down behind a neutral expression. The why didn't matter. Not now.

"Let's cut the bullshit," Lazarus said, switching gears. "Last trial we had, you paid off a juror. You know it and I know it. So don't sit there acting high and mighty. You're in the mud like the rest of us."

Gideon chuckled softly. "I am indeed." He leaned back in his chair. "I'll tell you one thing about Ms. Hartley. I've never seen anyone carry so much hatred for one person. When I mentioned your name, it was like lighting a fuse. There's a saying about hell and a woman scorned, isn't there?"

"There is," Lazarus replied, standing up. "I won't take up more of your time."

"Hold on," Gideon said. "I've answered one of your questions. You should answer one of mine."

Lazarus nodded. "Fair's fair."

"Did you know she was your daughter before all this?"

The phrase "your daughter" hit Lazarus harder than he expected. "No. Her mother never told me."

Gideon gave a sympathetic nod. "I'm sorry. I know how that feels, believe it or not. Have you tried connecting with her now?"

"That's two questions, Gideon."

A small smile flickered across Gideon's face. "So it is."

Gideon paused, leaning forward slightly. "I'll tell you this, though—there are people closely watching what happens here."

64

Piper sat on her balcony at sunrise and read everything they had in the *State of Nevada v. Denver Rose Hartley*. The case couldn't be clearer: She had been with Carlito at the chapel, Keri had given a detailed witness statement of everything that had happened between that time and the time they found her, and there were expert witnesses who were going to testify about human trafficking and the psychology of someone who engages in it. There were independent witnesses that saw the four of them together, not to mention that Carlito was under investigation for the murder of an ex-con at a local diner, something the prosecution was certain they could get a conviction on because of the number of witnesses, but it didn't matter much now, considering Carlito was dead.

She knew Gideon was a great attorney, if ethically challenged, but even this was too much for him. Maybe if he set it for a jury trial he could've confused the issues enough to get a couple jurors to acquit and get a hung jury, but he couldn't confuse the issues with Judge Hayes. Hayes had a degree in mathematics and was as logical a judge as she'd ever seen.

The sun came up. It wasn't much of a view this morning; the parking lot was underneath her, and she could see the parking stalls' roof, which had toys and bits of fluttering garbage on it, but she didn't mind. The place was hers, and sometimes that was enough.

She dressed in a suit and put on her ichthus necklace. Seeing it reminded her of her grandmother. She said a quick prayer for her.

The line to get into the court building was long, and she had to wait almost half an hour. When they were allowed to file in, one of the bailiffs at the metal detectors was yelling at anyone that came through. Piper just got through without arguing with him. She didn't have the energy to deal right now. All her mental focus was on this case because something didn't sit right, and when something didn't sit right, it meant she was overlooking something.

The courtroom was emptied; the bench trial had been scheduled for eight days, but she doubted it would take that long. Since there was no jury, things could be expedited: no jury instructions, no opening statements or closing statements if the attorneys didn't want to do them, and affidavits in lieu of long witness testimonies. It was efficient and clean but almost always resulted in guilty verdicts, so defense attorneys were loath to use them often.

She sat behind the prosecution table. James Porter came in, rolling a case behind him, with his assistant prosecutor, Tami, next to him. James didn't acknowledge Piper.

Gideon came in a moment later, dressed in a white suit with a blue tie. He looked more like a Colombian drug lord than a defense attorney, but it fit him in a way it wouldn't have fit others.

"Ms. Danes, good to see you."

"You, too, Gideon."

James glanced at the two of them and then turned his attention to Gideon. "You wanna talk?"

"Not unless you plan on dismissing these charges against my client."

James laughed. "Always spewing bullshit, huh, Gideon?"

Gideon's face looked like he was dealing with a distasteful teenager he no longer wanted to deal with.

Piper saw Lazarus at the back of the courtroom. She went over to him.

"Are you testifying today?" she said.

"First up."

She glanced back to see if anyone was listening and then said in a lower voice, "Something's wrong."

"I know."

The bailiff said, "All rise. Eighth District Court is now in session. The Honorable Franklin Hayes presiding."

Judge Hayes came out and took the bench. He gave a pleasant smile and said, "Morning everyone. Mr. Porter, I did receive your motions in limine, but, Mr. Malloy, I didn't receive anything from you."

He rose. "We have no motions at this time, Judge."

"Nothing at all?"

"No."

"Would you like a chance to address the State's motion?"

"No, Your Honor, we would submit to the court's discretion."

"Well, if you're certain, then, bailiff, let's bring out Ms. Hartley."

Denver came out dressed in a tight gray skirt and a blue shirt, her hair pulled back and a whisp of makeup on. The judge took a glance at her and lingered a little too long. The bailiff didn't have the compulsion to look away for decency, and he stared at her legs underneath the table from his spot leaning against the court clerk's side of the bench. Even James couldn't help but glance at her. Piper bet Gideon asked her to dress like that on purpose.

"It's magic, ain't it?" Lazarus said.

"Men certainly don't do that when I walk into a room."

The judge said, "Okay, I think we're ready to begin. We're here today for the matter of *State v. Denver Rose Hartley*, case number 224-cr-00756-NV. The matter is set for bench trial today. We have Mr. Gideon Malloy here for Ms. Hartley and Mr. James Porter and Tami Wax for the state and people of Nevada. As far as the State's motion in limine, I found nothing terribly objectionable. I will go through each point to make sure it's clear, but before I do, does anyone have any other issues that need to be addressed?"

James said, "No, Judge," without standing.

Gideon stood and said, "No, Your Honor."

The judge went into a reading of the issues that the State had presented in the motion. It was mostly things having to do with which witnesses could say what and the timing of how the evidence would be introduced. Nothing groundbreaking. Still, Gideon didn't object or argue any point. There were lazy attorneys out there who did nothing and watched their clients get convicted, but Gideon wasn't one of them. She had heard he once worked seventy-two hours straight on a case, without sleep, to make sure motions were done correctly before a trial.

"Okay," Judge Hayes finally said, "I think that's everything. Any other issues before we begin? . . . Excellent. Mr. Porter, the floor is yours."

James said, "We would waive opening statements and ask to call Detective Lazarus Holloway to the stand."

Piper watched Gideon. It was customary during a trial to invoke an exclusionary rule, which asked that no other witnesses be in the courtroom when one witness was testifying, to prevent witnesses from influencing each other. Gideon said nothing. Just calmly watched Lazarus.

James took to the lectern as Lazarus was seated and sworn in. He looked calm.

James waited a second and then said, "Your Honor, since we are in a bench trial, I'd like to waive all foundational issues and simply qualify Detective Holloway as the lead investigator on this, as well as being qualified in law enforcement investigation."

"Any objection from the defense?"

Gideon stood. "None, Your Honor."

"Then it's so recognized."

James nodded once and said, "Detective Holloway, we don't need to lay any groundwork here since there's no jury, so let's jump into it. Briefly tell us who you are and how you got involved with all this."

"I'm currently a detective with the Criminal Intelligence Unit of the Las Vegas Metro PD. I was approached by Detective Lou Hobbes on the seventh of June and asked to provide support on an active investigation."

"What was that investigation?"

"The murder of William Dalton and the kidnapping of Bradley Lowe and Keri Bines."

"What did Detective Hobbes tell you happened to get you involved?"

"Two individuals had crashed through the wedding chapel's doors, slit Mr. Dalton's throat, and then forced the two underage victims into the trunk of the car. It'll be easier if we play the video while I talk."

"Of course." James looked to his assistant, who worked with the clerk to get the screen down and the video playing.

"Tell us what's happening, Detective."

"This is the beginning of the ceremony. The perpetrators were outside waiting for everyone's attention to be drawn to the couple."

"Objection," Gideon said softly as he rose. "Speculation."

"Sustained," the judge said.

James said, "Tell us what's happening now."

The car crashed through the front doors. No sound on the video, but Piper could imagine the screaming. The car skidded to a stop, and then both doors opened. The driver and passenger looked like they kissed before getting out of the car.

"The driver, we believe, was Carlito Xibala; the passenger, the defendant." Piper caught Gideon's sharp glance—he had an objection brewing, but he held his tongue.

"What are we watching now, Detective?" James said.

"The driver walks by Mr. Dalton, who is pleading with them not to harm anyone."

Piper watched as Carlito slid the hunting knife across the minister's throat, like he was killing cattle.

"What are we seeing now, Detective?"

"The death of Mr. Dalton, and then you can see here Mr. Xibala, the driver, grabs Keri Bines and drags her to the car. He didn't look at anyone else, just went straight to her. She was the primary target."

They watched more of the video, and Lazarus kept speaking.

"Mr. Lowe ran up while Mr. Xibala was pulling her away, and the passenger in the vehicle came up behind him, bashed him in the head with her shotgun, and a struggle ensued. She overwhelmed him, then forced him into the trunk."

James said, "What evidence do we have on the identity of the passenger?"

"When Ms. Bines and some of the other witnesses testify, they will establish that the voice they heard from the passenger was the voice of the defendant in this case, Denver Hartley, and that when her mask was removed, it was revealed to be her."

"So this seems like a straightforward murder and kidnapping. Why did the intelligence unit get involved?"

"Witnesses reported that there were no license plates on the car, so Detective Hobbes couldn't go that direction, and there was no ransom notice or anything similar in the time that followed. Detective Hobbes felt the leads would grow cold, so he asked for the help of the CIU in relation to a bracelet we believe Mr. Xibala lost at the scene from struggling with Keri, and that's how I came to be involved."

Piper noticed that he hadn't mentioned Keri might be his daughter.

"And what was supposed to be your role?"

"I was to gather intelligence and help identify the perpetrators."

"Is that a typical role for the CIU?"

"Yessir. My job is primarily investigative support. I help find the things other detectives might overlook."

"And did you identify the couple?"

"We did."

"Please go into detail."

Lazarus outlined how he had tracked down the couple, what happened when they were tracked down, and then various details of what he knew about Denver Hartley and Carlito Xibala.

He talked about the shooting of Carlito and how it was still under investigation by Internal Affairs and the next steps they would be taking.

James hurried through some of it. Judges knew exactly what they were looking for in a bench trial: Did the prosecution present enough evidence of every single element of the offense to convince a reasonable person beyond a reasonable doubt that the defendant committed the crime? It was, in many ways, a very broad mandate, but Piper believed Judge Hayes would do his best to stick to it. As such, there was no need for an outlining of tiny details. Maybe that's why Gideon chose this venue? He thought they had a better shot in an appellate court and wanted to get the actual trial over with as quickly as possible?

"And what did the defendant do after Mr. Xibala was shot?"

Lazarus gave a quick glance to Denver, whose gaze hadn't moved from him.

"She ran to him. I then effectuated an arrest."

James nodded. "Thank you, Detective, that's all I had for now."

The judge looked at Gideon. "Cross-examination, Mr. Malloy?"

"Yes, Your Honor."

Gideon went to the lectern.

65

Gideon didn't carry a single note or file. He approached the stand like it was a casual conversation, as if it was him and Lazarus having a chat over coffee. It was the kind of tactic defense lawyers used to charm juries—making it look effortless. But in a bench trial like this, in front of Judge Hayes, there was no reason to avoid notes unless you were planning on something else entirely.

"Detective, let's start with the Reeves case from two years ago. Please refresh my memory about that. What happened there?"

Lazarus kept his face neutral. "It was a burglary ring. We apprehended a suspect—"

"A suspect that was later acquitted on all charges, correct?" Gideon interrupted.

"Yes," Lazarus replied flatly.

"And why was that suspect acquitted?"

"The appellate court ruled that the warrant was vague and overbroad, which led to evidence suppression."

"So, the man you arrested was acquitted because you failed to follow proper procedure?"

"The court found the warrant insufficient, yes."

"Not just insufficient, Detective. It was *your* failure that led to this supposed criminal walking free, wasn't it?"

Lazarus paused a moment, eyes locked on Gideon. "That's not how I'd phrase it."

"I'm sure it's not," Gideon said. "Let's talk about the Ujan trafficking investigation. Please tell us about that."

"Objection," James cut in. "Relevance?"

"How the detective conducts investigations is highly relevant, Your Honor," Gideon said smoothly.

"I'll allow it," Judge Hayes said.

Lazarus's expression remained neutral, but inside, he felt a flicker of irritation. Gideon was moving quickly, not giving him time to explain.

"We had reason to believe that Mr. Ujan was involved in a narcotics operation—"

"An investigation where you were reprimanded for excessive force, correct?" Gideon interjected.

"There was a misunderstanding—"

"I didn't ask for your opinion on it, Detective. You were reprimanded, yes?"

"Yes."

"And that led to you being mandated to take anger management classes, didn't it?"

Lazarus's head tilted slightly, a subtle sign that those who knew him well would recognize as a loss of composure. "Yes. But those records are sealed. How'd you find out about it, I wonder."

"Have you completed those classes yet, Detective?" Gideon's voice was calm.

"No, I haven't."

"So you're still under treatment for anger issues?"

Lazarus's gaze darkened. "I haven't started the classes yet."

"So, you're testifying in a case involving a murdered man, vulnerable minors, and you've been instructed to attend anger management classes you haven't even started yet. Doesn't that concern you, Detective?"

"Objection," James said, rising to his feet. "This is irrelevant."

"It speaks to his credibility, Your Honor," Gideon said, turning to the judge.

"I'll allow it," Judge Hayes said. "But Mr. Malloy, please don't stray too far."

Lazarus kept his eyes on Gideon, his tone icily calm. "My personal development doesn't affect how I conduct an investigation."

"Well, I suppose that's up for the court to decide," Gideon said, his smile barely perceptible. "Let's talk about substance abuse, Detective."

"Objection!" James snapped, nearly shouting.

Gideon stayed composed. "If Detective Holloway has had issues with substance abuse, it speaks directly to his ability to perform his duties, Your Honor. I have a duty to explore this on behalf of my client."

"I'll allow it," Judge Hayes said, though his tone indicated mild reluctance.

Gideon's eyes bore into Lazarus. "Have you ever sought treatment for substance abuse?"

"No."

"Not even after the Reeves case, when you were spotted at the Last Chance Saloon every day for a month straight?"

Lazarus's jaw flexed, a ripple of tension passing through his body. "No, I did not."

"Let's talk about Ms. Keri Bines. You're familiar with her, of course?"

"Yes."

Gideon paused, letting the silence settle over the courtroom. "You called her on June seventeenth, three days before her official interview, didn't you?"

"Yes."

"That phone call wasn't recorded, was it, Detective?"

"No."

"An unrecorded and undocumented conversation with the key witness. Not standard procedure, is it?"

Lazarus remained calm. "It was to set the appointment."

A small chuckle rippled through the courtroom from the gallery.

Gideon didn't miss a beat. "Let's talk about Ms. Hartley's alibi. Her mother, Maria Hartley, provided one for several nights in question, didn't she?"

"She did."

"But you never interviewed her, did you?"

"I didn't see a need to—"

"You *didn't see a need* to interview the alibi witness?"

"Her timelines didn't match with other evidence."

"So you decided her testimony wasn't worth checking? How many other potential leads did you dismiss without following up?"

"We followed all credible leads."

"Credible by whose standard, Detective? Yours?"

"Objection," James called again, though his voice held a weariness now.

"Withdrawn," Gideon said. "Detective, isn't it true that you decided, from the beginning, that Denver Hartley was guilty? And you built your entire investigation to fit that conclusion?"

"That's not how it works."

"Isn't it? In your own notes, you dismissed three potential suspects without so much as a phone call. Care to explain that?"

"They were cleared based on—"

"Evidence that we haven't seen presented in this courtroom," Gideon cut in, his voice growing sharper. "Now let's talk about the night you shot Carlito Xibala."

Piper stiffened, watching Lazarus closely. This was the moment Gideon had been building toward.

Lazarus's voice was steady. "I shot Mr. Xibala in the line of duty. It's under investigation."

"An investigation you've been suspended for, correct?"

"That is correct."

"So, here you are, suspended for an officer-involved shooting, testifying in a case where your credibility is paramount. Doesn't that seem odd?"

There was a heavy silence in the courtroom. Lazarus didn't flinch, didn't blink. "Odd how?"

Gideon stared at him for a beat too long, then stepped back from the lectern. "No further questions, Your Honor."

Lazarus locked eyes with Gideon as he stepped down from the stand. The two men didn't speak, but the tension between them was tangible—like a fuse had been lit.

66

As soon as the judge adjourned for lunch, Gideon walked swiftly out of the courtroom, his steps casual but with a purpose behind them. Lazarus, however, wasn't done. He followed.

The hallway was quieter than expected, most people already heading for their lunch breaks. Gideon had just turned the corner when Lazarus caught up with him.

"Malloy."

Gideon stopped, his back straightening slightly before he turned, his face betraying no surprise. "Detective," he said smoothly.

Lazarus stepped in closer, lowering his voice. "That was quite the performance."

Gideon gave a small shrug, his expression indifferent. "It's just business, Detective."

"Business? You dragged in personal shit that has nothing to do with the case. What the hell you playing at?"

Gideon's smile was as cold as ever. "The truth can be uncomfortable, Detective. You of all people should know that."

He turned and left. Lazarus followed him onto the elevator, pushing himself into the small enclosed space before the doors could close. A few people waiting were about to step in, but Lazarus stood in front of them, a quiet force, blocking entry. He reached for the Close button, ignoring the soft muttering from people left behind. As soon as the elevator started moving, he hit the emergency stop, and the buzz of the alarm echoed in the confined space.

"What are you doing?" Gideon asked, irritation laced in his tone.

Lazarus didn't flinch. His eyes stayed locked on Gideon. "What the hell was that?"

Gideon's demeanor was almost amused. "I'm sorry if you can't handle a cross-examination, Detective."

"I can handle them," Lazarus said. "I've handled a lot of them. From you, too. And I've never had one so weak. You had me followed on the Reeves case, didn't you? You knew damn well I was drunk every day. You could've torn me apart on that stand, but instead, you barely touched the issue and moved on. That's not your style."

Gideon's smile was thin, more a twitch of the lips than anything else. "Every case demands a different strategy, Detective."

"Why pull your punches? It wasn't just weak—it was intentional. You're hiding something."

Gideon's eyes flickered with something Lazarus couldn't quite place—amusement, maybe, or a hint of something darker. "You want answers, go talk to the prosecution. It's not my job to make your life easier."

Gideon leaned over and pressed the emergency release. The elevator jolted back into motion. As the doors opened on the ground floor, Gideon stepped out without a backward glance. Lazarus watched him go, the sense that something much larger was at play gnawing at him.

Piper was leaving as Lazarus stepped off the elevator. They didn't speak until they were outside, in the open air, where the scent of exhaust from the busy street lingered.

"What did you think of that cross?" he asked once they were on the courthouse steps.

Piper took a deep breath, glancing around before answering. "He hit all the right topics but didn't dig into any of them. It felt off."

Lazarus nodded, staring into the distance. "He held back. You ever seen Gideon hold back before?"

"Never," she replied.

He stayed silent for a moment, lost in thought. "I gotta run. Catch up with you later."

Piper didn't feel like eating. The knots in her stomach from court had settled in too deep. Instead, she sipped coffee slowly, letting the warmth ease some of the tension. Court still made her uneasy—she wasn't hardened to it like the seasoned prosecutors or defense attorneys, who seemed immune to the stress that came with courtroom battles.

She knew that Judge Hope Dawson wasn't on the bench today, and she suspected where the judge would be for lunch.

Piper had always been fascinated by the enigma that was Judge Dawson. A billionaire heiress who could've lived a life of luxury but instead chose a life of law. She had once imagined Dawson's life filled with glamorous events and jet-setting to exotic locales, only to find out the judge preferred seclusion. "Thought requires solitude," Dawson had told her once.

The country club was sprawling and pristine, with acres of manicured lawns and luxury dripping from every corner. The teenager working the entrance booth gave her a massive guest pass, clearly designed so the members knew who the nonmembers were.

Piper parked and made her way to the restaurant on the grounds. The tables were draped in cream-colored linens, the patrons looking like they had stepped off the pages of a high-end lifestyle magazine. Judge Dawson sat alone on the veranda, shaded by a large umbrella, with a small fan gently blowing a strand of her hair back and forth. A plate of half-eaten crab cakes sat in front of her along with a glass of wine.

"Do you know why I come here?" Judge Dawson said without looking up, startling Piper, who hadn't expected to be noticed so quickly.

"No," Piper replied, approaching the table.

Dawson looked up then. "Because there are certain crowds you can be in and yet feel completely alone. I like that."

"Sorry to interrupt, then," Piper said.

Judge Dawson grinned. "You're one of the few people I don't mind being interrupted by. Have a seat, Counselor."

Piper sat down across from her. "You come here every day, don't you?"

"Yes," Dawson replied, glancing around. "I like listening to people. It's amazing what you can learn just by listening. Everyone thinks they're unique, special, but deep down they're all the same. It's a comforting delusion they cling to. Human behavior is far more predictable than people like to admit."

Piper nodded. "I guess to each their own, Judge."

Dawson smiled. "You can call me Hope, Piper. We're past formalities." She took a sip of wine. "What do you do to stay curious?"

"I read a lot, pray, meditate. I try not to get lost in my head too much—it tends to slow me down. How about you?"

"I spend days lost in thought," Hope said, sipping her wine. "Most people wouldn't survive it, but it's a necessity for me. Detective Holloway is the same, you know. He spends more time in his own head than anyone out here."

"I wouldn't know," Piper replied. "He doesn't talk about himself much."

"He hasn't talked about the possibility of having a daughter?"

"No," Piper said, shaking her head. "He thinks she's better off without him."

Hope looked thoughtful, then changed the subject. "You seem distracted. Tell me what's on your mind."

Piper sighed. "I was in court today for Denver Hartley's trial. Gideon Malloy was . . . odd."

"How so?"

"I've seen him in court before and he's always aggressive, relentless. But with Lazarus, it felt like he was holding back. He touched on topics I know he could've used to do real damage, but he let them go. It's like he was performing, hitting all the right points but not driving any of them home."

Dawson nodded slowly, considering this. "Gideon is brilliant. Sometimes you don't understand a brilliant person's strategy until after the fact."

"I don't think that's what this was," Piper said. "It seemed deliberate. Like he wanted the transcript to reflect he did a good job without actually doing it."

"Could be burnout," Dawson said. "Law is a contentious profession. Contention is stress. Stress breaks people down as they age."

Piper shook her head. "I don't buy it. There's something else going on."

Dawson studied her for a moment. "And that's why you came here, isn't it? To discuss more than lunch."

"I wanted to hear your thoughts."

Dawson leaned back, crossing her legs under the table. "You're worried because you don't know what Gideon's endgame is. And that scares you because you think it could mean Denver gets acquitted."

Piper's silence was answer enough.

"Why does Denver scare you so much? You've dealt with violent offenders before."

Piper hesitated. "It's Keri. If Denver walks away, she won't let this go. She'll come after her."

Dawson nodded slowly. "Do you think Denver stands a real chance of being acquitted?"

"Yesterday I would've said no. But now . . . Gideon's confidence unnerves me. It's almost like he's laying groundwork for something bigger. I need to look into it—for Keri."

Hope Dawson sipped her wine, eyes thoughtful. "Just be careful what you look for, Piper. You might find it."

67

The next day, Piper woke early. A trait she didn't want to purposely cultivate, but it seemed to be thrust upon her as sleep became elusive. She dressed in a black suit, clasped her necklace around her neck, and said a quiet prayer. Her thoughts wandered to her grandmother, but before long, they drifted to Keri—a girl who never really fit in anywhere.

Piper finally nabbed Keri's medical records—a chaotic sprawl of therapists and medications, each a Band-Aid on a deeper wound. She'd seen it before: parents dodging the truth, shipping their kids off for a quick fix.

One incident stood out. When Keri was thirteen, Charlie and Amanda had sent her to a scared-straight wilderness program. The kind of place Piper had been working to shut down for years. Allegations of abuse ran rampant in those camps—kids went in with their problems and came out worse, traumatized. Keri had been stuck there for three months.

The courtroom wasn't as empty today. Piper noticed a reporter from the *Ledger*, Claude, sitting in one of the back rows. A crime-beat reporter who always wore shabby suit coats and worn-out jeans, despite his wife owning five McDonald's franchises. Claude had a habit of sticking his nose into the messiest cases.

"What are you up to?" Claude asked as Piper walked by, not bothering to get up.

Piper slid into her seat behind the prosecution table, turning just enough to acknowledge him without being rude.

"You know me, I just love court," she said.

"I didn't know you were involved in this one."

"I'm the guardian for the underage victim."

"No shit? How's she doing?"

Piper's gaze hardened. "She lost the boy she loved in about the most horrific way possible, Claude. She's struggling."

Claude gave a half-hearted chuckle. "Better to have loved and lost than never loved at all, right?"

"I have a feeling people who've lost love before don't feel that way."

He smirked but let it drop. "Probably not."

James and Tami entered the courtroom, looking focused. The judge arrived not long after, followed by Gideon.

Denver was brought into the courtroom. She looked different today. She was wearing a suit skirt, a crimson blouse, and black heels. It wasn't her usual look, Piper guessed, but it didn't really matter. What stood out were Denver's eyes—cold, piercing. They sliced through the room, drawing the gaze of nearly every man there.

Judge Hayes cleared his throat. "Okay, we are back on the record. Mr. Porter and Ms. Wax are here for the State, and Mr. Malloy is here for the defense. Mr. Porter, you may proceed."

"The State would like to call Dr. Sarah Chen to the stand," James said.

"Bailiff, please bring in Dr. Chen," the judge responded.

A moment later, an Asian woman in a sharp blue suit and with gray hair entered the courtroom. Piper thought she looked like the CEO of a Fortune 500 company. Composed, self-assured. Dr. Chen took her seat on the stand and was sworn in.

James stepped up to the lectern. "Dr. Chen, could you please introduce yourself to the court and briefly outline your qualifications?"

Dr. Chen nodded. "I'm Dr. Sarah Chen. I have a PhD in criminal psychology and a medical degree from Stanford Medical School. I specialize in human trafficking. I've conducted thirty-two years of field research and have over ninety published studies. I've also consulted for the FBI and Interpol on trafficking cases, and I currently teach at Stanford while consulting for various law enforcement agencies nationwide."

"We'd like to submit Dr. Chen as an expert in the psychology of human trafficking," James stated confidently.

"Any objections from the defense?" the judge asked.

"None, Your Honor," Gideon replied, his expression neutral.

"The court recognizes Dr. Chen as such. Mr. Porter, you may proceed."

James nodded. "Dr. Chen, as you know, this case involves human trafficking. Can you explain to the court the typical dynamics of human trafficking operations?"

Dr. Chen straightened. "Traffickers typically use force, fraud, or coercion to exploit their victims, either for labor or sex. They prey on vulnerable populations—minors, those living in poverty, people with disabilities, runaways. These individuals are often unable to defend themselves or don't have anyone looking out for them."

"And the size of these operations?" James asked.

"They can vary greatly. Some are small, involving only a couple of individuals. Others are large-scale, involving entire communities. One case I worked on in Thailand involved a city where tourists were being kidnapped. The entire town, from business owners to the mayor, knew what was happening but kept quiet because they were getting a cut of the profits. Around five hundred residents were complicit."

"And you've reviewed the evidence in this case?"

"I have, yes."

"In your expert opinion, is this case an example of human trafficking?"

Dr. Chen nodded firmly. "It is. The evidence points to Mr. Xibala and the defendant, Ms. Hartley, arranging to deliver the victims to a buyer. There was an initial contact here in Las Vegas, but for various reasons, the exchange didn't happen. Ms. Hartley then reached out to another contact, and a deal was made to take the victims to Mexico in exchange for a large sum."

"Do we know who they were selling the victims to?"

"We don't know for certain, but it's reasonable to assume it was a cartel. Since the legalization of marijuana in several states, cartels have been losing income and are turning to other illicit businesses. Trafficking is lucrative because of the large number of vulnerable individuals and the fact that people, particularly the younger generation, have become less cautious about meeting strangers online."

"Can you explain to the court the structure of a typical trafficking organization?"

"The best way to imagine it is like a spider's web," Dr. Chen explained. "At the center is the main trafficker—someone with deep connections in both the criminal world and legitimate society, unfortunately. They often have access to resources that allow them to operate undetected. There was a sheriff in Georgia, for example, who was found to be selling women arrested for prostitution to a trafficking ring in Florida. Stories like his aren't uncommon."

James nodded, urging her to continue.

"Branching out from the center are recruiters. These are the people who identify potential victims—runaways, addicts, undocumented migrants. They look for those that society is less likely to notice if they disappear. This case is different, though. Both victims—Keri Bines and Bradley Lowe—come from middle-class families who care about them. They weren't groomed or tricked. They were simply taken, which is very unusual."

"And what does that tell you?" James asked.

"It tells me that they were targeted specifically. This wasn't an opportunistic kidnapping—it was planned."

Piper felt a tightness in her chest as Dr. Chen spoke. To the doctor, this was all academic, an intellectual curiosity. But Keri had almost been sold into slavery. This wasn't a puzzle to be solved. It was Keri's life.

"Why were they targeted?" James asked.

"Detective Holloway, the lead investigator on the case, believes that the traffickers saw a wedding announcement in the *Las Vegas Ledger*. The paper often runs small features on weddings held at local chapels. We believe they saw the announcement, noted that the victims were teenagers, and assumed they would fetch a higher price on the market than older victims. And they were right."

James glanced at his notes, pausing briefly before asking, "Once a victim is identified, what typically happens next?"

"In most cases, that's when the grooming begins. Traffickers manipulate their victims psychologically, offering them promises of love, money, or a better life. In some cases, more direct threats or coercion are used. The goal is always the same: isolation."

"Isolation?" James asked.

"A person who is isolated is easier to control. By cutting off their victims from family and friends, the trafficker becomes the victim's entire world."

"And how does that compare to the situation before us?"

"This case fits the trafficking model. The organized selection of the victims, the use of a storage unit as a holding place, the planned border crossing—all of it points to trafficking, even if it's not exactly textbook."

James went into details about the psychology and implications of trafficking. Dr. Chen was calm and collected the entire time. Gideon had his fingers steepled and watched her with what seemed like almost preternatural concentration.

James turned back to the judge after a long while. "No further questions, Your Honor."

Piper glanced toward Keri, sitting quietly at the back of the room. She looked small, vulnerable.

Piper smiled at her, but she didn't smile back.

68

Gideon locked eyes with Dr. Chen, and she returned his gaze, composed.

"Dr. Chen," Gideon began his cross-examination, his voice smooth. "You've painted a rather chilling picture of the defendant as a cold, calculating trafficker. But I'd like to explore another possibility with you. Are you familiar with battered spouse syndrome?"

Dr. Chen nodded. "Yes, I'm familiar with it."

"Could you explain it to the court, please?" Gideon asked.

Dr. Chen shifted slightly in her seat, her body language barely revealing the recalibration of her thoughts. "Battered spouse syndrome is a psychological condition that can develop in individuals subjected to prolonged domestic violence. It's characterized by a cycle of abuse and the belief that they cannot escape their situation. Over time, the victim may develop learned helplessness, a condition in which they feel that any action they take will only worsen their circumstances. The syndrome is often misunderstood, even by those in the field of psychology."

James sat upright, clearly anticipating where this was headed.

"Dr. Chen, let's break it down for the court," Gideon said. "Can you explain the cycle of abuse that characterizes this syndrome?"

Dr. Chen's expression remained measured. "The cycle is typically divided into three phases: the tension-building phase, the acute battering incident, and the honeymoon phase. During the tension-building phase, the victim feels as though they're walking on eggshells, trying to prevent triggering the abuser. This tension escalates until it culminates in an acute battering incident, where the abuser unleashes violence—physical, emotional, or psychological. Afterward, the abuser may express remorse, making promises to change. This is the honeymoon phase, where they behave lovingly. And then the cycle repeats."

"And as this cycle continues," Gideon pressed, "what happens to the victim's psyche?"

"Over time, the victim's self-esteem erodes. They begin to believe they deserve the abuse, that they're at fault, and that there's no way out. This is learned helplessness. Even when opportunities to escape arise, the victim might not take them, believing it will only lead to worse outcomes or that they're incapable of surviving without the abuser."

Gideon nodded, leaning forward on the lectern. "So, Dr. Chen, is it possible for someone suffering from battered spouse syndrome to become complicit in their abuser's actions—not out of free will, but out of a distorted sense of survival?"

Dr. Chen paused for a moment. "Yes. A victim might comply with their abuser's demands, even if those demands are illegal or harmful to others, believing it's their only means of avoiding further abuse or harm."

"So, let's consider the possibility that Ms. Hartley, after years of abuse from her father, her husband, and later Mr. Xibala, as evidenced by her recent emergency room visit—let's say she believed that participating in his human trafficking operation was her only means of survival. She might have feared for her life or believed that refusing him would result in even greater harm to herself or to others. Would you say that's a possibility, Dr. Chen?"

Dr. Chen shifted in her seat again, a flicker of hesitation crossing her features. "It's a possibility."

Gideon pressed on, his voice steady. "We have no recordings of their private conversations, do we?"

"We do not."

"No psychological evaluations conducted during the time Ms. Hartley was under Mr. Xibala's influence?"

"No, nothing like that."

The Night Collector

"All we have are outward actions—and isn't it true that outward actions might not reflect someone's inner reality, especially if they're under severe psychological duress?"

"That's correct. Outward behavior doesn't reveal the full extent of a person's internal struggles, particularly in cases of severe abuse."

"Is it also true," Gideon continued, "that victims of battered spouse syndrome can sometimes be pushed to commit crimes they would never have considered before the abuse began? Crimes they might later deeply regret but, at the time, felt were necessary for survival?"

"Yes, that can happen," Dr. Chen replied, her voice neutral. "The victim's sense of reality becomes so distorted that they believe criminal actions are their only way out, or their only way to avoid worse harm."

Gideon's gaze went briefly to the judge before he leaned in slightly, his voice low. "And in those cases, Dr. Chen, in your professional opinion, do those victims deserve to be punished as harshly as those who commit crimes out of greed or malice?"

"Objection!" James shot to his feet.

Gideon ignored him and continued, his tone steady. "Or should we consider the full context of their situation, the psychological prison they've been living in, before passing judgment?"

"I said *objection!*" James's voice boomed through the courtroom as his hand came down on the table with a loud slap that startled the judge's clerk.

The room fell into a dead silence. All eyes turned to the judge as James, clearly trying to regain his composure, addressed him.

"Your Honor, I object on the grounds that this line of questioning is irrelevant and highly prejudicial. The defense is attempting to elicit a legal conclusion from the witness, which is beyond the scope of her expertise. Whether the defendant deserves a particular punishment is not for this witness to determine. It is the court's role to apply the law to the facts, not to allow sympathy for the defendant's situation to cloud that process. Furthermore, the defense's question is speculative and invites improper factors into consideration."

Gideon was calm, unfazed. "Your Honor, may I respond?"

The judge gave him a curt nod.

Gideon's voice was controlled. "The prosecution is correct that sentencing is the purview of the court. However, I'm not asking Dr. Chen to render a legal judgment. I'm merely asking her, as an expert in human psychology, to provide context that the court might find valuable when considering the defendant's state of mind and the factors that influenced her actions. The defense believes this context is crucial to determining whether the defendant acted under duress."

The judge sat back, weighing both arguments for a moment, before speaking. "I agree. The objection is overruled."

James clenched his jaw, unable to hide his frustration. "That's ridiculous."

"Mr. Porter," the judge said, voice stern, "you may want to rephrase that."

The tension between James and the judge was thick. Piper watched as they stared each other down, two egos on full display. It was a bench trial—there was no jury to influence. The judge had already heard the evidence, and the objection wouldn't change much. But James couldn't stand the idea of letting Gideon get one over on him.

James finally sat back down, visibly seething, and Gideon turned back to Dr. Chen.

"The context," Dr. Chen said carefully, "absolutely needs to be considered. Victims of battered spouse syndrome are not like typical offenders; their actions are often a result of extreme duress and psychological manipulation."

"Which would absolve Ms. Hartley of knowing participation in these crimes, correct?"

"Objection," James said again, but his voice was quieter now, his tone resigned.

Gideon gave a small, satisfied nod. "Withdrawn. No further questions."

69

The next witness in the trial was a gas station clerk who had interacted with Carlito and Bradley. His testimony was brief, recounting the terse exchange between Carlito and the boy, but it didn't offer much. The same went for the next few witnesses—diners at a local spot where Carlito had allegedly murdered a former inmate he'd done time with. Their testimony, while grisly, didn't land with the impact it should have. It almost didn't matter. Carlito was dead, and James hadn't charged Denver as an accomplice in that crime. But Gideon let the testimony drag on anyway, sitting back in his chair, quietly observing. He took the opportunity to allow James to paint Carlito as the psychopath he clearly was—a vicious, remorseless killer. It was clever. Denver's defense rested on the idea that she had been forced into this world by Carlito's sheer brutality.

When the day's proceedings wrapped up, Piper gathered her satchel, waiting for James and his assistant to leave first. She didn't like to be seen as hovering around, but she also had questions for him, things that were bothering her.

They walked to the elevators, James and his second chair, Tami, chatting about a different case entirely. Piper kept quiet. Once they reached the lobby, she held the door for James as he pulled his heavy case through. He gave her a quick nod of thanks.

"Can I ask you something, James?" she said as they headed out to the front steps.

James stopped, looking at her with an expression that was hard to read. "What's on your mind?"

"How do you feel it's going?"

"Fine."

"How do you think Gideon's doing?"

James shrugged, already turning his attention elsewhere. "Best he can."

"Do you think so? There were a few obvious lines of attack during his cross that he just . . . skipped. He didn't attack Lazarus's drinking, he didn't introduce evidence of threats or violence toward Denver from Carlito . . . I mean, he didn't really do much with substance."

"So?"

She was surprised by his indifference. "You don't find that odd for an attorney like him?"

"You're not in court as much as I am," James said. "These defense attorneys are all the same. It's about the money. I'd bet this lady screwed him on his fee and now he's stuck on the case. Judge Hayes won't let him withdraw, so he does a half-assed job. Happens all the time."

Piper frowned. She had seen Gideon in action before. Once, he had refused to let a bailiff unjustly arrest one of his clients, even going so far that the judge had him placed in handcuffs so they could drag her away without him interfering. That didn't seem like the kind of attorney who would phone in a defense just because he was stiffed on payment.

"That doesn't sound like Gideon to me," Piper said.

James's face twisted into an unpleasant grimace. "How many trials have you had with him? One? Two? I've had dozens over the years. Trust me, it's always about the money with guys like him."

Piper considered this but wasn't convinced. "One more thing. Why didn't you charge her as an accomplice in the murder at the diner?"

"I don't think she knew about it. And I'm already getting life. Why complicate things?"

James walked away, clearly done with the conversation. Piper stood there, watching him go, torn. She could let it slide, agree with James that this was just another case of a defense attorney going through the motions, or she could follow her gut and dig deeper, even if she didn't have the time or energy to spare.

"Damn it," she whispered, making her way to her car.

Gideon Malloy lived in a secluded area in the hills overlooking Las Vegas. The homes here were sand colored, surrounded by manicured lawns and perfectly spaced trees. The view of the city lights was distant, and the isolation felt purposeful. This was where people came when they wanted to pretend the rest of humanity didn't exist.

Lazarus stood outside Gideon's home, checking his phone for an update from Riley. The big man had eyes on Gideon's girlfriend's house; Gideon was spending the night there.

Lazarus walked up the driveway, his shoes barely making a sound on the stone path. As part of the Criminal Intelligence Unit, Lazarus had access to technology most people had never heard of. Surveillance was his job. Officially, they would have needed a warrant to enter the house. Unofficially, he had no intention of getting one, even if he could. He had already disabled the alarm system using a modulator—a piece of equipment only his unit had access to.

Sliding the glass door open, Lazarus stepped inside. The house smelled faintly of expensive cologne and the cool air was a sharp contrast to the desert night outside. The house was dark, but his eyes quickly adjusted.

He moved silently through the space, passing through the kitchen, past a bathroom that looked more like a spa, and eventually into Gideon's office. The door was locked, but Lazarus made quick work of it, popping the lock open with a tool he kept on his keychain for jobs like this.

The office was large, with a heavy mahogany desk and a black leather chair. A massive painting of Gideon adorned the wall, arms crossed with an American flag and the Constitution in the background, an eagle flying above him. Lazarus smirked to himself.

He began searching through the desk, though he wasn't exactly sure what he was looking for.

Papers, notebooks, pens—nothing out of the ordinary. Most of the drawers were empty. If Gideon was hiding something, it wasn't going to be out in the open. There was no safe that he could see, but Lazarus wasn't surprised. A guy like Gideon would probably keep anything important in a safety deposit box, maybe under a different name.

Lazarus moved to the bedroom next. It was decadent, to say the least. The bed was massive, with red velvet sheets and a gold-plated frame. A mirror hung on the ceiling above the bed, and Lazarus grimaced as he opened the nightstand, finding a collection of sex toys inside.

There was nothing useful here. No evidence that Gideon was hiding something. But Lazarus had one more source to tap—Denver herself.

Locking the doors behind him, Lazarus reactivated the alarm and slipped back into the night, the faint hum of the desert wind the only sound around him.

70

By Wednesday, Piper had filled four legal pads with notes, breaking down the evidence in her apartment every night. The prosecution was proceeding exactly as she'd expected. The parade of witnesses didn't stop, each one adding another puzzle piece to the case, but nothing earth shattering had emerged.

Another gas station attendant was trembling as he recounted how Carlito had threatened to kill him. His voice cracked as he described the wild, desperate look in Carlito's eyes. Gideon Malloy's cross-examination was sharp, picking apart the timeline and suggesting that the witness's fear might have clouded his memory. But just when it seemed like he was getting the witness to bend to his narrative, he pulled back, letting some ambiguity linger. It was as if he was only willing to push the defense so far.

By the afternoon, a truck driver had taken the stand, his weathered face grim. He testified about seeing Denver at a rest stop near the Mexican border. He'd noticed how the male suspect—Carlito—hovered protectively around the vehicle, one hand always resting near his waistband.

Then came the most gut-wrenching testimony of the day—a woman who needed tissues before she even spoke. She had been the first person to find Brad's body. She described the scene in halting, broken sentences: the body of the teenage boy—the same age as her son—broken and lifeless, lying crumpled on the ground. Gideon was gentler with her, almost sympathetic in his cross, suggesting that the scene was chaotic and traumatic, leaving room for doubt about the clarity of her memory.

Brad's mother had to leave the courtroom.

By the time Judge Hayes called it a day, exhaustion was etched into everyone's faces. "I think we can stop for this evening. What do you think, gentlemen?" the judge asked.

James nodded, rising from his seat. "Good with us, Judge."

Gideon followed, his movements slow, as if deep in thought. "That should be fine."

The judge's gavel came down with a quiet authority. "Then court is adjourned until eight-thirty tomorrow morning."

Piper gathered her belongings, but as she made her way out of the courtroom, she wasn't headed home just yet.

———

It was past dinner time when Piper pulled up in front of the Bines's house. The sun had set, and the hot Nevada evening made her mouth dry. She chewed gum to keep herself from feeling parched as she made her way to the front door.

She raised her hand to knock, but the door swung open before she could. Amanda Bines stood in the doorway, a look of surprise quickly replaced by a warm smile.

"Oh my goodness," Amanda gasped, placing a hand on her chest. "You startled me! I'm so sorry."

"I'm the one who should be sorry," Piper said with a small smile. "Didn't mean to scare you."

"No, it's fine. I get startled easily these days."

"I was hoping to talk to Keri for a bit, if that's all right," Piper said.

Amanda hesitated before nodding. "Oh, of course. I was just about to head to the store. She had a couple of friends over earlier and seemed . . . lighter. She even laughed. First time since she's been home."

"That's a good sign," Piper said, her tone encouraging.

Amanda called into the house. "Keri! Piper's here to see you!"

"Okay," came Keri's voice from another room.

Amanda grabbed her purse. "Charlie should be home soon if I'm not back before you leave."

"Thank you."

Piper stepped into the living room, where Keri was curled up on a brown leather couch, the glow of the television reflecting in her tired eyes.

"Hey," Piper said, taking a seat on the far end of the couch.

"Hey," Keri mumbled, not looking away from the screen.

"What are you watching?" Piper asked.

"Some cooking show. It's stupid."

Piper nodded, letting the silence stretch for a moment. "What would you rather be watching?"

"I don't know. Something with action, I guess."

"You like excitement, huh?"

Keri's jaw tightened slightly. "Used to."

"Things feel different now?"

Keri shrugged, her fingers twisting the remote in her hands. "Everything's different."

Piper leaned back, her posture relaxed but her gaze intent. "I get it. I went through something last year that changed everything for me, too."

Keri finally turned her head, curiosity sparking in her tired eyes. "What happened?"

"It's a long story," Piper said softly. "But I remember feeling like I'd never be normal again. Like I was carrying this weight no one else could see."

"Did it go away?"

"Not really. It just . . . changed. I carry it differently now. Some days, it's barely there. Other days . . ."

"Other days it's all you can think about," Keri finished, her voice low.

Piper nodded. "Exactly."

Keri hesitated, then said, "I keep thinking about Brad."

"That's natural, Keri. You loved him."

Her shoulders shook, and Piper resisted the urge to reach out, letting Keri find her footing.

"I'm scared all the time," Keri said.

"Being scared doesn't make you weak," Piper said gently. "It makes you human."

Keri's eyes met Piper's. "Will you be there? At the trial tomorrow when I have to testify?"

"Every step of the way," Piper said. "You're not alone in this."

Keri let out a shaky breath, a flicker of relief crossing her face. For the first time since the trial began, her lips curved into a faint smile.

After a moment, Keri said, "I meant to tell you something I remembered. About when I was kidnapped."

Piper straightened slightly. "What is it?"

"I was waiting in the car one time, and Carlito took Brad into this gas station. Someone called Denver, and she talked to them for a minute. She mentioned something called *the Pit*."

"The Pit?" Piper asked.

"Yeah. I remember it because I asked her what it was and she told me to shut up." Keri's lips tightened, the memory clearly uncomfortable.

Piper's mind raced. *The Pit* had a ring to it she didn't like. Could be nothing. But just in case, she filed it away, her instincts telling her it mattered.

71

The next day, Piper arrived at court early, well before anyone else. The courtroom was quiet and she sat staring out the window, her eyes unfocused on the brick wall of the adjacent building. The sunlight that filtered through the glass felt tainted, polluted by the oppressive atmosphere of this section of the courthouse.

Gideon Malloy was the next to arrive. Piper glanced at his wrist, noticing a bright plastic Donald Duck watch.

"Why Donald Duck?" she asked, breaking the silence.

Gideon looked at his wrist and smiled faintly. "A gift from my nephew. It's uncomfortable and turns my wrist green, but it gives a certain impression that I like."

"Humble?"

"Yes, down to earth. I usually wear it for jury trials, but it's turned into a bit of a good luck charm."

A bailiff—an older man built like a bookshelf—gave them a brief nod before unlocking the courtroom doors. Piper knew she wouldn't get another moment like this, so she took a chance.

"I'm sure this is a violation of some ethical rule, but I'm going to ask anyway. What are you doing, Gideon? This isn't like the trials I've had with you before. Something's off."

Gideon looked like he was about to say something but hesitated. Instead, he offered, "It is what it is, my dear."

Half an hour later, the courtroom was packed. More media had shown up—two cameras, several beat reporters. Piper recognized a few, including Claude, who once again plopped himself into a seat beside her, behind the prosecution table.

Claude let out a short breath. "Got a favor to ask, Pipes."

"What? And don't call me Pipes."

"This case. It's hot. Two middle-class white kids kidnapped at their wedding and taken to Mexico to sell? It's the kind of stuff that freaks out middle-class America. They like to believe crime happens to other people, but when they see someone like their own kids on TV, something shifts. Something gets triggered."

"And you make more money selling books and getting clicks, right?"

"That's neither here nor there."

"What exactly are you asking, Claude?"

He spread his arms out on the bench. "I wanna talk to her. An interview."

"You can't be serious."

"I am."

"What would make you think I'd let you interview my underage client?"

"Because I pay."

"We'll pass. Thanks."

"I'm serious. I'll give her five grand. That's a lot of money for a kid. She could put it away for college."

"No."

"Ask her first."

"I don't have to ask her. I'm her guardian."

Claude leaned back, undeterred. "Fine. Ten grand. Final offer."

Before Piper could respond, James Porter entered the courtroom, followed closely by his assistant, Tami. James took one look at Claude and scowled.

"Claude, get the hell back to the audience seats," James said flatly.

Claude stood up, hands raised. "Man, no love on this side of the room."

The judge entered, and everyone stood. After taking his seat, Judge Hayes glanced at the attorneys. "Good morning, Counselors."

"Good morning, Your Honor," James and Gideon both replied.

"We are back on the record in the matter of Ms. Denver Hartley. Ms. Hartley, good morning."

Denver smiled softly.

"Mr. Porter," the judge continued, "my understanding is the victim in this case will be testifying today?"

"That's correct, Your Honor."

"And we have the victim's guardian here as well. Good morning, Ms. Danes."

"Morning, Your Honor," Piper replied.

"Any objections or comments before we proceed?"

"No, Judge."

"Excellent. Let's bring Ms. Bines out."

The courtroom door opened and Keri entered, flanked by her mother. Amanda took a seat in the audience, and Piper noticed Claude eyeing her. She hoped he wouldn't be stupid enough to approach Amanda for an interview.

Keri took the witness stand, looking small and out of place. A kid in a room not made for kids. James Porter approached the stand with a gentle but purposeful demeanor. Keri's small frame was tense, her eyes darting nervously around the courtroom.

"Please state your name for the record," James said, his tone calm.

"Keri Bines," she replied softly.

"Do you know the defendant in this case, Ms. Bines?"

"Yes."

"Who is she?"

Keri's voice wavered slightly. "She and her boyfriend kidnapped me."

James nodded. "Keri, I'd like to ask you some questions about the experience you went through. Let's start with the night of June fifth, the night of your wedding. Tell us what you remember."

Keri swallowed hard. "I was marrying Brad, and we decided to do it at a chapel near his house. His dad was friends with the owner, so we rented it. We set it for June because that was Brad's favorite month."

"And Brad is Bradley Lowe, correct? The deceased victim in this case?"

"Yes."

Keri stared ahead, dissociating as she spoke. "Her boyfriend, Carlito, crashed through the front doors in a big black car. He got out wearing a horrible mask . . . a skull. She wore the same thing."

"What happened after they crashed into the chapel?"

"The minister tried to talk to them, but Carlito pulled out a knife and cut his neck. The minister fell over." Keri swallowed again. "He was a nice man."

James nodded again but didn't dwell on the trauma. "What happened next?"

"They grabbed me and Brad and shoved us into the trunk of the car. We were in there for a long time."

"What was the first thing you remember after being taken?"

"I was crying, hitting the trunk. Brad took my hand and said it would be okay. I could tell he was scared but he was trying to stay strong for me. He was always thinking about me." Keri paused, her voice breaking.

James kept his voice calm. "What happened next?"

"They took us far away. We were locked in some basement or something, and then they put us in the car again one day and drove for hours. When we finally stopped, we were at a storage place. They tied us up with ropes." Keri's eyes flicked toward Denver, then quickly away. "Carlito brought us a bucket and some toilet paper, but she said we should just be left to shit ourselves."

James cleared his throat, clearly uncomfortable at a young girl using profanity. "How long were you tied up in the storage unit?"

"I think two days. But they moved us to another place. I don't know why."

"And Brad was with you the whole time?"

"Yes. He tried to distract me by playing games like I Spy." Keri gave a shaky laugh. "He was such an idiot."

There were no tissues on the stand, and Keri's eyes were welling up. Piper gestured subtly to James's second chair, who handed some tissues to the bailiff to bring over to Keri.

James asked Keri about the storage facility and the specifics of what she saw, but Piper could tell the girl was slipping in and out of dissociation. Her mind was pulling her away from the pain, protecting her.

Keri recounted the horrors at the motel, including watching Carlito calmly shoot a man. Piper felt a wave of anger and sadness as she listened. The casual way Carlito and Denver had treated these kids, planning to sell them like livestock, was unimaginable.

Finally, James asked, "Did Carlito ever sexually assault you, Keri?"

Keri shook her head. "No. I think he just wanted the money." She looked at Denver again. "But she didn't care if we died."

72

When Keri finished testifying, Gideon rose from his seat without prompting and made his way to the lectern with the quiet confidence of a man who had done this a thousand times. He didn't touch the lectern, didn't lay anything on it—just stood beside it, as if it were an anchor keeping him grounded but not needed.

"Ms. Bines," Gideon began, his voice deceptively soft, "that's quite a story you've told us. Terrifying. But I have to wonder how much of it is true."

"Objection," James muttered without even looking up.

"Overruled," the judge said quickly.

Gideon smiled, showing a lot of teeth. He had the room now. "Ms. Bines, you said my client wore a skull mask. But in your initial police statement, you described it as a ghost mask, like from the movie *Scream*."

"I'm pretty sure it was a skull."

"Pretty sure?" Gideon repeated. "You mean you don't remember? But you just gave us such vivid details. What else might you be misremembering?"

"Objection. Argumentative," James cut in, his voice sharper this time.

"Overruled. The witness may answer."

"I'm not lying," Keri said. "It happened just like I said."

Gideon let the silence hang for a beat longer than necessary, pacing slightly in front of the stand. "Because your story seems to change with each telling."

Keri straightened. "It was a skull mask. I'm sure it was a skull mask. My story didn't change. They look a lot alike."

Gideon gave a slow nod, as if he were humoring her. "Ms. Bines, let's talk about the night you claim you were taken. That was your wedding night, correct?"

Keri nodded. "Yes."

"And how old are you, Ms. Bines?"

"Fifteen."

"And in the state of Nevada, to be married at fifteen, you need a judge's approval, correct?"

"Yes."

"And you got Judge Hope Dawson's approval for your marriage?"

"Yes."

Gideon picked up a paper from the defense table and held it up. "I have here your wedding application. Your Honor, may I approach the witness?"

"You may," the judge responded.

Gideon walked over and laid the document in front of Keri. "What is this, Ms. Bines?"

Keri glanced down. "It's our application for a wedding license."

"And could you read the section that states the reason for a minor marriage?"

Keri didn't even look down. "It says I'm pregnant."

"But you're not pregnant, are you?"

"No."

"You never were, correct?"

Keri looked down at her hands. "No, I wasn't pregnant. We said that so we could get married."

"So, you lied on an official application?"

"Yes. It seemed like the best way."

Gideon let that sink in before he continued. "I'd like to bring up a little incident that happened at school. You were arrested for drugs at one point, is that right?"

"Not arrested," Keri said. "The school cop gave me a warning. It was a joint in my locker."

"Did you tell the officer right away that it was yours?"

Before Keri could answer, Piper stood up. "Your Honor, I don't see how this is relevant. Any reason they had for getting married has nothing to do with the kidnapping."

"It goes to the credibility of the witness, Your Honor," Gideon said.

"I agree, Ms. Danes," the judge said, looking directly at Piper. "The objection is noted. Though, as you are not a party, I will take judicial notice."

James shot a glare at Piper as though she had overstepped, but she didn't care. If he wasn't going to protect Keri, she would.

Gideon returned to Keri. "Did you ever see the person wearing the mask take it off at the chapel?"

"No," Keri said.

"So, you never saw their face?"

"I saw it later, when they got us out."

"Were they still wearing the masks?"

"No."

"So two people with masks put you in the trunk, and then you claim my client and Carlito Xibala got you out, correct?"

"Yes."

"But you never saw the people underneath the masks?"

Keri hesitated. "No." She shook her head, then glanced at Denver. "But I know her voice. When she took me from the chapel, she said, 'If you scream, I'll kill you in front of your family.' It was her voice. I know it. I know her voice real good."

"Let's talk about this trip to Mexico now, Ms. Bines," Gideon said.

The aggressive, relentless cross-examination continued to grind down on small, insignificant details. Keri's frustration grew, evident in the way her eyes darted back and forth, trying to keep her composure.

Gideon pounced on every hesitation.

"But you said earlier that it happened so fast you didn't see everything."

Keri's face was flushed now. "I . . . I remember . . ."

"Objection, badgering the witness," James finally said, rising to his feet.

"Sustained," the judge said, his irritation seeping through. "Mr. Malloy, knock it off."

For the first time, Gideon's relentless demeanor seemed to soften slightly.

Piper had to stand several more times throughout the remainder of the cross, mostly to remind Keri that she wasn't alone. Each time, James shot her a warning glance, but she didn't care.

After another hour of cross-examination, Gideon finally finished. He had tried to poke holes in Keri's memory, but it wasn't enough. She had held up well against his aggression.

When Gideon sat down, James rose for a redirect. His strategy was clear: rehabilitate Keri's testimony, cover every point Gideon had attacked and reinforce the consistency of her story.

Gideon seemed uninterested now, sitting back calmly at the defense table next to Denver. He didn't even appear to be listening. Denver, on the other hand, wasn't moving. She stared at Keri with unsettling calm, her hands folded neatly in front of her on the table.

After about twenty minutes, James wrapped up his redirect. "Ms. Bines, are you absolutely certain that the defendant in this case, Denver Hartley, the woman sitting right there, is the one who kidnapped you, threatened to kill you, and attempted to smuggle you across the border to Mexico?"

Keri didn't hesitate. Her voice was clear, unwavering. "Yes. It was her. I'm sure."

A small, almost imperceptible grin touched Denver's lips.

73

It was dark when Lazarus glanced at the clock on his dash and realized he'd been parked in front of the Bines's house for three hours. The quiet suburban street was still as glass.

This was Americana at its most polished: manicured lawns, porch lights casting warm halos, and the faint scent of watered grass. He imagined holidays, birthday surprises, and family trips—things as alien to him as the surface of Mars. Lazarus had always felt like an outsider. It had taken years of pain to understand that everyone else was, too.

His phone buzzed. Piper.

"What are you still doing up?" Lazarus asked, leaning back in his seat.

"Couldn't sleep. You ever heard of something called *the Pit*?"

"No. Should I have?"

"Keri remembered hearing Denver mention it in a phone call. I think it could be tied to trafficking."

Before Lazarus could respond, his eyes caught movement down the street—a lone figure, hands buried in the pockets of a hoodie, moving under alternating pools of light and shadow. Something about the walk felt wrong. Too casual, too measured.

"Lemme call you back," he muttered, already hanging up.

The figure drew closer, sneakers crunching on stray gravel. Lazarus's hand hovered near his sidearm, his breathing shallow. The man passed

Amanda's house, continuing down the sidewalk without a glance. Lazarus exhaled, tension momentarily easing.

Still, his instincts screamed. Something wasn't right.

He would call a unit to watch the house; there was no point in him sitting here all night. There were bigger things to worry about, like Deadeye vanishing after being granted bail. Lazarus had followed the court proceedings, watching in disbelief as the fumbling prosecutor all but handed the judge an excuse to let the man walk. Now Deadeye was in the wind, and Lazarus's contacts hadn't heard a whisper.

The figure stopped.

Lazarus froze, watching as the man turned, his hooded head tilting toward Amanda's house.

"Now what are you doin', partner?" Lazarus muttered to himself.

The man darted toward the fence, vaulting it in one smooth motion.

"Shit."

Lazarus bolted from the car and sprinted up the street. He reached the fence, leapt over without hesitation, and landed hard in the backyard. He drew his weapon and held it low as he scanned the yard.

Wide, grassy, with playground equipment rusting under the faint glow of a porch light. The patio had wicker furniture, and sliding glass doors led into the kitchen.

No one was there.

Lazarus checked the sliding doors and windows, keeping his movements quiet. It didn't make sense. There wasn't enough time for the man to get out of sight. Six seconds at most had passed from when he jumped the fence to when Lazarus landed.

He stood still, closing his eyes and listening.

Traffic hummed in the distance. A plane droned overhead. Laughter drifted faintly from a nearby house.

The sound of a door sliding open behind him made him whirl. Amanda stood there, wrapped in a robe, her eyes wide with confusion.

"Lazarus?"

He quickly tucked his weapon behind him. "Sorry. Didn't mean to wake you."

"What's going on?"

"I thought I saw something."

"In my backyard?"

"Yeah." He hesitated. "I've been watching your house. Just for now, until I can get a detail out here."

"Do you want to come inside?"

"No, no," he said, shaking his head. "I've got some things to catch up on. Go on back to bed."

Amanda nodded slowly and slid the door closed. Lazarus walked around the house, scanning the yard one last time. He couldn't shake the image of the figure—fluid, deliberate, lifelike.

The chill crawling up his spine wasn't just from the possibility of danger.

He'd seen things before. Shadows, movements in the corner of his vision. But those were dreams. What if this wasn't?

A fear buried deep in his psyche clawed its way to the surface: the fear of losing his mind and not knowing it. Something that had haunted him since childhood.

He called his assistant and asked for a protective detail at the Bines's home.

As he hung up, he cast one last look over the yard, the shadows playing tricks on his eyes. He wasn't ready to admit what scared him most—that what he'd seen might not have been real.

74

For Piper, the days in court were a blur of witnesses. Most of their testimony rehashed what had already been covered: forensic techs, firearms experts, the medical examiner's team, EMTs, and paramedics who were the first responders at the scenes. Bystanders added a few more details, but none that changed the trajectory of the case. It felt like an endless parade, and by Friday evening, everyone was exhausted.

The Pit gnawed at Piper's focus. Lazarus's Vice contacts confirmed it was worse than she'd thought—a digital cesspool, invisible unless you knew the way in. Guns and drugs were just the start; ads peddled kidnappings, hits, burglaries and worse. She'd barely dug in but it already reeked of despair. If Carlito and Denver were hired, the Pit was a likely source.

As the day wound down, James stood and addressed the judge. "Your Honor, under Rule 1182, we'd like to submit these affidavits from eleven witnesses in lieu of their testimony."

The judge didn't bother hiding his fatigue. "Any objections?"

Gideon didn't even look up. "No, Judge."

"Then have my clerk mark them. Let's go ahead and take a break for today. I'll review the affidavits in chambers over the weekend. Thank you all."

The judge banged the gavel, signaling the end of the day. James groaned as he stretched his back, while Piper gathered her things. She glanced at Gideon, who looked as fresh as he had at the start of the trial.

He sat at the defense table until the bailiff arrived to escort Denver back to her holding cell. He didn't seem the least bit tired.

"How many more witnesses do you have?" Piper asked James.

"I'm going to review everything tonight and decide if we need anyone else. At this point, it's getting redundant."

"So you're going to rest on Monday?"

"Possibly."

Piper looked over at Gideon again. "Is he going to let her testify?"

James shook his head. "I don't think I've ever seen Gideon let one of his clients testify."

The doors to the courtroom creaked open, and Lazarus stepped in. Piper grabbed her satchel and followed him out into the hallway.

"How's it going in there?" he asked as they walked down the hall.

"We'll probably wrap the prosecution's case on Monday. What have you been up to?"

Lazarus exchanged a glance with James, who had just exited the courtroom and was heading toward the elevators. "Runnin' down a few things. How's it looking?"

"There's no way she's going to be acquitted. Gideon must have something planned for an appeal. There's something we've missed."

Gideon approached them, nodding to Lazarus. "Detective."

"Gideon."

"I have a request of sorts. Ms. Hartley would like to speak with you at the jail tonight."

"Why?"

"She says she wants to speak with you alone. I advised her against it, of course, but she insisted. I think it's a terrible idea, but she asked me to extend the invitation."

Lazarus hesitated before nodding. "I'll go tonight."

"Thank you." Gideon gave a slight nod and walked toward the elevator.

Piper turned to Lazarus, her voice hushed. "Letting her talk to you without him there is malpractice."

"I know," Lazarus said, watching Gideon as the elevator doors closed. "Maybe that's his play—do a bad job, then have another attorney appeal the case."

———

Later that night, Lazarus sat alone at the Last Chance Saloon, a glass of absinthe glowing faintly in front of him. The dim light above the table cast a greenish hue over his hands as he swirled the liquid, watching it catch the light. Bass wasn't working tonight—it was his son's birthday. His son, who had been killed years ago with a hammer.

No suspects. No arrests. Lazarus had obsessed over the case for months, searching for meaning. But some things didn't come with reasons. They just *were*.

He drained his glass, left a bill on the table, and headed for the jail.

The facility was quiet when he arrived, the kind of silence that pressed down thick and heavy. Visiting hours were over, but Gideon's paperwork had already cleared the way. After a brief back-and-forth with the guards, Lazarus was led to one of the attorney-client rooms.

Inside, the hum of the air conditioner filled the cold, sterile space. The table and benches, bolted to the concrete floor, felt more like an interrogation room than a meeting space. Lazarus sat down and took a hit of his vape, his thoughts steady as he waited.

Denver entered, flanked by a female guard. Even in her orange jumpsuit, with no makeup and her hair pulled back, she looked like a force of nature—like a beautiful storm about to break.

She took her seat across from him.

Lazarus held out his vape pen for her. She took it and inhaled deeply, her movements deliberate and unhurried.

"You wanted to see me?" Lazarus said, breaking the silence.

She leaned forward, vapor curling from her lips. "I want you to know," she said. "It's not fun when you don't know."

"And what is it I don't know?"

"That I'm going to take what you love. That's the only way the universe has balance."

Lazarus studied her. "You're talking about Keri," he said. "Why? She's not the one who pulled the trigger."

"She's the one you care about," Denver said.

"I don't even know her."

She grinned. "And you'll never get to."

Lazarus leaned back, exhaling a plume of vapor. "It's charming you think you're the first person to sit there and threaten me. But I got news for you, lady—you ain't original. Pain is old hat to me."

"Not this kind of pain," she said, her eyes narrowing. "I'm going to hurt your soul."

He tilted his head, studying her as if seeing her for the first time. "You talk like this is personal. But Carlito wasn't your family, was he? Lover, yeah, but not family. I thought you two were more . . . business."

"You don't know shit about me."

He let out another plume of vapor. "This right here—this rage, the need to burn it all down—it don't come from nowhere. What happened to you? Before Carlito?"

For a moment, she didn't respond.

Then she leaned closer, her voice dropping to a whisper. "Sleep tight," she said, blowing him a kiss before knocking on the door for the guard.

Lazarus sat there as the door clanged shut behind her. The vapor hung heavy in the room, but he didn't move. He took one last drag, staring at the spot where she'd sat, his mind working through her words.

75

James approached the lectern, pausing to take a sip of water from a plastic cup. He straightened his tie, his gaze steady as he looked toward the judge.

"Your Honor, over the course of this trial, we've presented not just evidence, but a narrative of unthinkable cruelty and loss." His voice was measured but firm, filling the quiet courtroom. "The facts before you paint a clear picture of the defendant's guilt, but I ask you to consider the human cost behind those facts."

A faint rustle came from the gallery as someone shifted in their seat. Keri sat beside Amanda, her hands clasped tightly in her lap. Amanda placed a reassuring hand over hers, but Keri's gaze stayed fixed on James.

"Keri Bines and Brad Lowe had their lives irrevocably altered," James continued. "One life ended, another forever scarred. We've heard Keri's testimony and seen her struggle with the trauma inflicted upon her. Yes, her story may have inconsistencies, but isn't that to be expected from someone so young, put through such a nightmare?"

He stepped forward slightly, his tone softening. "The defense has tried to discredit Keri, to paint her as unreliable. But I ask you to consider the courage it took for her to sit in this courtroom, to face her tormentor and to relive the worst moments of her young life. That's not the action of someone spinning tales. It's the painful honesty of a survivor seeking justice."

James glanced at Denver, who sat at the defense table, her expression calm and unreadable. Gideon Malloy leaned back in his chair, fingers steepled in front of him, watching James with an almost predatory focus.

"Mr. Malloy wants you to believe that this was a case of battered spouse syndrome, that Ms. Hartley had no choice, no agency. But let's not forget: She wasn't a helpless victim. She was a willing partner. This wasn't a woman acting under duress. It was a woman making choices—choices that led to armed robbery, kidnapping, and, ultimately, death."

James placed his hands on the lectern, leaning in slightly. "Ms. Hartley had opportunities to escape, to seek help, but instead, she chose the gun, the getaway car, and a path of violence. The facts show us a criminal duo, not a victim and her abuser. Justice requires that we hold them both accountable for their decisions."

James straightened. "So, I ask you to consider not just the letter of the law, but its spirit—to protect, to serve, to bring justice to those who cannot defend themselves. Find the defendant guilty, Your Honor, because she is guilty."

He stepped back, smoothing his jacket as he returned to his seat.

The judge nodded. "Thank you, Mr. Porter. Mr. Malloy? Any closing statements?"

Gideon rose slowly, adjusting his tie with meticulous precision. His movements were deliberate, almost theatrical. He approached the lectern, his expression one of quiet confidence.

"Your Honor," he began, his voice soft but commanding, "we have heard a tragic story in this courtroom. A story of youth cut short, of trauma and pain. No one can deny the suffering Keri Bines has endured. But it is not the role of this court to heal wounds or soothe pain. It is to determine truth and dispense justice based on facts, not emotions."

The room was eerily still. Even the distant hum of the air-conditioning seemed to fade.

"The prosecution has painted my client, Denver Hartley, as a monster," Malloy continued, pacing slightly. "But I ask you to look beyond the inflammatory rhetoric and consider the glaring holes in their case. We have a traumatized teenager whose story has changed multiple times. We have physical evidence that doesn't match her testimony. We have timelines that don't quite add up. And we have a woman—Denver Hartley—who was herself a victim of Carlito Xibala, a man whose viciousness was evident to everyone who encountered him."

Denver sat motionless, her hands folded neatly in her lap.

"Yes, Keri Bines has suffered," Malloy said, his tone softening. "But does her suffering give us the right to condemn a woman who was bullied into actions she didn't want to perform? Does trauma justify overlooking the inconsistencies, the lack of corroborating evidence, and the reasonable doubt that saturates this case?"

Amanda shifted in her seat, her grip on Keri's hand tightening.

"Your Honor," Malloy said, his voice dropping, almost intimate now, "it would be easy to succumb to emotion. To let righteous anger at the fate of these young people cloud our judgment. But that is not justice. That is vengeance. And vengeance has no place in this courtroom."

He paused, letting the words hang in the air before continuing. "I implore you to look at the facts. To consider the evidence—or rather, the lack thereof. Where is the proof that my client acted of her own free will? Where is the proof that she wasn't just as much a victim of Carlito Xibala as anyone else? What evidence have they provided that shows, beyond a reasonable doubt, that Ms. Hartley wasn't terrified for her life?"

Malloy turned slightly, gesturing toward the gallery. "The burden of proof lies with the prosecution, and they have failed to meet it. They've given us a story, but they've not given us proof. And proof is what justice demands."

His gaze shifted back to the judge. "Eventually, Carlito Xibala would have killed Denver, just as he killed Brad Lowe. Ms. Hartley was trying to survive, not thrive. Don't take away her freedom based on speculation. Ms. Hartley is a victim herself, Your Honor, and I urge you to find her not guilty of these absurd charges."

Malloy returned to his seat with measured steps, the faintest trace of a smile on his lips as he sat down.

The judge nodded once. "Thank you, Mr. Malloy. If there is nothing further, I will take all of this under advisement and have a verdict for you tomorrow morning. Court is adjourned until then."

76

Lazarus saw things older than time. The sky bled crimson, and the earth split open, swallowing everything—innocent and guilty. Sunlight, burning bright and angry, peeled the skin off screaming bodies, their bones left in the wind before shattering to dust. He was always an observer, never a participant, trapped in these visions that tore through his mind like some fever. He drifted, powerless to change a thing.

The familiar weight of sleep paralysis clung to him as the nightmare faded and his room came into focus. He could wiggle his fingers. Movement returned, and he forced himself to sit up. The night terrors never got easier. No amount of experience toughened him against these kinds of wounds.

Drenched in sweat, he peeled off his shirt and checked the clock. Five a.m. Too early for most but not for him. The courthouse wouldn't open until eight, but he didn't mind. He liked sitting in the parking lot, watching the sun claw its way over the horizon. There was peace in waiting.

Showered and dressed, a white shirt and red tie hanging off his frame, Lazarus headed out. As he locked his door, Isaac's mother emerged from the apartment across the hall. He'd only seen her a handful of times—she was a skittish woman, quick to dart away, like a mouse afraid of being crushed.

She hesitated, wringing her hands. "Um . . . you're a cop, right?"

He turned to face her. "I am."

"Can I ask you something?"

"Sure."

She swallowed hard, avoiding his gaze. "If they put a drug charge on you, can they take your kids away?"

"Depends. What kind of drug charge?"

"Oxy," she said. "I had surgery and got hooked. They pulled me over with my son in the car. My public defender says the judge could take him."

"It's possible. If the judge thinks you're a danger to the kid, they can place him in state custody."

Her eyes dropped to the floor. "Okay, thanks." She scurried off, got into her car, and drove away.

Lazarus watched her disappear. Everyone had their battles, even if no one else saw them. He tried to remember that. Tried to keep his humanity intact, even when it felt like the world was doing everything it could to tear it away.

He got to the courthouse early, as usual. Bluegrass played softly through his car's speakers as he vaped, the scent of leather filling the space. He rolled down the window slightly, letting in the cool morning air. A minivan pulled into the lot, and a group of Mormon polygamists filed out. Lazarus recognized them—there was a small sect that lived nearby. Their homemade dresses, hair pinned in styles from another century, made them impossible to miss.

They reminded him of his own childhood. Growing up in the deserts of Utah with a survivalist polygamist sect, waiting for the collapse of the world. At night he used to imagine it—the buildings crumbling, blood running in the streets, the earth reclaiming everything. He never feared it. Even as a kid, he understood extinction was the rule, survival the exception.

The courthouse opened, and Lazarus headed inside. He flashed his badge to the new bailiff—who was eager to prove himself—and took

The Night Collector

his usual spot by the windows in the hallway outside the courtroom, watching the sun creep over the mountains.

"Some people find the scenery ugly." Gideon's voice came from behind. "I've always found it beautiful. Empty. Like another planet."

Lazarus didn't turn. "I grew up in deserts. Don't know how to live any other way."

Gideon stood beside him, adjusting his cuffs. "You lived in New Orleans for a time, didn't you?"

"Yeah. That's where I learned how to be police."

"I started as a public defender in LA," Gideon said, almost wistfully. "Thankless, grinding work. But nothing shapes you like difficulty."

Lazarus turned to him. "Why so chatty today, Gideon?"

Gideon smiled, the picture of relaxation. "It's a good day. The trial's over, and I'm flying to Jamaica tonight. Can't imagine a better reason to be in a good mood."

Lazarus said nothing. Instead, he watched as Amanda and Keri Bines emerged from the elevator. They moved through the building like they were made of glass, fragile and barely holding it together. Reporters and media were already coming in behind them, buzzing like flies.

Lazarus let them pass, staying by the windows as the courtroom filled up. He eventually followed, leaning against the back wall, watching. Keri and Amanda sat near the middle, Molly and Justin Lowe behind them. Molly looked broken. The weight of her son's death had crushed her.

The judge came out, his face a mask of professionalism.

"Morning, everyone. We have a packed courtroom today, but please make room for court staff . . . Thank you. We are on the record in the matter of Denver Rose Hartley. Counselors, any issues before we proceed?"

James rose first. "One matter, Judge. Mr. Malloy will likely file a notice of appeal today and ask that Ms. Hartley be released pending that appeal. We'd like to address that."

"We're not there yet, Counselor. We'll discuss it when the time is right. Ms. Hartley, please rise."

Gideon and Denver stood. James shot them a glance, his chest puffed out like a man who knew he had already won. Lazarus scanned the room. The seasoned veterans—the bailiffs, reporters, clerks—were calm. They knew how these things went. But the newcomers—Keri, Amanda, the Lowes—looked terrified.

"I have reached a verdict," the judge began, his voice steady. "As to count one, kidnapping in the first degree, I find the State has not met its burden beyond a reasonable doubt. The defendant is found not guilty."

The room should have exploded, but the shock held everyone still.

Keri began to cry, her sobs muffled against Amanda's chest. Molly Lowe, her face twisted in anguish, clapped her hand over her mouth to stifle a scream. Her husband sat in silence, frozen in disbelief. Piper's mouth hung open, and her thoughts struggled to catch up.

Lazarus glanced at Gideon. He didn't react. Just sat there, fingers steepled, the picture of calm.

The judge continued. Count after count. *Not guilty. Not guilty. Not guilty.* When it was over, the only conviction was for reckless driving, and that carried no jail time.

James stood, his face pale with fury. "Your Honor, we ask for a judgment notwithstanding the verdict."

The judge gave him a weary look. "That's only for jury trials, Mr. Porter. You're asking me to reverse my own ruling."

"We are."

"Why would I do that?"

"Because you're wrong."

Lazarus watched the judge's face twitch with anger, but beneath it, there was something worse—shame.

"Counselors, approach."

Gideon, James, and Piper went to the bench. The judge hit a button, sending static through the speakers, but Lazarus could still make out some of James's words—*appeal, bullshit, judicial complaint, jackass, abuse of discretion.* Gideon said nothing, letting James rant.

When they returned to their seats, the judge sighed. "Thank you for your time. Ms. Hartley, you are free to go. Court is adjourned."

77

Piper remained seated as the courtroom emptied, unsure what had just happened. A gnawing in her gut had told her something was wrong—she had known Gideon was holding something back; but she had assumed it was a technicality or a loophole for appeal. She hadn't expected . . . this.

Claude sidled up to her, his voice casual but cutting. "How about that interview now?"

She brushed past him. In the hallway, Amanda was clutching Keri, both of them sobbing. Lazarus was guiding them through the throng of cameras and reporters. Piper trailed behind, her mind too foggy to process much.

They descended the staff stairwell quickly, silently. Lazarus led them to the parking lot, and the moment they stepped outside, Amanda stopped.

"What just happened?" Amanda's voice was shaky, disbelief cracking through.

Piper exhaled slowly, choosing her words with care. "It means . . . she's free to go."

"So it's done? Just like that?"

"I'm afraid so."

Keri, her voice thin and trembling, asked, "So she can just show up at my house now?"

"No," Piper said quickly. "I'll file a protective order. I'll make sure she's not allowed near you."

"Like you said she'd be in prison for the rest of her life?"

Piper couldn't answer. She had no explanation, no reassurance that would make this better.

Lazarus looked toward the courthouse entrance, where more cameras were spilling out. "We need to leave."

Together, they walked Amanda and Keri to their car. Piper wanted to say something comforting, something to dull the pain, but the words wouldn't come.

Amanda drove off, a ghost of herself. Keri's tear-streaked face lingered in the rearview mirror as they disappeared.

Lazarus paced, hands on his hips, his frustration crackling like electricity. "What the hell was that?"

"I don't know," Piper said, shaking her head. "I've never seen anything like it."

"Me neither." Lazarus's tone darkened, and he started walking back toward the courthouse.

Piper followed, trying to reason with him. "Think about what you're doing."

But Lazarus was already pushing through. The clerk behind the desk protested as they neared the door. "Excuse me, you can't—"

Too late. Lazarus burst through the door.

Judge Hayes looked up from his desk, irritated. "This better not be what I think it is."

The clerk appeared behind them, flushed. "Judge, I tried to stop them—"

"It's fine, Darci. I'll handle it." Hayes waved her off, his eyes fixed on Lazarus.

The door closed, leaving them alone with the judge.

The Night Collector

"You have something to say, Detective?" Judge Hayes's voice was calm, but there was an edge there, something dangerous.

Piper stepped in quickly, positioning herself between Lazarus and the judge. "We just wanted clarification, Your Honor. You can understand how this verdict would affect the victims and their families. They deserve to know why."

"I don't have to explain anything beyond what I already did."

"Of course," Piper said, keeping her voice measured. "I'm just hoping for something to take back to them. Something they can try to understand."

The judge removed his glasses and placed them on his desk. "Tell them whatever you feel is the truth."

Lazarus said, "I don't think 'The judge has his head up his ass' will make them feel better."

Piper felt her stomach drop. *Damn it, Lazarus.*

Judge Hayes rose from his chair, his calm demeanor dissolving into anger. "You think you can come into my chambers and accuse me of—"

Lazarus cut him off. "I'm not accusing you of anything, Judge. I'm telling you. You're either corrupt or you're too stupid to realize how wrong you are."

The judge's face flushed with fury. "You have the audacity—"

"Maybe we can—" Piper tried to defuse the situation, but it was too late.

"You come in here and think you can stand in the chambers of a—"

Piper stepped in again. "We just wanted clarification, Judge. That's all. If you're not willing to provide it, we'll leave."

The judge took a breath, pressing his thumb and forefinger to the bridge of his nose as though trying to stave off a headache. He sat back down, exhaling slowly. The moment of anger passed, though his patience was clearly thin.

"Based on the evidence," he began, his voice measured again, "it was clear that Ms. Hartley was more a victim than a participant in the kidnappings. The signs of battered spouse syndrome were compelling, and the prosecution failed to prove willful intent on her part. Therefore, I found her not guilty. Now leave."

"That's bullshit and you know it," Lazarus said.

"That was the evidence presented," he countered, his face impassive.

"The only evidence presented was from the prosecution. Gideon barely did anything. I've never seen a verdict so—"

"Choose your next words carefully, Detective." The judge's tone was ice.

Lazarus held his gaze, unflinching.

Piper grabbed Lazarus's arm gently. "Thank you for your time, Judge," she said and pulled Lazarus toward the door.

Once they were back in the hallway, the clerk glared daggers at them as they passed. Lazarus's pacing resumed the moment they were out of sight, his anger bubbling over. Piper knew this side of him—when Lazarus truly lost his temper, the energy that radiated off him was raw, uncontrolled.

"Lazarus, we need to leave."

"That was on purpose," he said, his eyes dark.

"What do you mean?"

"That decision. You can't make a ruling like that and think it's just. Question is who's pulling the strings."

"Don't mistake stupidity for malice. A hotheaded Metro detective told me that once."

"Yeah, well, that was before I watched a judge throw all common sense out the window."

"Well, maybe it's not for no reason."

Lazarus stopped pacing and stared at her. "Right."

"I'm going to Amanda's house to check on Keri," Piper said. "You should come with me."

Lazarus shook his head, turning away. "No. You go. I'll catch up later."

78

Riley eased into Lazarus's car with a groan, the crackle of his knees loud. Lazarus pulled out of the apartment complex and headed back toward Metro PD headquarters, the soft hum of the music filling the space between them. Riley, staring out the window, hadn't said a word since they'd left.

"You don't need me for this," Riley finally muttered.

Lazarus glanced over. "I talked to Williams. They're marking you on indefinite leave. That way, you don't have to go through the hiring process again when you're ready."

Riley sat quietly for a moment, then said, "Thanks."

When they arrived at the station, it was late. A few uniforms stood by their patrol cars, chatting. One of them recognized Riley, tried to engage him in small talk, but Riley ignored them. His heavily bearded face passive.

"You shouldn't grow a beard," Lazarus remarked as they entered the building. "It's almost too manly."

Riley smirked, a fleeting expression. "It's just laziness." The two exchanged a glance, and then Riley added quietly, "I won't always be like this."

"I know," Lazarus replied, though what he really thought was, *I hope to hell that's true.*

They entered the CIU offices, Lazarus swiping his keycard to unlock the door. The room felt more modern than the rest of the station, outfitted with new Macs and devoid of the usual clutter. No greasy takeout containers, no stale coffee cups—none of the usual grime that came with long shifts at police desks.

Lazarus sat down at his sleek glass-and-steel desk. He liked that it felt cold, hard—a war room, not some cozy office.

"You sure about this?" Riley asked, leaning on the desk, which creaked under his weight.

"You not?"

"You find anything, it's not admissible," Riley reminded him.

"I don't need it to be. I just need to know what's there."

"And if there's nothing?"

"No harm, no foul."

Riley sighed, the kind that carried the weight of years of experience. "If they find out, you'll lose your badge. They'll probably charge you."

"If you want out, I understand."

Riley shook his head, grumbling. "Sucks having friends."

Lazarus grinned, punched a few keys on his keyboard, and waited.

———

An hour later, the warrant came through, complete with a forged signature from a federal judge. Judge Patrice Clemens. It was shockingly easy to pull off, a reminder of just how dangerous the power behind a badge could be.

Lazarus filed the warrant electronically with the phone company, giving him access to Judge Hayes's private cell phone records, office lines, and emails.

"I can't believe how easy that was," Lazarus said, leaning back in his chair.

"That should tell you something," Riley said. "No way they don't bust you at some point."

"At some point. But who the hell knows if I'll even be alive by then. Life's nothing if not unpredictable."

"Remember that when you're working at a car wash."

"You think if I lost my badge, all I could do is work at a car wash?"

"What else can you do?"

Lazarus grinned, scanning his screen as the records and emails downloaded. "I can hunt, fish, build, track. Give me a piece of land, and I wouldn't need people anymore."

"Then why don't you do that now?"

The download completed, showing all the incoming and outgoing calls, voicemails, and texts from Judge Hayes's phone. Lazarus could already picture the judge's face if he ever found out about this. Riley was right—he probably would find out. Which meant Lazarus had to uncover something worth the risk. Something embarrassing enough to make the judge back down if he ever got wind of this.

As the software churned through the data, linking phone numbers to names, addresses, and employment, Lazarus began sifting through the details, flipping quickly through the information.

Riley sat nearby, silent, until the quiet stretched too long. "Find anything?"

Lazarus didn't look up from the screen. "Mostly calls to his wife and kids . . . but this is interesting."

"What's that?" Riley leaned in.

Lazarus pointed at the screen. "Look at the phone's location when he received this call. Recognize that address?"

"Where is it?"

Lazarus stood up, grabbed his keys off the desk, and headed for the door. "Somewhere it shouldn't be."

79

Lazarus killed the engine outside Judge Hope Dawson's cliffside mansion, the weight of the night pressing on his chest. The thick file on Denver Hartley lay open on the passenger seat, her juvenile records. Every case, without fail: "Judge Hope Dawson presiding." Every disposition a gentle slap on the wrist, a nudge down a path of escalating violence.

This wasn't a judge being lenient. This was grooming.

What are you playing at, Hope?

He stepped out into the warm night air.

The chime of the doorbell echoed through the house, a sound swallowed by the vast silence of the cliffside. The door swung open, and there was Judge Dawson—tousled hair, silk robe barely tied at the waist, and a wineglass held like an accessory. Her eyes, sharp and calculating, showed no surprise. She had been expecting him.

"Detective Holloway," she purred, raising her glass in mock welcome. "To what do I owe this late-night pleasure?"

"We need to talk," Lazarus said.

"Of course," she said, stepping aside. "Come in."

He followed her into the circular living room, where desert tones blended with the cold steel of modern design. The sprawling neon lights of Las Vegas shimmered in the distance like a mirage. Lazarus's gaze wandered to the balcony—the same balcony where Dawson's ex-husband had taken his fatal fall. The whispers about his death had never gone away, but Hope had come out clean, as always.

"Celebrating something?" he asked, taking the beer she handed him without asking.

"My divorce anniversary," she said with a dry chuckle, clinking her glass against his bottle. "To freedom, Lazarus."

He took a long sip, eyes narrowing. "Funny thing about freedom. It can disappear in a blink."

Her gaze flickered, just a second of something darker behind the practiced smile. "True," she said, settling herself on the couch. "But I doubt that's why you're here. So, why don't you tell me what's really on your mind?"

Lazarus set the bottle down on the table between them. "Hayes came by here the day after he got Denver's case. Seems like an odd coincidence, don't you think?"

Dawson's expression remained still, unreadable. "Judges meet socially all the time, Lazarus."

"Sure. Except this wasn't a social visit. We both know Hayes threw the case because you've got something on him. The real question is why you'd risk it for a street kid like Denver."

Dawson's lips curled into a slow, deliberate smile. She stood and moved toward the balcony, her silhouette framed against the electric hum of the city. "You give me too much credit," she said, her voice soft.

Lazarus stepped closer, eyes locked on her. "I read the files, Hope. Every time she got into trouble, you were there. You let her walk, over and over again. You've been grooming her for years. Why?"

She didn't answer right away. Instead, she took a slow sip of her wine, letting the silence stretch. "You know what I see when I look out at this city?" she finally said. "Rot. We're being led by the weakest, the most easily corrupted among us. Power doesn't corrupt; it just reveals who's been corrupt all along."

"And brainwashing a kid to be your tool since she was nine makes you the cure?"

Dawson turned to face him, the city lights casting an eerie glow on her features. "This isn't about Denver," she said, her voice turning cold. "This is about survival. My brothers are trying to take everything from me—my father's empire, my reputation. If they win, this city will rot faster than it already is."

"Using a kid makes you no better than them."

A flicker of anger crossed her face, but she quickly masked it.

"Keri's mother," Lazarus said, "you're close with her. You keeping tabs on me, Hope?"

Judge Dawson's smile faltered, just for a moment. "You're a precision tool, Lazarus. Just like Denver. You've always been useful when I needed you to be."

"Why did you convince her to kidnap my daughter?" Lazarus stepped closer, his voice rising. "What do you get, Hope?"

Dawson's eyes glittered dangerously in the moonlight. "Justice, Lazarus. Real justice. Not that watered-down version you cling to. Denver, Carlito, my brothers—they're all just symptoms of a disease, and I'm the only one willing to do what's necessary to cure it."

"You don't get to decide who lives and dies."

"I already have."

"You have no idea what you've done," he said, his voice tight. "I'll take you down for this."

She stepped closer, her voice low. "Do you ever think about Owen Whittaker?" she asked, the name freezing Lazarus in place.

"What?"

Her gaze sharpened, locking onto his. "I've been mulling over the thought of petitioning the courts to reconsider that case—especially the nature of his death. Such a pity, isn't it, that only the two of you were present? Convenient, really. There's no evidence left to *prove* you murdered him unjustifiably. But imagine if that case were brought back to light . . . if every moment leading up to his final breath were reexamined in detail. What do you suppose we might uncover?"

The words hit Lazarus like a blow to the gut. Memories he'd buried, compromises he'd made—Dawson had always known exactly how to pull his strings.

"We're alike," she said. "We both want justice. We're both willing to go as far as necessary to get it."

Lazarus felt the weight of every secret, every dark corner of his past. He stared out at the city below.

"Why my daughter?" he asked. "What does this have to do with me?"

Dawson leaned back, her gaze distant, a faint smile curling her lips. "Have you ever considered that some lives are meant to orbit others? Like planets, pulled into place by invisible forces. I just give that force a name." She paused, her voice lowering to a near whisper. "And I always know where my stars are."

Lazarus's eyes darkened. "I'm going to bring you down for this," he said, his tone flat, dangerous.

Dawson's smile returned. "Then I guess I'll see you in prison. How many men have you put away over the years, Detective? Think they'll give you a warm welcome?"

She tossed back the rest of her wine and turned toward the house. "Go home, Lazarus," she said, her voice fading as she walked away. "Before you do something you can't take back."

Lazarus stood alone on the balcony, the city sprawling beneath him like a distant nightmare. He'd known she was dangerous. But now he realized she was something worse.

80

Riley sat sweating in his truck, the desert heat lingering even in the dead of night. The air inside was stifling, but he barely noticed. His eyes were fixed on the house three doors down, across the quiet street. The moon hung as a silver crescent in the sky and offered little light. Streetlamps dotted the road, but they did little to cut through the shadows that gathered around Denver's mother's house.

She had picked Denver up from jail earlier that day, and Riley had followed them ever since. Twenty years on the force had shown him all kinds of things, but seeing someone like Denver Hartley walk free, with that much evidence stacked against her, rattled him. Something was wrong—something big. Someone with serious juice wanted her out, and that made her dangerous.

Movement caught his eye. The silhouette of a woman—Denver's mother, still clinging to her youth, with sparkling jeans and bright-blond hair. She looked like Denver but older, a ghost of what Denver would become. She moved through the living room and passed the window. Riley raised his protein shake to his lips, trying to focus.

A sound.

His hand froze halfway to his mouth. Something outside. A soft, muffled noise. Something bumping against something else—plastic on rubber? His eyes went to the side mirrors. Nothing. He turned back to the house, scanning the front door, the windows, the driveway.

Fifteen minutes later, the lights inside went out. Riley's heart was pounding, and he didn't know why. Maybe it was the heat. Maybe it was the darkness. Maybe it was the way everything felt wrong, like the air was thicker tonight, harder to breathe.

He pulled out his phone and flipped through old photos. His kids at a waterpark, splashing around and laughing. His wife and him on a date, her arms around him as they smiled for a picture. Another photo: him holding a powerlifting trophy, her beaming with pride beside him. It felt like another life. A stranger's life.

His throat felt dry. He scrolled to her number and pressed Call, his thumb hovering over the screen as it rang. His wedding band caught the faint glow of the phone, a reminder of the life that was slipping from him.

"Hello?"

"Hi," he said, his voice cracking.

A pause. He could hear her breathing on the other end.

"I told you," she began, "you could pick the kids up early on Friday."

"I'm not calling about that." He leaned out the window, letting the warm night air hit his skin. It didn't help. "I just . . . wanted to talk."

A long, tired sigh from her side.

"Don't hang up," he said quickly.

"Hang up? I should never talk to you again, Kevin. Wade told me you assaulted him. And Lazarus punched him, too. I should call the police, but I know how you guys like to stick together." Her voice was ice, and he could almost feel her slipping further away.

"I didn't . . ." His words caught in his throat. "I lost my head. How would you have felt if you found out something like that?" He swallowed hard, the pain in his chest building. "I don't blame you."

Silence.

"Don't call me again unless it's about the kids, Kevin." The finality in her voice hit him like a slap. "I can't do this anymore."

The line went dead.

The Night Collector

Riley stared at the screen, at the picture of her smiling at him from better days, from the mornings when she would kiss him before he left for work. He'd called her to tell her how much he missed those kisses, how much they had meant, but he hadn't found the words.

There it was again. The noise.

Closer this time.

Riley's head snapped up. His eyes scanned the street, his pulse quickening. Shadows shifted, but nothing moved. He turned back to the house, his eyes narrowing as he scanned the front porch, the driveway. The lights were still off. Everything was still.

His gut twisted with something dark.

Slowly, Riley opened the driver's side door and stepped out into the night, his boots crunching softly on the gravel. He glanced around.

"Someone there?" his voice bellowed.

He stood quietly a long time and didn't hear it again. A cat maybe.

As he got back into the truck, he felt something cold press against the back of his skull.

In a second, a thousand thoughts raced through Riley's mind. He wondered if it was true what they said—that you never heard the shot that killed you.

Then the world went black.

81

Lazarus sat with Piper at the Last Chance Saloon, the loud hum of voices and clinking glasses wrapped around them like a blanket. The crowds were thick tonight—just the way he wanted it. Chaos outside, chaos inside. Anything to drown out his thoughts.

"You know what I want on my tombstone?" he asked, heating up the absinthe spoon with a lighter, his eyes distant.

Piper looked at him, sipping her beer. "What?"

"'The individual.' That's all. Simple. The crowning achievement of a life. What about you?"

"I don't know. Maybe 'She made a difference.' Something like that."

He let out a cynical chuckle. "Make a difference . . . You really think there's such a thing? Maybe we're just hamsters hopping from one wheel to the next, thinking we're getting somewhere."

"Even hamsters can do good things," Piper said, scanning the room.

She was different from everyone else here, Lazarus thought. Most people in this world looked at others and calculated what they could get from them. But not her. Piper looked at people like she was searching for someone to help, someone she could save.

"You're a good person, Danes. You don't belong in this line of work."

"What do you mean?"

"There are people out there that use people like you as cannon fodder." He smiled faintly, a ghost of bitterness crossing his face. "People like me, too, apparently."

"What are you talking about?"

He almost told her right then. He could feel the words on the tip of his tongue, but something stopped him. If Piper knew everything, she'd become a target—a threat.

"Stay away from Judge Dawson," he said.

"Why?"

"Do me a favor—don't work on anything she brings you. Don't take her calls, don't meet with her. Just stay away."

"Tell me why."

"Trust me."

"You're scaring me now."

"You should be scared."

Piper's eyes lit with realization. "Is she the reason Denver was acquitted?"

Lazarus didn't say anything. Silence was enough of an answer.

"Lazarus, talk to me. She knew, didn't she? Gideon too. I wonder who else—James?"

He shook his head. "No. James was blindsided, just like the rest of us. Dawson had dirt on Hayes. Gideon didn't care as long as his client walked free. That's why she hired him. It wasn't random that Hayes was assigned to the case."

Piper stared into her beer. "Where's Denver now? Do you have someone watching her?"

"Riley's keeping an eye on her."

"Are you sure about all this, Lazarus?"

He paused, the weight of everything bearing down. "She knew Keri was my kid. She knew Denver from years ago, molded and shaped her like clay as a weapon to be used whenever she wanted."

"Why would she have your daughter kidnapped?"

"I don't know, but I'm gonna find out."

Piper leaned in, keeping her voice low. "We have to go to the DA—tell James. File a complaint with the bar and the judicial commission about Judge Hayes."

Lazarus stared at the table, swirling the last of his drink. He didn't answer.

"That's what we're doing, right?" Piper pressed.

"No."

"What?"

He shook his head. "We're not doing a damn thing."

"How can you say that?"

"Because that's just how it is," Lazarus said, finishing his drink in one long pull. "I'm drunk. I'm goin' home."

"You're not driving, are you?"

"I'll take an Uber. You wanna split one?"

"No . . . I think I'll stay a little longer."

He studied her, a flicker of concern passing over his face. "You sure you wanna stay here alone?"

"I don't feel like going home right now."

Lazarus nodded, rising from the table, stumbling slightly before catching himself. "I'll call you tomorrow."

He walked over to the bar and leaned in close to Bass. "Keep an eye on her for me, would you?"

"No problem," Bass said, wiping down a glass. "You all right?"

"One of them days."

Lazarus pushed through the crowd. Two men were arguing near the door, something about a game of pool gone wrong. One of them tried to say something to him, but he didn't stop. Didn't care.

Outside, the warm desert air clung to his skin, the night alive with the hum of neon and distant traffic. The moon hung low, nearly full, casting long shadows across the empty street. He walked out to the curb. The crushed glass in the pavement sparkled under the streetlight like stars. He sat down, pulled out his vape, and took a long drag, watching the vapor curl into the sky.

He pulled out his phone and opened the Uber app, when he felt a sudden, burning fire in his side.

His breath caught in his throat, the pain shooting up through his ribs, his lungs. He gasped, fingers fumbling at his side, coming away slick with blood. His vision blurred as he tried to stand, but his legs gave out beneath him. The pain—unbearable at first, then strangely warm. Numb.

"Wait for me in hell," a voice whispered in his ear.

She twisted the blade in his side, and he choked on a scream as the world spun around him.

She slashed again, and he grabbed the blade, feeling it cut deep into his palm, warm blood spilling over his fingers. Voices echoed in the distance—people coming out of the bar—and Denver was gone.

Lazarus fell back onto the pavement, the black blood pooling around him like oil in the moonlight. He lay there, staring up at the stars, the warmth leaving his body. He could hear the distant sound of people shouting, running toward him, but their voices grew faint, like echoes in a tunnel.

The blood wasn't stopping.

Piper watched the bar patrons, half listening to the hum of conversations and laughter. Some of them started to get rowdy, voices rising with alcohol-fueled bravery. But Bass, with a single look, would shut it down. It didn't matter how big or tough they thought they were; when Bass glanced at them, they turned into kids afraid of disappointing their father.

She thought about going home, but there was nothing waiting for her there. It was too quiet, too warm and clean—like a body without a soul. She missed her grandmother more than she could ever express. The little things that had once seemed so mundane—the smell of cooking, apple-scented air fresheners, Sunday breakfasts, short walks in the park, and long talks about books—were now all she wanted. The smallest pieces of life became the ones you craved most when they were gone.

Piper stood, deciding she was done being around people for the night. A coffee shop near her condo stayed open late, and the idea of hot chocolate and jazz sounded like exactly what she needed. It felt safe, a small escape from the noise in her head.

She walked over to Bass to say goodbye, but he was caught up in a conversation with two women, their voices frantic. Piper only caught a few words, but it was enough to make her pause—something about calling the police because someone was hurt. Her first instinct was to find Lazarus, assuming he was still here, but then her mind stilled, her face slackened, and she turned to the front entrance. Without another thought, she hurried outside.

A small crowd had already gathered near the curb where Lazarus lay on his back. His body was still. One man crouched beside him, pressing a T-shirt against the wound in his side. Blood was seeping through it fast. Two others stood nearby, phones glued to their ears, frantically calling for help.

Piper froze, her heart pounding in her throat. Her instincts screamed at her to run to him, to help, to do something—but before she could move, one single, horrifying thought slammed into her, freezing her in place.

Keri.

82

Keri Bines stepped onto the porch, spotting her mother slouched in a chair, drink in hand. Amanda was drunk—Keri could always tell. Her mom opened up about her past when Charlie wasn't around, like the alcohol gave her enough courage to talk about things she normally kept locked away.

"Come sit with me," Amanda said, her words slurred.

Keri sighed but sat beside her. The night was thick with the sound of crickets. The dim yellow glow from the lawn lights cast long shadows across the porch.

"How you feeling, kiddo?" Amanda asked, her gaze distant, lost in the past.

"Okay."

Amanda gave her a wistful smile, brushing a strand of hair away from Keri's face. "You're so beautiful. Not just on the outside. You're strong, so much stronger than I ever was."

"Mom . . ." Keri said, her voice tinged with frustration. She hated this drunken, emotional version of her mother.

"No, let me finish," Amanda insisted. "You're strong. I should've believed that. You were strong enough to learn the truth about your father, but I kept it from you. I didn't think you could handle it. And I'm sorry."

Keri's heart skipped. "What about my father?"

Amanda hesitated, then swallowed hard. "That detective, Lazarus . . . we knew each other before, back when he first came to Las Vegas. He didn't have a place to stay. We met in a bar. I was different then. He was wild, reckless, and brilliant . . . and I fell for him. Hard."

Keri's stomach twisted in knots. She already knew what her mother was about to say.

"He's my father?"

Amanda nodded, her face crumpling with guilt. "Yeah, he is. I'm so sorry I didn't tell you, Keri."

"You made me think he abandoned me!" Keri stood, her body trembling with rage and confusion.

"I had to," Amanda said, her voice shaking. "He hurt me so bad, Keri. I couldn't let him do that to you, too. I couldn't let him break you the way he broke me."

Keri's anger flared, but before she could respond, Amanda's head jerked violently, like a rag doll in a crash. The sickening thud of a baseball bat meeting skull echoed. Amanda's body collapsed onto the porch, blood already pooling beneath her.

For a moment, Keri couldn't process what she was seeing. Her mind went blank. Her muscles froze in place.

Denver stood over Amanda's body, breathing hard, the bat spattered with blood. A wicked grin spread across her face as she licked the blood off her lips.

Keri wanted to scream, but the sound caught in her throat. She was paralyzed—trapped in some nightmare where she couldn't move, couldn't make a sound.

Denver's eyes locked onto Keri, her grin widening, savoring her fear. Keri's heart felt like it was ready to burst. It broke the trance, and she bolted off the porch.

She didn't look back. She knew Denver was faster, knew she wouldn't make it to the neighbors. Instead, she cut through the backyard, sprinting toward the back door. Fumbling with the lock, she managed to get inside and slam it shut just as Denver's footsteps pounded behind her.

She locked the door and dashed to the front, locking it, too. Her breath came in ragged gasps, and her vision blurred with tears. She threw up on the living room carpet, her body convulsing from fear.

Keri ran to the window, her hands shaking as she looked out. Her mother was still outside. Tears poured down Keri's face. The sound of the bat cracking against bone kept replaying in her mind, making her want to scream.

A loud crash from the kitchen snapped her attention back inside. The window. She gasped and ran to the front door, unlocking it in a panic. She yanked it open, and Denver was already there, swinging the bat. Keri ducked, the bat missing her by inches and slamming into the doorframe with a loud whack.

Keri scrambled to close the door, but Denver wedged the bat in, preventing it from shutting. Denver's hand shot through the gap and grabbed Keri's throat with an iron grip. It felt like her neck was caught in a vise.

Denver squeezed harder, her strength inhuman. Keri's vision blurred. Bright spots of light flashed as she tried to pry Denver's hand away, but her strength was fading fast. Her lungs screamed for air.

Her body went limp. Pain faded into numbness.

And then nothing.

83

Keri Bines woke to the pounding in her skull. She blinked, staring at the ceiling, disoriented. The living room came into focus, and she saw Denver, sitting on the couch with her mother's blood spattered on her. The bat was between her legs, and her eyes were vacant, lost in a dark place.

"What do you want?" Keri's voice was shaky.

Denver didn't look at her. "I was going to kill you while you were out. Bash your brains in."

Keri pushed herself up, feeling a sharp sting settle deep in her bones. "Why didn't you?"

Denver sat silent for a moment, then nudged the bat with her foot so it clattered to the floor. "I don't know."

Keri's heart raced. She saw a small opening.

"It won't bring him back. Nothing will."

Denver's face remained expressionless, her voice cold. "You know that cop's your dad, right?"

Keri nodded slowly. "Yes."

"He's dead."

The words landed like a punch, but Keri didn't react. She couldn't. Not now.

"Why do you like hurting people?" Keri asked, her voice trembling.

Before Denver could answer, headlights swept across the living room wall, casting long shadows. A car pulled into the driveway.

"Don't move," Denver hissed.

Denver sprang to her feet, went to the window, and peered out.

Piper was out of the car, hurrying to the porch. Keri watched her through the window, her heart pounding so hard she thought she could hear it. Piper knocked, then rang the doorbell.

Denver's voice was low, filled with threat. "Don't make a sound."

"I won't."

Keri slowly started backing toward the bat, keeping her eyes on Denver. She was only a few feet away now.

"Keri?" Piper's voice came from outside. "Are you home?"

Denver motioned for Keri to come to the door. Keri glanced at the bat again.

"Get over here," Denver whispered, her tone lethal.

Keri swallowed the fear. She got up and went to the door. Denver stood behind it.

"Keri?"

"I'm fine, Piper. I just want to be alone."

"Where's your mother?" Piper asked, her voice closer now.

"She's at a friend's house with Charlie. Just go away."

"Can you open the door so we can talk?"

Keri glanced at Denver. "No," she said.

"Keri, please open the door."

"I can't."

A long silence.

"I'm not leaving until I see you're okay."

Denver squeezed Keri's arm painfully, eyes filled with venom. She whispered, "Open it. Slowly."

Keri unlocked the door and cracked it open, enough to see Piper standing there with a warm, worried smile.

"You okay?" Piper asked.

"I'm fine," Keri said, her voice robotic. "What do you want?"

"I wanted to check on you. Your mom wasn't answering her phone."

Denver tightened her grip and whispered, "Let her in."

Keri's mind spun. As she went to open the door wider, she saw Denver pull a gun from her waistband. Panic surged through her and without thinking, she slammed the door into Denver's face.

"She's here!" Keri screamed.

Denver roared, backhanding Keri hard. She fell to the floor, her vision swimming. Denver lunged for Piper, grabbed her hair, and dragged her inside, slamming the door shut behind her.

Keri's eyes darted to her mother's body, now tucked away in the corner. Blood was everywhere. The room felt like a nightmare.

Denver hit Piper with two brutal punches, sending her reeling. Then she grabbed a floor lamp, swung it like a club, and struck Piper again. The gun clattered to the floor.

Piper was on her side, gasping for breath. Denver moved in for another blow, but Piper reached into her pocket, then sprayed mace directly into Denver's face.

Denver screamed in agony, clawing at her eyes. Piper, bloodied, stumbled to her feet.

"Run, Keri," she gasped.

Keri scrambled for the door, but Denver caught her by the hair, yanking her backward. She fell hard, the breath knocked out of her.

"Leave her alone," Piper yelled.

Denver's eyes were wild, filled with fire. "She's gonna die."

"Denver, listen to me," Piper said, her voice steady despite the chaos. "You've been used your whole life. By your father, by your husband, by Carlito. But you don't have to be the person they made you. You can be better."

"I don't want to be better."

"Stop." Keri's voice came from behind her. She was standing, the gun in her hands, shaking. "Stop it now."

Denver smiled. "You gonna kill me?"

Keri's hands trembled. "Yes."

"Really? You ever fired a gun before? You ever seen what it does to a person? It's not like the movies, kid."

"Leave me alone!" Keri screamed, tears streaming down her face. "I just want you to leave me alone!"

Denver took a step closer. "Then shoot me. You have to kill me if you want me to stop."

"I will."

"Go ahead."

Piper took a step toward Keri. "Don't make her do this, Denver."

"She has to," Denver snarled.

"No," Piper said, her voice soft. "She doesn't."

Denver's expression wavered, her eyes flicking to the ground for a moment. Then, with a roar, she charged. Keri screamed, but her finger froze on the trigger.

Denver reached for the gun, a shot went off, and two of her fingers were blown off. She howled in pain, but it didn't slow her. She tore into Keri, clawing and thrashing.

Piper jumped onto Denver's back, and they tumbled to the floor. Denver swung wildly, her fists like hammers. She hit Piper again and again, blood splattering with each blow.

Keri stood frozen, the gun shaking in her hand.

Suddenly, a hand reached over her shoulder. Amanda, bloody and battered, gently took the gun from Keri's trembling grip. She raised it.

Denver paused, sucking in ragged breaths. Amanda's hands shook, but her aim was steady.

Piper, bleeding and gasping, seized her moment. She raised the mace and sprayed it into Denver's face—directly into her open mouth.

Denver screamed, blinded by pain. She leapt, but the sound of a gunshot cut through the air.

Amanda had pulled the trigger.

Denver froze, her eyes wide in disbelief. A dark-red stain bloomed on her chest, growing larger. She fell to her knees, glaring at Piper with pure, boiling hatred.

And then she collapsed.

84

Sitting in the back of the ambulance, Piper felt detached, her mind floating in a haze of confusion and exhaustion. She couldn't get a straight answer. Was Lazarus dead? Was Denver? Were they both? The paramedics avoided her questions with the usual platitudes, telling her to lie back and relax, to stop worrying, that she had fractures and bleeding.

The hospital was a blur. Nurses came and went, stitching her up, giving her something for the pain, and she drifted in and out, catching only fragments of what they were saying. Lazarus was in surgery; that much she gathered. But no one knew if he was going to make it.

Hours passed like days, and when Piper woke, the pain hit her. Her head throbbed with a deep, primal ache, like something vital had been ripped from her body. She pushed herself up, the hospital gown sticking to her sweat-dampened skin.

Piper swung her legs over the side of the bed, but the room spun, forcing her to sit back down. After a minute, she stood, gripping the edge of the bed for balance. The nurse at the station saw her.

"You need to get back in bed, sweetie," the nurse said, hurrying over.

"I want to know where the officer is. Lazarus Holloway. Where is he?"

"He's upstairs right now. But you should get some rest."

"I thought he was dead. I need to see him," Piper said, her voice firmer than she felt. "Please."

The nurse studied her for a moment before nodding. "Okay."

They made her sit in a wheelchair, hospital policy apparently. Piper hated it, but she was too drained to argue. The ride up the elevator was quiet. The nurse wheeled her down a dimly lit hallway, stopping in front of a small room at the end.

When they entered, Piper's heart sank. Lazarus lay motionless in the bed, tubes and wires snaking from his body, his chest rising and falling with the mechanical rhythm of the ventilator. His face was calm, eerily serene, like a mannequin version of himself.

Keri Bines sat beside him. A magazine lay discarded on a chair across the room, along with her purse.

"Where's your mother?" Piper asked softly.

Keri wiped at her eyes, sniffing. "Downstairs with Charlie."

Piper took a seat on the opposite side of Lazarus's bed. "Is she okay?"

Keri nodded. "She's gonna need surgery. But they said she'll be all right."

Silence fell between them, broken only by the soft beeps of the machines keeping Lazarus alive. His chest rose and fell.

"They said he's in a . . . whatever, whatever they do to keep you asleep," Keri said after a long pause.

"An artificial coma," Piper replied.

"Yeah. What does that mean?"

"It means they need to do more surgeries. It keeps him stable while they work."

Keri's face was pale. "My mom says he needs a liver transplant. But they're hard to get for alcoholics. And he is one."

Piper stared at him, her throat tightening. His face was different now—older, etched with deep lines. His brow, always furrowed in thought, was smooth, peaceful.

Keri's voice cracked as she asked, "Is he really my dad?"

Piper nodded, her heart heavy. "I think so, yes."

"Is he going to die?"

Piper didn't have an answer. "I don't know."

The room felt quiet and cold. The scent of antiseptic and sickness lingered, clinging to everything. Piper thought it would be an awful place to die.

"It would make sense," Keri whispered, her voice barely audible, "that I'd find my dad just to watch him die. Story of my life."

Piper reached out. "You're not cursed, Keri."

"Yeah," Keri said, wiping at her tears with the back of her hand. "Sure as hell feels like it."

85

Judge Dawson had received word earlier that morning—Denver Hartley was dead, Lazarus Holloway was barely clinging to life, and Kevin Riley had been murdered in his truck, shot through the driver's side window. So much death. It clung to the city like a thick, sticky fog, choking everything. Death was loud, disruptive—unlike the quiet precision she preferred. But she knew there were times when quiet wasn't an option.

She'd thought about visiting Lazarus at the hospital, but his physician had informed her he was in a chemically induced coma, the single-pass dialysis machine working desperately to save what remained of his liver and kidneys. He would need a transplant, they said, or he wouldn't survive.

It would be a pity if he died. The world would be less interesting without him in it.

That morning in court, her mind wandered, though outwardly no one could tell. She appeared as engaged as ever, but her thoughts were a million miles away, weaving intricate patterns, always returning to the same center. It wasn't random, like other people's idle musings—it was controlled, deliberate. Every idea carefully examined, every plan meticulously considered.

Was there guilt? Maybe. But Lazarus's life was a price she was more than willing to pay. She had endured too much for this life to let anyone take it from her. Her brothers were closing in, threatening to strip her of everything: her home, her career, her political future, even her sanity. That couldn't happen—not after the life she'd lived, after the degradation she'd survived at the hands of her father. The man who had broken her fingers when she misbehaved, breaking an additional one if she made a sound. She had learned quickly that there was no avoiding the second break. It was inevitable. And he did it because he enjoyed it.

And now her brothers wanted to take from her what she had built out of the wreckage of that life? No. She would *not* allow it.

After court, she went to the country club—a solitary meal of chicken salad, hardly touched. The conversations of the other patrons usually provided a distraction, an amusement. Today, they were nothing but noise. Humanity itself made her feel sick. The hypocrisy. The self-righteousness. And at times, herself included.

She went home to a dark and silent house. After kicking off her heels, she poured a glass of wine and stepped onto the balcony. The night air was cooler than usual, a faint breeze brushing against her skin.

"Sneaking into people's homes is dangerous," she said without turning around.

A voice answered from behind her, calm and amused. "What's a little surprise visit between friends?"

She paused, her hand resting lightly on the railing. She didn't turn.

"It's a beautiful house," the voice continued. "I'd buy it just for the quiet."

Hope Dawson finally turned, her expression unreadable. Seated on her pristine sofa, the man looked as out of place in her home as he did in the world. Pale skin, a thick black beard, and milky, sightless eyes behind glasses. He always reminded her of a reptile—Deadeye was an apt name.

"The quiet is temporary," she said smoothly. "We humans have a way of filling every space."

"I couldn't agree more," Deadeye said, a smile tugging at his lips.

"Would you like something to drink?" she offered.

He shook his head, his fingers tapping his cane—a silver eagle head glinting in the dim light. "I'm fine."

She folded her arms, her voice turning cold. "May I ask why you thought it prudent to sell Lazarus's daughter?"

He grinned, that reptilian smile that made her skin crawl. "I gave your girl instructions on where to take her. Simple transaction. I would've taken custody and gotten Lazarus to drop this bullshit with me. But your girl decided to have a little payday instead. Gotta say, it was pure balls to screw us both, don't you think? Gotta respect that."

Hope's stomach turned. People like Deadeye, Carlito, Denver, her brothers—they were the disease. They rotted cities from the inside out. She had told Denver only to kidnap Keri and deliver her to Deadeye, to use her as leverage against Lazarus, but Denver couldn't resist the temptation of turning the girl into another commodity, like she had been her entire life. Her instability had been an asset . . . until it hadn't.

He shrugged. "You should've just told me where the girl was. What the hell were you thinking, sending someone that unhinged? I had twenty men that could've done better."

She took a deep breath. "Denver does have a flair for the dramatic," she said, almost wistfully. "Well, had."

Deadeye chuckled, leaning forward. "She worshipped you. She told me you were the only one who ever treated her like a human being. You really got into her head. I respect that."

Judge Dawson studied Deadeye for a moment, disgusted by the way he wore his cruelty like armor.

"You're just a thug. You only understand power that comes from the barrel of a gun," she said. "I collect people, not guns."

He pulled a silver tin of snuff from his pocket. "I probably should've killed you the minute you knocked on my door," he said. "But getting me out of custody like that? Now, that was a trick. You'll have to show me how you pulled it off sometime."

She grimaced. "You won't last long enough to learn any new tricks."

"That right?"

"You could've let this go, taken witness protection and disappeared. But you couldn't do it. You let ego get in the way. That's why men like you never last."

Deadeye smirked, taking a pinch of snuff. "You're something else. You played her until the day she died." He took another pinch and sniffed. "Real ruthless bitch, aren't you?"

"If you ever use that word to describe me again, I'll kill you," she said, her tone as calm as ever. It wasn't a threat. It was a promise, and Deadeye knew it.

He raised an eyebrow but didn't argue. "This whole thing turned into a mess," he said, shaking his head.

"What about my brothers?" she asked, cutting through his ramblings. "The lawsuit is approaching discovery, and your efforts have been . . . disappointing."

"They're clean. Sure, they own a few escort services, but nothing that'll help."

"What's your plan, then?"

Deadeye stood, brushing off his suit. "You don't need to worry. Your inheritance is safe."

"They'll never agree."

"They don't have to."

She nodded, satisfied. "Thank you."

He moved toward the door, then paused. "What did Holloway do to you, anyway?"

"Nothing," she said.

"Nothing? You gave me his daughter, and he didn't do a thing?"

"He was useful. A tool, just like you. That's all."

Deadeye shook his head, chuckling. "You belong on this side of the law, Judge."

She didn't respond.

He said, "You know, my mother was from Iceland. She used to tell me stories about the *Náttsafnari*—the Night Collectors. They're these ancient beings creeping through the night, stealing people's secrets

The Night Collector

while they sleep, collecting them like trophies and using it against them. They're in love with the goddess of chaos. Sound like anyone you know?"

"Good night, Phineas."

He gave a mock salute with his cane and left.

Once he was gone, she turned to the city, watching as the neon lights flickered in the distance.

Hope Dawson understood Las Vegas better than anyone. The streets and sewers, the desperate and delusional, the self-made heroes and the beggars all played their parts. She knew the men ranting on street corners about invisible enemies and the polished ones on TV selling out the city for a chance at power. The whole city was a theater of madness wrapped in a gaudy package of neon. When the world finally collapsed, places like this would be the first to fall. The whole thing was an illusion, pretending that nature had tamed Armageddon.

But Armageddon came for everyone eventually.

Unless people like her, those with vision and the willingness to do what was necessary, delayed it. Stopping it was impossible—everything went extinct sooner or later. Nations, species, entire worlds. But the goal wasn't to stop the inevitable, just to push it back. Humanity had that much power at least. To hold the line a little longer and slow down the descent into the flames.

Deadeye had called her a lover of chaos. He couldn't be more wrong.

She didn't love chaos. She loved this city. Adored it. Like a lover adores every inch of flesh. She loved every broken street and glittering tower and worn-down building. And she would never let anyone take it from her. Not her brothers. Not men like Deadeye, who claimed power but didn't understand it. Not foolish betrayers like Denver. Not Lazarus.

Not anyone.

She sipped her wine, eyes glowing in the reflection of the neon lights like fire.

86

Keri Bines sat quietly at her father's bedside. *Father.* The word hit her differently now as she looked at a face so similar to hers. Her mother had always told her that her father left before she was born, never trying to reach out. For years, Keri had dreamed of meeting him, sometimes imagining screaming at him until she was hoarse and sometimes imagining a man who would understand her, who would protect her. She tried not to be mad at her mother, but she couldn't shake the ache of what she could've had.

Brad had been the only person who truly understood her. Having a father back then might have changed everything. Now, as she watched the rise and fall of Lazarus's chest, the thought of losing him just as she'd found him was unbearable.

The hospital room felt smaller, the pale walls closing in on her. She didn't want to leave, couldn't go back home—not to that living room with bloodstains still on the carpet. Her mother would have to deal with that. Maybe they could sell the house and leave it all behind.

Keri stood, twisting her stiff back, and stepped into the hallway. The fluorescent lights buzzed faintly, the stillness of the hospital almost unnatural. A clock on the wall read past one in the morning. She decided she wasn't going home tonight. She'd sleep here, no matter what anyone said. She hadn't seen the police officer assigned to watch the room for a couple hours, and she wasn't going to leave Lazarus alone.

At the end of the corridor, she bent down to take a sip from the drinking fountain. The cool water calmed her briefly, but as she turned back toward Lazarus's room, unease crept in.

When she stepped inside, she froze.

A man in blue scrubs stood next to her father's bed. He had scruff on his jaw and wore glasses that caught the faint light from the monitors.

"Is something wrong?" Keri asked.

The man flinched slightly and turned, flashing a quick smile. "You scared me," he said, his tone light. "No, just checking on him. Visiting hours are over, sweetie. You should go home."

Keri's eyes flicked to the pockets on his scrub top. Something was sticking out—a syringe.

"No," she said, her voice firm. "I'm staying with him."

The man's demeanor shifted instantly. He straightened, his face hardening into an emotionless mask. His eyes locked onto hers, cold.

"Okay," he said flatly. "Now you can't leave."

For a moment, neither of them moved, the air between them crackling. Then Keri bolted.

"Help!" she screamed, her voice echoing down the corridor. "He's trying to kill him! Someone help!"

The man cursed behind her, his footsteps heavy as he chased her.

Keri ran, her heart pounding, legs burning. The nurse's station came into view, but it was empty.

She glanced back. He was gaining.

The police officer assigned to Lazarus's room rounded the corner, his eyes narrowing as he caught a glimpse of the man.

The man skidded to a stop, glancing between Keri and Lazarus's room. For a second, Keri thought he might attack the cop, but instead he spun and sprinted toward the stairwell.

"Stay here," the cop ordered, taking off after the man.

Keri ignored him, doubling back toward Lazarus's room. She ran inside, her chest heaving, tears streaming down her cheeks. Her hands shook as she frantically checked the IV tubes and monitors. Everything seemed intact, but her mind raced with what-ifs.

A nurse rushed in. "What happened?" she demanded, gently pushing Keri aside.

"A man—he was dressed as a nurse," Keri stammered, her voice trembling. "He had a syringe. He was going to hurt him."

Another nurse and a CNA entered, both moving quickly to check Lazarus's vitals. Keri stumbled back, her adrenaline draining, leaving her legs weak and unsteady.

A second police officer ran past the doorway, his radio crackling with updates about a lockdown. The first nurse glanced at Keri, her tone sharp. "Get her out of here."

Keri didn't resist as someone gently guided her into the hallway, her thoughts spinning. She was ushered into a small lounge, where she collapsed onto a couch. Her breaths came shallow and fast as the reality of what had just happened sank in.

She didn't know how long she had been on the couch when the police officers came back. Their faces were drawn with exhaustion, but their voices were calm as they took her statement, listening carefully as she recounted everything.

"You did good," one of them said, his tone kind. "He's safe now."

Keri nodded, though the words felt hollow. She wondered if "safe" was something she would ever feel again.

"You should go home. Get some rest," the officer added gently.

She shook her head as she stood. "I'm staying."

Without another word, she walked back to Lazarus's room. The hospital staff exchanged concerned glances, but she ignored them. Inside, the faint hum of the monitors filled the quiet space.

She sank into the chair beside his bed, her hand brushing his. His breathing was steady, his chest rising and falling in the glow of the machines. He was still here. Still alive.

She sat back, watching him, the silence heavy but no longer unbearable.

About the Author

Victor Methos's journey into the world of law and justice began at the age of thirteen, following a profound personal experience where his best friend falsely confessed to a crime after enduring an eight-hour interrogation. This pivotal moment steered Methos toward a future in law, culminating in a law degree from the University of Utah. Starting his career as a determined prosecutor in Salt Lake City, he soon established Utah's premier criminal defense firm, showcasing his prowess in more than a hundred trials over a decade.

One case in particular left an indelible mark on Methos, inspiring his breakthrough bestseller, *The Neon Lawyer*. Transitioning from the courtroom to the writer's desk, Methos has since dedicated himself to crafting gripping legal thrillers and mysteries. His exceptional storytelling has earned him the prestigious Harper Lee Prize for *The Hallows* and an Edgar Award nomination for Best Novel for *A Gambler's Jury*. He currently resides in southern Utah.